The Lady Anne Elliot

T.F. FIG

ISBN
978-1-961601-93-2 (Paperback)
978-1-961601-94-9 (eBook)
978-1-961601-92-5 (Hardcover)

The Lady Anne Elliot

TABLE OF CONTENTS

Foreword..vii

Chapter 1   All She Deserves 1
Chapter 2   Weddings!..26
Chapter 3   Fulfilled Dreams...47
Chapter 4   It's Twins 66
Chapter 5   Time Goes by So Quickly..........................89
Chapter 6   Changes... 112
Chapter 7   It's War 134
Chapter 8   Margret Anne 158
Chapter 9   Knighthood 179
Chapter 10   Fitzwilliam..223
Chapter 11   Royal Events 250
Chapter 12   The Autum Years.....................................288
Chapter 13   Honors For Anne......................................302
Chapter 14   Anne Is Gone From Us............................325

FOREWORD

Jane Austen, a most beloved author, passed away far too early. With only six novels written, all of which are considered classics today, we all hoped for more in the way of tales. She once said, "There are so many characters to describe, many stories to be told."

Millions have opinions of which of the six novels is their favourite. Like most, I fell in love with all her works. Miss Austen had a central theme around her stories and characters. She would say about her characters, "After a bit of trouble, they get all they desired." And so, her novel *Persuasion* starts a beloved story. In the end, Miss Anne Elliot and Captain Frederick Wentworth engaged, and the story ends, leaving the rest of their lives to the imagination of the reader.

Like many lovers of Miss Anne Elliot, we wonder what her life would have been like had Jane Austen continued the *Persuasion* tale. The Lady Anne Elliot continues the tale to its end.

This novel begins with Anne accepting Captain Wentworth and ends with her passing. The story starts where *Persuasion* ended. Anne receives a letter from Captain Frederick Wentworth. In it, he professes his love for her and proposes. She goes in search of him to finally encounter him at Camden Place, after a frantic search on the streets of Bath.

CHAPTER 1

All She Deserves

"Sir, I am in receipt of your proposal and have a mind to accept. I will accept."

"Are you certain?" asked Captain Wentworth (engaged to her eight years earlier where she was easily persuaded out of her promise by the Lady Russell and family, breaking both their hearts.) This proposal represented a single chance for both at love.

"I am determined, sir … and nothing and no one will ever change my mind!" said Anne lovingly as they kissed in Frederick's embrace.

Frederick could see Anne was exhausted in her rush to find him, but neither wanted to leave each other's side. If they went into Camden Place, they would have no privacy or time to speak.

"There is a tea room just a few streets from here where we can sit to a cup of tea and refresh ourselves. Do you feel up to a very short walk, Anne?" asked Frederick.

"Yes," replied Anne taking Frederick's arm for the first time, as they walked slowly in that direction.

"It has been eight long years since last we could talk openly, and this will be the first and very important conversation with my captain since then …"Anne thought to herself as they slowly walked along the streets of Bath.

As Anne and Frederick walked along the stoned streets of Bath away from Camden Place, Frederick thought "no doubt the Lady Russell would be awaiting Anne's return in readiness to weave her influence into recent events. My Anne seems determined and I am confident no influence will deter us this time."

It had rained all morning, but by noon the rain had stopped, though the skies were filled with leaden gray-covered clouds. The street, still wet, was filling with folks walking and enjoying the out-of-doors until the next shower, when they would rush indoors again.

"Cousin William would propose to play his gambit of pressing his marriage proposal upon me at the planned evening's gathering in Camden Place. Frederick and I need uninterrupted time to talk and plan," thought Anne as she looked into Frederick's eyes, having just moments ago accepted him.

Frederick was very attentive to Anne, careful not to over-strain her as they walked. The sun shone at times in between the breaks of a very fast-clearing sky. Both knew they needed time to plan and organize themselves for the challenges of opinions from family and friends that would come as a result of their pending announcement of engagement.

It had been eight years since last they talked from the heart. Years older, Anne and Frederick were more sensible now of their desires for happiness in each other, both determined there would be no surprises in their plans to marry this time around. "I will not be so shy this time with my captain," thought Anne.

"My dear, the tea room," said Frederick.

Anne was pleased with Frederick calling her 'my dear". "It will be the little things I will love most," noticed Anne.

"Frederick, I was amazed at the rumour of me marrying Cousin William. It is true Cousin William has singled me out for special attention and has proposed just the other night at the concert where we talked that evening. I had not answered him. I do not love him, but was attracted to the idea of becoming mistress of my beloved Kellynch Hall, my home. I thought of missing my chances with you…

"This evening at Camden Place we have a family gathering to include the Dowager Viscountess, the Lady Dalrymple, and her daughter the Honourable Lady Carteret where Cousin William is expecting an answer to his proposal. He will be disappointed," said Anne earnestly looking into Frederick's eyes. Earlier in the week, I was called upon by Admiral and Miss Croft who explained to me the extraordinary circumstances of Captain Harville and Louisa Musgrove's engagement. What a surprise. It gave me hope. I could scarcely have imagined, explained Anne.

"When the Admiral announced your arrival at Bath only the day before, I hoped it was to see me. In all of this, we chanced to meet in the sweet shop where I trusted you would understand my meaning that I would be at the pump rooms for a concert that evening. I was put out since Cousin William was escorting me back to Camden Place. This was awkward for me since it was you I wanted to be with.

"When you arrived at the concert, I went to you to open my heart…but the Lady Dalrymple and her daughter arrived and in the commotion, I lost touch with you until you stood to leave. I came to you a second time to entreat you to stay and talk with me but Cousin William followed me, giving you only the option to withdraw. It was then he asked me to marry him, and I gave no answer but hinted this was not what I wanted,

"I received your note explaining the business you needed to discharge on behalf of the Admiral and hoped it was your way to see me. When you asked about marriage rumours and returning to Kellynch Hall, I knew this was my chance, and I quickly put to rest any rumour of this kind, hoping you would understand my meaning that I was quite unattached. I love you and always have been constant, even when there was no hope," declared Anne.

"I came to Bath after I found Louisa had directed her affections to Harville. I inadvertently entangled myself with her because of my selfish pride and hurt feelings over our failed engagement of years past. I wanted to hurt you only to realize you are the only one for me. I became aware of the entanglement with Louisa after my friend Benwick explained to me the situation of my conduct.

"I made clear to him. I had no intentions toward Louisa Musgrove. She is a sweet girl to be sure, but I love you. Surprised, he suggested a course of action, and it was for me to leave Louisa in the care of Harville and visit my brother with the hope Louisa, being young, would propose her attention to another. It seemed to work.

"After a talk with Benwick, he suggested I would leave Lyme for a while, and I did just that, returning, after some weeks, distraught at the possibility of being bound to marry someone I regarded but not loved. Benwick explained the change in Louisa's affections. 'I wrote to you of Harville's engagement to Louisa Musgrove. She has accepted him and they are to be married as soon as possible. You must not have received the letter", said Benwick.

'No, I did not; then am I free to follow Anne at Bath?' I asked him. 'Yes, and I am off to Bath tomorrow. Will you accompany me then?' asked Benwick. I came to Bath at all possible speed to propose to you," said Frederick, his face animated, Anne noticed, from across the small café table.

Tea was served, accompanied by small finger sandwiches. The café - still mostly empty - gave Anne and Frederick the privacy they required to continue to talk frankly over the soft candlelight.

"While here, only one day, I heard rumour that you and your Cousin William Elliot were to be engaged shortly, but nothing was public as yet. I wondered if I lost my only chance at happiness and all because I was hurt and acting childish. I had to know if I still had a chance with you. I am the source of the fanciful rumour," explained Frederick, holding Anne's hand.

"After our conversation this morning at Camden Place, which was interrupted by my sister Mary and the Lady Russell, I ran after you but was again interrupted by my friend Harriet Smith, who related to me Cousin William's exploits with the point of setting up Mrs. Clay as a mistress in town, after marrying me. The scheme was in the hopes of protecting his inheritance of my father's baronetcy title. You see, Mrs. Clay was intending for her father to marry her, and if she had a son the boy would be next in line for the baronetcy title. I was liked well enough by my cousin but just incidental to him at securing his goal," related Anne.

"If I had known you ran after me, I would have stopped for you, but I didn't know dear Anne.

"I arrived at your apartments at Queen Square where I found Captain Benwick in receipt of a note you commissioned him to deliver to me. He mentioned you, and the Crofts were on the way to the pump rooms when he begged his leave to attend to his appointments. As I read your note, I found the words I only dreamed about these eight years long. My thoughts and feelings told me my whole happiness depended on finding you quickly. So I made all haste to the pump rooms, discovering only the Admiral and Mrs. Croft there. They mentioned you were off to Camden Place in search of me. I set off worried I may find you after you encountered the Lady Russell, who persuaded me not to accept you those many years ago. Breathless, I found you only a few yards from Camden Place talking with Charles. I was relieved and anxious to give you an answer to your proposal, and so…here we are," described Anne.

"Anne, I am sorry we missed each other, and I am glad for your determination to find me. I believe nothing will deter us this time. I know it. I feel it," said Frederick confidently.

"Frederick, eight years ago you proposed to me, and I accepted. At just eighteen I was easily persuaded to break our hearts. I took the advice of friends and family that this offer was a most imprudent marriage proposal. Lady Russell said, 'You are but eighteen. We are in the middle of a war, and you are engaged to a naval officer who has no title, no fortune, no connections. This would not be allowed".

"With the whole of my family and friends on the side, I was influenced. I suffered loneliness and deep sadness every day for these eight years, believing I had lost my only chance at happiness. All I had were the papers for my authority to know of your wellbeing, but I was never inconstant, although I saw no circumstance that would make it possible to have this chance again," said Anne.

"The breakup of our engagement almost broke my heart, dear Anne. I focused on my career and amassing wealth so this would never be the case again. I convinced myself of my abhorrence for the weak-minded. I never thought I would be able to win you again until these circumstances where my sister and her husband, the Admiral, were to let Kellynch Hall, and my discreet inquiries about the Elliot family found you still unmarried. I was against the letting of the Hall at first but then realized life might be giving us a second chance at happiness. I found ways in conversations to learn from you. However, I wanted to teach you a lesson. I didn't realize you had suffered as well these eight years long in breaking off the engagement.

"You were not at the first supper party with the Musgroves and this vexed me that you would care for a child not your own in this case. I made the best of the evening knowing I would have to direct the conversation in a way that would give me leave to go to the Uppercross the next day. Perhaps, I would catch a glimpse of you.

"That morning at Uppercross, with the excuse of hunting with Charles, I arrived early. I could hardly recognize you. You were more beautiful and mature now, but aloof from life. I could see in your eyes the Anne that I loved, but my hurt feelings would not allow me to go to you straight away. I realise this doesn't make much sense. I am glad we are here now. This is what matters," said Frederick.

"I agree and will be at your side from this day forward," said Anne smiling as Frederick caressed her hand.

"Shall we talk about this evening? We have much to plan" suggested Anne.

"Yes, what do you suggest?" queried Frederick.

"Well, we have a supper party at Camden Place with the entire family attending, including the Dowager Viscountess, the Lady Dalrymple, and her daughter the Honourable Lady Carteret, as well as the Lady Russell. I suggest you escort me to Camden Place, then return later in the evening where we announce to Father privately, at first, my engagement to you. With his blessing, we announce our news to family and guests.

"I will work on Lady Russell, in the interim, in my apartment to gain her support for you. I will stay in my rooms until your arrival, so I do not have to encounter Cousin William and any unpleasantness. My dear Captain, no matter how the evening goes, I will honour our engagement. I am determined." Anne said decidedly, as Frederick squeezed her hand affectionately at hearing her words.

"Then it is settled. Let us put on a good show for your family and guests," replied Frederick as they stood up to leave the tea room and walk toward Camden Place.

"It seemed so hopeless only a day ago, and now I am in your arms, and we are engaged," said Anne as she and Frederick walked slowly along the cobblestone streets, not noticing the hustle and bustle of Bath and walking slowly enough to stretch the moment before they would have to part.

"It is all I could have hoped for my dear," replied Frederick, walking closely.

"It has been too long since I felt calm and protected. To think Frederick will be mine all the days of my life," thought Anne, taking a deep breath that brought a feeling of complete happiness and warmth.

Arriving at Camden Place in the early evening now, Frederick turned lovingly to Anne. "I shall return in two hours, my dear."

"I will be waiting on you, my Captain. Be assured all will go your way this evening. I give you my word," said Anne with a kiss as they embraced.

Anne stood at the door watching Frederick call a carriage and waved until he was out of sight, heading in the direction of Queens Square.

Anne entered Camden Place to find Lady Russell had been waiting for her. "Anne, where have you been? I was worried. You left with such haste and have been gone for almost five hours," inquired Lady Russell.

"Good afternoon Lady Russell," replied Anne, composed and curtsying as is customary. Her countenance changed. She glowed, and the Lady Russell noticed without comment.

"Your father and sister are out at the moment. Now is the time to tell me all that has transpired," requested Lady Russell.

Servants were about preparing for the evening's events, setting flowers, arranging furniture, and cleaning. "Will you walk with me to my apartment Lady Russell?" asked Anne.

"Yes, of course, child," replied Lady Russell.

They walked together up the stairs to Anne's apartment not saying a word. With the door closed behind them, Anne related the story of Cousin William's offer of the proposal of marriage. "You should accept him, Anne. It would be a very advantageous marriage to be sure," said Lady Russell.

"Perhaps not dear Lady Russell," replied Anne, determined yet calm. "There is this business of Mrs. Clay…"

Anne related the exploits of Cousin William and his proposed mistress to the shocked expression of Lady Russell.

"Anne, what will you do?" asked Lady Russell.

"Frederick will announce his intentions to marry me to Father this evening," said Anne, holding back the details of the day still.

With a surprised look, Lady Russell asked, "Anne what is this news?"

"Frederick proposed to me today, and I have accepted him. We spent the afternoon together catching up. Eight years is a long time to wait, but Frederick has been constant and now that he has wealth and rank in the navy, nothing stands in our way. No one but you, Frederick and I know of this happy news," said Anne.

Lady Russell looked at Anne, in the now early evening candlelight, noticing her happy countenance and serene manner. "I haven't seen this joy in you in such a long time. I almost forgot just how handsome you can be. You reflect your mother's beauty," stated Lady Russell.

"Dear Lady Russell, since Mother's death you have been like a mother to me, and I have been grateful for your kind attention and guidance. I have a request for you. Would you hear me out?" asked Anne.

"Yes, of course, dear child," replied Lady Russell.

"I would like you to rally to me and my Captain's side in this matter. Tonight, we will make our engagement known to Father first, asking for his blessing, and then announce it to the family. Do I have your support Lady Russell?" asked Anne, taking Lady Russell's hand.

"Well, if you are a determined child. Of course, I will support you with all my heart. What will you have of me?" asked Lady Russell.

"Father will need some encouragement after we announce to him our intentions. Frederick is honourable, kind, and loving to me. He fulfills all that society requires with fortune and rank. I also would like you in our lives after we are married. I expect we will take a small house in the neighbourhood near Kellynch Hall. What do you say dear Lady?" queried Anne, searching Lady Russell's eyes.

"Anne, I love you like a daughter and know well of your unhappiness these long years. I wish you happy and support your wishes in this case. Frederick does meet the requirements. He is honourable and a gentleman. It will be as you ask," responded Lady Russell, smiling as she embraced Anne.

"Thank you, Lady Russell," replied Anne.

"I must leave now child to prepare and return this evening," said Lady Russell.

"I will ready myself and wait here until my Captain's arrival to avoid any unpleasantness with my Cousin William. Frederick and I will enter the drawing room together where we will speak to Father privately and tell him of our happy news. My hope is that Father will accept my Captain and introduce Frederick formally to the family as my betrothed. If this news goes badly in father's eyes he will not make the announcement, which is when I will need your assistance in convincing him of the good points of this match. Even if he accepts Frederick, he will look to you for an opinion, and it is my hope you will give him your good opinion," requested Anne.

"You are so sensible Anne, and quite determined I can see. You have thought this through very well indeed. I will do all I can to guide events to your wishes. Have courage all will go well," replied Lady Russell.

"I will also speak privately with Father and Elizabeth about my cousin's exploits with Mrs. Clay and of his proposal to me, along with his worries about the baronetcy title in the hopes of saving embarrassment for all concerned," commented Anne.

"Yes, that would be wise Anne. These things must be done with delicacy to not make the mood unpleasant. I should like to be present to assure this."

"Of course," replied Anne.

"Until this evening my Anne, and congratulations, truly" exclaimed Lady Russell.

"Until this evening Lady Russell, and thank you," said Anne bowing as Lady Russell departed.

Anne prepared herself with the help of a servant for the evening's events. She did all the things that can be done to look her best. Her hair and face were made up with care and the dress she selected had never been worn. It reflected happiness and cheer, yet had a simple English elegance. It was a soft cream colour with white ribbons and lace, just enough detail but not too much. She wore her mother's jeweled necklace and matching bracelet, with small flowers braided to resemble a crown in her hair. She was ready for the evening and to impress her Captain.

While she completed preparations, Anne had a few moments to write in her diary of the day's events and her feelings. "Frederick was kind and gentle with me as in our original days. The words in his note washed away eight years of pain and loneliness. For the first time since I can remember I feel alive again. No matter the events of the evening I will be with Frederick, and that is what matters to me most," wrote Anne as she carefully placed Frederick's note declaring his love for her within the pages of the diary. Anne knew this saving would be only the first of many such mementos she would keep over a lifetime.

Anne could hear the Musgrove's arrival being announced and knew she would have guests in her apartment soon enough. She put her diary away in preparation for Louisa and Henrietta. A knock at the door brought Anne to her feet. "I am glad for the distraction since I feel a bit nervous about the events of the evening. It is perfectly natural considering I am to be engaged," thought Anne opening the door. "Please do come in," said Anne.

Sister Mary rushed in with cousins Louisa and Henrietta. "Anne! William is just arriving behind us. Will you not go to him?" asked Mary in that way of father's manner. Before Anne could respond she was saved, answering through the interruptions of Louisa and Henrietta and their wedding plans, the dress, and how Benwick stole Louisa's affections.

"I wish you happy Louisa. Truly, you have chosen a good man surely," said Anne.

"Will you come shopping with us tomorrow Anne? My dress must be perfect, and you have such good taste, Anne. Please come?" asked Louisa.

"I will come with you. Of course, I shall. If also to see wedding dresses and designs," responded Anne.

Mary thought she must have a proposal from Cousin William to be announced this evening since it was the talk within the family and having no reason to suspect otherwise.

Just then, the Dowager Viscountess Lady Dalrymple and her daughter the Honourable Lady Carteret and Cousin William Elliot were announced.

"Anne, will you go down to William?" asked Henrietta, with Anne focused on Louisa's excitement over her upcoming marriage plans.

"We are off to the drawing room. Will you come with us Anne?" asked Louisa.

"I shall be down momentarily. Please go ahead," replied Anne as, just then, Captain Frederick Wentworth was announced.

"Who invited him?" asked Louisa.

"He is my particular guest this evening, cousin. Shall we go down to the drawing-room?" suggested Anne making final adjustments to her dress, leaving her visitors confused and unaware of her plan for the evening. They all set off out of Anne's apartment and down the staircase in the direction of the drawing room. Anne made sure she would be last in the group down the stairs.

Frederick looked magnificent in his dress uniform, standing tall and commanding. This was the first time Anne had seen him in his formal royal navy captain's attire. Mary, Louisa, Henrietta, and Anne approached Frederick, greeted him, curtsied, and bowed as is customary.

For a moment, the group made small talk about the uniform and how handsome Frederick looked. Frederick congratulated

Louisa and Henrietta on their upcoming weddings and accepted invitations to attend. During this time, Frederick stole glimpses of Anne, standing just to the back of the group, their eyes embracing their spirits without even a hint of their connection to the rest of the group. "After eight years long it is still there and strong," thought Frederick.

Finally, Mary, Louisa, and Henrietta exhausting all subjects, gave their leave to enter the drawing room to find Sir Walter, Elizabeth, the Lady Dalrymple, Lady Carteret, the Musgroves, and Cousin William, who was having a quiet conversation with Mrs. Clay no less.

"No one suspects William," said Mrs. Clay.

"Good, I will have to marry Anne since this is my duty, but it is you I love," declared William, looking down leaving Mrs. Clay uneasy with the sincerity of the plan.

"I wish you would marry me instead so we would not have to hide from society," replied Mrs. Clay discreetly.

"Perhaps so, but I am bound by society's rules in this case and must marry a lady," replied William coldly.

"Then it will be as you have planned. Have you decided on apartments for me and my children in town?" asked Mrs. Clay.

"I have not settled on this quite yet, but soon," replied William.

"He is not honourable. What am I doing in this case?" thought Mrs. Clay.

"I will use her until I can discard her from this family," thought William to the entry of Mary, Louisa, and Henrietta all smiling and full of cheer.

"Anne, you are so beautiful," said Frederick as he offered Anne his hand, leading her to step down the staircase.

"And you Frederick take my breath away. I don't believe I have ever seen you in this dress uniform," said Anne.

"Is it too much my dear?" asked Frederick.

"No my Captain, quite the contrary, you will have the stage this evening, and I am glad of it!" replied Anne.

"Do we have the Lady Russell's support?" asked Frederick.

"Yes we do, with all her heart," replied Anne.

"That is indeed good news and a surprise," mentioned Frederick.

As they turned, the Lady Russell was announced and entered. "Lady Russell good evening," said Anne with a courtesy as Captain Wentworth bowed.

"May I introduce to you formally Captain Frederick Wentworth of His Majesty's Navy? Captain, the Lady Russell," said Anne with a pleasant air.

"Anne, Captain Wentworth, good evening, may I speak with you both privately?" asked Lady Russell discreetly. Anne directed them to a small drawing room at the side of the entry.

Lady Russell began, "Give me leave to say, congratulations on your engagement. I wish you both happy."

"Thank you Lady Russell," said Frederick and Anne together, as if one.

"I thought it best to ask your father into this room where you can announce, to him, your plan of marriage," suggested the Lady Russell, encouraged to continue by Anne.

"If it does not go well we can work on him here rather than create a spectacle with the gathering looking on in the drawing room. What do you think of this plan Anne?" asked Lady Russell.

Frederick and Anne were surprised but pleased Lady Russell had rallied to their cause.

"Yes this is an acceptable plan," responded Anne.

"Have no worries, I shall be at your side," said Lady Russell on her way to ask a nearby servant to request the presence of Sir Walter in this side room.

The servant entered the drawing room and approached Sir Walter as he was deep in conversation with Elizabeth, the Lady Dalrymple, and Lady Carteret, "Sir, the Lady Russell requests your presence in the side parlour for a private audience."

"This is highly unusual. Ladies if you will excuse me a moment I shall not be long," said Sir Walter, bowing before turning to leave his guests momentarily.

"Ah, Lady Russell what is so urgent as to take me away from my very important guests?" asked Sir Walter as he entered the room. "How might I help you dear Lady?" he exclaimed in that fashionable but pretentious way.

"There is an announcement to be made Sir Walter, and your blessing to be given. Anne, Frederick would you explain," requested Lady Russell, standing at Anne's side and with Frederick on the other side.

"Sir, I have this day proposed to Anne, and she has accepted me. We would like your blessing and announcement of our engagement this evening," stated Captain Wentworth, standing tall and erect, commanding the attention of everyone present.

"Captain Wentworth? I am confused here; I expected your acceptance of Cousin William this evening. Are you sure Anne?" asked Sir Walter, gazing into a small mirror at himself.

"Yes, Father. I would like to introduce to you my future husband Captain Frederick Wentworth of His Majesty's Navy. I have accepted him and ask your blessing," said Anne as Frederick put out his hand in a gentlemanly gesture toward Sir Walter.

"This is a very advantageous marriage proposal for Anne, Sir Walter. There are wealth, rank, and other considerations," exclaimed Lady Russell as Sir Walter shook Captain Wentworth's hand.

"Well then, welcome to the family Captain Wentworth. The Lady Russell's opinion carries great weight with me as you can see. Congratulations daughter, I wish you happy," commented Sir Walter to his daughter and Captain Wentworth.

"This has gone well," thought Anne.

"Has a date been set?" asked Sir Walter.

"Not as yet father, but certainly after Louisa and Henrietta's weddings" replied Anne confidently.

"What is to be done with Cousin William?" asked Sir Walter.

"Father, I have some disappointing news about our dear cousin," commented Anne.

"Shall I call for Elizabeth and Mary? They should hear what you are about to say," stated Lady Russell.

"Yes, please do Lady Russell," replied Anne.

With Elizabeth and Mary in attendance and wondering what could be so important that they leave their guests, Anne proceeded to detail the exploits of dear Cousin William, Mrs. Clay, and William's proposal to her.

"Ah, I see," said Sir Walter as Elizabeth and Mary were startled at the news, half expecting Anne to announce her engagement to their cousin.

"Why did not Cousin William talk to father about his worries about Mrs. Clay?" asked Elizabeth.

"You may have put this to rest with a few words," followed Mary.

"Mrs. Clay is handsome enough to be sure, but a nobody, and not enough to tempt me into matrimony," replied Sir Walter.

"Elizabeth, Mary," said Anne. "I would like to formally introduce you to my future husband Captain Frederick Wentworth of His Majesty's Navy. I have accepted him this day."

"Anne, are you engaged? Father?" said Elizabeth looking confused, breaking up her plans to lure Captain Wentworth into her influence this evening.

"Yes sister, just this day," replied Anne.

"Congratulations to you both, I wish you a happy sister. Welcome to the family brother," said Mary.

"Congratulations sister. Father, we must return to our guests. What will they think of us leaving them alone like this?" asked Elizabeth, distracting herself, for the moment.

"Yes, we must," replied Sir Walter.

"Let us not create a scene this evening. Elizabeth, would you ask Mrs. Clay to leave tomorrow? Do so in a very civil way. Set arrangements for her transport to her father's house. Let me talk with Cousin William personally on the matter Anne just explained. During supper, I will propose a toast of the happy news of Anne and Frederick's engagement," detailed Sir Walter.

"Captain, I will introduce you to the Dowager Viscountess, Lady Dalrymple, and her daughter, the Honourable Lady Carteret since these will soon be your relations as well. Shall we return to our guests now?" hinted Sir Walter as all agreed.

"Sir Walter, is it convenient to visit with you privately tomorrow?" asked Frederick.

"Yes, son you may of course," replied Sir Walter as Anne discreetly thanked the Lady Russell walking in the direction of the drawing room.

Anne and Frederick entered the drawing room together, the last of the guests. With all the pieces in place, the plan was set. Frederick commanded notice of his presence in the drawing room. His dress uniform projected the power of the empire to this social circle. Anne, breathless at his stature and power, felt momentarily unsure of herself.

Decorated by His Majesty, even Sir Walter and Lady Dalrymple stood in his honour. The entire set of single women in the room moved toward Captain Wentworth, save for Anne as she conversed easily with Lady Russell. Frederick and Anne's eyes met periodically, and all was communicated in a glance. "He only has eyes for me," she knew in her heart.

Anne talked to one of the servants discreetly, asking that Captain Wentworth be seated across from her, and to sit Cousin William and Mrs. Clay together away from her and Frederick, as well as to keep this plan quiet. The servant acknowledged the plan with Anne, and all was set for supper. Cousin William, occupied by Elizabeth and Mrs. Clay's attention, left Anne and Captain Wentworth to converse.

"William is hoping to speak with me later in the evening but father will announce our happy news at supper," mentioned Anne. Aware of William's scheme now, one can see the discreet gaze between Mrs. Clay and him.

"Thank goodness Harriet made me aware of his plan. I must thank her in some special way," thought Anne, gazing discreetly at Cousin William and Mrs. Clay while in conversation with Frederick.

"What a surprise it will be," said Frederick.

"I am glad of it my Captain. I have asked the servants to seat you across from me at supper," replied Anne.

"Dinner is served!" announced the Butler. Sir Walter moved quickly to the Dowager Viscountess Lady Dalrymple to escort her and Elizabeth into the dining room, followed by the Lady Russell and the Honourable Lady Carteret, then Mary and the Musgroves, and it was Anne with William at her side and Captain Wentworth, followed by cousins Louisa and Henrietta.

To Cousin William's surprise, he was not seated across from Anne, who would be customary and right under the obvious (to him) circumstances. Rather, Captain Wentworth was seated across from Anne, and he was left with Mrs. Clay across the table and away from Anne, with Louisa and Henrietta in between. "He looked quite put out," thought Anne, smiling at her Captain and paying him all her attention.

Supper went well with much in the way of good and amiable conversation. Anne found herself light and happy again after such a long spell. She would catch herself glancing at her Captain and when their eyes met, she realised she knew what he was communicating to her. No words were needed. They were close again. With the meal almost at its end, Sir Walter stood up to offer a toast.

Most of the party expected the toast to be in honour of the Viscountess, but to their surprise, Sir Walter announced the engagement of a beloved daughter. Cousin William anticipated it to be Anne's way of accepting his proposal, confused as to seating, was ready to stand for congratulations all around and move to Anne's side. Anne kept her eyes strictly on Frederick, sending him all the love in her being, at that moment. They were as one.

"I would like to announce the engagement of my daughter Anne, to Captain Frederick Wentworth of His Majesty's Navy," said Sir Walter, raising his glass with all his surprised guests and family, and to a stunned Cousin William.

Mary, smiling at the news, Charles shouting congratulations to Anne and Captain Wentworth, cousins Louisa and Henrietta at Anne's side in a blink of an eye congratulating her and wishing her all the happiness.

"When is the wedding day Anne? Why did you not tell us?" asked Louisa.

"We haven't set a date yet, but surely after your return from honeymoon. I could not speak of it until Father gave his blessing," replied Anne smiling broadly.

Anne received the compliments of the Dowager Viscountess the Lady Dalrymple and her daughter the Honourable Lady Carteret, as well as that of the Lady Russell.

"This evening's events are something I could not have imagined," thought Anne.

All the years of loneliness were over, and it hit Anne hard. All the happiness and joy just burst out of her heart and showed in the happy tears falling from her eyes. Lady Russell, Sir Walter, and even Elizabeth, and Mary could not help but be happy for Anne.

She looked so different now, as she kept her eyes on Frederick sitting stately and elegant in his chair. "She does look like her mother at times," said Sir Walter quietly to Lady Russell.

"Yes, indeed. And how I miss the Lady Elliot," replied Lady Russell.

Cousin William sat with Mrs. Clay across from him quietly, not knowing what to do, but to congratulate Anne and Frederick, his chance had passed. His scheme had failed. "But there is the baronetcy, I must protect this for me," thought William, not knowing Sir Walter and the Elliot's had a full account of his scheme with Mrs. Clay.

Elizabeth, watching Mrs. Clay, could see the littleness there and realised the truth in Anne's telling. She decided to let the evening go to its conclusion where in the morning she would ask her 'former' friend to leave Camden Place, in that dignified manner as father had asked.

With supper over and the men off to the library for brandy and smoke, and the women left to the drawing room, everyone commented on the happy news. They all conversed on the prospect and what they would do to assist in the happy event and even suggested dates for the event, save Mrs. Clay. With the evening late and the guests now happy to greet their beds, all gave their leave to retire, with their carriages waiting outside.

"Good night and safe ride home," said Sir Walter to the Dowager Viscountess the Lady Dalrymple and her daughter the Honourable Lady Carteret.

"Good Evening Anne, Frederick," said the Lady Russell taking her leave, and then the Musgroves and finally Cousin William.

"My dear, may I visit with you tomorrow?" asked Frederick.

"Yes, of course. I will be about Bath with the Musgroves in search of wedding dresses with an eye out for my wedding dress until later in the afternoon," replied Anne.

"Excellent, until tomorrow," said Frederick giving his leave and thanks for a pleasant evening, kissing Anne's hands before he departed.

With Camden Place quiet now and its residences ready for bed, Anne wrote in her diary in the quiet and the candlelight, "How wondrous this day has been. I will never forget even a moment of it in the whole of my life." Closing the diary and blowing out the candle in her apartment, she retired to bed.

The next day, happy with most of the events of the previous evening save two, Sir Walter began to look at Anne somewhat differently. "Perhaps she is an asset to the family, even if she is unorthodox in her manners at times and my treatment of her may have been too harsh. She is after all an Elliot and does look like her mother. She is handsome enough and can't be all bad," he thought.

After breakfast, Elizabeth asked Mrs. Clay to leave, giving the excuse, "With my sister Anne's engagement and the wedding of two cousins this will leave me little time to attend friends."

"Is there something I did Miss Elizabeth?" asked Mrs. Clay.

"Since you will be moving to London sponsored by my cousin you will also be busy," smiled Elizabeth.

Embarrassed, Mrs. Clay understood the full meaning. The scheme was exposed. She would be on her way back to her father's house by afternoon with not another word said.

Sir Walter sent Cousin William a note asking for his attendance this morning to speak on a matter. At his arrival and in private, Sir Walter related the secret events and the dishonour of this plan to that of the family and in particular, to Anne. In a dignified way, he asked William to explain himself. Cousin William accepted responsibility for all and apologised to Sir Walter. Sir Walter also asked Cousin William to apologise to Anne for his scheme.

"And we will hear no more about it. I have no plans to marry and foster a son. So, you see cousin, the title is not in jeopardy," said Sir Walter.

Sir Walter reminded his cousin; "family connections are always worth preserving," while also advising that Mrs. Clay was asked to leave only this morning with no direct mention of the knowledge of the scheme.

"You may catch Anne now before she is engaged in the day's duties," said Sir Walter.

"I will ask her for a moment," said Cousin William begging his leave.

William Elliot related all to Anne and took personal account for his action, asking her indulgence in this case. Anne not trusting, but for her breeding, decided to preserve the relationship.

"I forgive you, cousin. Let us hear no more of this matter," said Anne.

"I wish you and Captain Wentworth happy in your plans to marry," said William, begging his leave to depart from this uncomfortable moment.

With William gone, Anne wrote a note to Harriet thanking her for all she did to explain Cousin William's scheme, saving her and the family much embarrassment. Anne also announced her engagement to Captain Wentworth.

"I will come to visit you within a few days dear Harriet. As you can imagine I am quite busy with Louisa, Henrietta, and now my engagement. Your dear friend, Anne."

Frederick arrived for a private meeting with Sir Walter. "Frederick why are you meeting privately with father?" asked Anne, happy to see him.

"My dear, there will be very few times I will ever keep my activities from you, this is but one of them, and I ask your patience and leave in this case," replied Frederick.

"Of course," said Anne. After an hour, Frederick and Sir Walter emerged from the small study in high spirits and very amiable in conversation and manner, smiling.

"We shall see you for supper then Captain?" asked Sir Walter.

"Yes, and with pleasure Sir Walter," responded Frederick.

The announcement of Anne's engagement was applied to the papers, with many congratulations received from around the Navy. Frederick was well-known and respected. Anne had no idea she would marry into such a large naval family, with so many well-wishers yet to be met.

In the next days, Anne found time to visit with Mrs. Smith and Nurse Rooke, who played no small part in exposing Cousin William's true meaning.

"Because you shared this knowledge with me, the family could avoid embarrassment. Thank you both," said Anne, holding a cup of tea.

"You are a dear friend Anne; I am glad of it and all the happiness to you and Frederick. He is truly a good man," said Harriet.

The Admiral and Mrs. Croft were stunned at learning Anne was the girl in the county Frederick was engaged to eight years earlier. They, now knowing the details, gained a deeper respect for Anne as a result of all the events leading up to the engagement. Anne had been tested in the most challenging ways, with Louisa thought to be Frederick's intended, and she has shone through it all.

Benwick and Harville, upon notice, sent their congratulations to the happy couple.

"Harville and Louisa's wedding will take place first, in a fortnight, at the parish church near Kellynch Hall. Then it will be Henrietta and Charles Hayter's turn," said Lady Musgrove to Anne.

"Then it will be late summer when Frederick and I may marry, at the Kellynch parish church of course," said Anne.

"Yes, by then Louisa and Henrietta will be back from honeymoon and the whole family rested and ready to attend," said Lady Musgrove.

Anne spoke to Frederick that evening at Camden Place. "Frederick, I talked with the Musgroves today and was able to determine when it would be convenient to set our wedding date. After the Musgrove's daughter's weddings and honeymoons it looks like mid-July, when everyone is back and rested," said Anne.

"Mid-July sounds wonderful. Some fellow naval Captains and officers wish to attend and be part of the happy affair. We will be sure to have the details settled in the next weeks, so we may secure our friends for the date," commented Frederick.

"Of course my Captain," replied Anne.

"Also my dear there are so many officers planning to visit here at Bath in the next few days I am considering leasing the pump rooms for an evening where we may host them perhaps in a private ball. What do you think? Sir Walter likes the idea, of course, more attention on himself and the family, and he doesn't have to pay the expense. His words to me, 'I see this assembly as an excellent opportunity for our society here in Bath".

"Yes, I can help with this," said Anne.

Elizabeth looked on thinking, "Perhaps there is a wealthy captain for me." aloud she added, "We must invite the Lady Russell, the Dalrymples, and other important personages in our society. Let us also invite many ladies to assure dancing for the officers."

"This will be the ball of the season," smiled Frederick to Anne.

On the evening of the ball, Anne and Frederick received the hearty congratulations of his naval colleagues. Frederick introduced Anne to many well-known and not-so-well-known officers in the service of His Majesty.

"Frederick, it seems you are well respected and loved by those across the services," commented Anne.

"I am fortunate to be sure," replied Frederick.

There was much in the way of dancing and music, the atmosphere light and gay with amiable conversation and good food.

Elizabeth was much admired by the officers, but one Captain Warwick singled her out. Even Anne and Frederick noticed the forming attachment.

"May I visit you at Camden Place Miss Elliot?" asked Captain Warwick.

"Yes, you may. When shall I expect you?" asked Elizabeth.

"Would tomorrow mid-morning be convenient?" replied Warwick.

"Yes, that would be acceptable," returned Elizabeth almost shyly.

Sir Walter, too much engaged to notice any but himself during the evening, as senior officers gave him and the Lady Dalrymple diversion with stories of the crown and His Majesty.

The ball was a success.

"I have met so many new friends, my Captain," commented Anne.

"You have an extended family with me, my dear," said Frederick.

In the meantime, Cousin William, determined to marry into the Elliot family, set his sights back on Elizabeth. The next day, after the ball, he arrived unexpectedly at Camden Place and was seen being very attentive to Elizabeth.

At mid-morning Captain Warwick arrived as expected. "Would you announce me to Miss Elizabeth Elliot," asked Captain Warwick to the servant as he was led to her in the drawing room.

"Good morning Miss Elizabeth," said Captain Warwick, bowing in greeting and to Cousin William's surprise.

"Good morning Captain Warwick. Thank you for coming. Cousin, I would like to introduce Captain Warwick of His Majesty's Navy. Captain Warwick, William Elliot my cousin," announced Elizabeth with a hint of a proud brow in her voice.

"How things work out for the best in the end. I am fortunate among women to be able to marry the one I love. The battle for Elizabeth's affection begins, in earnest, with Captain Warwick and Cousin William both persistent suitors indeed. I wish my sister good luck. I am surprised at the improved Elizabeth, who is attentive and patient at times with me. I will open the way for Elizabeth to be a close part of my happiest of days to come," writes Anne in her diary before blowing out the candle and retiring for the evening.

Sir Walter was impressed with all the attention showered on the family with Anne's connections to Captain Wentworth. "The navy has many a personage linked to aristocracy and the royal line. Of course, these connections can only be perceived as beneficial and right under the circumstances," thought Sir Walter, Baronet.

Elizabeth, typically cold to Anne over the years, treating her more like a servant than a sister, could not fight the sisterly bonds with a wedding looming. "My sister is engaged and I want to be a part of this event," thought Elizabeth as she lay in bed in her candlelit bedroom.

CHAPTER 2

Weddings!

A letter had come from the Crofts to Anne asking her to be their particular guest at Kellynch Hall during the week of Louisa Musgrove's wedding. This was a delightful surprise for Anne on several points. She would be able to reside at her beloved Kellynch Hall, visit with the always pleasant Crofts, spend time with Frederick, and attend Louisa's wedding.

"This would be a very amiable circumstance indeed," wrote Anne, and she accepted.

Sir Walter and Elizabeth were invited to stay at Lady Russell's estate just in the neighbourhood. Captain Benwick, Harville, and Warwick would stay at Kellynch, making this a very merry party indeed.

The Musgroves made final their preparations at the church and Barton Hall, where they would hold the wedding party. The Musgrove estate is large to be sure but not formal enough for these affairs, and no one knew the Crofts so much as to ask for leave to have the ball at that estate. Louisa had her dress. Mother and sister organized the church, the after-ball, and the invitee list. Anne was crucial with advice and little details like the flowers, the vicar, the psalms to be read and the music to be played. The men did what was expected and that was to show up on time, be dressed for the occasion, and be in good spirits, attentive and patient with the proceedings and women. All was ready.

During the week Anne and Mrs. Croft were the centre of attention at Kellynch Hall. With five naval officers and two women, one could hardly guess at this excellent circumstance. Anne was loved by one, dear friends with two and admired by the others at the party.

At the first supper, the conversation turned to Anne and the eight years previous. "Anne. I am determined to uncover the details of eight years ago and this business of an engagement to our dear friend Wentworth," commented Benwick.

"Ah, that was a time when I was very young, sir, and easily persuaded by those in my circle. You see. I was very much in love with my Captain, but my family disapproved of the match owing to several reasons. They were against the match due to Frederick being a young naval officer going off to war, with no fortune, title, and no connections. This would be most imprudent a match. It broke my heart and that of Frederick when the engagement was broken off.

"I spent eight years having the papers as my authority on Frederick's wellbeing and only my wish to be with Frederick someday. I thought this to be impossible, my chance gone," explained Anne.

"I wondered why you were so driven for the coin Frederick. I now understand the purpose of your focus," mentioned Harville.

"Miss Anne, I admit I am an admirer of yours. In the last months, I watched what I thought was the courtship of Louisa and Frederick while you patiently and with much grace endured the suffering of not having Frederick to yourself. It took great strength and the courage of any naval Captain in the heat of battle surely to remain composed," commented Admiral Croft, acknowledging Anne.

"Well my dear, said Mrs. Croft, it is good of you to notice and admit to such power that a well-bred lady possesses in times of trial."

"Yes, I admit it openly, how could it be otherwise," replied Admiral Croft, smiling at Mrs. Croft and Anne to the grins of his male guests.

"How are your plans for the wedding coming along Anne?" asked Mrs. Croft.

"Frederick and I have decided on the date for the wedding, our honeymoon…"

"You will have your reception and after ball here at your home, Kellynch Hall of course," interrupted Mrs. Croft.

"It would only be right," stated Frederick.

"Dear, would it be considered a slight to invite Sir Walter and Elizabeth to stay at Kellynch Hall the week of Anne's wedding?" asked Admiral Croft to Mrs. Croft.

"Let us ask Anne. Anne what do you think about the matter?" asked Mrs. Croft of Anne.

"I can enquire with Father on your behalf. I don't see any impediments. It is very kind of you surely," replied Anne.

"Of course, you will be invited to stay," commented Mrs. Croft.

"Thank you Mrs. Croft for your kind regard toward me," said Anne.

"Not at all Anne," replied Mrs. Croft.

"Tomorrow is the church meeting over Louisa and Harville's wedding. We are considering a walk to the church, weather permitting. Are our women up for an easy walk with four naval officers as escorts Mrs. Croft, and Miss Elliot? You will of course be under our protection all the way through," said Harville.

"Yes, I believe we would enjoy the company of four officers of His Majesty's Service," replied Anne cheerfully.

"So it is settled," commented Benwick with a smile.

"The Admiral shall go ahead by carriage and on the return trip, he can take Anne and me if it comes to that," said Mrs. Croft.

The rest of the evening was all ease as Anne and Mrs. Croft retired, leaving the men to tales of war and conquest late into the evening.

The next morning was bright with the sun after a few days of rain. Later that morning the group would make their way to the church meeting, arriving in the company of the Musgroves, Sir Walter, Elizabeth, and Lady Russell.

"Anne, might I sit with you this morning and talk of our wedding details? I have many officers wishing to attend, we have much to do," explained Frederick.

"Of course my Captain. Have no worries," replied Anne.

"Miss Elliot, will Elizabeth be at the church today?" asked Captain Warwick shyly, turning to her.

"I believe so sir. I am expecting an invitation to dine at Lady Russell's this evening and will discreetly extend an invitation to this party. What do you say to that sir?" exclaimed Anne.

"Many compliments to you Miss Elliot," replied Captain Warwick.

Mrs. Croft, Anne, Frederick, Harville, and friends had a pleasant walk to the parish church where they were met by the Musgroves in force, Lady Russell, Sir Walter, and Elizabeth. As expected, Lady Russell extended her invitation to dine not only to Anne but the Crofts and guests, as well as the Musgroves and the vicar. This was indeed a very generous offer extended by Lady Russell. "This is a mending of the fences for the pains of eight years previous," thought Anne.

The mood at the church was very light and positive and one could see the ease and love that existed between Louisa and Harville. All wished them happy as the practice ceremony concluded. At its end, the vicar declared all to be ready with each person knowing their part. "Until Saturday," announced the vicar.

On the walk back Mrs. Croft, Anne, and her officer escort stopped in the village at the local shop to pick up several small items, with Anne walking to the dress shop to look at ribbons.

When everyone was done they all met and walked together to Kellynch Hall in high spirits and expectation of a good and amiable supper at Lady Russell's this evening.

After a while, at Kellynch Hall, "What is it Anne?" asked Frederick, over a cup of tea.

"It is hard to believe at times we are engaged, the family is in support, and all the things you already do for me. I like it when you call me 'my dear'. I am truly happy my Captain," exclaimed Anne.

"And so am I my dear," replied Frederick, as the carriages arrived to convey them to the Lady Russell's estate.

"The evening's events at Lady Russell's estate were as expected. There was much in the way of easy conversation and amiable feelings among all the guests present. The vicar had taken an unexpected nap after a bit too much wine. Anne was asked to play the pianoforte.

Lady Russell made an extra effort to assure Captain Wentworth was well engaged in pleasant conversation with her. To her surprise, Anne could see her Captain make great efforts to be attentive to Lady Russell, with his ease of conversation and polite nature. "I was pleased to see the two most important people in my life getting along so well," thought Anne.

All the captains present, for that fact, successfully engaged Lady Russell, being experienced through many societal events. The Crofts moved adeptly from one group to another throughout the evening, assuring a conversation with all the attendees. "Even Elizabeth and Father relaxed enough to smile and extend a hand of friendship," thought Anne.

Elizabeth and Captain Warwick got on famously indeed, her Captain never leaving her side the whole of the evening; nor did she want him to. "I wonder though if she has made up her mind. If so, she has not felt the need to tell me her happy news as yet. Cousin Elliot is to arrive tomorrow. I shall be interested in the goings on if not to be a support for my sister," wrote Anne in her diary.

The next couple of days flew by more quickly than Anne wanted. One of the days it rained all day, leaving Anne and Frederick to spend the whole of the day together. Anne found she could tolerate Frederick quite well. "He is never underfoot but just there when I will talk with him on the many subjects of no consequence, and those only important to the female sex. I wonder if you know I can't do without you now, my dear Captain," thought Anne sitting across from Frederick that evening reading beside the fire.

The morning of the wedding was busy with last-minute preparations. Captain Benwick, at Kellynch hall, dressed in his naval uniform for this formal affair. He seemed relaxed but with a heightened sense of focus. His Captain friends assured him he was in good cheer and had all his wants fulfilled.

Louisa, at the Musgrove estate, went about her business in a way instructed by her mother, who, by the way, seemed more nervous than the daughter to be married. Her sister prepared all her clothes, and her breakfast and organized the servants, assuring she would not have to worry in the least. After breakfast, the servant came into her room to prepare her hair while others laid out her dress. All was in readiness for an early afternoon ceremony as the carriage arrived ahead of time, and the driver and attendants prepared the box for the bride.

Even the sun came out as light fluffy clouds slowly crossed the sky every so often. It was a warm and pleasant day by English standards. The parish church was being worked on since before dawn, with flowers and ribbon being set, pew books being arranged and last-minute touch-ups being completed. The church was ready by the time the vicar came to inspect the progress several hours ahead of time.

"During last night's supper at Lady Russell's, Louisa asked me to come to her at Uppercross to help with her preparations. Frederick. The carriage is here to take me. I shall see you at the church then?" said Anne to Frederick.

"Of course my dear," Frederick commented while taking her hand and kissing it. Frederick accompanied Anne to the carriage, waving as it left for the Musgrove estate just across the hedge row.

This would be a simple but elegant ceremony for Louisa and Captain Harville. Near Uppercross was Barton Hall, where the reception and after-ball would be held. This would be an easy ride or walk from the church. With a quiet now that seemed to take hold, everything was in readiness at the church just before the ceremony.

Some of the villagers and neighbours began to gather near the church for a glimpse of the proceedings. The Musgroves had many acquaintances and well-wishers. As guests began to arrive, they were greeted by family and friends and had a quick chat outside the church just before entering its doors.

With all in attendance now, Wentworth and Benwick arrived as planned. Just after that, another carriage approached the church carrying Louisa, her mother, Henrietta, and Anne. As all the occupants came out one in turn from the carriage, Anne could be found lending a hand in straightening the veil and helping to set the train back as preparations were made for Louisa's entry.

Captain Wentworth, as best man, stood to the right of Captain Benwick. Anne imagined herself at that moment, "Yes. I can see it; how nervous I will be," she thought.

Just that quickly the ceremony was over and the newly married couple exited the church as everyone wished them happiness, throwing coins into the air as is the tradition. They were all off to Barton Hall for the reception and after the ball. Frederick found his way to Anne's side and like a familiar couple, Anne laid her hand in the fold of her Captain's curved arm. They strolled toward Barton Hall together with the whole wedding party.

Neither one said anything for a while. They just enjoyed the stroll, thinking about what it would be like on their special day. "A beautiful ceremony," said Anne finally, holding Frederick's arm tightly.

"Yes, indeed," replied Frederick.

Villagers knowing Anne paused to exchange greeting with her, bowing and moving on quickly. Most of the wedding guests decided to walk along the lane because the day was so lovely in sunshine and temperature and Barton Hall was only a short walk away. The carriages could be seen empty and slowly going on ahead to the hall.

Barton Hall was a stately manner on any day but especially today with the garden trimmed and rooms ready for the wedding party with food, candles, musicians, and people. As the evening came and the air-cooled fires were lit, servants could be seen running here and there, guests arriving and leaving at a steady flow. Music could be heard playing to those that danced. The event was a success with much in the way of enjoyment and celebration.

Anne, escorted by her Captain throughout the evening said, "I have missed Kellynch Hall." Anne opened up to Frederick about her feelings about her childhood home and the many memories. "My hope has always been to one day return to live in my childhood home. When we are married, since Kellynch may not be possible, perhaps we can take a house nearby. If that would be agreeable with you Frederick," commented Anne.

"Of course my dear Anne," replied Frederick, smiling at another wish coming true but still a secret of his and Sir Walter. Frederick was to purchase Kellynch Hall for Anne.

In the meantime, Frederick would act otherwise. "We will engage a solicitor to see what houses might be available in the neighbourhood," he commented.

The evening went well and it was time for the happy couple to be off to honeymoon, a fortnight in Scotland. The Crofts asked Anne to stay on at her apartment at Kellynch Hall for a few more days, so accommodating now that they knew the story of Frederick's regard and their pending wedding. Anne agreed.

"Anne, I am to leave for a couple of days to town on important business matters. When I return, I would be happy to escort you back to Bath. Would that be acceptable?" asked Frederick.

"That would be wonderful," replied Anne.

Unbeknown to Anne, Frederick would be making the final arrangements to complete the purchase of Kellynch Hall, a surprise wedding present for his dear bride. Frederick, off to town, engaged his solicitor in signing the papers directly.

Upon his return, Frederick spoke to Sir Walter about the advantages of this scheme. "This purchase will do two things for you, Sir Walter. It will free you of debt immediately with a considerable fortune to spare and keep Kellynch Hall in the family. Of course, once Anne and I are married, we will keep apartments at Kellynch for Elizabeth's and your particular use."

"This is all to my advantage sir. I see I am dealing with a very honourable man, thank you, Captain Wentworth," said Sir Walter as they shook hands.

The purchase of Kellynch Hall would be a dream come true for Anne and the expense of it would not dent Frederick's wallet since he had a considerable fortune in Spanish Gold. Sir Walter would come back to Kellynch Hall during the winter months since Bath would be nothing during these months and Sir Walter agreed that all was to be kept confidential for the sake of Anne's wedding surprise; not even Elizabeth had an idea.

Lady Russell wished Anne to have a grand affair. "You have suffered much Anne," said Lady Russell.

"Like my mother, simple and elegant is best in these affairs," said Anne.

Lady Russell, not deterred, saw her challenge to be that of two parts, first a modest country affair at the parish church and second at Kellynch Hall with its Grand Ball and Reception rooms. The reception would be more in the way of lavish. This would satisfy Anne and her wishes, and Sir Walter's need for pomp and circumstance on this very special occasion.

Lady Russell revealed her plans to Sir Walter and Elizabeth, "Let us make a good showing of it Lady Russell," said Sir Walter.

Sir Walter and Elizabeth gave their blessings to Lady Russell's plan. Lady Russell had a word with the Crofts on the plan and brought Frederick into the circle of confidence. "I am a supporter of this plan, Lady Russell. How can I help?" asked Frederick.

"First, keep this confidence," said Lady Russell, "and leave the planning to me and your sister. This will be yours and Anne's day."

Lady Russell reviewed the wedding plans, focusing on the church ceremony, with Anne. Anne, content the wedding at the parish church would be simple and elegant, with the reception and after-ball at Kellynch Hall to be a bit more to satisfy Father and Elizabeth, approved the plan.

"I will keep a few surprises to my confidence but Anne would get all she desired that special day," thought Lady Russell.

"The invitation list should include Dowager Viscountess Dalrymple and the Honourable Miss Carteret, Cousin Elliot, the Musgroves, the Crofts," said Sir Walter to Lady Russell.

"The Musgroves and the Crofts want to help with the wedding preparations," mentioned Anne smiling.

"I shall indeed put them to work. You can be sure," replied Lady Russell.

"There is Captain Warwick, he asked to escort me to the wedding and after the ball, and I accepted," commented Elizabeth, as the room went silent, wanting more information.

Elizabeth, now, the aim of intensified attention from Captain Warwick and Cousin Elliot, was undertaking to decide her happiness where both are equal in wealth, connections, and family. "What will you do with both suitors Elizabeth?" asked Lady Russell as those in the room looked on with raised eyebrows.

"I just don't know. I haven't made any decisions as yet. Nor have either made me an offer," replied Elizabeth.

The Lady Russell remained silent but attentive.

"It would be appropriate to invite several Admiral Croft's colleagues, of the Admiralty, to the wedding. Captain Wentworth is well respected and up-and-coming in these circles, and it is only right to do so. Shall I provide you with a list Lady Russell?" queried Mrs. Croft.

"Of course, Mrs. Croft" replied Lady Russell, as tea was served.

"Anne, I realise you want the wedding to remain a simple country ceremony, but many important and prominent personages will come to this wedding so it is only right that the reception and after ball at Kellynch Hall be sufficiently grand," commented Sir Walter.

"Yes Father, I agree," said Anne.

Captain Wentworth served Lady Russell a cup of tea as she sat at the drawing-room desk among many papers detailing the wedding plan and invitee list. She realised how dear Anne was to her, and Frederick, not so unaware of Lady Russell's guilt was attentive to her, which was only right under the circumstances.

"Thank you Lady Russell for all your help in this matter," said Anne.

"Not at all child, it is the least I can do, and I do have Mrs. Croft's assistance so it is not too much," replied Lady Russell.

Captains Benwick and Harville offered Frederick help with his wedding preparations. One very important detail to be managed was to manage the work with tradesmen to restore Kellynch Hall to its full glory, while Frederick and Anne were on honeymoon, with the work being completed just before their return to their Somerset home. "I have engaged several tradesmen and detailed all the work to be done. Here is the list of repairs and changes," said Frederick confidentially to Benwick and Harville.

"Quite a lot of work here Wentworth!" said Benwick.

"I have talked to sister and Admiral Croft on the daily noise to expect," said Frederick.

"Does Anne know of this scheme?" asked Harville.

"No, nothing at all," replied Frederick.

"What a surprise it will be then," commented Benwick.

"Right, we will perform our maneuvers well," said Harville.

Mrs. Smith, a particular guest of Anne's, helped with some simple wedding tasks, asking Nurse Rooke as well to seal invitations, dispatch notes, and organise servants for the after-ball. "Anne, thank you for inviting us as your particular guests, it is wonderful to help with your wedding and leave Bath for a few days," commented Harriet.

Anne wrote in her diary, "In less than a month my Captain and I will be married in the parish church at Kellynch. Bath is quiet these last few days, and I should be glad of it because tomorrow a party of us will be off to town in search of my wedding dress. I will travel with Lady Russell and Elizabeth to her estate near Kellynch; spend the night, where Louisa and Benwick, my Captain and Lady Russell, as well as Mary and Charles and I will make for a three-day trip to town (London). All this, in search of the perfect wedding dress, but Frederick insists on me having my heart's desire, and I must confess I will indulge just this once."

In town, at accomplishing their mission, they attended a play and an assembly before returning to Lady Russell's estate, and now just that quickly they were safely in Bath.

"As it is raining quite a lot these last few days I have had no choice but to think of the wedding. In just a fortnight I will be married to my Captain, and we will be off to honeymoon. I am all at once happy beyond words and nervous over the thought," wrote Anne in her diary.

"Henrietta's wedding was solemn as is only right of the wedding ceremony and the reception and after ball lacked a bit of music and dancing that one would expect of these happy occasions. I suppose, perhaps, this was due to the marrying of a country curate. All in all, and for the most part the occasion was a pleasant affair. It will be something to be noted but not necessarily remembered. Thank goodness Lady Russell will have none of this in my case" continued Anne in her diary.

"In less than a fortnight you will be married," said Lady Russell.

"I am so very excited and afraid all at the same time," replied Anne.

"Do you have doubts?" asked Lady Russell.

"No, I am sure of my Captain and my feelings. I suppose it is the nature of a woman to worry about the important events of our lives," commented Anne.

"The wedding will go well Anne. In a few days, you will be at my estate with your family around you. Frederick will be just up the lane at Kellynch Hall. And with the parish church there in between our estates and the village, nothing can go wrong," explained Lady Russell with a broad smile.

"Of course dear lady," replied Anne.

Sir Walter and Elizabeth made Lady Russell's estate the only option for staying on two points, in particular. Since the Musgrove estate was too 'rural' compared to that of Kellynch Hall and lacked the civilised amenities required of a gentleman with title, it would be beneath the dignity. On the second point, Kellynch Hall was not an option because it was not right that the bride and groom reside under the same roof before the marriage. Lady Russell's offer to stay at her estate, in the neighbourhood was acceptable on both points.

On the trip to Lady Russell's estate, it seemed every point was considered many times to assure not to have missed any essential detail. After some resistance, Anne settled into the review of the passing countryside and enjoyed the discussions in the carriage. There was very little else to do on such a ride. Elizabeth assured the invitee's list was complete while Lady Russell focused on all the social aspects and standards to be observed, as well as the timing of the events.

After a couple of days at Lady Russell's, Frederick and the Crofts were invited to supper. Frederick and Anne paid great attention to each other but did not neglect their fellow guests.

"I can't help thinking my Captain, which of my all-important nothings should I tell you first," said Anne.

"Well, my dear start at the beginning. I am all ears for you," replied Frederick.

After some days of nearly constant rain, the sun was out in all its glory. Anne woke to Lady Russell, Elizabeth, Mary, and Louisa's prompting and breakfast, which was brought up to her room. It was her special day!

Lady Russell, ever prepared, went through the events of the day. Louisa was the most fun of the group. So young and exuberant, she always had a smile and enjoyed life's happiest moments. "For someone nervous over the events to come there is no better medicine than the distraction of youthful enthusiasm," thought Anne, engaged in the distraction. Anne was glad for all the attention. The morning was flying by quickly. Henrietta arrived adding to the excitement of the moment.

It was soon time to prepare. Anne's dress was readied. While she sat, the final touches to her hair were made. Louisa and Henrietta helped Anne fit the wedding dress to a chorus of 'oohs' and 'ahhs". With the dress on, the jewelry was then put on carefully. "Some of the pieces are mothers and very sentimental," commented Anne.

There was one surprise piece, which came in a box wrapped in pink sheer silk and matching soft ribbon. "My dear Anne, I am so happy I can hardly speak of this joy. Thank you for waiting for me, for marrying me this day. Let us go forward and love each day together. Your Captain," read Anne with tears in her eyes now; and just that quickly she was ready.

Lady Russell noticed the usual nerves. "My dear Anne, it is normal to be nervous but don't let the moments be lost to them. Enjoy each, pause, and remember. This is your day, your time, your moment. All of your supporters are here and around you." Elizabeth listened attentively. Her admirers were heating up and she expected her day to come soon. She was learning well what to expect in this case.

"You ought certainly to live in this moment dear sister," commented Elizabeth to the surprise of Lady Russell and Anne.

"What wisdom from someone so steeped in her affairs," thought Anne as she smiled in acknowledgment.

The church filled with arriving guests and the expected onlookers of the event gathered across the lane in several places. Frederick's arrival marked the closeness of the ceremony to its beginning. Dressed in the full Royal Navy uniform of His Majesty's Service, this would only be the second time Anne would have seen him in this way. Many officers were in attendance and dressed in uniform, fully lending power to the ceremony to come and awe in the local villagers.

Many of the guests stopped Frederick to offer him congratulations, advice on the institution of marriage and to see his nerves on this day. Captain Warwick arrived with Elizabeth as expected and their coming heralded the soon arrival of Anne.

"Captain Wentworth, it is time to take your place at the front of the church sir," said the Vicar.

Captains Benwick and Harville escorted Frederick to the front of the church, using small talk to keep his nervousness in check. "My friend, you have nerves of steel in the heat of battle, fighting pirates and with the sword. Why would this be any different?" asked Harville.

"Yes, this is certain," smiled Frederick.

Anne peaked out of the window to see her carriage ready and waiting to take her to the church up the lane. "Are we ready? It is time," exclaimed Lady Russell.

"Yes, let us be off then and give a grand performance for our guest," replied Anne.

Lady Russell, Louisa, and Henrietta exited the rooms. At the bottom of the stairs, Sir Walter awaited his daughter, escorted by Lady Russell. "I shall not be sorry to be seen with you my dear!"

commented Sir Walter, his way of telling Anne she looked very presentable. Into the carriage and off to the church they went. All was quiet on the three-minute ride as the bride arrived at the church.

The carriage attendant opened the doors and laid the steps out for the passenger exit. Sir Walter exited the carriage first, and then the Lady Russell. Louisa and Henrietta helped Anne carefully out of the carriage. Sir Walter covered Anne's face with the sheer veil, giving her an angelic look in all that dress. One could hear the standing onlookers sigh in admiration at her vision. Many there knew her from childhood.

The church went hushed as the signal that Anne had arrived and was about to any second now, appear at the entry. Anne, looking so beautiful and vulnerable in her gown, was visible to those in the church. Anne looking at Frederick thought, "How handsome he looks; do I deserve him?" Steadying her nerves she said to her father with a smile "I am ready father."

For the first time in many years, to Sir Walter's surprise, he felt pride at the moment. The soft sound of a violin began playing, giving Sir Walter the cue to step forward.

In a tender and rare moment, Sir Walter said to Anne, "I remember your mother holding you just as if it were yesterday, and now…you are about to be married, how I wish you happy Anne."

With a tear in her eye, Anne felt moved and astonished at his sensitivity. She gathered up her composure, knowing for certain if she had any more surprises today she would just break down uncontrollably.

The sun, high in the sky, glistened through the stained glass windows, creating a rainbow of colours in the church. All eyes were upon her now with many a comforting smile. Anne walked down the aisle with her father as Henrietta fussed over her dress with last-minute adjustments. Looking magnificent on the day, even Sir Walter, Elizabeth, and Mary were surprised at her beauty and elegance, they were proud to be seen with her.

The Elliot countenances were on full display, as Anne arrived at Frederick's side.

Frederick noticed just how small and slight Anne was and how vulnerable she was at the moment. He determined he would shield her, to lend her his protection all the days of his life.

"Who gives this woman away?" asked the vicar, his voice clear and true.

"I do, Sir Walter Elliot, Baronet," responded Sir Walter. Frederick extended his hand and Sir Walter placed Anne's small hand into his.

"Sir, I have taken care of Anne all her life. I now turn her over to your care. Be gentle with her, she is a good girl," said Sir Walter to the startled and pleased looks of Anne and Frederick.

"I shall care for her sir. All the days of my life sir," replied Frederick, giving Anne power and strength, as Sir Walter acknowledged his comment and withdrew to the closest pew, so he might view the proceedings.

"You may kiss your bride," said the vicar to cheers and applause. The wedding ceremony went flawlessly. Anne was beautiful, Frederick perfectly tall in his Royal Navy Uniform, and the church packed and completely silent during the most precious moments. And just that quickly they were married and led to a side room where they signed the church register. For the first time, Anne signed "Mrs. Anne Elliot Wentworth," to the congratulations of the vicar.

The guests filed out while Frederick completed the formalities and had some final words with the vicar. The newlyweds were led out of the church. As they walked out, they were met with many cheers of congratulations, and coins in the air. The sun peaked from behind the clouds to a spectacular country scene as they stepped into the carriage, and they were off to Kellynch Hall where the reception and after ball was to be held. There would be plenty of food, drink, music, and dancing, as this was not a country curate being married and the Elliot name to be upheld.

The reception ball was impeccable in its music, dancing, ceremony, and excellent conversation. There were so many well-wishers and much in the way of amiable feelings. Anne danced with Frederick all night and when she was not she was introduced to many of the navy officers and their wives, engaging in conversation and making new friends and acquaintances. Sir Walter was entertained with stories of His Majesty and court where many an Admiral was required to attend. Elizabeth experienced firsthand the social circle her dear Warwick traveled and realised he was a man of connections.

All of a sudden it was dawn before the last of the guests retired from the ball, each wishing the newlyweds happy on their honeymoon and hoping to see them upon their return.

"It has been a magical day from its beginnings to its end, truly," wrote Anne, later in her diary.

Anne and Frederick would leave in a matter of hours for a month-long honeymoon. Frederick, not afraid of travel across the sea, would take Anne to Spain and Italy. Anne thought this to be an adventure of a lifetime as she had hardly left the English countryside and ventured into London only rarely.

"I would never have even thought of such a travel but for you Frederick," said Anne yawning at this long day and night of celebration.

The final guests, having not retired completely as yet and seeing it was just past dawn, presented their compliments and departed, leaving Sir Walter, Elizabeth, the Lady Russell, and the Crofts to a quiet hall. They conversed about how wonderful the ball had been, the amiable guests, the general splendour of the hall, the wedding, and that Frederick and Anne would be leaving on honeymoon for a month full before they would see each other again.

"Don't forget to wrap yourselves well so as not to catch a cold," said one guest.

"I am not sure that it is good for the health, all this coming and going," said Sir Walter, hinting at perhaps his not wanting Anne to leave.

Sir Walter told Elizabeth, in confidence, of Frederick's purchase of Kellynch Hall as a wedding present for Anne. "Captain Wentworth purchased the property at considerable cost. Now the Elliots are out of debt and have a modest fortune to live on. Perhaps a bit of economy this time. Anne does not know yet of the gift. A condition of the sale, of course, is the use of the home during the winter months, and summers can be spent in Bath."

Elizabeth smiled. "I can see my brother is quite generous, and I am glad of it," replied Elizabeth discreetly. With her newfound respect for Anne and liking of Captain Wentworth, she would find these circumstances to be very amiable indeed.

The happy couple, now in travel attire, took a bite of breakfast and conversation before they would leave on their honeymoon. "I would expect a nap will be the first task above all," said Admiral Croft in his jolly way.

"Yes, we are awake if only for the excitement of the moment," replied Anne with a happy note. They waved as the carriage left to take them to Portsmouth and their ship to their first destination, Spain.

To Anne, the carriage seemed to glide along the English countryside. "Anne, my wish is you will learn of the sea and places outside of England so you may know me better and gain a broader experience of the world," said Frederick.

"This will be the first I set foot on a ship and in another country for that fact. I am very excited and nervous," replied Anne.

Within a couple of days, work began to restore Kellynch Hall to its full glory. Captains Benwick and Harville took this task seriously since Frederick was a dear friend, and now Anne. Elizabeth and Sir Walter provided advice to the pair with histories and tales of interest in the guiding of the restoration work. Anne and Frederick invited Sir Walter and Elizabeth to stay on at Kellynch as long as they liked, and they graciously accepted the offer.

The work progressed well and would be completed two days before the couple returned. Sir Walter, surprised at the restored beauty of Kellynch Hall, described childhood memories of his family seat. "See here Benwick, the Lady Elliot had her first pains of birth as we rushed to her aid and conveyed her to our apartments there, and this was where Anne was born," said Sir Walter reminiscing.

The gardens were made pristine again. All the rooms were polished to a shine. New furnishings replaced the old and tattered ones in the drawing room. Some pieces were repaired and cleaned while others were replaced entirely. The library was restocked with books and little touches, and pictures of the family placed about the rooms. Even a commissioned painting of Anne and Frederick during the wedding ceremony was completed and hung prominently at the entrance. The floors were polished and cleaned, and the wood glowed now. With the windows clean inside and out, the out-of-doors shone through and when the sun peaked through the clouds, streams of light poured in, creating many shades and beams.

Flowers were everywhere. The Crofts moved into a quiet apartment on the west side of the great house as Frederick didn't want them to leave the hall, but they wanted to be out of the way.

Final preparations were made to ready the place for Anne and Frederick's return. It was late afternoon when a carriage was seen half a mile up the lane in the direction of Uppercross since that was where the happy couple had decided they would stay while they decided on the purchase of a small country house in the neighbourhood, or at least that was what Anne thought.

A few weeks earlier, "The next weeks would surprise Anne certainly…" thought Frederick.

"Frederick, the trip to Spain has changed me somehow. I can't help but replay it in my mind. I have written every detail in my diary, so I never forget," said Anne as the ship at sea made for Italy.

"I hoped you could experience a little of what I know in the navy, my dear. I am glad to hear it," responded Frederick.

CHAPTER 3

Fulfilled Dreams

In general, Anne could hardly contain all the experiences she encountered abroad on her honeymoon. She sat this evening reading her diary reviewing many of her recent adventures. "Have no fear, my dear Anne. I am with you every step. I believe these experiences will broaden your horizons and deepen our connection," said Frederick as he boarded the ship to Spain with Anne at his side.

"I have hardly been outside of the village with short infrequent trips to London and Bath, let alone boarding a ship to Spain, my Captain. This is all new to me, but I shall have confidence with you at my side," read Anne from her diary, remembering how wide-eyed she was at all the hustle and bustle of an active port town.

"Is this going to and from normal Frederick?" asked Anne.

"Yes, dear, many ships load and unload cargo here from around the world. The cargo is then distributed to London and other cities. In turn, goods are shipped from here from our manufacturers for transport around the world. Mostly, goods go between our colonies and some to our allies and trading partners.

Trade is important to the empire. The need for a strong Navy is apparent. Do you see?" asked Frederick.

"Our honeymoon will be important in two respects. First, this is our honeymoon, and it is just you and I together. I have waited eight long years for these days. The second point of gain is you're experiencing the sea and having adventures, with me, in other countries, you have only read about. You will encounter different cultures in Spain and Italy, the food, people, the countryside and even the weather! One will get to know the sun quite well, unlike in England," replied Frederick smiling.

"I look forward to all the experiences my Captain," read Anne remembering.

"Barcelona was magnificent my dear Captain. The warm evenings, supper in the out of doors, the people, and the food, were so different and pleasant at the same time. I could hardly keep up with all the new ideas and views to be seen and experiences to be had. And now we are off to Rome, and I want so much to see all the sites, and drink in all the culture and people. I don't feel so small as before. What will the food be like Frederick?"

"Italy is quite different than Spain in language, food, and culture, but not so different as to be a great contrast. You will love the food. There is a dish called pasta. It is made of boiled flower strings, cheese, and tomatoes on top. It is very good for the taste. The weather will be quite warm and sunny there too. Look at you, you are quite sun-bleached and freckled now. Very beautiful and healthy," commented Frederick as they reached the Italian port.

The port was busy with large and small vessels about. The Mediterranean Sea was the deepest blue with a matching sky. The town was full of colour, with flags and banners of all sorts hung about. The people were friendly and the smell of the food glorious, making one hungry instantly, the culture just penetrated one.

"We hired a carriage for Rome and lodging for the fortnight of adventures to come. I wished for a proper cup of tea but there was none to be found in the foreign lands. They had a hot drink called coffee that could be found in London but certainly not throughout England. One could become used to this drink, especially the Italian make of it. I have stored some of the seeds that are crushed and placed in boiling water then strained into a cup and drank with a touch of milk," read Anne from her diary.

"My dear we have arrived," said Frederick.

Closing her diary now as they arrived at the lodging, they stepped out to a warm early evening where it was not quite dark and not quite full sun. An attendant met them at the door and saw to the cases while Frederick escorted Anne into the lodging. Anne noticed it was quiet and clean, rooms were like apartments, and some common rooms where breakfast and supper would be served to guests. "This must be a new idea in lodging and very convenient indeed," said Anne as she and Frederick were led to their apartments for the fortnight.

"Sir, supper will be served in the half hour. Please feel free to attend should you be hungry. Shall I come for you?" said the attendant.

"Yes please, we will freshen up first. We are quite starved I assure you," smiled Anne to the smiling servant.

The attendant knocked on Anne and Frederick's door and escorted the couple to supper. There they met other couples from London and other guests from Spain and Greece. They all knew some broken English, which was enough to hold a simple and enjoyable conversation.

"Shall we walk my dear before we turn in?" asked Frederick.

"Yes, that would be lovely. I am still affected by the rocking of the ship at sea," replied Anne, taking Frederick's arm on the way out of the lodging.

"You have done so well Anne. On the ship, you have not been too seasick, and you have taken in all the experiences with eagerness, and all of this without a good English cup of tea," joked Frederick.

"Frederick, how can people be so different and the same?" asked Anne.

"That is the question. Culture and language may separate us but in the end, people are what they are. We are born, grow up, marry, raise children, and live with all the problems and happiness that we stumble into on the road of life," replied Frederick.

"Eight years ago I could not have imagined this for us. You have grown so much in maturity and experience and are gracious to share it all with me. Thank you, my dear Captain," said Anne, holding Frederick's arm tightly as they strolled along a quiet street in Rome, Italy.

The next morning a carriage was waiting for them after breakfast. Frederick had organised a day of touring. They would tour the Roman ruins and have lunch at a local café, as well as shop in the local store. "My dear, like in Spain, let us buy a few items that will remind us in years to come of our experiences here," said Frederick. The next day was the Vatican and castles of note.

"Caio bene," said Anne, thanking the lodging attendant at supper. "Caio Seniora," returned the attendant in a natural manner of the culture.

"What is this? A new language my dear?" asked Frederick, smiling approval.

"It seems these strange and wonderful words can't help but be learned," laughed Anne, so relaxed and glowing.

"The fortnight flew by with many singular experiences of note. And now we are on board a ship viewing the coast of our beloved England," wrote Anne in her diary.

"Oh, this small and precious island," thought Anne.

Arriving at Portsmouth, Anne commented on her surprise at the lack of sun and warmth in the weather, smiling in jest, and determined to find, after a month, a proper cup of tea. Frederick managed the bags - some of which had special mementos of their adventures - directing the carriage attendant.

Once the bags were secured and a carriage hired for the trip to the Musgrove estate the next morning, Frederick and Anne set out in search of supper and lodging for the evening.

"You have grown so much in your manner my dear Anne," said Frederick.

"In what way my Captain?" asked Anne.

"Well, a month ago I would have led the way in search of supper. Now just a month later you are at my side eager to investigate all the possibilities and discuss the decisions to be made. A true-life partner, commented Frederick, with his broad smile and look of approval.

"I didn't notice sir, but this is true," replied Anne as they settled on an inn to stay the night, enjoying supper across the street at a small and quaint tea room, while realising the next step in their life was about to begin.

They settled in for the evening. "Even though we are on a bed on solid ground, I still feel a rocking feeling," said Anne to a laughing Frederick.

"In a few days the rocking will go away my dear," replied Frederick smiling.

In the morning, finishing breakfast, "Ah, I have missed my tea. I am right as rain my dear," said Anne as the hired carriage arrived early to take her and Frederick to her home county. On their way and in the morning rain so common, the carriage moved along the King's Highway unimpeded.

"Frederick, perhaps tomorrow we may engage a solicitor to begin inquiries for houses in the neighbourhood of Kellynch? What say you?" asked Anne.

"This sounds like an excellent notion my dear. We shall proceed thus," replied Frederick while he thought of the surprise he would present to his beloved wife.

"How will I explain the strange and wonderful places of Spain and Italy, the voyages and the port cities? The people, the food, and the culture. Can my acquaintances conceive of such ideas?" asked Anne.

"I believe much will be lost in translation but your saving grace will be my sister since she has traveled abroad and will know well most of your adventures. How she will talk with you over many cups of tea about what you saw, ate, places visited, and culture differences," commented Frederick.

"I am glad we have some gifts for her of our travels that will bring back a memory or two," said Anne yawning, before closing her eyes and drifting off to sleep, head leaning on Fredrick's broad shoulders, he felt protective of Anne.

Anne awoke to discover they had reached their destination, the Musgrove estate. They pulled up now to pouring rain.

"Welcome back dear ones! Welcome back!" exclaimed Mrs. Musgrove, covered by a shoal holding an umbrella. "I have hot tea and supper for you both! You must tell all, or perhaps you need rest, maybe tomorrow morning," cried Lady Musgrove, with Louisa looking on and excitedly taking Anne's hand.

It was early in the evening and over a cup of tea it would be proper as a guest to provide initial descriptions of what was done, seen, and known during the honeymoon since all would be eager to listen. Even the servants hid in the shadows straining for the words, living the moments themselves as described.

After a sufficient start to the descriptions of places, food, and people, Anne and Frederick begged to withdraw to their bedroom for the evening, leaving their host breathless at such talk, but they were tired and needed time to rest and refresh. "Good evening everyone, it is good to be back," said Frederick before leaving the drawing room and retiring for the evening with his Anne.

In the morning and well rested, Frederick set off on a few errands, leaving Anne at the Musgroves to describe to the woman folk and Mr. Musgrove the places of Spain and Italy. Frederick met with Benwick, who reported on the readiness and completed work at Kellynch Hall.

"We are expecting the arrival of Sir Walter and Elizabeth this morning in preparation for the surprise of Anne that Kellynch Hall is her wedding present. Pray, how was the honeymoon? How did Anne fare with the rocking of the ship?" asked Benwick.

"The honeymoon was more than I could have hoped and Anne had some sickness but quickly gained her sea legs. I will buy time by engaging a solicitor on a search for houses in the neighbourhood. See you soon my friend," said Frederick, leaving and thanking him.

Frederick proceeded with a solicitor and the searching for a small house in the neighbourhood, if not more than to keep up the air of searching. Having located a local solicitor, Frederick confidentially informed him of the scheme, who then acted out the part quite well after a small fee for his time was settled on.

"A few houses in the neighbourhood may be available Mrs. Wentworth and for ones you are interested in it will be a couple of days before we can view them," said the solicitor as Anne listened, disappointed.

"My Captain, we have not yet visited your sister and Admiral Croft. We must keep our obligation in this matter," commented Anne.

"As a matter of fact, my sister and Admiral Croft will be dining with us this evening here at the Musgroves," commented Frederick.

Anne pondered that she had been in the neighbourhood a few days now and had not even seen Kellynch Hall as yet.

Supper with the Crofts in attendance was lively and full of conversation about the adventures abroad. Frederick mentioned to his sister how Anne had missed Kellynch Hall and wished to see her childhood home. "Well my dear, you must come over for supper later this week," said Mrs. Croft.

"Thank you, with pleasure," responded Anne.

The next day was sunny, mostly with a cool wind as Anne thought of the sunny and warm Mediterranean coast. A carriage arrived that would take Frederick and Anne to the solicitors for a conversation over possible choices of homes in the neighbourhood.

"Dear Anne, I have been remiss in presenting you with a wedding present," said Frederick.

"Not at all my Captain, You have given me all good things, and I am grateful for all of it," replied Anne.

"Thank you my dear for the kindness of your words. Still, I would like to address this oversight. To do this properly I would like to blindfold you. May I?" asked Frederick.

Anne, with a puzzled look, replied, "Of course, blindfold me? If you must my Captain."

With Anne secure in the carriage and with the blindfold on, Frederick made small talk on all matters of no consequence. He, with hand gestures, directed the carriage up to the next lane where in just a few moments then came upon the Kellynch estate. Around a bend and along the entry the carriage came to a stop whereupon Frederick stepped out and with his hand guided Anne safely out of the carriage.

"My dear I would like to present to you your wedding present," announced Frederick as he untied the blindfold over Anne's eyes.

Confused Anne replied, "Where is it Frederick, do we go inside Kellynch Hall?"

"My dear Anne, Kellynch Hall is your wedding present!"

Anne stood as if frozen for what seemed like more time than should be allowable under the circumstances. She turned to Frederick with tears in her eyes as the impact of returning to Kellynch Hall and as its mistress fulfilled the most secret and precious of dreams fulfilled. "Has this come true?" she thought, holding Frederick so tightly now he had to take a deep breath as she let go. He could see his gift was well received indeed.

"My dear, let us tour the grand house. Much work was done to repair and restore the place at our leaving for honeymoon, and now it is done."

Anne could not speak out of her complete joy. "There are moments in life that are remembered above all for my sex, my Captain and this will be one of them," said Anne softly as she looked about, turning at each step as they entered the hall.

The Hall looked magnificent, every corner pristine and new. The wood and furnishings were no longer unattended and dusty. The grand staircase was polished like new. The bedrooms and study are all fine in their newer state. Entering the drawing-room, Anne found Sir Walter, Lady Russell, Elizabeth, Mary and family, the Musgroves, and Captains Benwick, Harville, and Warwick.

"Congratulations Anne," said Sir Walter as everyone in attendance raised their glasses to the happy couple.

"Thank you all," said Frederick.

"For the first time in a long while I feel like I have come home," Anne said to Frederick so that only he could hear.

Frederick was pleased with himself this day, washing away the pain of the last eight years finally, and was happy with Anne.

Anne, feeling completely joyful, slipped away to tour the house again on her own. "It is all so familiar and filled with memories, yet now with all the improvements so new and ready for a lifetime of fresh memories," Anne thought to herself.

Even the gardens were renewed with a lovely terrace area making the house seem to open to the garden as if entering a large room. "I will love this spot in spring and summer months," thought Anne, standing on the terrace enjoying the view. "It reminds me so much of the Italian and Spanish home designs I have become familiar with. Like a daydream, I could not have imagined a better circumstance," mused Anne.

Returning to the party, in the drawing room, Anne moved to Frederick's side. "Frederick, thank you for this. I have for some time dreamed of coming home or to the neighbourhood at least. Now I will be the mistress of my beloved childhood home and the thought of this is beyond words to me. Thank you. I love you dearly Frederick," she said, looking deeply into Frederick's eyes.

"I knew for some time of your love for this place. What better spot to settle? When I spoke to your father about the purchase of Kellynch, keeping it in the family, settling his debts, and giving him and Elizabeth apartments he thought this very amiable, and the arrangements were set very quickly. The scheme would leave him with a small fortune. It would secure Kellynch, and he and Elizabeth could winter here. It was to everyone's advantage. I am glad you are pleased my dear," said Frederick.

"I am not just pleased. I love it, and I love you, Frederick," said Anne.

"My dear you look a bit flush. Are you okay?" asked Frederick.

"I believe it to be all the excitement and surprise. I will sit a few moments before we supper.

At dinner, Frederick and Anne were left this first night to themselves. Having a quiet meal with Anne, Frederick related how he and Sir Walter talked of this sale that day in Bath, talking privately at Camden Place after the announcement of their engagement. Of how Captains Benwick and Harville were charged with managing the restoration of Kellynch Hall to its full glory, and how he wanted to tell her so much but knew to keep the secret.

"I am glad of you Frederick and glad to be here at Kellynch Hall. I have never wanted to leave this place. It is my childhood home. I am home now and with the one I love, there could not be any better condition," said Anne.

Anne continued. "We must plan a supper tomorrow night, and I insist on the Harvilles, the Benwicks, and the families be invited for their first dinner at Kellynch."

"Then my dear, as mistress of Kellynch, this is perfectly possible," replied Frederick.

The next morning Lady Russell called on Anne and Frederick as was only right and the duty of a neighbour. "Anne, I am so happy to see you back in the neighbourhood," exclaimed Lady Russell.

"Lady Russell, do come in. Thank you. Cup of tea?" asked Anne. After some very amiable conversation, Lady Russell took her leave to return this evening for Anne and Frederick's first formal supper party at Kellynch Hall. "Shall we see you this evening, Lady Russell?" enquired Anne.

"Of course and with pleasure," responded Lady Russell.

"Lady Russell made no secret of her pleasure to see her neighbours restored back at Kellynch Hall," said Frederick.

"She was sorry to see us in Bath. It hit her particularly hard," replied Anne waving as Lady Russell's carriage moved steadily up to the lane toward her estate.

The evening came quickly with last-minute preparations for the supper party. As supper time approached, guests began to arrive. First, it was the Harvilles and Benwick. Anne thanked them for the superb supervision of the restoration work throughout the house and grounds. "Even Sir Walter admired the showcase Kellynch has become, and we all know how particular father is," said Anne.

Benwick and Harville were modest about the effort but were glad to have helped her and Frederick in any way. Lady Russell arrived in good cheer and was quickly engaged by Sir Walter and Elizabeth in conversation, freeing Anne to review the final preparations for the supper.

With all the guests in a very amiable mood, one of the attending servants announced dinner was to be served, as all the guests were directed to the now restored dining room. Lady Russell commented on the general splendour of the room. Nameplates at each setting organised guests as to where to sit, as supper was served in courses.

Lively conversation followed, full of stories of the honeymoon, the surprise wedding present of Kellynch Hall, and the restoration work done on the house. Anne and Frederick could see the evening going along famously and were content with the close group of friends.

"Anne, you look a bit flush again. Are you okay?" asked Frederick.

"Perhaps it is all the excitement of these days," commented Lady Russell.

After a short time, Anne felt rather ill, so much so that she was taken up to her apartments. Everyone thought this was only natural with all the excitement.

"Poor Anne just needs rest," said Mrs. Musgrove.

Frederick, monitoring the situation, saw her nausea persist, and with Lady Russell at his side, she advised a surgeon be called.

"Frederick, attend your guests and when the surgeon arrives, have him sent here. At the news, I will call you; have no worries," said Lady Russell,

As Frederick left the room as instructed, Lady Russell turned to Anne. "Anne, are you thinking what I am?" commented Lady Russell.

"Yes, I may be with child. It might still be too soon to know for sure. Frederick has no idea," replied Anne looking slightly ashen in skin colour.

The surgeon arrived quickly since he lived just outside the local village. He was escorted to Anne's rooms where Anne and Lady Russell were waiting. After a time, the surgeon advised Anne she was quite pregnant. Lady Russell smiled broadly in congratulations.

"Young lady, you are healthy and with child but need your rest. You are eating and breathing for two now, moderation is best in these circumstances. You need not be bedridden, but too active a lifestyle is not healthy for you and the baby," advised the surgeon.

Lady Russell had a servant call Frederick at once. When Frederick arrived Anne asked him what names he had picked out for his child to come. Stunned at the question he asked, "Dear, are you with child?"

"Sir, your wife is quite pregnant," said the surgeon smiling with congratulations. "She is healthy but a more modest lifestyle would be best now until the birth. I will make myself available to be called quickly and will schedule to see you again in a fortnight," said the surgeon to Anne.

Frederick was elated, smiling so broadly that it was difficult not to be hurt by it.

At Anne's side on the bed, he held her softly, kissing her and putting his arms around her. "Frederick, the guests must be worried, it is best you tell them the news since I am advised to rest here," commented Anne.

"Yes, of course, my dear," replied Frederick.

"I shall go with you, Frederick, and return to Anne shortly," said Lady Russell, with Anne's approval.

"I shall wait here and complete my prescription for you Anne," said the surgeon.

"Anne, pregnant? Congratulations, Frederick!" said Benwick. The guests and family overhearing the news shouted with surprise and pleasure.

"The surgeon also mentioned she is quite healthy, and this nausea is to be expected considering her condition. He prescribes rest and ease during this time of bearing, and that he will be available in the moment and return in a fortnight to check on Anne and the baby," said Lady Russell.

Almost instantly Mary and Elizabeth asked Frederick and Lady Russell if they could visit Anne. "Yes, but quietly," responded Lady Russell as they walked excitedly up the staircase to the apartments, followed by Mrs. Musgrove (Anne's former nanny) and Lady Russell.

Frederick asked everyone for patience. "Anne will regain her strength in the next days when she will be up and about and can take visitors to the house," said Frederick.

Frederick went upstairs to check on Anne, and they embraced again at the news of their first child. Lady Russell again offered her hearty congratulations. Those of the family and friends invited to the evening supper, just before they took their leave, sent their congratulations as well.

"I will return tomorrow to attend you," said Lady Russell like a mother to a daughter.

"Thank you, Lady, I will look forward to your visit," replied Anne.

Anne recovered quickly in just a few days, while Lady Russell oversaw her treatment, coming to her each day in a routine. "With Christmas fast approaching and it being customary to hold a ball for the neighbourhood at Kellynch Hall, would you help me, Lady Russell?" asked Anne.

"Of course, child, leave all the details to me and Frederick. We will review the plan with you, but no running this way and that," ordered Lady Russell.

"Yes, of course," replied Anne happily.

"With the house in good repair, this should be one less item on the list. Shall we begin with the guest list? The invitee list should be what is expected with the inviting of those in the neighbourhood, and this year some of Frederick's naval friends would love to attend and should be invited. Of course, the eligible females in the neighbourhood will want to be informed of the attendance of officers at the ball. A single woman is always interested in the possibility of interacting with single respectable gentlemen in a way that is acceptable to society. A ball is that opportunity."

"They can practice being on display, conversation, and playing and singing at the pianoforte," commented Lady Russell.

"There is one Captain Warwick, in particular, we want to be invited for the sake of my sister Elizabeth, you see," added Anne.

The day of the Ball had arrived. Lady Russell and Anne checked with staff on all the final arrangements and inspected all the rooms to be used. Sir Walter and Elizabeth spent the day preparing themselves and awaiting their special guests. Mary arrived early in the day with the pretense of assisting but really just sought all the attention—her health, the latest gossip, and more.

Lady Russell managed her to a number of time-consuming tasks of no consequence for the cause of saving Anne's strength.

The Admiral and Mrs. Croft, out of the way in their apartments at Kellynch Hall, were excited for the evening's events. "This circumstance of Anne's return to Kellynch Hall and our staying on in these apartments is akin to acquiring a family without the expense," commented Admiral Croft approvingly.

"Yes, we are quite comfortable, and we will be involved in the lives of Anne and Frederick. And at this time of life what better circumstance could one wish for?" replied Mrs. Croft.

The Crofts were looking forward to seeing some old naval friends who had been invited and were eager for the evening's course of events. Frederick spent some regular time with Admiral Croft talking over the latest naval topics and advising Frederick on a career path. Lady Russell, after the final ball arrangements were complete, took her leave and spent the rest of the day tending to her affairs and preparing for the evening ball, leaving Anne in the capable hands of Mrs. Harriet Smith and Nurse Rooke.

"I am glad you accepted a cottage on our estate, Harriet," said Anne to Harriet and Nurse Rooke.

Anne invited Harriet as a particular guest to the ball, secretly hoping a gentleman might notice her. Harriet, in Anne's estimation, was quite attractive and accomplished, and with her health no longer an issue, it seemed time for her to get back into the fray of life. Anne was sure to secure a proper gown for Harriet for the evening's event and gained Harriet's approval in its design and material. All was set.

Anne made final checks on all the arrangements with the staff, the orchestra, food, rooms, refreshments, arrival arrangements for guests, dancing, fires in the fireplaces, and more. Harriet and Nurse Rooke advised Anne to retire now to rest an hour before getting ready for the evening, preparing her hair, and putting on her dress.

All seemed set for the evening as she rested in her apartments. There Frederick read the admiralty news and naval affairs tablet he received regularly. "Admiral Croft has advised me to join a number of admiralty committees at the naval war college. He assures me my efforts will move my career along," commented Frederick.

"What will that mean, my captain?" asked Anne.

"It will mean once a month I will spend the week in Plymouth attending to the business of the admiralty," responded Frederick.

"You seem determined on this matter," replied Anne.

"Yes, my dear it is a duty to the navy, His Majesty, and England. It must be done," said Frederick earnestly.

"You will be safe on shore?" asked Anne. "Yes, of course," replied Frederick.

"Then nothing stops you, and you have my full support in this," replied Anne.

"All is set for the evening," Anne announced as Frederick smiled.

Anne turned to Harriet. "Isn't it time for you to get ready, Harriet?"

"Oh dear, yes," replied Harriet, as she and Nurse Rooke begged their leave.

"Better go then. I shall return for the ball," said Harriet.

"Of course! Harriet, see you this evening. Thank you for all your help," replied Anne smiling.

As it tended to get dark early this time of year, candles were lit. Fires were set in preparation for the evening's festivities. One could feel the growing anticipation and excitement, as preparations for the arrival of the first carriages began with lighting the pathways and entry pieces. As Anne looked around, servants were buzzing about with final fixes. "We are ready, my captain," said Anne.

In the distance, Frederick and Anne could see the first carriages approaching up the lane.

"Air, it is the Musgroves," noted Anne, as she and Frederick greeted their guests politely and with all the civility required in these society events.

As the rest of Mary's family arrived, followed by more carriages, Sir Walter insisted Anne and Frederick take a break from greeting guests. Although this was thought to be unusual, considering Anne's condition, all would be forgiven by the guests.

Anne was grateful, since she could not stand for extended periods as yet, but was gaining more strength each day now and bearing the pregnancy well. Tonight would be a test of endurance for sure, and she would need to ascend the stairs periodically to find quiet and rest from time to time.

The navy arrived in force as Sir Walter, always questioning of such people, greeted them with all civility and in a most gentleman-like manner. Elizabeth spent a little more time with her captain Warwick in her greeting, as expected.

Sir Walter and Elizabeth were relieved by Anne and Frederick as the bulk of guests arrived, including some particular guests, whereupon Sir Walter and Elizabeth escorted them to more private rooms; the Dowager Viscountess Dalrymple, the Honourable Miss Carteret, and William Elliot. Tire Viscountess loved the navy at court and took no offense whatsoever in mingling with them now here, to Sir Walter's surprise.

Anne paid special attention to Sir Walter's particular guests so as not to injure family relations and relations with her father and sister in any manner, and to accord all the attention required of their station in society. "Relations are always worth preserving," said Anne to Frederick discreetly, smiling.

The evening progressed very well, as Anne and Frederick made the rounds to all the guests talking with each in that personal way that engenders the maintenance of or creation of true friendships. Tire dance floor was frill and the music played a delight to the ear. Frederick reminded Anne to rest every so often. "I will sit with you, my dear. The guests may get along without us for a moment or two. I would also like to dance once with my wife," said Frederick.

Elated to dance with her husband at least once, which was her hope for the evening, she replied, "Shall we dance now my captain?"

"Is it not only right and proper that the man asks the woman to dance?" responded Frederick smiling.

"I am your wife and have broader liberties than that of a single woman with a gentleman," responded Anne smiling back.

"Yes, it seems you do, my dear. However, do not strain; let us just be together," commented Frederick, waiting for a slow and short dance they might attempt for Anne's sake.

The officers, of course, received much attention from the full gathering of eligible women at the ball. As considered proper and only right, they unselfishly and prudently asked all those willing to dance and behave as perfect gentlemen in form and manner. The ladies who remained at evening's end declared those wonderfill stories that explain how attentive an officer was to them to declare the evening a great success. The single women were most satisfied indeed as attention was paid and their honour upheld.

The evening quickly turned to dawn as many guests gave their leave with many thanks to Anne and Frederick for the wonderful evening. As the last of the guests left, all proclaimed the evening a rousing success. "Well done, Anne," commented Frederick. "You seem tired; it is time for you to rest, my dear."

Before Anne retired, she set the servants on the massive task of cleaning up, hoping that by the time she awoke late in the day, she may find a house that was back in order. Taking her leave and with a cup of tea in hand, she ascended the staircase for her bed as Frederick followed her, leaving the servants to themselves and the task set before them.

"Anne is so much changed this last year, I would hardly recognise her," said Elizabeth.

"Yes, indeed," responded Sir Walter.

"She has gained confidence and patience in her manner," described Elizabeth.

"Frederick has done wonders for her and in such a short time," said the Lady Russell over a cup of tea.

"He is a gentleman in many respects and pays us great attention, assuring our enjoyment. He is as fine a brother as ever there was," said Elizabeth sitting by the drawing room fire. All there could agree they would not be sorry to be seen with Anne or Frederick.

CHAPTER 4

It's Twins

Five months later Anne was bearing her pregnancy well, fitting into Kellynch Hall with no bother at all and still discovering, to her delight, that which was worn out and broken from neglect had been restored in her beloved home. "How dear Frederick has been to me. I love him so now," thought Anne.

At regularly scheduled visits the surgeon confirmed Anne's health. "Frederick, the surgeon will visit today," said Anne.

"Are we healthy dear?" asked Frederick.

"I believe so, I feel good and have followed all his instructions," commented Anne.

"I shall stay close to Kellynch Hall for his news my dear," said Frederick. The Lady Russell regularly at Anne's side sat quietly reading but aware of the conversation.

"Mrs. Anne," said a servant after knocking softly first to gain entry. "The surgeon has arrived and is waiting in the drawing room."

"Thank you, send him up please," said Anne.

Frederick went on the task himself, entering the drawing room from the study to find the surgeon there waiting. "Sir, how are you today?" asked the surgeon.

"Very well, thank you," replied Frederick.

"How has your wife been these last two weeks?" asked the surgeon.

"Quite well I must say. Shall I escort you to her?" asked Frederick as they left the room.

"Mrs. Anne, how have you been?" asked the surgeon.

"Very well thank you," replied Anne, with Lady Russell looking on. The surgeon began his examination, taking a little more time than usual and going over a test or two a second time.

"Your ankles are a bit swollen, but this is normal considering the state you are in. You are not in discomfort from this?" asked the surgeon.

"No, this comes on late in the afternoon when my feet are up," replied Anne.

The surgeon seemed quieter than normal, eventually writing notes in his journal, particularly tracking Anne's progress over the pregnancy.

After a time, and with more prodding and checking to concerned looks by Anne and Lady Russell, the surgeon asked Anne to allow him further tests. When these were over the surgeon was intently writing in his journal. His unusual manner caused Anne and Lady Russell to be concerned over the possibility of unfortunate conditions that had not been stated, and not yet confirmed by the surgeon's actions.

"My dear Mrs. Anne I have to inform you of a development in your pregnancy."

Anne and Lady Russell showed concern and both held their breath at his words.

"You are pregnant with twins!" said the surgeon. "And both babies seem to be quite healthy indeed and with strong heartbeats," stated the surgeon firmly. "I didn't notice, until now, the second heartbeat. Congratulations!"

Anne was frozen, speechless. "Twins, are you sure Sir?" asked Lady Russell.

"I was very careful and checked more than once. One can now hear two distinct heartbeats. I confirm two babies in your belly. My warmest congratulations madam, you and the babies are quite healthy. The babies seem to be growing normally," said the surgeon smiling.

"What a surprise this will be for Frederick," said Anne to Lady Russell, holding her hand.

The Lady Russell, devoted to the family, was beside herself at the news. She was renewed in her many years with purpose thinking of Anne quite as if her daughter by blood. Lady Russell in Anne and Frederick's eyes has become in many ways an Aunt, doing all the things to be done by a relationship.

"Shall we inform Frederick immediately Anne?" asked Lady Russell.

"Perhaps we will wait till we lunch and make the announcement then. Let us only say I am quite healthy and all is well," replied Anne, then asking the surgeon to lunch with the family and guests.

Anne lunched with Frederick, the Crofts, Lady Russell, and the surgeon. As Mary, Louisa, Henrietta, and Lady Musgrove arrived together "quite unexpectedly" knowing the surgeon was due and wanting to confirm Anne and the baby were well.

"Please lunch with us?" asked Anne of the Musgroves.

"This would be a pleasure, especially since your cook is so adept at tasty meals," replied Louisa.

"The latest news is I am quite healthy!" exclaimed Anne to the smiling group of women and men.

When in the course of normal conversation and in quite a natural way Anne said to Frederick, "Our children will need…".

Frederick corrected her with "our child."

Anne looked at him in that special way that only she and Frederick may know, yet leaving everyone aware of that special bond. Without a word, Frederick jumped to his feet and asked Anne her meaning.

"I am confident I am pregnant with twins dear. The surgeon has confirmed this, have you not sir?" asked Anne of the surgeon as he nodded in agreement.

"Yes, Mrs. Anne is pregnant with twins and quite healthy," replied the surgeon.

After a pause in conversation and in the appropriate way, the room erupted into many congratulations, as Anne related the details that led to the events with the surgeon just that morning. "The surgeon said, after much prodding and listening, giving me a puzzled look, he could distinctly hear two heartbeats, and both babies and I were quite healthy. Lady Russell and I held our breath," said Anne.

The surgeon confirmed Anne's account in the discovery of this fact. Meanwhile, Lady Russell sat back glad to be part of the family, just enjoying the conversations back and forth and drinking in the moments.

"The family must be informed of the news," said Lady Russell as Anne, in the next days, informed the relatives and close friends by note of the news of twins.

All were very excited for Anne and Frederick, and many a congratulatory letter arrived at the door throughout the next days. Anne kept to her regime of not over-working herself and resting frequently.

"Frederick we have so many plans to make in the next few months. There are names, rooms to pick, clothes, nurses to find. Perhaps I can convince my dear friends Harriet and Nurse Rooke to assist me with the children. We have that empty cottage at the end of the lane we can use and Harriet would be glad to leave Bath permanently. What do you think of this, my Captain?"

"I like the idea of it. We shall go along one step at a time, and I am sure Lady Russell will also want to be at your side every step of the way. Remember let us not overdo it," replied Frederick.

In the next few days, Anne picked out rooms for the children. "If girls, I want my rooms in my growing up to be used. If boys we have hardly used guest rooms," said Anne to Frederick.

"What if we have a boy and a girl?" commented Frederick.

"Well then we have more work to do my Captain," said Anne in reply, smiling at the prospect.

"That you and the children are healthy is the most important to me," said Frederick earnestly.

Lady Russell asked Anne to give her leave to help with the children. "It is not common for a lady to attend to these duties Lady Russell, however as you are the dearest of friends it shall be as you wish," agreed Anne.

Lady Russell was pleased with herself at the prospect of helping with the children. "What else is there for me at this stage of life than to be of service?" asked Lady Russell.

"Lady Russell, you will need assistance, and just now I have written a post. I could help a dear friend and secure the care of the children all in one transaction. Through a note just this morning, I requested the assistance of Mrs. Smith and Nurse Rooke of Bath to assist so the children are not overtaxed.

"That is a great plan," commented Lady Russell, knowing Mrs. Smith to be a sweet-tempered, gentle woman with knowledge of society, but whose husband's passing left her in reduced circumstances. "Mrs. Smith, Nurse Rooke, and I will be quite a team for the twins. I look forward to this," replied Lady Russell.

"We will inform you of Mrs. Smith's response to this proposal. I am sure she will accept. We would like her to take the empty cottage on the property and quit Bath," said Anne.

Some days later, a note arrived from Harriet and Nurse Rooke, having gratefully accepted all the provisions of employment with the benefit of the cottage. "They thank me for the opportunity and send their warmest regards to you Frederick," said Anne.

"Wonderful, then this is settled. Let us inform Lady Russell of the news," commented Frederick.

Mrs. Smith and Nurse Rooke were glad for Anne's offer to quit Bath and would move to the cottage on the Kellynch Hall estate as soon as convenient. Anne informed the housekeeper of her plan to use the cottage for Harriet and Nurse Rooke, whereupon she asked it be cleaned and prepared for occupancy as soon as possible.

Anne, the center of attention these next months, basked in her pregnancy. Elizabeth, used to this role in their society, and not receiving all the attention, was a bit put out and subdued as a result, so Anne, sensitive to circumstances, involved Elizabeth in all the arrangements and the sisters both remained quite content with the coming events.

Anne's sister was amazed at Anne's ability to make things right in all circumstances. "You are so much like mother in many ways Anne. You were too young to remember. You seem to work things out properly, applying economy and moderation at every step, unlike me, but I am learning the lesson, even if slowly," related Elizabeth to Anne's surprise and astonishment.

Elizabeth was being courted by both William Elliot and Captain Warwick to the point of exhaustion. Each day one would arrive with some plan of amusement, and even both arrived on the same day at times, leaving no time to oneself. What started as a dream come true was now a confusing and challenging state of affairs, difficult to manage, and that which could not go on much longer.

"It would not be respectable to either man and for the sake of your sanity you must choose your suitor sister," said Anne at Elizabeth's insistence of advice. "In their favour, they are both quite wealthy, well tempered, all in all, acceptable prospects everyone must agree. So equal in many respects but who to pick; there was the incident with Mrs. Clay to take into account where Cousin

William is concerned," thought Elizabeth, "and a handsome and attentive Captain Warwick to consider who is honourable to the core."

"I want to also have love in the marriage. This seems very agreeable since money and connections are not an issue," said Elizabeth to Anne. I can see the effects of love on your marriage making this a very amiable affair for you and Frederick. You chose well indeed sister," commented Elizabeth earnestly.

"Our relationship as sisters is so very different now than in the past sister. I am married and with child, two as a matter of fact! Frederick, once a 'nobody' in my father and your eyes, has earned great respect with him and you both, and I certainly benefit from this change in opinion," thought Anne pleased.

William Elliot and Captain Warwick were regular visitors to Kellynch for Elizabeth's sake. "Today, William, next week it is Captain Warwick. Elizabeth here, Elizabeth there, I am quite exhausted over the matter sister," said Elizabeth to Anne.

"I long for a more normal existence. What shall I do?"

"Choose sister, for all our sakes, choose and be done with it," replied Anne with a smile.

"Sister, tell me your thoughts on the matter. Who would be best?" asked Elizabeth trusting.

Startled at the request Anne thought a moment, "I do not want to injure my sister's chance at happiness and so must be careful with my advice. Taking into account Elizabeth is favourite to father and his happy approval will be crucial to my sister's happiness and their long-term relationship."

"The shock of one naval officer, where the father is concerned, may be enough, save the excellent gallantry of Captain Warwick. Furthermore, there is the matter of William and his focus on position and title, and yet he seems to have formed a sort of attachment to your sister. It appears to me your Captain Warwick loves you and William perhaps loves you. As well as you are favourite for one and not the other is to be considered. In the end, only you can make this fateful decision. On any decision, I will support you with all my heart, and wish you happy!" said Anne frankly.

"I have observed Warwick is ready to settle and raise a family. He would also move into the neighbourhood, further extending the close circle of family and friends who live locally here. He has a very amiable character and friendship with Frederick and the Musgroves.

Frederick and Warwick served together you know. He surely has all this on his side," said Anne.

"William perhaps is not so keen on the Musgroves, there is that consideration," noted Elizabeth.

"Captain Warwick would have to be my consideration. I have known this for some time and just wanted your opinion on the matter. But poor William, I can't help but think of his disappointment. Well at least he will inherit the baronetcy one day and there are plenty of eligible women in society just looking for a single man with fortune and title," said Elizabeth.

"He will be fine, let me assure you, sister! We will maintain the family connection and keep it all amiable," said Anne.

"Thank you, sister. I suppose I have made up my mind. It is settled. I will ask my Captain to visit with me," exclaimed Elizabeth.

"We will invite him to supper when it is convenient for you Elizabeth," offered Anne.

"I simply guided Elizabeth to her own decision on the matter. That way we will never have a falling out," thought Anne.

"So, is it to be Captain Warwick then?" asked Anne.

"I am afraid so. The poor man, he does not know what he is in for in my case," smiled Elizabeth.

Harriet Smith and Nurse Rooke arrived at Kellynch Hall, a few days hence, quitting Bath. Anne greeted them warmly calling for tea to be served. "Harriet, remember the day you provided me the crucial information about William, saving me and the family from being so manipulated?" said Anne.

"Yes, I do. I was glad to be the one to tell you since this was quite an unbelievable telling by any other means," replied Harriet.

"You look so very much with child," said Nurse Rooke smiling.

"I assure you, I feel it as much these days," replied Anne.

"Are you and the babies healthy?" asked Harriet.

"Yes, we are very healthy. Just the normal aches and pains of bearing two children in one's belly" smiled Anne.

"Then we should be glad for this," replied Harriet.

"How was your travel here from Bath?" asked Anne.

"Uneventful and quite smooth a ride," said Harriet.

"I am very glad you accepted our offer to stay on at the Kellynch estate cottage and help with the children," said Anne.

"This is a happy circumstance for me and Nurse Rooke. We could not have arrived at any other decision," said Harriet.

"You are both dear friends indeed and very welcome here," said Anne.

"Thank you, Anne," replied Harriet sincerely, with Nurse Rooke tipping her head.

"I would find it hard to place the children in the hands of strangers," commented Anne.

"So, it is to be twins then?" asked Harriet with a smile.

"Yes, I am afraid so. Lady Russell will be helping quite a lot, as she considers me almost a daughter in this affair," said Anne.

"Wonderful, I like Lady Russell. She has been very kind to me even in my circumstances," replied Harriet.

"Shall we go to the cottage? I had the servants clean and prepare the living place. It should be stocked with food, bedding, a fire going, and a housewarming present from Frederick and I," said Anne.

"You shouldn't have," said Harriet.

"Of course, we should have, we are long-time dear school friends after all. You and Nurse Rooke saved me from a most imprudent marriage proposal indeed. It is the least I could do," said Anne.

"Let us walk through the garden since it is close by and the weather is very pleasant indeed," said Anne."

This is a wonderful cottage! Are you sure Anne?" asked Harriet.

"Yes, Frederick and I are determined to have you both in our lives," said Anne.

After a short tour of the place, Anne turned to Harriet and Nurse Rooke. "Good night then, shall I see you in a couple of days? This will give you time to settle in when I can take you on a tour of the big house and the children's rooms," stated Anne.

"Yes, of course, and Thank you again, Anne. Please give Frederick our regards," said Harriet as they settled into their new surroundings, thinking how fortunate they were to have Anne's friendship.

After a few days to settle in, Harriet and Nurse Rooke assisted Anne and Lady Russell in preparing for the arrival of the twins. The house was all abuzz at the coming event, even the servants were extra careful to ensure everything was just within reach when Anne needed something.

"The house servants are very fond of you Anne, especially as you treat them very well and are respectful in all their circumstances. It seems they are now quite attached to and protective of you," noticed Harriet, who benefited from this great treatment, as a dear friend of the mistress.

"Yes, I am quite aware of this and careful not to take advantage of my house staff," replied Anne discreetly so as not to be overheard.

Lady Russell, not sure of the idea of Harriet and Nurse Rooke realised at once how valuable they would be and how easy to work with they are. "This will be a great bonus on all matters concerning the children. Harriet and Nurse Rooke have a great common sense and simple approach that makes them a blessing to all concerned. They fit right in," commented Lady Russell.

"Yes, and they are dear friends. It was my hope it would be so for you Lady Russell," said Anne.

"I see Mrs. Smith is a woman of breeding and is not so wholly unfamiliar with society. If it were not for the unfortunate circumstance of her husband's untimely death, she would be in better circumstances. I understand your friendship in this case," said Lady Russell.

"Yes, it is a good thing to show her compassion and respect," said Anne.

"Yes indeed," replied Lady Russell.

Nine months fast approached with Anne wanting the babies out now. Everyone gave their opinion readily as to whether the twins would be boys or girls together, or a boy and a girl.

"Frederick wanted Anne and the children healthy at its end and is never far from me these days," wrote Harriet in her diary one evening.

They decided on names – the first boy to be Frederick II, the first girl to be Margret Anne. If a second boy his name be Fitzwilliam, or Elizabeth Mary if a second girl.

"I hope and pray for them Frederick," said Anne on a quiet evening as they lay in bed, Anne on her side with a set of pillows wedged under her belly in strategic places so she would be comfortable.

"Our hearts will be beating in the both of them," commented Frederick.

"Even though they are not born yet, we live for them now," replied Anne.

The surgeon arrived every few days now as time became close to the blessed event. "Anne is doing quite well under the circumstances," said the surgeon to Frederick.

"We all hope for her and the baby's health sir," said Frederick.

"All seems well under the circumstances. Expect the blessed event in the next few days," commented the surgeon.

"We have a guest room for you so you need not have to travel so much these coming days," recommended Frederick.

"Thank you, sir, this would be very convenient to be sure." replied the surgeon.

"One of the servants will find you later today to arrange for your personal and medical items to be picked up and delivered to your rooms here," said Frederick.

"That will be very good sir. If you will excuse me, I will attend to your wife," said the surgeon as he departed up the staircase.

The morning of the first day of spring Anne awoke to pains in the back and water in the bed. Frederick, call the surgeon, Lady Russell, and Harriet! I think it's time…" cried Anne.

"At once my dear," replied Frederick as he called to one of the servants, asking that they assist Anne by straightening the room while others were charged with calling Lady Russell, Harriet, and Nurse Rooke. Frederick took on the task of fetching the surgeon himself.

"You are in labour madam," diagnosed the surgeon as he ordered the servants to bring hot water, clean sheets, clothes, and other particulars.

"Frederick, has Lady Russell, Harriet, and Nurse Rooke been called?" asked Anne with some notice of pain and wincing.

"Yes dear, they will be here shortly I am sure," replied Frederick in his calm manner.

Each friend quickly arrived to attend to Anne and the surgeon. The surgeon, experienced in such a circumstance, talked to Anne about the birthing, so she remained as calm as possible. "All will go well, Mrs. Anne. Follow my instructions and trust Mother Nature will tell you what to do. Women folk have done this before, that is the good news," said the surgeon. Nurse Rooke listened intently as the surgeon instructed her in what he would be doing and needing at each stage.

A day of waiting began, as the family was informed and many arrived to assemble in the drawing room, awaiting news of the births while consuming many cups of tea and biscuits. Every so often, one could hear the shouts of pain at the staircase, wondering if it had begun or had ended.

Nurse Rooke and Harriet assisted the surgeon with the birthing as the first child began to show. Harriet, holding Anne's hand encouraged with "push now."

Nurse Rooke, at the surgeon's side, followed his instructions with some level of expertise, having experience with birthing previously. "Nurse Rooke, you are quite adept and are following my instructions closely," mentioned the surgeon.

Lady Russell and Elizabeth watched the proceedings, ready to take the babies, clean and clothe them, once the surgeon completed his work, and they were breathing and ready for their open hands.

Anne gave birth to the first, "It's a boy!" said the surgeon. The surgeon cut the cord and holding him by his feet, slapped his bottom whereupon a loud cry could be heard. "Perfectly healthy," said the surgeon, examining him closely.

Anne, relieved at the sound of it, prepared to push out the second child. Nurse Rooke took the baby and cleaned its tiny mouth and nose then handed him to Lady Russell and Elizabeth. "Here comes the next. "It's a girl!" said the surgeon with a spank on the bottom whereupon cries could be heard. "They both look very healthy Mrs. Anne mentioned the surgeon, checking on the work Lady Russell and Elizabeth had done as the babies were placed with Anne for the first time.

"A handsome son and a beautiful daughter," thought Anne holding them close as they slept in her arms. Everyone in the room was at once elated and exhausted. The surgeon and Nurse Rooke tended to Anne while the room was cleaned for visitors.

"Frederick will be the first to meet his son Frederick II and daughter Margret Anne," said Anne with a tired but proud voice.

"My nephew and niece are perfect," thought Elizabeth as Anne placed them with Elizabeth and Harriet. Lady Russell helped Anne sit up before Frederick was called to visit.

"Lady Russell, would you call Frederick, I am ready to see him," said Anne softly now.

"Yes of course child," replied Lady Russell, leaving for the drawing room.

Lady Russell walked down the staircase and into the drawing room where Frederick stood instantly, and was at her side in a blink. "Lady Russell, what of Anne?" asked Frederick.

"Anne is well and so are your children. The three of them wish to see you, sir," offered Lady Russell as Frederick walked out of the drawing room at a quick pace and up the stairs.

After Frederick had left the drawing-room, Lady Russell announced the birth of Frederick II and Margret Anne.

"Anne and the children are healthy after the birthing," said Lady Russell. All assembled shouted their congratulations, hoping to see Anne and the new arrivals. "It will be a few moments before the surgeon will allow you up for a quick visit. Anne and the infants are exhausted as you might imagine."

Most of the family was present, knowing how close Anne was to giving birth. They were either at Kellynch or the local area staying with relations, waiting on the news, prepared to give their congratulations.

"My Captain, I would like to present to you Frederick II your son, and Margret Anne your daughter," said Anne smiling.

"They are beautiful and so small. How are you and the children?" asked Frederick as he sat on the bed beside Anne.

"We are well, just a bit exhausted as you can see," replied Anne.

The surgeon nodded in confirmation of the condition. "Can you not see Frederick II is the image of his father and Margret Anne will have both of us in her features," said Anne proudly.

"Yes, quite right my dear. I see it now," replied Frederick.

Elizabeth gently took Frederick II from Anne's arm and placed him in Frederick's. "What do I do?" asked Frederick.

"Support his head and hold him close my Captain," answered Anne with a smile.

After what seemed a moment or two, Elizabeth placed Frederick II back into Anne's arms as Harriet placed Margret Anne into Frederick's now curved arms. Frederick quickly learned to support the head and hold the bum secure.

"Your daughter sir, Miss Margret Anne Wentworth," said Anne as Frederick gazed into the tiniest of eyes with wonder. After a few moments Frederick looked at Anne lovingly and without words expressed his deepest emotions and connection to her and his newly born children.

"Shall we have a quiet visit by those waiting in the drawing room?" asked the Lady Russell. "Yes, so I and the babies my rest for the evening" replied Anne. Elizabeth, Lady Russell, and the surgeon went in the direction of the drawing room to invite the gathering to visit quickly and presented their many congratulations. They repeated to the gathering the events that led up to the perfect births of Frederick II and Margret Anne, with the surgeon nodding. "Shall we go?" said the surgeon as the group walked slowly up the staircase to Anne's room.

Anne looked radiant and exhausted and having every right was kissed deeply by Frederick just before the gathering arrived to be let in. "Well done dear, well done," said Frederick tenderly.

The group of the family entered as Anne, holding both babies, introduced Frederick II and Margret Anne through many congratulations and wishes of happiness. Louisa and Henrietta rushed to the front to see the precious gifts. Frederick knew his children were on the way but the full realisation didn't hit him until Anne said "My Captain. Your son has your chin and hair." All agreed.

Frederick remarked, "Our daughter has your eyes dear."

He would soon settle into fatherhood.

Frederick could not have been happier and the connection between Anne and Frederick couldn't be closer than at this moment. The family wishes all the happiness, as Anne realised how fortunate to have much in her life. Initially frustrated, and after some trouble, she has gotten all she desired, and so has Frederick.

The next days were filled with Anne's recovery, two additional hungry mouths to manage, and every few hours as is normal for infants, they were fed and cleaned. Lady Russell and her assistants, Mrs. Smith and Nurse Rooke managed all the details, freeing Anne to recover rapidly and only to breastfeed her new arrivals, Anne insisted no wet nurse. "The surgeon said the mother is the key to the child's health, especially in the first weeks," repeated Nurse Rooke.

Anne, an attentive mother in every respect, spent as much time with her children as possible and saw to as many details of their daily affairs as her health would allow her. "I am so excited about my little man and daughter. There are so many expectations in me for them. I now know personally how a mother may have hopes for their children, wanting to give them all that can be done to their advantage," said Anne.

"Every mother who loves truly has that same wish," replied Lady Russell.

Lady Russell had practically moved in to help with the children. Like a close aunt, she was already talking about schooling for the boy and finishing school for the girl. "Perhaps the naval academy for the boy?" she suggested.

"Let us first catch our breath from the birthing Lady Russell," commented Anne with a big smile and grateful demeanour.

Harriet and Nurse Rooke were a great help to Lady Russell, who was glad for them. Anne could just enjoy the moments and be happy to have such faithful friends near at this time. Frederick managed the house affairs and would be at Anne's side just at the right times and places so as not to interfere nor be bothersome to the affairs of mother and infants, but just enough to support Anne. "He is wonderful," said Anne when asked how Frederick coped with all this confusion and upheaval.

Elizabeth, on the other hand, would be overwhelmed and moody at times with the giving of constant attention to the children and believing children should not be seen nor heard. With her relationship growing more serious she may one day have her child and this, she recognised as good training for her for a circumstance she may even wish for in the bonds of marriage. "Thank you Elizabeth," said Lady Russell with unexpected assistance from Elizabeth with the wrapping of Frederick II.

Lady Russell, not used to pacing her time, was assured so she may attend her duties and responsibilities; that this be a joy and not a chore. Harriet and Nurse Rooke relieved Lady Russell at regular intervals. They had grown in their regard for Lady Russell and were watchful not to overstrain her in helping with the children. They would both free Lady Russell multiple times a day so she may attend to her duties, and when she returned, tell her in detail of all the events while she was gone. Lady Russell, grateful, had Harriet over for tea several times now and quite considered her a valued acquaintance.

Elizabeth, with all her worldly-wise airs and opinions, was very tender with her newly born cousins, happy to spend time holding them and helping in general ways but not in the changing, feeding, or bathing as yet. Anne watched over time as her sister took on the role of aunt to her blood kin and how it matured her to the more real points of life and lessened the draw of the trivial.

One afternoon Elizabeth said to Anne in confidence, "Captain Warwick and Cousin William have each asked for my hand. What do I do, Anne? Who do I pick? How can I be sure?"

"If you have to ask, that is your answer. When you know it is right no one can say otherwise," responded Anne gently.

Anne, much more capable of providing good advice now that the children were born and having regained her strength, began to steer Elizabeth to her own heart. Anne's strategy was to help her sister make her own decision in this case. "Sister, what does your heart tell you? Who do you see a happy life with now and forever?" asked Anne.

Elizabeth responded, "I like William, but I love Captain Warwick. I admire and look up to him. William is entertaining. I am the surest of Warwick of the two. I will have to work on Father for his blessing since this is another navy man who may be knocked about one day with all that wind and sea. However, I feel love and respect for him, a partnership. He makes me feel safe and without a care in his arms," explained Elizabeth.

"Well then sister you have answered your question. As for Captain Warwick, he is fortunate indeed. I and Frederick wish you happiness beyond measure and will be glad of your announcement. In the meantime, I will not speak of this to anyone until you give me leave," said Anne earnestly.

Elizabeth later discovers of family connection with respect to Captain Warwick. found a distant connection in the Royal line. Her Warwick was a third cousin on the Queen's side of the family and is recognised at court. "Warwick, why have you never mentioned your connection to the royal family to me?" asked Elizabeth.

"Well, my lady I did not think it needed to be said quite frankly," replied Captain Warwick smiling.

Elizabeth used this connection to further her cause with her father and convince him to accept her choice and give his blessing to their union. When this was secured, she would ask her Captain Warwick to approach her father on the subject, asking for his blessings, and the announcement of engagement to be made public.

Elizabeth wrote a note to Captain Warwick asking him to dine with her and the Wentworths as her particular guest. It was this special evening she would tell him of her decision to accept him and plan to gain her father's blessing.

Anne asked Elizabeth if she might tell Frederick of the proposal between her and her Warwick. "Sister, may I inform my Captain of this happy circumstance and your plans for the evening? Perhaps your Warwick has nerves. Frederick, as a trusted friend, would be able to talk with him in the way men do. What say you?" asked Anne.

"This is a good idea sister. Would Frederick approve of my decision?" asked Elizabeth shyly.

"He will be very glad for you sister and wish you and Captain Warwick every happiness!" commented Anne.

"Then pray let us tell him at once," exclaimed Elizabeth.

Frederick came to them at his usual time to visit with Anne and the children. "Brother, I would have a word with you," called Elizabeth.

"Of course sister, what would you have of me?" asked Frederick.

"Captain Warwick has proposed to me, and I have decided to accept him. This evening I will tell him of my decision and father of this happy circumstance. My Warwick will ask Father for his blessings and announce our engagement publicly at once. What do you say to this?" asked Elizabeth shyly.

"Sister, I am very happy for you and Warwick, but I am not surprised. Warwick explained to me, wanting advice, his intention of a proposal, and your gracious dinner invitation. He is very happy and hoping you will put him out of his misery at once. One could not but see. I am so happy for both of you. You have chosen well. Warwick is a good man of great character, and I do believe he loves you dearly. You will both be very happy," said Frederick to the surprised women smiling at the compliments. "How can I help in your plan sister?" asked Frederick.

"You have already dear brother in giving me confidence in my decision and plan," said Elizabeth.

"Then, I am glad of it and look forward to your announcement this evening!" exclaimed Frederick.

"I believe he will be acceptable to Sir Walter. Especially, if he moves into the neighbourhood and there is no loss to father of your company," explained Frederick smiling.

Captain Warwick arrived at Kellynch Hall to greetings from Anne and Frederick. "Good luck," said Frederick as Elizabeth granted a private audience with her Captain in a side parlour room. Upon emerging, Captain Warwick entered the drawing room and asked Sir Walter for a moment of conversation in the study, leaving little doubt of his intentions where Elizabeth was concerned, and because Elizabeth had a conversation with her father earlier in the evening concerning a certain proposal. Sir Walter expected this to touch on the certain subject of his proposal to his daughter.

Sir Walter and Captain Warwick entered the study whereupon Captain Warwick explained Elizabeth's acceptance of him and his proposal to marry. Sir Walter asked Captain Warwick about his connections to the Royal family, his wealth, and his work in Majesty's Naval Forces. "Sir, I see no impediment to you marrying my daughter. I suppose you have talked with Frederick and Anne about this plan?" asked Sir Walter.

"Anne and Frederick wish us happy and are great supporters. Do I have your consent to marry sir?" asked Captain Warwick.

"Indeed you do son-in-law. My hope is for you both to settle in the neighbourhood. Let us have a drink over this before we return to the drawing room. Congratulations!" added Sir Walter, lifting a glass.

"They have been in the study for quite some time," commented Elizabeth in a concerned tone.

"Have no worry sister. Father and Warwick are still talking, and that is a good sign," said Anne.

Finally, the study door opened and Sir Walter and Captain Warwick walked into the drawing room in very amiable spirits. "I have an announcement to make." Anne, Frederick, Lady Russell, and the Crofts were in attendance, with Elizabeth at Captain Warwick's side. "I would like to announce the engagement of my dear daughter Elizabeth to Captain Warwick of His Majesty's Navy," said Sir Walter, raising his glass in a toast as everyone in attendance expressed their heartiest congratulations.

All present talked with the happy couple personally and again wished them happy and many congratulations. Excitedly, Elizabeth and Warwick gave their thanks. Supper went well this evening with much talk of the engagement and the twins.

Frederick, being friends with Warwick and married to Anne, had the privilege to know the goings on at Kellynch Hall and inside the Elliot family. "My Captain, why did you wait to advise Captain Warwick on the matter of Elizabeth and Sir Walter?" asked Anne.

"I believe patience to be a very good strategy in this case," replied Frederick.

"I was just wondering," commented Anne.

"I decided to say nothing until Warwick mentioned his happy circumstance to me. When he did approach me on the matter he asked it be kept confidential until Sir Walter announced it of course, and I respected his opinion. I congratulated him nonetheless, giving him every confidence Sir Walter would rally to the plan. Elizabeth is handsome to be sure and connected to a family with a title, and he is wealthy and connected to the royal family. I saw no impediments here," said Frederick as Anne, proud of her Captain, listened.

"Elizabeth asked me to sit in with father as she told him of Warwick's offer of marriage and her acceptance of his proposal. To everyone's surprise, Father mentioned he only a few days earlier talked to Captain Warwick asking when he would propose to Elizabeth. Warwick said he had made an offer, and she was considering it."

The next day, Elizabeth invited Cousin William to lunch at Kellynch Hall through a note sent that morning. It was only right that he heard from her of her intention to marry her Captain Warwick. He has been a gentleman to her in all respects, and it was to be expected that she return the same in the manner of treatment. She was determined to be respectful in this case.

"I have made my choice cousin. I have accepted Captain Warwick. We are both very happy," announced Elizabeth.

"He is indeed fortunate dear lady. Will I expect a wedding invitation then?" asked William.

"Yes, of course, cousin," responded Elizabeth.

"I wish you both happy," said Cousin William as he departed.

At supper that evening, Anne, Mary, Louisa, and Lady Russell offered to help Elizabeth with the wedding plans. "Thank you, There is much to do. I will need all the assistance I can get, said Elizabeth.

"We have some experience in these matters," commented Lady Russell with a smile, looking at Anne and Louisa with understanding glances back at her.

"Yes, I suppose you do!" exclaimed Elizabeth.

"We can start tomorrow with your ideas for the wedding, church, and ball. One thing we have learned is not to wait, there is much in the way of planning to do if one is to have a happy and memorable day," said Anne.

"The theme is to be simple but elegant. I enjoyed your wedding Anne. The church is just up the lane of course. And the ball must be here at our family hall. What do you say?" asked Elizabeth, hoping this was acceptable.

"Yes, to all of this, with Anne's approval…" replied Lady Russell, happy for the amiable circumstance.

"Of course sister, we will make this a very happy day indeed," commented Anne.

"Let us soon decide on the day of the blessed event since this will be crucial to our plans," commented Louisa.

"Yes, we have much to do," replied Elizabeth.

Sir Walter, quite pleased with himself to have both daughters well placed in marriages, looked over those seated at the table enjoying the moment. "Captain Warwick, will you take a house in the neighbourhood?" asked Sir Walter.

"That is our intention sir. I will not take a daughter away but add a son-in-law to this happy group," replied Captain Warwick.

"I will introduce you to my solicitor if this is convenient. He seems to know well the state of all the properties in the neighbourhood and what they sell for," mentioned Sir Walter.

"I would like to be close to my sister and father. If this is acceptable?" commented Elizabeth.

"This is very acceptable my dear," replied Captain Warwick.

Elizabeth and Anne made eye contact. "Elizabeth would also miss her newly born niece and nephew," thought Anne.

"Father you may not be so inclined to travel to Bath now that your family has settled here," mentioned Anne.

"I believe you may be right. Perhaps a fortnight in Bath would be sufficient to satisfy my need for travel and for getting away now that my daughters are settled," responded Sir Walter.

"You, of course, have a place here at Kellynch Hall," mentioned Anne.

"And with us, wherever we settle Father. So you see, have no fear for apartments and a place to stay, it is all settled," commented Elizabeth smiling happily.

CHAPTER 5

Time Goes by So Quickly

"How days turn to months and time flies by in these happy times," said Anne to Frederick.

Married life had become routine, and the spring and winter balls at Kellynch had become a neighbourhood expectation. Elizabeth's wedding had come and gone. After the honeymoon, Elizabeth and Warwick happily settled into the neighbourhood and are frequent guests to Kellynch Hall.

With three daughters married, Sir Walter was well-occupied with visits from family, friends, and dinner parties. Perhaps not so lavish as in the past and he is much older now.

Life had settled quite comfortably with all the anticipations of a gentleman and lady living a country life, the raising of children, and the running of the estate is the focus of the daily affair.

"Frederick visited the Admiralty twice a month at Plymouth as is customary for his rank and responsibilities. He was active with three naval committees; that of Tactics and Strategy, War Games, and Fleet Operations Planning (well beyond my knowledge), still, it all sounds so important," wrote Anne in her diary.

Guided by Admiral Croft, whose experience told him there would always be another war, he mentored Frederick carefully. "In the quiet times it is best to put one's hands in, in shaping the next generation of the navy warfare," said Admiral Croft to Frederick. "One has time to gain the confidence of senior naval leaders before the rush to battle and lateness in the hour. One thing is true, war is coming. One does not always know the appointed date, but it will come," advised Admiral Croft.

Anne missed Frederick terribly during his monthly duties with the Admiralty, but noticed Frederick was much improved on his return to Kellynch Hall as he had expended energies he would not have otherwise utilised. "You are young and vigorous. Although the time away is a sacrifice, I feel you need this Frederick," said Anne.

Every so often Frederick would take Anne with him to Plymouth for naval balls and assemblies, while at other times he was quite busy with naval affairs. Plymouth left a lot to be desired for society events if they were not sponsored by the Navy. It was after all a town focused on His Majesty's service, charged with the protection of the realm.

While at Kellynch, Anne had the children to occupy her days and thoughts, along with the help of Harriet and frequent visits from Lady Russell and Elizabeth, and of course, Father and the Crofts, while Frederick was away. It was in these times that Anne worked to create such a warmness and pleasure for Frederick's return, making him welcome in every way. Anne well remembered life before Frederick and was grateful for all she possessed through her beloved husband.

"The children are growing fast and too soon they are walking, running, climbing and talking…" Anne wrote to Frederick.

Anne and Frederick were very happy. "To marry for money and connections is one thing but with love, it is so much more," said Anne to Frederick one evening, and just that quickly Anne was pregnant again.

"My dear, is it possible to have twins again?" asked Frederick jokingly.

Looking at Frederick with pleading eyes, Anne responded, "May this not be the case, one set of twins, whom I love with my life, is perfectly enough, thank you very much!"

"As long as you and the baby are healthy my dear," replied Frederick, smiling and proud.

At breakfast one morning, Anne said to Frederick, "How far we have come Frederick. I now know what the nausea sickness means, and we are not so panicked as before."

"Truly. My dear, experience is the best of teachers," replied Frederick.

"We had better dust off the names we decided on those many months ago when the twins were born." Anne agreed, holding Frederick's hands in the throes of a bout of nausea.

"Come rest my dear," said Frederick.

It was time for the spring Ball at Kellynch Hall. This spring would bring lots of challenges in pulling off another successful ball and also managing the hopes for a new and healthy child so close to birthing. The house staff now knew how to plan balls and all the preparations went like clockwork. With the ball set for mid-May and a baby in June, the timing seemed perfect. Frederick would adjust his travel away to the Admiralty to ensure he would be at Kellynch Hall for the crucial birthing period.

The surgeon had become a family friend these days, and his regular visits every two weeks now alerted all of a soon-to-come child. His good reports of Anne and the baby's health allayed any fears. "Anne now knows what to expect and paces herself well so as not to over-strain," said the surgeon to Frederick.

Lady Russell and her two helpers, Harriet and Nurse Rooke, worked out so well for Anne and Frederick. They quite instinctively know what to do and where to be to assure Anne had very smooth days, with Frederick II and Margret Anne well in hand.

With the ball date quickly approaching, the house staff became busy with all the preparations. "Have all the invitations gone out?" asked Anne of the house manager.

"Yes ma'am, the last of the invitations were dispatched yesterday morning. We have begun to receive acceptance notes just today. See here in the register." replied the house manager.

"Yes, I have forgotten we agreed on a register to keep track of our guests. Thank you," said Anne.

Elizabeth, quite adept at preparations for a ball, offered her assistance in assuring all the details were accounted for. Anne genuinely appreciated her sister's help and told her of such.

With a month yet to the birthing, Anne went into labour ahead of time, and with days until the Ball and Frederick went to the Admiralty, the house was in an uproar over the speed of events. Lady Russell stepped in to manage the situation. "Quickly, send this dispatch at all possible speed to Plymouth where one will find Captain Wentworth. Call for the surgeon to Anne's side. Give this note to Harriet and Nurse Rooke; ask them on my behalf if they would assist Anne and the surgeon. Take this note to Elizabeth asking her to notify the family of Anne's condition about to give birth," commanded Lady Russell in a calm and experienced way.

With each servant gone to their tasks, Lady Russell focused on Anne, now well on her way to giving birth. "Anne you may have the child before the surgeon arrives. In this event, there is Nurse Rooke who understands the birthing, since she is a midwife and assisted with the birth of the twins. We will be okay if it comes to that," said Lady Russell calmly, keeping Anne quiet and without tension.

To add to the confusion, the room was being prepared quickly for the birth. Since the birth of the twins, preparation was undertaken with experience, with everything laid out for the surgeon. Elizabeth stopped her wedding planning, so she could come to Anne's side.

"Frederick has been informed and is no doubt on his way back to Kellynch Hall. He is hoping all is well and sends his love," commented Lady Russell reading from a return dispatch, from Frederick.

"Will my child be born healthy?" asked Anne of Nurse Rooke, since the surgeon had not yet arrived and the child was not waiting to be born.

"It all looks quite normal dear lady. Have courage we will carry on without the surgeon, and he can take over when he does arrive," replied Nurse Rooke.

"Now, push…," said Nurse Rooke.

Anne began birthing in the early evening. Nurse Rooke guided the procedure as Lady Russell held Anne's hand, helping her through it all on one side and Elizabeth on the other. In just a moment the baby was out and the cord tied. With a slap, he began crying.

"You have a son, Mrs. Anne," said Nurse Rooke, handling the baby, and a very healthy one at that. Nurse Rooke handed the baby to Harriet who assisted with cleaning and clothing the newborn.

"Congratulations ma'am," said Nurse Rooke.

Harriet carefully handed the wrapped child to Anne, "ten fingers and ten toes," she stated to a happy and exhausted Anne.

"Thank you, Harriet, thank you, Nurse Rooke," replied a relieved Anne.

"To be born so early is not as uncommon as one would think. You both seem very healthy, and I expected an easy birth and healthy mother and child at the end of it, Mrs. Anne," said the surgeon as he arrived and examined both the child and the mother.

"Well done Nurse Rooke. Well done all of you! Truly, I could not have done better in this case," commented the surgeon.

"Thank you, doctor," replied Nurse Rooke, tired but relieved all went well for mother and baby.

Nurse Rooke, Harriet, and Lady Russell got to work on tidying the room and preparing Anne for visitors. To change the subject, Anne thanked Elizabeth for putting a pause on her wedding plans until after the birth. "This leaves you little time to complete your plans," said Anne.

"The biggest decision I have my sister is where to buy my dress. Bath, London, or the big warehouses, and this is nothing to the birth of a cousin. It could have waited surely another day or so. Let us focus here," said Elizabeth as all agreed.

In the carriage on the way back to Kellynch Hall, Captains Wentworth, Warwick, Benwick, and Harville talked about marriage and gave their opinions about the general convention as the carriage sped along the country lanes.

Frederick was all alone in his thoughts about his Anne. "In this moment she could have given or is giving birth, and I wanted so much to have been there for her," thought Frederick as the carriage moved swiftly along the King's Highway, late in the day now.

A servant informed Harriet that Frederick and the men were just arriving. Frederick, on his way up the stairs walked into Harriet, who was out to intercept him and give him the news of a healthy son and to ask his patience while they prepared Anne, the baby and the room for visitors. "Just a few precious moments more sir?" asked Harriet.

"Of course, would you tell her I am here," said Frederick in a happy tone.

"Of course sir," replied Harriet walking back into the room.

Anne overheard the conversation and smiled. In just moments she would present Frederick with his newest son, Fitzwilliam.

Anne and the baby were ready to receive Frederick. At that Lady Russell appeared to invite Frederick to visit his wife and newest child. "Both mother and child have come through the event very well," exclaimed Lady Russell.

Anne, seeing Frederick entering the room burst into tears, "Please meet your son Fitzwilliam," said Anne handing him his child. Frederick, holding this new arrival and littlest of bundles, looked first at his son and then at Anne. It was a precious moment indeed, leaving little to be said.

Now ready to receive guests, Captains Harville, Benwick, and Warwick presented their hardiest congratulations and compliments. Louisa and the Musgroves, came flying into the room with all the pomp of a circus, so cheerful and expectant. "Just beautiful Anne! Just beautiful truly! And what is his name?" asked Louisa.

"Fitzwilliam Wentworth," answered Anne.

The next day Anne awoke early, exhausted from having been up most of the night feeding Fitzwilliam and worrying about the upcoming ball. After breakfast was served in her apartments she called her house staff to find all the ball plans in order.

"Miss Elizabeth has been supervising the tasks on your behalf, Mrs. Anne, with the Lady Russell overseeing all. Have no worries all is in order." Even Frederick had pitched in to ensure the final arrangements were completed on time.

As was customary, neighbours called in on Anne, many offering assistance with the arrangements for the ball. "So many friends, such consideration and kindness," Anne thought to herself. She had five days to regain her strength for the night of the ball, sleeping when the baby slept and waking to feed and change him when he was awake.

"Rest today and tomorrow. Eat hearty soups, meats, and breads and all will go toward regaining your strength Mrs. Anne. Then we shall see your strength the night of the event," said the surgeon optimistically as he provided a detailed note of instructions for the cook on Anne's behalf to ensure she was eating healthily.

"Father arrived from Bath to greet his new grandson into the world. Sir Walter seems so proud of his healthy new relation, and even the Dowager Viscountess Dalrymple sent the Honourable

Miss Carteret to present her congratulations. Miss Carteret, uncharacteristically to that of her station in life, asked me how she might assist me in this time," wrote Anne in her diary. Anne was moved by how life had afforded her such a change in fortune and how people now treated her.

Those around her found strength and stability in her countenance, and she took great care in her appreciation.

The night of the Ball arrived, however, Anne was unable to attend. Being so close to birthing and still tired, she would have to remain in her bed. Close friends could visit her the upstairs for a time, and she prepared just for this with regular reports from staff, assured all was set and the evening planned to go very well by all accounts. Many visitors presented their congratulations to Anne and Frederick on the birth of Fitzwilliam.

"My dear, how are you this evening?" whispered Frederick, before realising Anne was asleep. He slipped out, not wanting to awaken her or the baby since sleep was still at a premium at this stage of young Fitzwilliam's life. "You are such a mother," thought Frederick.

The next several weeks went by, with Anne on her feet now taking care of her duties, while Frederick returned to complete his work at the Admiralty. This day was unusual in that Lady Russell sent a note that she was not feeling well. "Have no worries though, I will rest at the estate and should be well enough in a day or so," wrote Lady Russell.

Unconcerned, Anne sent a return note of well wishes for recovery and a visit on the next day if she was not up to visiting Kellynch Hall. The next day, however, there was no Lady Russell, not even a note sent. Anne traveled the short carriage ride to the Russell estate, finding the Lady Russell asleep and servants attentive, and the house in order. "Our Lady will be on her feet on the morrow Ma'am and we expect she will be on her way to Kellynch since this gives her the greatest pleasure," said the housekeeper.

"Has the surgeon been called to look in on the Lady?" asked Anne of the housekeeper.

"No ma'am our Lady insisted this not be done," replied the housekeeper.

After a few days and still no visit from Lady Russell, Anne ventured to her neighbour's estate, careful not to overstrain herself. Arriving at Lady Russell's estate, Anne quickly assessed the gravity of the situation, discovering Lady Russell to be quite ill and weak. Anne decided to call for the surgeon and send a dispatch to Frederick of the situation. She also sent a note to Nurse Rooke to assist, since she was on her estate and could come quickly. Nurse Rooke arrived in all haste.

Anne, at Lady Russell's side, did all she could, assuring the surgeon was on his way, and informing family and close friends through notes written and dispatched by servants. The staff organised to see to every comfort. While Lady Russell rested, Anne noticed her breathing to be labored. She remembered how she was such a dear friend to her mother and when her mother passed on she became, in fact, her mother. Lady Russell was much more than a neighbour, a dear family friend, she was family as surely as blood kin. She has been the dearest of the family to her over these years.

Frederick, who was completing his work in Plymouth, quickly returned home to Anne's side to assist Lady Russell in any way. "You also feel it?" asked Anne of Frederick.

"Yes dear, I do. I have never forgotten how she rallied to my side in our reunion. And she has been with us every day since at Kellynch Hall," responded Frederick.

Lady Russell accepted Frederick quicker than Anne's family once she realised Anne's intent and his suitability to marry. Over the years, her kindness and care of his children breathed life into her as she became more a part of the Wentworth family. "She has become family in every respect," mentioned Frederick. To himself, he thought how much he and Anne would miss her if she should leave them.

"I am sorry to say Lady Russell is at the end of her life. Be with her now in her last moments," advised the surgeon in the most gentle of ways.

Anne and Frederick remained at her side, Anne holding her hand and Frederick close by. Lady Russell opened her eyes to speak to Anne, "Have no worry child. I feel no pain. Your mother and I were such great friends. She helped me through so many difficult times, that is why I was so devoted to her and when she passed, then to you for her sake. I became attached to you, and you saved me from desolation, giving me life through your lovely children. I have been so happy these last few years. I felt like a part of your family and lived each day in such happy circumstances. Thank you, Anne, Thank you, Frederick," said Lady Russell softly and out of breath.

"Rest now dear lady," said Anne softly.

"Frederick, I am sorry I didn't see the value in you at your first proposal to Anne and in fact, delayed your marriage eight years because of it, leaving you and Anne empty and alone for so long. Love won out in the end as is only right. You are the best of men, of husbands, and a great father. It has been an honour to know you and be welcomed into your family. Thank you both so much. I don't want to go but time has set a date for me. I love you and will think of you always..."

With that Lady Russell closed her eyes once more, never to open them again in this life.

The great lady passed away, and Anne felt this deeply. Lady Russell and Anne were not just friends but family. For the first time in her life, Anne was without Lady Russell. Life suddenly seemed a little lonelier, a little darker somehow, and she held Frederick and her children closer these days. "Living my life, enjoying the precious moments more deeply is my priority," wrote Anne in her diary.

Lady Russell's funeral service was wondrous. After days of continuous rain, the sun shone bright in the sky and all was new and glistening. The vicar's words were light and hopeful of all meeting again someday. So many came from far and near. All walks of life.

To Anne's surprise, she discovered later in life Lady Russell did so much good for so many, and these folks wanted to pay their respects. Even those not knowing Anne approached her simply to thank her for her compassion and love of the Lady Russell. They talked of her regenerated hopefulness and light that was the direct result of Anne, Frederick, and the children. Anne was touched and felt less sadness and more hopeful. After the service, the family reassembled at Kellynch Hall for a light supper and early night.

That night Anne dreamt of Lady Russell. "As if Lady Russell wanted me to know she was happy again Frederick. I would like to share it with you," said Anne of her dream.

"Hold on to this memory dear. It is a gift for you. Tell me more of it," replied Frederick holding Anne close.

"Lady Russell was so young and full of life. My mother was with her, and even though I do not remember my mother in her youth, I knew in my being it was her when our eyes met. They were all smiles, and light and hope, two best friends. There were cups of tea on a wood-painted garden table and lots of sun and warmth," said Anne as she related the dream to her Frederick.

Astonished, Frederick felt the lightness of this vision and exclaimed "This is our hope to one day meet again."

"Write this telling in your diary so when you miss her, you can remember this moment," said Frederick.

As Anne lay in bed she thought about all the good Lady Russell had done for so many in the neighbourhood, the less fortunate. With her gone now, someone would need to take up the cause. "Lady Russell, with such economy and moderation, assisted the less fortunate," commented Anne to Frederick. "I am determined to be of such service on behalf of the Wentworths in the name of Lady Russell. What do you say to this, my Captain?"

"I think it a worthy idea my dear. I trust your judgment completely in this matter," replied Frederick.

The next morning Anne called on Harriet to take on Lady Russell's role with the children. Harriet, humbled, consented. Elizabeth, much changed these days, was in Anne's sights to help her organise assistance for the less fortunate in the neighbourhood, taking up where Lady Russell left off.

Elizabeth, not used to this type of work was at first hesitant, but with Anne at her side, she explained this in fact, would raise her status through thinking of others. Elizabeth agreed and Anne set about being of service in the way Lady Russell had. Anne felt her spirits rise knowing she would keep Lady Russell's spirit alive through her charity. She contacted several village volunteers who worked closely with Lady Russell and assumed her role.

Another few years flew by with abandon. "It seems when one is happy time moves so quickly like the sands in the hourglass it never stops nor slows on the joys," wrote Anne in her diary.

"The children are growing and it is time to prepare and make decisions about Frederick II and Margret Anne's formal schooling. Frederick.

"Frederick II, like you, will go to the Royal Naval Academy for three years, receive a Royal commission at the rank of ensign, and be assigned an active ship to begin his career. I received his acceptance letter this morning. It seems the Navy has plans already for our son," said Anne.

"Yes, this is true. Even I was surprised," replied Frederick.

Margret Anne would attend finishing school for as many years, then return home and be presented as eligible to society.

"My Captain our children are growing up!" exclaimed Anne with a tear in her eye, wanting so much to relive these last years. "If only we could slow the march of time."

"Fitzwilliam would be a year after, his character being different to that of his older brother, he is more like Sir Walter in outward manners and form of the aristocracy, but he loves finance and business, with a mind as keen as yours Frederick, yet upon different matters entirely. Kings College, perhaps business and the law to begin may be the path for him dear?" queried Anne.

"Only time will tell with that one, his mind is keen and quick. We do know the navy is not for him," Frederick agreed.

Anne and Elizabeth went into the local village, a not-so-common event. As they walked along from shop to shop, they were bowed to and curtsied to. Hats were tipped, and they were smiled at by many residents who paused and gave way to their presence.

Wondering what this unusual behaviour was about, Elizabeth commented, "This is more civility than one would think normal?"

They stopped to chat with one of their charity agents who they met strolling along the lane and lived in the village. She was a volunteer helping Anne and Elizabeth maintain Lady Russell's charity programs for the less fortunate in the area.

"Good Morning Mrs. Todd," said Elizabeth.

"Good morning Your Ladyship, Mrs. Elizabeth," replied Mrs. Todd curtsying. Anne mentioned the unusual manner of people this day in politeness and civility. Mrs. Todd explained that these common folk benefit from the charity programs. "They are mothers and children, fathers and young men who benefit from the charity. The village is flourishing because of the helping hand provided by the charity. Your work helps a lot of people, and you are very much revered by the community for your kindness and compassion. Did you not know this dear Lady?" queried Mrs. Todd.

"No, not at all," mentioned Elizabeth surprised.

As ladies, they could not be talked to directly, unless properly introduced. "These folks, upon notice of who you are, simply present themselves in the only way acceptable to society, which is with a bow, a curtsy, a smile, and giving way to you. They are very grateful and honour you for all you do. As we all do," said Mrs. Todd earnestly tipping her head and curtsying sincerely.

Anne was moved, and Elizabeth uncharacteristically broke down, with tears in her eyes, not realising until now that all she was doing for Anne through the charity was impacting people in such a profound and positive way.

"You have been doing such good work here, but you have always kept your distance so as not to know the details. Your charity, Mrs. Anne, Mrs. Elizabeth has a positive impact on the communities in the parish, and many bless you for it," said Mrs. Todd.

"If you would permit me and for only a moment, let me tell you of some of the ways you have helped. Would you walk with me?" asked Mrs. Todd.

"Yes, of course," replied Anne. "See the village school, just there, that simple building? You make that possible for all the village children. With more village folk working, thanks to your apprentice charity, the village will soon be able to pay for the schoolmaster and maintain the building. Your surgeon donates time, once a fortnight, with an open surgery where those less fortunate may come for treatment free of charge. There are apprentice jobs opened to teach the young men a trade. Many stay in the village applying their trade here. Some families have lost jobs and need a hand to keep a roof over their heads and foodstuffs until they find work; they find help through charity. Your charity assists in these ways throughout the parish now."

"See there ladies, that mother and child? The father was injured in the last war. That would have meant homelessness for him, her, and the children but this home houses several widows and families, giving them a chance to raise their children and survive. You have made this possible." This family is now learning a trade through charity, and paying their way with lodging and food, as well as volunteering with charity work, giving back, and putting to use their new skills. You do quite a lot, Ma'am. We are all grateful for you and Miss Elizabeth," said Mrs. Todd as she begged her to leave with a deep bow and turned to go about her business.

Elizabeth, standing close to Anne, realised how much she could do with so little to help the common people. Turning to Anne, she said, "How did you know this would affect me so?"

"You seemed ready to give and I thought this would be the perfect way. You are different now sister, life isn't all about you all the time. Your work has lifted the less fortunate, and now they look up to you because you extended a hand even though you did not have to. It seems we have made many friends," said Anne.

Elizabeth, with this realisation, wiped her tears from her eyes, determined to be an even better person going forward in this respect, as she walked along with Anne, secretly in awe of her sister, to many a bow, smile, and curtsy.

With the shopping completed and so many standing aside to put them at the front of queues, they felt humbled and loved as the carriage arrived to fetch them back to Kellynch Hall with onlookers waving them a good day.

At dinner, Elizabeth related all the events of the day to family and guests present of their exploits in the village. A special guest at supper was Captain Warwick, who was moved and realised the influence Anne has had on Elizabeth. "She is of better character for the association, and I honour you Anne for it," thought Warwick.

Mary, hearing of the events, asked if she might be of assistance to the charity works, and it was agreed she would be set to work, perhaps even forgetting her illnesses as a result. But like Elizabeth this would be a journey of realisation for Mary, thought Anne, although she had little idea how much she would grow and how humbled she would be to know of the transformation from despair to hope people would make because of her efforts.

Anne and Elizabeth looked into each other's eyes, knowing all too well the growing Mary would make. Just then Louisa asked if she might participate and then Lady Musgrove and Henrietta.

Anne, speechless for a moment, consented to the offers of help. "I will organise a lunch meeting for the charity where you will learn about the works, and we can assign each of you areas of organisation and responsibility. This is a fun endeavor. One of hope and love and care, ladies," said Anne proudly.

Frederick, watching all of this unfold realised Anne was such a positive influence in the lives of friends and family, as well as his life. As dinner concluded Anne and Elizabeth set a date for tea when all the women and volunteers might get together at Kellynch Hall to talk about the charity, receive their assignments and manage charitable events and service, as well as be introduced to the energetic parish volunteers who do much of the front line work.

Elizabeth and Captain Warwick had now set the date for their wedding. With the birth of Fitzwilliam and Lady Russell's passing, it was only right to wait till now. Captain Warwick and Elizabeth told Anne and Frederick of their plans, and Anne planned a family dinner where the announcement and final preparations could be made for the happiest of events.

Anne and Elizabeth held a lunch and tea where they and their new charity recruits gathered for assignment, planned charitable events, and discussed ideas. Parish volunteers were introduced after discreet instructions to put aside social rank for the sake of treating many of the volunteers with respect and courtesy. "It would be very difficult indeed to expect frank discussions if social rank were introduced in this setting. Our volunteers are common folk it is true, and they are in awe of our rank. By our treatment of them and in this case the setting aside of rank for the sake of the charity work they are enabled with much more power to do the task," instructed Anne to nodding and attentive relatives. The meeting was a success, and all was settled for moving charity efforts forward.

Elizabeth slipped and hinted as to the purpose of the family dinner that evening and was queried until she gave in and admitted she and Captain Warwick had set a date for their marriage since it was delayed due to Lady Russell's passing. Now the time was proper to marry. All were excited and bound to silence through many discreet congratulations.

Supper at Kellynch Hall was always special with all the history in the surroundings and on the walls. Furthermore, it was not often the whole family was together in one place these days. Just before dinner was served, in the drawing room, Elizabeth and Captain Warwick asked for the attention of the gathering and announced that a date for the marriage and invitations would go out the following fortnight. Everyone was excited and supper conversation revolved around the wedding event and how all might participate in the happy day. Elizabeth was the center of attention and deservedly so.

Before long the village and surrounding area received wind of the happy event, one servant telling a family member, a family member telling a wife, a wife telling a neighbour, and so on. Much of the goodwill for the family, through all they do for the less fortunate, led many a volunteer to approach the vicar to assist with the cleaning up of the church, the yard, decorations, and much more in the way of tasks usually left alone. The vicar was overwhelmed, not realising until now how loved the family was and how Anne and Elizabeth were so well regarded by all. The parish folk asked that this be a surprise only revealed on that special day, and it was agreed.

He knew this would be no ordinary ceremony; many villagers would line the road, wave and shout well-wishes as a surprise for the bride and groom, and also for the whole family. He promised to keep the secret and help in the arranging.

The vicar felt honoured to know of Anne and Frederick. Since they had come to the neighbourhood together they had raised the hopes and faith of people in the area. He was also very impressed with the Wentworths. "Their actions have spoken louder than any words," he said to the congregation "and although they are not often to church here in the village, as you can imagine how busy an active Captain is in his Majesty's Navy and Anne with all the children, a large estate and the charity to manage this leaves little time even on the Lord's day. They are about the Father in heaven's business though, that is clear to see," said the vicar.

The night before Elizabeth's wedding had arrived, Anne and Elizabeth, Mary, Louisa, and Henrietta spent time together talking about all the expectations of marriage. Over cups of tea and soft candlelight, they dreamed of the morrow and the ceremony to come, hoping for sunshine and laughter, of the reception and after ball at Kellynch Hall. "Your honeymoon is yet to be decided?" asked Anne.

"I think it will be a tour of Scotland and Ireland for us," said Elizabeth.

"Are you nervous?" asked Louisa.

"A little," replied Elizabeth shyly.

"Warwick is a grand fellow, good in manners and attentive to the ladies. He will make a good husband, and sister. You have chosen well indeed," said Mary.

"Thank you, sister," responded Elizabeth.

"A gift," presented Anne.

"Oh, you shouldn't have," replied Elizabeth.

"I didn't, this is a special delivery from your Warwick," replied Anne to the eager eyes of all the ladies present.

"Open it, open it, let us see what is in it," said the group.

Elizabeth opened the package, careful not to tear the soft blue paper, to find a hand-painted portrait of her Warwick with a lock of his hair. All the women sighed at the thoughtfulness of the act.

"We have yet to purchase a home in the area. There are several choices," said Elizabeth changing the subject still not use to displays of honest emotion. Anne mentioned that the late Lady Russell's estate was up for sale or let, adding how wonderful it would be to have a sister as a neighbour. "This is on our list of homes to tour, upon our return," replied Elizabeth.

"In the meantime, Kellynch Hall can be your residence," said Anne.

"It is such a happy place with many happy memories sister. Perhaps that is why a decision to purchase has been difficult," replied Elizabeth.

The sun rose quickly this short and restless night for Elizabeth. Anne expected her to be nervous as breakfast was brought to her room but to her surprise Elizabeth was all smiles and much in the way of being relaxed, almost serene in her manner. Anne could see the happiness pour out of her and was glad of it. "Truly your Warwick is a lucky man, sister."

They chatted over a light breakfast as all the sisters and cousins arrived at her side. Elizabeth finished breakfast and began to get ready for the wedding and ride to the church. Work began on her hair, and when completed the wedding dress was fitted properly, along with shoes, ribbons, and flowers. "You look grand indeed," Mary said, breathless.

"Your dress is traditional yet modern to the times," said Harriet, adjusting a ribbon.

"The veil is just hinting at how beautiful your face is today. The man will fix his eyes on you, that is certain," said Louisa. The servants finished helping dress Elizabeth, leaving one behind just in case something was missed. However, Elizabeth was ready and all was prepared with little mishap to consider.

The carriages arrived and all were poised for the ride to the church. As the women carefully escorted Elizabeth down the staircase, they exited Kellynch Hall and boarded their rides. Unbeknownst to them, several hundred villagers and folk of the surrounding area lined the way to the church for a mile on both sides of the lane. Sometimes several persons deep, they waited patiently for the carriages, determined to wave and shout their good wishes to the family, holding flowers to throw on the path ahead.

Elizabeth was now ready and seated, as the carriage lurched forward slowly. A dispatch rider was sent ahead on horseback to notify those at the church of her leaving the hall and being only minutes away. All those lining the country lane where the bride and family were to pass saw the rider and knew Elizabeth, Anne, and family were on their way in the carriages to follow. Only Frederick and Warwick were already at the church, as was only right and proper for the ceremony.

Elizabeth was in the lead carriage with Anne, Mary, and Louisa, with cousins in another carriage just behind. As the carriages left it soon became apparent to the occupants the roads were filled with well-wishers. So many, in fact, Elizabeth, Anne, and the whole family, for that matter, waved the whole way to the church, happily thanking all for coming out to wish them well.

For Mary, Mrs. Musgrove, Louisa, and Henrietta this was a humbling experience, and they felt the full force of the positive work of Anne's charity to the local communities and were truly moved and grateful for their involvement by the sight of the local folk and to know her and be the object of this affection.

Elizabeth's special day was graced with sunshine in June. Lane after lane people waved and sent many wishes for happiness and goodwill. Approaching the church, Anne noticed how immaculate the church grounds were, with many new flowerbeds, and commented on how revived the church looked. She was told later of the many volunteers who worked the week over to repair, straighten, prune, plant, and polish every inch of the church for the wedding.

Anne relayed to Elizabeth and party the news and all were moved at the signs of respect and goodwill everywhere. "It is now time to enter the church," commented Louisa.

There was surprise music that was not planned for; it seemed the local orchestra that was engaged for the balls at Kellynch Hall twice a year wanted to give this present to the family. The music was soft and ethereal, making the ceremony wondrous in feeling and atmosphere. "How very fortunate we are my Warwick," said Elizabeth with tears in her eyes.

"Very fortunate indeed my lady," replied Warwick, kissing her hand.

With the ceremony concluded, the bride and groom followed the vicar into sacristy to sign the church register, while the gathering made their way back to Kellynch Hall for the wedding reception, waiting upon the arrival of the bride and groom. Anne and Frederick stayed behind to witness the signing and escort the happy couple back to Kellynch Hall.

"So, it is done my dear heart. We are married," said Warwick.

"It seemed all so natural and meant to be. I am glad about it and have hope for our future. Perhaps, children one day soon?" queried Elizabeth, searching Warwick's eyes for an answer.

"I am betting on it my dear," replied her Captain smiling and curving his arm for her hand as he escorted his bride out of the church and onto the waiting carriage where Anne and Frederick stood in wait for them.

There were still groups of parish folk waiting along the lane waving and cheering for them, sending their congratulations to the newlyweds. The short carriage ride to Kellynch seemed even shorter today as they arrived at the after-ball amongst cheers of goodwill and many guests.

The reception at Kellynch Hall was sufficiently grand, all invited were able to attend, giving their congratulations and hopes for happiness. There was much in the way of dancing and conversations, renewing of friendships, and catching up. All was amiable and fine throughout the evening.

Anne managed all the events from behind the scenes. Sir Walter, the proud father, fluffed his feathers, as was expected, and was in good form as he escorted the Dowager Viscountess, the Lady Dalrymple, and the Honourable Miss Carteret assuring only the 'somebody's' would be introduced, although many had the privilege of speaking with the Viscountess since she was not so bothered about meeting people and knowing their stories. She especially had a weakness for the men in uniform attending the ball and made herself available for conversation.

Miss Carteret, a little more familiar with Anne, now that she had helped with Fitzwilliam's birthing, broke away from Sir Walter's party to chat with Anne and Mary. "Anne, how is Fitzwilliam coming along?"

"Quite well. The children are here with Harriet, able to see the events while still being out of the way. He is growing so fast, we are blessed with him. Thank you for enquiring," replied Anne.

"Not at all," commented Mrs. Carteret.

"How are you these days?" asked Anne.

"Very well thank you," replied Mrs. Carteret as a gentleman approached, bowed to all, and asked Miss Carteret if she was inclined to dance. "I believe I shall sir," replied Miss Carteret. "Ladies," said Miss Carteret leaving.

Frederick moved to Anne's side, noticing she had a tear in one eye; "Are you well Anne?" asked Frederick.

"It seems my dear Captain these last years are slipping through our hands like sands pouring through our fingers. I just can't seem to slow the passage of these most happy moments."

"We must enjoy each moment, be grateful for all, and live for now," said Frederick squeezing Anne's hand.

Shall we stroll through the garden? The evening is glorious and the ball has taken a life of its own. I am sure we will not be needed for a few moments," said Frederick, offering Anne his arm.

"Yes, that would be lovely," as they silently walked across the room and slipped through a door onto the garden.

"The ball is going so well, and Elizabeth is as happy as any bride on her wedding day. You should be proud of all the work and planning you have done on her behalf. She will never forget this day, nor will Warwick," commented Frederick.

"Thank you, my Captain. It is true sister and I have not always seen eye to eye, but in these last few years, she has changed, ever since we married. You have helped bring this change about," replied Anne.

"I wish I could account for her change. I believe your confidence and patient manner have won her over," said Frederick. "I am so very proud of you and grateful you chose me," said Frederick, holding Anne close to kiss her softly in the moonlight.

The ball's events concluded at dawn with thoroughly exhausted guests, and with the bride and groom boarding a carriage that would take them to their honeymoon. They were farewelled with cheers, waves, and smiles. All the guests commented on the general splendor of the ball and the happy couple, the music and dancing, and plenty of interesting conversation to be had by all.

In the days following, Anne received many notes of thanks and compliments for organising the fine event. It would be a fortnight before Anne would see her sister and brother-in-law. "I will remember this wedding; so wonderful and momentous, full of hopes and all the happy wishes for Elizabeth and her Captain Warwick. It brought me back to my special day when my Captain expressed his love for me in this very garden under a full moon. He still loves me as ever," wrote Anne in her diary.

CHAPTER 6

Changes

Admiral Croft took ill. It was sudden, and he passed away in his sleep one evening. This was a shock to the family. Mrs. Croft lost her best friend and her spirits were low as would be expected. All the women in the family, including Anne, did all they could not to leave her alone at this delicate time. Each lady took their turn keeping her company, showing great compassion, and patiently hearing her out throughout the day. Mrs. Croft, in these last years, developed excellent friendships that were now supporting her in her time of need.

Admiral Croft's wishes were to be buried at sea as was customary for some of the older sailors. Frederick made all the arrangements, escorting Mrs. Croft to Plymouth and taking her on board the H.M.S. Laconia specially assigned by the Admiralty for this solemn task. Many who attended the ceremony replaced regular crew, taking on the crew tasks notwithstanding their rank, so they might attend. The H.M.S. Laconia never looked better. The Admiral's body was carried aboard, with ceremony, wrapped in the Union Jack, and placed carefully on deck. Mrs. Croft broke with tradition to stand by her husband's remains.

Frederick, barking orders to set sail, could not help to notice how small and frail she looked at the moment. Captain Benwick, also seeming to notice, stopped what he was doing and took her arm so that she might lean on him.

It was a brisk wind and cloudy morning when the Laconia laid a course just south of Plymouth port where with pomp and circumstance Admiral Croft was laid to rest in the one place he loved most, the open sea. Mrs. Croft felt it deeply as Frederick at her side ordered Admiral Croft's body released into the dark waters, with gun and canon fire rocking the ship.

Frederick consoled Mrs. Croft. "You have us now sister. You are not without family," said Frederick.

"Thank you, Frederick, thank you and Anne for all you have done," replied Mrs. Croft in a tried and lonely tone. "These last years have been a happy retirement for us since you, and Anne returned to Kellynch Hall. We wished it would go on a while longer," whispered Mrs. Croft.

Anne waited on shore as the Laconia docked late into the dusk, taking Mrs. Croft's arm as she disembarked a navy frigate for the last time. "Dear sister, please let me escort you to our apartments. We will stay tonight and leave for Kellynch tomorrow. Will this be acceptable?" asked Anne.

"Thank you, this is very acceptable. Can we stop at the cathedral for prayers, if this is not too much?" asked Mrs. Croft.

"Not at all, it would be an honour," replied Anne with Frederick now at her side.

Each of the officers, presented their final condolences, with some sharing a funny story or two for the last time. When they were done they formed a line to the waiting carriage where the door was opened and Mrs. Croft, Anne, and Frederick were whisked to the cathedral for prayers.

Upon the return to Kellynch and not too soon, Mrs. Croft emerged from isolation and resumed her role in the family conversations and suppers together. Life at Kellynch Hall settled down to a normal pace and even keel. "These are glorious days. How I wish them to last and last…" Anne wrote in her diary.

With the children growing up so very quickly now, they would soon be off to schools and careers. Anne, felt the winds of changes in her heart when she looked in their eyes so full of hope for the tomorrow. "Life is unfolding like an open road before them. Oh Frederick, how can I ever let them go, how can I stand my heart breaking knowing they will be off soon," said Anne.

"We will never let them go, my dear. They have our hearts in them forever and ever," replied Frederick, holding her hand tight, as he and Anne sat watching the children, each in their interest.

"We are so connected to each of them and each other," wrote Anne to her sister.

This morning Frederick II, like on Father's Day, would be off to the Naval Academy. His bags were packed and he spoke of nothing else. He was ready for the great adventures life would hold for him. Frederick was proud of his oldest son's accomplishments as he took his first steps into the world. Anne fussed about seeing her firstborn still as that little one that clung to her so tightly at birth and for far too short a time. "Don't worry Mother I will be back for Michaelmas and spend all my time with you," said Frederick II as Anne hugged him deeply as any caring mother would.

Frederick shook his son's hand, "You are a man now son, and ready for all the challenges to come, go with my love and blessings. I am very proud of you and look forward to reports of your progress at the academy," said Frederick.

"Thank you, father. I will make you proud," replied Frederick II, almost as tall as his father.

Frederick II turned to his twin sister with a smile and there were hugs all around. Fitzwilliam, in awe of his brother, hugged him tightly. "This will be the first time we are not all together. Write to me. Tell me about your exploits. I will be interested," commented Frederick II.

"I will," replied Margret Anne hugging him a final time.

"I shall brother," replied Fitzwilliam shaking Frederick's hand.

At that Frederick II walked toward Mrs. Croft standing to the side of Frederick and Anne, and in the gentlest of tones said "I so wished the Admiral could have seen me off. We talked of this moment often and what to expect at the Academy. He is with me in spirit and so are you dear Aunt."

"Good luck Frederick," said Mrs. Croft as they hugged

"Good Bye Frederick, Good Luck, Write when you're able son," said Anne holding her Captain's arm tightly. The carriage so quickly crossed the crest of the hill and was gone from sight, now into the world. Frederick, holding Anne's hand, saw her bravery, but she was shattered and hiding it well. Margret Anne, realising her mother's deep connection to all of them, came to her side, knowing in just a few days she would be off to finishing school, and that she must make the most of this time.

The next few days flew by for Anne and Margret Anne. They awakened this morning knowing another was to be off to finishing school by the afternoon. It would be two months before she would next be home again at Kellynch Hall. Anne felt her heart break as she knew life would never be as it was. "My only girl is to go out into the world my Captain," said Anne.

"Frederick II and Fitzwilliam were always there and now how quickly all has changed and with the quiet of a gentle breeze everything is different," wrote Margret Anne in her diary under candlelight and to the early dawn hours.

Anne knocked on her door and came into the room as Margret Anne chatted away about both everything and nothing, save how much she would miss everyone. Holding back the tears, begging time to stop and reverse, Anne said "I can remember that innocent time when all of you would run into Mummy and Daddy's room in the early morning to play on the bed. We would spend the day together on many adventures in the garden and on walks."

At breakfast Anne and Frederick fussed about all the arrangements, assuring themselves everything was set and ready for Margret Anne's safe passage. This was more a distraction, leaving only to the last minute the going away of another beloved child. With Henrietta arriving, this signaled the closeness of the hour.

"Write often Margret Anne, for my sake," said Anne, both mother and daughter letting the tears flow.

"It is a woman's way," thought Frederick feeling his heart break but doing everything not to show it.

"Father, have no worries, I will write often and see you in just a few months. I promise," said Margret Ann, hugging her father tightly.

"Mother, we are bound as a mother and daughter should be. I have learned well from you and will use all you have given me. I love you," said Margret Anne.

"And you, be safe and go with God child," replied Anne, hugging her child close.

"Father, I will miss you. This finishing school business will be done with quickly, and I will be home once more," said Margret Anne hugging her father.

"Goodbye for now brother," said Margret Anne.

"See you soon sister," replied Fitzwilliam.

In the carriage Margret Anne, with Henrietta and Louisa as an escort, waved with tears in her eyes, "I will miss you all. I will write and be back in two months to visit for the holiday!" she exclaimed as the carriage bounded up the lane and out of sight.

Anne walked into the hall arm-in-arm with both her men. She was never accustomed to not seeing her children and so all the more important were the times when they were all home on a visit to enjoy every precious moment.

Months had gone by quickly, and Fitzwilliam would be off to Cambridge University tomorrow. He was leaving a year early as a result of brilliant schooling and test results but may return more frequently and promised to do so as he could.

Of the boys, he was closest to Anne. "You are off to college tomorrow son. Do you have all the arrangements completed?" asked Frederick.

"Yes, father," replied Fitzwilliam. Fitzwilliam spent most of the evening with their mother and father, so he would not lose time away.

Despite his calm manner and aloofness, Fitzwilliam was very closely connected to his mother and father. "This will be the first time away from you and standing on my own. This seems like a big step," said Fitzwilliam.

"Remember what I have taught you of the ways of the world, and all will go well for you son," instructed Frederick earnestly.

"I shall father. I will focus on my studies and not the distractions of the larger towns and the folk there," replied Fitzwilliam.

"That is a good son. I hope and pray for your success and safe return," commented Anne, not wanting to be too emotional but working hard not to show how much her heart was breaking.

With Fitzwilliam off to Cambridge, the morning was left to just Anne and Frederick. "It has been years since it has just been you and I. We will have to get used to this again my dear," said Frederick.

"Yes, my Captain. It is you and I and I am glad of it. I remember the days early in our marriage when we lived for each other, this does not bother me. It seems strange to go back to it again after so long a time. I am sure I do not like this business of leaving," replied Anne.

"Well, shall we lunch together, then take a stroll through the lanes since the weather is so glorious?" asked Frederick.

"Yes, let's do dear," replied Anne as they walked into the hall.

"I enjoyed our walk this day. It has been long since we have had such time together, for each other," said Frederick.

"I worried we would have forgotten why we love each other but our closeness has not changed over the years, and we fit like hand and glove," replied Anne.

"Shall we go into supper?" asked Frederick.

"Yes, of course. We are alone for the first time in many years; all we have is each other and our closeness," replied Anne.

"It is not so bad really. And with frequent visits from the children it will all go well," said Frederick.

"You are all I ever wanted my Captain. The children were extra and more than I could have hoped," commented Anne.

"Yes, they are a love in our lives. I wonder what each is doing now. Frederick II is about the academy classes."

"Margret Anne would have settled in her room, meeting fellow girls. Some good, some not so good she will discern. Tomorrow will bring a new set of lessons in language, economy, and the running of a home," replied Anne.

"Fitzwilliam will start classes next week, so he will be as busy as well," commented Frederick.

"So you see we have done well in the raising of the children. It is only natural for them to go out into the world, children truly are on loan" said Anne.

Anne gave so much to the children, and now they were off into the world. She felt it. Frederick was to go to the Admiralty for a fortnight and asked Anne to accompany him, not wanting her at Kellynch alone at this sensitive time. He could arrange time around his schedule of work to spend time with her as well as have breakfasts and suppers with her in Plymouth.

Secretly, he missed all the noise and excitement of the kids and couldn't bear to be away from Anne just now himself, but as a man, he neglected to say it. Anne, knowing Frederick well, supported him. She knew his heart was broken too.

"Yes, dear it will be good to travel with you to Plymouth," answered Anne as they tried to support each other in this time of change.

It had been some months now and Margret Anne was soon to complete finishing school for the term. She would arrive this morning for holiday and take up residence at Kellynch Hall. With only one term to go, she would be home soon enough. "We will plan Margret Anne's coming out ball. I am so excited to have, at least one of my children back in my life soon," said Anne to Frederick.

"I am also excited dear. I have missed her," replied Frederick.

Anne felt so grateful to Margret Anne for her understanding and support these last years. All the children knew how deeply Anne felt for them and so made the effort to stay in close contact with her. Letters would arrive every week telling in some detail, of all the goings-on in each life. "I am fortunate Frederick, with the children wanting to be free to enter the world but considerate of my longing for them and including me in all their adventures," said Anne.

"We are indeed fortunate. What is there to live for but each other and our children in the end?" commented Frederick.

Frederick II arrived home after success at the Naval Academy. A graduate and a commissioned ensign awaiting assignment to a Frigate, he was much changed now. "You look so much like your father when we were just courting," said Anne at supper with her Captain looking on.

"So tall and poised," said Margret Anne, having arrived just this evening.

With a welcome home glint in his eye, Frederick II commented, "How I miss our old friend Admiral Croft and the many chats about adventures and lessons of sea voyages past and full of advice for the future. I experienced much he described so well,.

"Still, you have your dad to be grateful for this," commented Mrs. Croft with a smile to Frederick II. He is a great seaman and high in the admiralty.

"Sister will you be staying?" asked Frederick II.

"I will be here for a fortnight then return to school to finish the final months and return home for good. That is the plan. Do you miss me?" replied Margret Anne.

"Yes, sister you have found me out," answered Frederick II.

"Then brother let us spend the day together tomorrow and catch up on all we have been about. What say you?" asked Margret Anne.

"With pleasure, I look forward to our time" replied Frederick II.

"The twins do have a special bond. They feel it, particularly when they are apart for long periods," mentioned Anne discretely to Frederick's concurrence.

Fitzwilliam had graduated from university and was working on business ventures as an intern in London. Frederick received regular reports on Fitzwilliam's progress in the business world and was astounded at the results. He could see a great talent with money and business.

"Fitzwilliam asked me to invest a small amount in his business startup, and I agreed. Sooner than expected the investments returned my investment with a profit equal to ten times and more of the original investment. I can attest to Fitzwilliam's talents indeed," said Frederick.

Fitzwilliam was fast becoming known to society as the boy with the Midis touch. Fitzwilliam, with great insight, yet cautious with all his investments told his investors investments are fickle things requiring constant attention else one may lose as much as they have gained. His role was to reduce risk through attention, although sometimes loss was inevitable. Investors were lining up to give him funds to invest and manage and seemed well pleased with his results thus far.

Fitzwilliam quickly amassed a fortune for the family, nearly doubling its proportions and enjoying great success with his start-up business venture. Instead of holding the money personally he just added to the family fortune.

With the weekend upon them and Fitzwilliam's arrival, the family spent some rare family time together. Even after Frederick talks with him about personal wealth, Fitzwilliam tells the family, "I don't work for personal gain but for my family. I am glad we can stay in Kellynch and support of mother's charity work and that my success has secured the family financially. This is what I can contribute in this case and I am glad if it."

"Thank you, son we are all very proud of you. Is it acceptable to use some of the funds for charity work?" asked Anne.

"Yes, Mother by all means," answered Fitzwilliam.

Anne and Frederick savoured every moment of these days, knowing they could and would change in a moment. The siblings wasted no time catching up on each other's news and spending every moment possible together, each sensing and knowing how lucky they had been. Kellynch, their home, had such wonderful memories of growing up and family together.

Frederick received a dispatch one evening from the Admiralty notifying him of his promotion to Admiral. In the same dispatch, Frederick II received orders of assignment to a frigate. He was to prepare for sea immediately. "You know Captain Harville well son. He is a good and steady captain. Watch him well and learn. He will teach you all he can in handing off his lessons to the next generation," said Frederick.

"Yes, Father I shall. He is almost part of the family," replied Frederick II.

Margret Anne and Fitzwilliam gathered near Frederick II knowing and without a word the world was changing around them as life would sweep them from each other.

So quickly Frederick II was on his way to Plymouth and the sea. "Goodbye for now. I will see all of you when I make port at Plymouth again."

Anne, better prepared for departures now, gave him all her love and wishes. He would be first to come to Plymouth for Frederick's promotion ceremony then he would set sail with Captain Harville on the HMS Valiant for a nine-month voyage to the East Indies, crossing at the Cape twice.

In Plymouth, all was hustle and bustle, as the Wentworths settled into temporary apartments, save Fitzwilliam, who would billet on the Valiant. The next day was the promotion ceremony and Frederick II's first sea voyage. "We will all see you off son. It is one of the few privileges of an Admiral you see," said Frederick at supper with Captain Harville in attendance.

"Have no worries, Admiral, I shall personally look after your son," said Captain Harville smiling at Anne and Frederick.

"This is nothing but a normal tour of duty," said Captain Benwick, who would be accompanying the Valiant on its tour in his ship.

The subject changed to that of old times, growing up, and manhood, "What a happy circumstance we have all lived through a lifetime of friendships," said Frederick.

"To the Wentworths and the Navy," said Captain Harville.

Frederick's promotion ceremony went well and with naval precision. The surprise was in young Prince James making the presentation of promotion since he had graduated from the academy and was now an ensign and about to go to sea.

Frederick, now an Admiral, turned his attention to seeing Frederick II off on his first voyage. "Good luck son, stay close to Harville and learn," said Frederick.

"I shall Father," replied Frederick II saying goodbye to the family. The Wentworths returned to Kellynch Hall one less this time.

It had been a year and Frederick II had made great progress in the ranks and was now being considered for the rank of Captain. Captain Harville's reports to Admiral Wentworth of Frederick II's natural abilities at sea were upbeat. "Like father like son; it is a pleasure to have your son aboard and be the one to teach him of finer sailing and command," wrote Captain Harville.

On May 2nd, Frederick II was given orders of promotion to the rank of Captain assigned to the Valiant while awaiting his command. "There are no words of thanks for all you have done for me Captain Harville," said Captain Wentworth at supper on board one evening at sea.

"It was always my pleasure Frederick II. Good luck and God's speed in all your endeavors. I will be watching your career closely, and will be glad to serve at your side if it should come to that," replied Captain Harville.

"Captain Frederick Wentworth II," said Admiral Wentworth as Anne, Margret Anne, and Fitzwilliam looked over the proceeding, so very proud.

"I can't help remembering once in the garden you were stuck up a tree branch crying for my help, and now you are a Captain in His Majesty's Navy. I am very proud of you brother. God's speed in all your voyages," said Margret Anne emotionally.

"Son I am glad you will come home with us on leave until you are given a command," said Frederick.

"Let us not waste this time but study tactics and strategy I have developed over these last years," commented Frederick privately.

"Yes father, I was hoping you would offer such insights. I am ready and eager to learn. I hear from those that know you have advanced the art to a new level, and with rumblings across the sea with tensions slowly building I expect your plans will be much needed," replied Frederick II.

"Perhaps, only time will tell," answered Frederick.

One day in the study at Kellynch as they poured over the orders of battle and newer strategy and tactics changes Captains Harville, Benwick and Warwick visited unexpectedly. "Shall I leave you gentlemen to this then?" asked Frederick II.

"No son what we will talk about concerns everyone here, Captains all. Please keep this conversation confidential though and let us close this door for privacy," motioned Frederick.

The Admiral talked of recent events and the brewings in Europe, "I called you all here because I have grave news for you. It looks like the inevitable may be just off the horizon, war gentlemen," said Frederick in a calm and focused manner.

"How ready are we for engagement?" asked Captain Harville.

"The newest ships are completed and seaworthy. The latest strategies and tactics are drawn up. Recruiting levels are below sufficient but this can be remedied. One is never completely ready, but we are as ready as can be expected. My hope though is the diplomatic route will succeed in talking all the parties out of this, but we shall see while preparing in the meantime for the worst.

"Many Captains and officers would like to be briefed on the incredible work you have done at the admiralty these last year's Admiral. Those who have caught a glimpse of the work call it brilliant. Each of us would like to learn from you, so we may better prepare, win, and survive the next conflict should it come to that," said Captain Benwick as young Captain Wentworth took note of the love and respect his father had gained with his peers.

"Yes, let us organise reviews and briefs with as many captains who wish this. My son can help since he has been briefed intensely in all of these plans since their inception and now has great insight into the strategies," commented Frederick.

"I will do whatever is asked of me father," replied Frederick II. All present were impressed with his quick and sure manner of service to his superiors.

"Has Frederick II been granted his command?" asked Captain Harville.

"We are close to a decision gentlemen," replied Frederick deep in thought over organising command orientations and briefs.

"We have much to do, and I will depend on each of you in the task ahead. Do I have your concurrence gentlemen?" asked Admiral Wentworth.

All concurred.

"Let us spend this week getting each of you acquainted with orders of battle while we plan briefing command," mentioned Frederick.

"Father, can we not use Kellynch Hall as the place for briefings? We can organise groups of commanders at a time. The Hall is off the beaten track, maintaining discretion in our task and each of us is available and close in the neighbourhood to assist," suggested Frederick II.

"That is a very good idea. Would you organise the logistics, as well as be available to offer instruction with our captains here present?" questioned Frederick.

"Of course father! I will begin immediately to the task," replied Frederick II.

"Good man," commented Captain Benwick.

Suppers were lively affairs with much in the way of amiable discussions on topics other than what was going on behind closed doors.

In the next days and months, many naval officers of the highest ranks spent many hours a day behind closed doors in the study at Kellynch Hall, with another group arriving shortly after. So much so that Anne enquired over this business of the study and hours of discussions behind closed doors.

"Father is home unexpectedly," said Anne to Frederick.

"That is a surprise since he likes Bath this time of year and with Elizabeth living her life now it is his preferred distraction. Is he doing okay?" asked Frederick.

"For some time now he is slowing in pace and his health is now all one would want. I think he is more tired these days but he won't admit it" replied Anne in a quiet tone.

"You are worried dear?" inquired Frederick.

"He is not long for this world I fear..." said Anne changing the subject.

"My Captain, I am glad for your many visitors. Is there a special reason for such goings on?" asked Anne one Sunday at supper with the family knowing Monday would bring the next group of officers to Kellynch. They stay for three days and are gone where Kellynch is quiet until the next group arrives eager for the meetings and exhausted at its end.

"My dear family, it seems war the worst of all circumstances may be upon us if the diplomats do not agree soon. In preparation,

I have the responsibility of how this next conflict is to be fought on the seas. This has been my task these many years, Frederick II, Benwick, and Harville have been briefing and instructing commanders concerning such plans. It is my intention not to wait until the battle is upon us but to train, teach, and mentor the command and prepare now for what may come. Please realise what I have just explained to you is in the most confidential tone. Keep this a secret, lives will depend on it not only in the Navy but throughout the realm. Spies are everywhere that is why these groups arrive and leave by night, " commented Frederick gravely.

"Well, then my dear Captain…how can I help?" asked Anne.

"You are helping. Each of you is. Anne, you make the house welcoming and light, and that allows commanders to focus on the task at hand while here. You have managed the house staff to assure our guests are well taken care of, in every respect; assuring dispatches are presented to the right commander, and more. Fitzwilliam, you have done wonders for our finances, and this is no inexpensive endeavor. I hope the Navy will reimburse us for the expense, but I will not bet on this case. And Frederick II your work in our briefings, and the insights you have brought have helped many a Captain gain confidence and respect for you and your talents and the plans that have been drawn up. You see, each of you has supported His Majesty's Service in your way, and I thank you for it, truly. I ask you for your continued help since this will go on a bit longer," commented Frederick.

"Well then my Captain we shall all continue in this way then," stated Anne.

"My dear, several important members of the Admiralty will visit next week to receive their briefing on the progress of the learning and preparedness of the command. It would be prudent to keep the relatives away during this time as it might bring up questions at the sight of such high officials. Especially since one of the personages will be the Minister of the Navy himself," stated Frederick.

"It shall be as you have asked," commented Anne.

They agreed not to speak of it to spend all the happy times they could before it broke in the news, and even then not speak of Kellynch Hall and its place in the preparations for war. "We may have some months of pleasure, let's not waste it on this business completely," suggested the Admiral.

"Family first, then it is the Admiralty," said Frederick II as they raised a glass to it.

Family and friends were regular visitors after all the briefings were completed. Charitable events and planning meetings all occurred at the expected times. Elizabeth gave birth to a healthy baby boy. The Warwicks are proud parents and Anne is asked much advice about the raising of children and to be the godmother. Life seemed so normal one would never know what was brewing just below the surface.

One evening, with just Anne and Frederick by the fire in the drawing room, Anne asked Frederick "There is more than normal activity for the navy these days. I am sensing something has been decided. Do you want to tell me?" She asked with hesitation but knew time was short and he and Frederick II did well to conceal this in the happening.

One of the servants signaled to approach Anne and Frederick, "I fear Sir Walter has passed," mentioned the servant discreetly and with care.

Anne and Frederick rose to follow the servants to Sir Walter's apartments to find the servants laid Sir Walter on the bed in a dignified repose. "He looks as if asleep" mentioned Anne quietly.

Frederick held Anne close since he understood the strange relationship she had with her father. After marriage he seemed more in the way of a loving parent and enjoyed the grandchildren so there was some feeling to this event.

"I will send word to the family of father's passing. There are arrangements to be made and a date to be set to lay him to rest," said Anne organizing the affair as a distraction.

"I will ask one of the servants to notify the vicar and have him come," mentioned Frederick with Anne's concurrence.

A few days later and with the family assembled a quiet ceremony was performed and Sir Water was laid to rest in the family plot in the churchyard.

"It seems as if an age has passed, we are in new and unknown territory now," expressed Anne.

Frederick, there tall and strong at Anne's side with her children standing with her just there.

The days flowed by with peaceful and sweet moments. Everyone makes an effort to enjoy every moment. Knowing the storm that lay on the horizon would change their world forever.

"The long-awaited storm is here my love, my life. War seems the only option, and we are but instruments of will now. I have been assigned Fleet command with the protection of England itself on the high seas. Frederick is in my command and His Royal Highness Prince James is an officer on my vessel. I have done all so in the hour of most need, we are not rushed in planning but prepared and confident in our roles. I believe we are more prepared than in all history for what is to come. However, as it is in war, one cannot tell the grave events that come and take us." Anne moved to Frederick's side, holding him tightly as ever before. They sat there by the fire silent the rest of the evening.

At breakfast, after reading the latest dispatches that arrived, "The young Prince is to visit here on his way to the King. He is expected tomorrow for lunch," said Frederick.

"Frederick, I… the house is not ready, the Prince, so much to do," said Anne

"Don't trouble yourself, my dear. I have met the Prince many times now. He is quite normal really and likes less fuss in these matters. I have talked with the cook about lunch arrangements. All is set. If you would be at my side that is all I ask of you. He will arrive in the morning hours where I will brief him on the orders of battle and what to expect at sea.

My dear let's not disturb the children with this news until the last possible minute," suggested Frederick.

"Does my young Captain know of this business?" asked Anne

"Yes, he knows of the possibility, and he has kept his promise not to mention it," commented Frederick.

Anne cried all night on and off. She wanted to hold Frederick with all her might, knowing war could bring the worst of news. Although he was one of the most skilled seaman and tacticians - a warrior of the first order - she would worry for him and her young Captain. "I will pray every day for you, please come home to me, and bring my son home with you," she asked Frederick softly one morning at dawn, just when the house was its most still.

"We all pray my dear to God's speed in this endeavour. All that can be done is now in place, requiring only good command and a steady hand at the helm."

At full morning Anne prepared the house as best as possible for the royal visit. "Frederick it is time to tell Fitz of the visit, may I?" asked Anne.

"Yes, please do. I will be in the study with our son preparing the plans for presentation," commented Frederick. None of the relatives were notified for fear news of war would spread, endangering the family and leaking the preparations for readiness. Only the immediate family in the hall was made aware of the pending visit and the reason. The house and ground staff were reminded that all the events that occurred at the house were not to be talked about, not even with family, especially now when war was being pressed on the realm.

"We have been fortunate father that we have had no leaks of Kellynch's role in the preparation to defend the realm," said Frederick II.

"Very fortunate, even the village folk, not knowing anything directly have noticed many commanders coming and going, and have kept a close eye on strangers, not hinting or providing any information but calling the sheriff to look into their business here. Yes we have been very fortunate indeed," replied Frederick.

Early afternoon brought several soldiers to the property. "My Captain, there are royal marines on the property and at the door," said Anne.

"I shall attend to this, my dear. It means the Prince is not far from Kellynch Hall. As you can imagine his protection is of the utmost importance. There are no reports of incidents but this is precautionary," stated Frederick on his way to greet the marines and give his leave to spread throughout the property.

"They are quite polite. I have never seen that type of uniform," commented Anne.

"These are specially trained guards. They are assigned to the royal family. They are extremely attentive to their safety."

The Royal carriage arrived an hour later. All the proper greetings and introductions were made with all the civility accorded for the circumstances of any high personages arriving at a private home. The Prince went into the study with the Admiral, Captain Wentworth, and his escort Admiral Knight to discuss the Prince's assignment to the command vessel and possible fleet operations expectations. Admiral Wentworth, in full dress, briefed His Royal Highness on the order of battle. After some hours, emerging from the study, they entered the drawing room to find Anne and Fitzwilliam and the just-arrived Elizabeth, her child, and Captain Warwick.

All there were stunned at the sight of His Royal Highness Prince James, save Anne, who greeted him upon arrival, and of course Fitzwilliam. "Shall we lunch?" asked Anne.

"Yes please I am famished," stated Admiral Knight with His Royal Highness smiling in agreement. They all entered the dining room for lunch. Fredrick used to sitting at the head of the table, sat further down to give way to the young Prince as was only right. Fredrick sit at the Prince's right and Admiral Knight at his left, then Captain Warwick, Captain Wentworth and Anne, and the rest of the family.

In full uniform, all the officers impressed the family with the force of their allegiance to the young Prince, one day to be King of England. "How far we have come and how much we have to lose," thought Anne, worried.

Conversation was easy as all subjects were discussed but that of the coming war. The Prince and Admiral Knights departed, and, looking at Frederick, Fitzwilliam asked, "What is going on, this is really out of the ordinary?' before answering his question "I have lived long enough now to know the signs of war, when are you off?"

"In the fortnight we take up our commands. We kept it from family to spend as much time as possible in the quiet happiness we so enjoy. However, alas it can no longer be a secret, so there you are," said Frederick, Anne with tears in her eyes now, while Fitzwilliam, standing at his brother's side his hand on his shoulders. "Fitzwilliam, you will be the man of the house while we are gone, I could not know a better man. Protect your mother and sister and guide this family son as we don't know what the future will bring."

"I shall write a note tonight to ask Margret Anne to come home with all speed and spend time with the family," said Anne, collecting herself.

"Son, courage is not the lack of fear but in the doing of what is right despite it. Your courage will be the support for this family while we are gone to war. Your mother and sister will depend on it," said Frederick softly knowing his son to be a different type of warrior in the way of business matters and not in the fighting and killing.

Fitzwilliam pulled himself together and took the stance his brother Frederick II held as Anne could see his steadiness take hold. They would all depend on it. Elizabeth took Anne's hand from across the table, squeezing it in support and not saying a word, All was understood as the women feared for their men's lives.

Anne and Frederick spent time together talking over all the things one must upon the circumstances coming about and quite out of their control. They both spent every moment with the children they could. With all the uniforms put away, the family spent these last weeks in blissful peace. Like old times, they stood together loving and enjoying each other, only desperately.

The night before departure, a special supper was arranged by Anne and Margret Anne. Quite the woman now and all grown up, Margret Anne understood the gravity of the next months, or possibly years of trials and danger. She wanted a final special occasion before the storm began.

As the whole family arrived to sit for the meal the admiral, Captains Warwick, Wentworth, Benwick and Harville were the centre of attention throughout the evening. "Such conversation, such civility, such love, as the evening finished so very quickly," thought Anne as she lay in bed awake, not wanting to miss even one moment with Frederick.

They lay awake together. The children downstairs sat by the fire reminiscing about their childhood in these last moments before the dawn. Have no fear, I will return. Father is brilliant and I am his son," stated Frederick II. As each sibling held hands sharing each other's strength, they prayed one last time.

Dawn broke and they decided to go into mother and father's room hoping they might be awake and finding them as such. "It has been many years since last all the children came to visit us in our rooms in the early morning. Thank you for this moment," said Anne in a soft voice as they sat on the bed and talked about all manner of things not including the war.

After breakfast and with the sun up now, "My dear how I will miss you, write often. I will live for your words," said Anne to Frederick.

"Your life is my being my dear," replied Frederick through Anne's tears as she squeezed her admiral and her captain tightly.

"The carriage has arrived to take you to Plymouth, sir," said one of the house servants. Anne and Frederick walked out to the box where the family said their last goodbyes. As the box lurched forward Anne waved until all she could see was the last of it as it crested the hill taking two of her most precious men away. They were off to war, while the women and the youngest son waited in the quiet for news…

CHAPTER 7

It's War

Admiral Wentworth recalled to duty, took command of fleet operations aboard the command vessel the H.M.S. Excalibur. His orders were to halt all possible attacks upon England by sea and deny access to the shores of England itself. The sea war had begun.

At his side, Captains Harville, Benwick, Warwick, Frederick II, and ten other Captains, were each briefed and familiar with Frederick's strategy and tactics. Each knew the plan as brilliant and all of them were confident in Admiral Wentworth's command ability. Other commanders through the fleet familiar with the orders of battle had the same confidence and drilled their crews in the strategies and tactics until it was second nature.

"If we are to war, and we want to prevail and make it home safe you are our best hope," said Captain Johns of the HMS Plymouth at a meeting of the admiral and captains aboard the Excalibur. They would support Admiral Wentworth in every way possible.

"All the crews in our command have been drilling in all aspects of the orders of battle and are ready Admiral," stated Captain Harville.

Quietly, Prince James, heir apparent, boarded the Excalibur. Ranked an ensign, the young Prince was noticed by some of the Captains, who bowed before their Prince. Admiral Wentworth stood fast as was proper, and in these circumstances as his superior officer, but with great respect and love for his Royal Highness the Admiral, stood to his right.

The young Captain Wentworth was ready and had prepared all his life for just this moment as he watched his father in the latest brief. Even then with strong emotion, he had great confidence in guiding his ship. His crew was quick-acting and experienced in Admiral Wentworth's approach to the coming battles. Captain Wentworth allowed each officer to brief him and the other officers under his command on their understanding of the orders of battle and their responsibilities and preparations.

Aboard the Excalibur, "Tell me of the key points in this scenario, Captain," said the Admiral to each well-studied Captain under his command. "We are ready gentlemen. Please ensure Captains further into the fleet are just as adept. Let us continue to drill in secret, find weaknesses, and strengthen them in preparation," commanded Admiral Wentworth.

The sea war broke out, and other fleet commanders sent word of battles and tactics used by the enemy as well as the status of forces to Admiral Wentworth. He replied with orders that resulted in the quick defeat of the enemy in these early engagements. "The Admiral hasn't wasted his time during the peace but spent many years working on the newest tactics, the latest approaches to engagements. The early results of his work demonstrate innovation and original approaches to defenses, confusing the enemy. Defense and attack patterns so unique and brilliant is resulting in the saving of ships, lives and winning battles decisively," remarked Admiral Extese, to the Admiralty in Plymouth.

Admiral Wentworth's orders of battle were requested by other fleet commanders and were quickly adapted and implemented at once throughout the navy when other commanders received wind of the early results.

The Captain's Corp. gained a deep respect for Admiral Wentworth's dedication and obvious superiorities in this respect, learning and following his methods exactly. Visits from other admirals and captains were common aboard the Excalibur who requested a brief on the orders of battle and tactics.

Admiral Wentworth keeps his son close, continuing to teach him the basis of war tactics and defensive strategies while they await their turn in the conflict. The H.M.S. Excalibur was the crown jewel in the conflict, and it was only a matter of time before the most powerful enemy fleet would take aim and attack their position. "I have given you every advantage over potential adversaries, giving you the benefit of years of navy experience," thought Frederick of his son as he observed him pouring over an aspect of the battle plan.

Frederick II, like his dad, learned quickly. "What makes Captain Wentworth interesting is he not only understands the tactics and strategies but adds his flair to the equation. The obvious intent is harder to read by the enemy until it is too late. This will make him a formidable foe indeed," said Captain Warwick to other command Captains as Admiral Wentworth listened.

"Not until his first battle will he know what steel he is made of," said Captains Benwick and Harville to Admiral Wentworth.

"It all looks good so far," commented Captain Harville, like a mentor should.

"We shall continue to drill throughout this command gentleman. We are on the razor's edge here. Let each Captain determine readiness and rest periods for their crews. However, let us not be lax, for the crucial battle is just over the horizon," commented Admiral Wentworth.

Prince James executed his duties flawlessly and regardless of rank. The crew was careful with the Prince, going about their routine duties, sometimes working side by side but never crossing the line and always respectful of His Highness. "The Prince is gaining valuable experience and much respect through his daily experience aboard the Excalibur," wrote Admiral Wentworth to the Admiralty.

The Admiral briefed the Prince, specifically on tactics and strategies, defenses, and fleet operations. "This will win battles, save ships, and save lives," said Prince James to Admiral Wentworth.

"That is our hope, Your Highness," replied the admiral. The Prince, impressed with the commander, was glad to be aboard his ship. In trusting Admiral Wentworth so much the Prince let his guard down periodically when only with the admiral, speaking frankly and with candor, and quite at ease. "Thank you admiral for your service to my father and this realm, it has not gone unnoticed," said the Prince one evening during a rare supper alone with Admiral Wentworth.

"Thank you, Your Highness," replied the Admiral.

In interacting with those aboard and with visiting captains and admirals, His Highness gained an acute awareness of the differences in Admiral Wentworth, Benwick, Harville, Wentworth II, and Warwick their readiness for battle sharper as they helped those that were just grasping the plan to master it. The Prince greatly valued Admiral Wentworth and his dedication to his father the King.

Captain Wentworth II, on board the Excalibur often learning and strategising with the admiral and in the Prince's presence Frederick II, was very well acquainted now with the Prince. The Prince could see all the traits within the son of his father and was aware the navy would be in good hands for the next generations should they all survive this conflict. The Prince and Frederick II were of similar age and became good friends, and often found talking about something or other.

Letters to Anne and their family were as frequent as possible. Frederick, devoted to Anne, told her all he could of Frederick II. Anne wrote almost daily of everyday life accounts, mentioning how normal events move along at their Kellynch Hall. "My letters must be nothing to your work my Captain," wrote Anne.

"I long for the normal my dear and live for your country tales and am glad of it. Tell me every detail," returned Frederick. Frederick II wrote regularly but less frequently at times as is the case with the younger generation. A reminder note from my mother gained quite a response in writing when letters were not so frequent.

There were several quick engagements with the fleet ships. "The enemy is testing our readiness gentlemen," wrote the Admiral to his commanders and captains corp. Now using the Admiral's tactics and strategies the skirmishes were quickly suppressed, and the fleets gained confidence in these strategies and dedicated themselves to the plan even more so than before. Admiral Wentworth learned of a major engagement about to break out in his sector of the sea. It would determine whether the Royal Navy continued to rule this part of the ocean or failed in its mission. "Gentlemen, failure is not an option. It seems the war will come to us, and we are ready for this grave moment," said Admiral Wentworth, attending a Captain's meeting.

Every preparation was made. Drills were executed flawlessly and all was in readiness. Admiral Wentworth ordered small behind-the-lines war games to be carried out to ensure understanding and execution of tactics in battle-like conditions. The fleet was on station and standing by just a hair's breadth from pulling the trigger.

"Admiral Wentworth your command is resupplied, weapons at the ready. Ships deployed as planned and crews are clear as to plan. Patrols are monitoring the seas in all sectors with no reported enemy contacts," read the morning brief. The Admiral dispatched the latest intelligence report to all Captains, "Be vigilant, do not let the quiet before the storm lull you to sleep."

"Intelligence is now consistently reporting that the enemy is amassing forces in this area at an alarming rate and is maintaining position just over the horizon, just out of sight. It is a matter of time gentlemen. Patience, but prepare your crews for the worst. Admiral Wentworth, Fleet Command."

At dusk one evening the enemy fleet was spotted on the horizon. "Intelligence indicated similar numbers of ships. Eighteen heavily armed vessels and at the centre smaller light ships of the force Admiral" reported the intelligence chief.

"What are they protecting at their centre?" thought the Admiral.

"Orders are sent out to the fleet to dispense attack plans, guards all night, batteries in ready status, prepare for sneak attack tactics from the enemy. All scout ships to positions to monitor enemy movements and small ship incursions,

Admiral Wentworth Fleet Command."

Captain Wentworth talked to his officers, checking all possible preparations. He ordered twenty-four-hour guards to be relieved every two hours. He also ordered the crew in a rotating fashion to rest as much as possible in between shifts and continuous over-the-side checks for sneak small ship incursions, as well as distribution of armory supplies, to be completed at all possible speed and posted marines to all critical points on ships keeping sight of any threats.

The Admiral, up all night, checked and rechecked every detail of the battle plan, studying every aspect to the last minute to ensure his fleet had every chance of victory and every opportunity to save the lives of his men and ships.

The prince, restless, came into the war room, as he could not sleep. "So very suddenly this young ensign, His Royal Highness the Heir to the Empire, confirms his bloodlines and all the instinct that can't be taught show through at the crucial hour," thought Admiral Wentworth.

"No need for sleep," said Prince James. The Admiral bowed to His Highness for the first time as they spoke of preparations and expectations of the fight.

The Prince showed his true command of the battle vision, acknowledging the Admiral's brilliance and stewardship of His Majesty's Fleet, thanking him for his dedication, and wishing him God's speed. The admiral asked the Prince to spend the day at his side, as it was only right to be seen with the Fleet Commander. "I expect the enemy commander has been informed by their spies our command and control vessel is in these waters. They will come for us," said Admiral Wentworth. "Your command is steady. The orders of battle are brilliant and we have great confidence. The enemy will fail! I believe it!" replied Prince James.

"Strategies are much more complex now, protection of the Prince, winning the battle, conserving our crews and ships, all a very sensitive balance to be sure," said the admiral to Captain Wentworth.

"To your ship son, I fear in a few hours begins the longest of days."

"We are all ready Father," replied Frederick II as Prince James looked on, understanding the gravity of the moment.

As morning broke the crews needed no prompting to get to stations. No one was hungry but the admiral did make time to take tea with his Prince and some of his senior officers. "It is the British way to act with some order and civility in these cases. We are after all not savages," said Lord Norton.

Shortly after tea, the enemy made the first moves of engagement, showing themselves on the horizon. The fleet held positions until the last possible moment so as not to alert the enemy of the trap being set for them. Each Captain knew their part, holding steady to orders, waiting like a cocked pistol searching for the whites of the eyes.

Finally, the sound of cannon, loud shouts, and the engagement was in full play. The command ship used coded flags to communicate moves and positions while receiving regular intelligence reports on enemy positions, the size of ships, and battle progress. With the engagement afoot, enemy ships were being captured, sunk, or taken under surrender. All was going to plan so far with the strategies being beyond the grasp of the enemy to counter in any effective way. Royal Navy losses were minor with more in the way of injuries and damage than the of loss of the whole ship.

The main enemy force made their move and began bearing down on the command sector with the bulk of their sea forces as a last resort and trying to save the day. Captains Benwick, Harville, Warwick, and Wentworth were in a perfect position, and as planned intercepted the hoard of vessels. The combatants were enjoined and the battle raged for the next few hours. For a period, valiant men on both sides fought to the height of their abilities equal to the task, each knowing this was the battle and what was at stake.

After a while, the Admiral's tactics and strategies began to take hold and his ships like pieces on a chess board, as it were, held the superior positions, taking enemy pieces one by one. The enemy commander, seeing the writing on the wall decided to make his boldest move yet in a final effort before it was too late.

The Admiral could see his son had what it takes in battle. Frederick II demonstrated his dad's stock running deep in his veins. He fought on instinct' knowing where to be and what to do and those little particulars that can never be taught but spell success or failure in battle. "His understanding of the orders of battle and the loyalty of his crew made his vessel a formidable foe," said Prince James to the proud Admiral. Admiral Wentworth acknowledged the Prince but was focused on his whole fleet and their welfare in this battle while secretly keeping his son's status close in mind and heart.

Captains Benwick and Harville noticed and trusted Captain Wentworth to protect their rears as they battled the main incursion forces. He and his crew were skilled and without fear, as they repelled one attempt after another.

Just as the enemy assault began to lose some momentum, a single ship in the center of their force slipped through the pattern of defenses and quickly made for the command ship. Seeing this move, Admiral Wentworth perceived quicker than any other the gravity of this gambit.

"That was the enemy's real plan all along, brilliant move. Overtake the command ship and cut off the head." At that same moment, Captain Wentworth II ordered his ship to intercept this threat. HMS Valiant instantly changed course to intercept and engage the enemy. In a straight line, the HMS Valiant moved to block the enemy advance.

Captain Wentworth used his experience and judgment gained to repel what seemed like an all or nothing attempt to overthrow the gains made in the day's battle thus far. HMS Valiant engaged the enemy ship, denying access to the command vessel only a few hundred yards away. Captain Wentworth ordered a second change in course to cut the intercept time and explained the enemy's plan to his officers en route. His crew looked at him and responded instantly to his commands. He ordered cannon fire just below the decks of the enemy vessel as they approached…the battle was fierce close-in fighting with cannon fire from both ships tearing at the hulls.

The HMS Valiant quickly disabled the shooting effectiveness of the enemy ship, but it rammed the Valiant and used gabbling hooks to keep in close quarters. The enemy was bent on hand-to-hand combat this day and the Valiant crew would have to stand firm.

The admiral and prince had front-row seats to this engagement. Not being able to do anything and having the bigger sea battle to manage, Frederick's focus was on the whole command but secretly praying for his son and his crew. "In his first major engagement his son is to be tested to the fullest," thought Admiral Wentworth, a worried father assessing the overall fleet progress.

"This single enemy ship aimed to ram and then board the command vessel for hand-to-hand combat with the intent of killing the young Prince and the admiral. If unopposed they would have succeeded with dire consequences to this battle and the sea war. Now is the time and this is the place we stand for King and countrymen," announced Captain Wentworth, holding a sword in one hand, barking commands, and pointing with the other hand.

Captains Benwick, Harville, and Warwick were aware of Captain Wentworth's engagement but were unable to aid him until they dispatched their foes. Each of them focused on their engagement, hoping their young Captain's steel would not bend. In the meantime, while commanding their men harder to end the engagements to assist the junior Wentworth and crew.

Quick thinking and commands by Captain Wentworth maintained his ship between the command vessel and the enemy. A mortal battle ensued at close range, both Captains able and confident, as hand-to-hand combat broke out on the decks of both ships. Cannon fire slammed into and through the sides of each frigate. Enemy marines boarded HMS Valiant to sword and shot and were repelled time and again, like waves to the shore.

Captain Wentworth's crew, confident and focused, began to win the day as the enemy ship, heavily damaged now, took on water slowing its movements. Its crew lost poise and began abandoning ship, while others fought on. A moment later, there was a surrender with what was left of the living and wounded aboard and in the water.

The battle was won, but at a heavy cost to the ship and crew. "Captain Wentworth was stabbed through from the back by a dying enemy sailor. Seriously injured, he continued to order that all be secured. As he barked his final commands fighting the loss of consciousness, he showed no signs of injury to give the crew every confidence in the final moments. He only gave in when we arrived and relieved him" relayed Captain Harville to Admiral Wentworth.

"Both, I and Captain Benwick took up positions at his side as we completed the work Captain Warwick reached the young captain first."

"It seemed our young Captain fought the most serious and crucial engagement, in the most important battle of the seas and. this could have determined the course of the engagement and perhaps the sea war," commented Captain Benwick earnestly.

Winning their respective battles, Harville, Benwick, and Warwick had come alongside the HMS Valiant, heavily damaged and barely seaworthy, and grappled to the enemy vessel, to clean up the mess and relieve Captain Wentworth and crew. Finding him seriously injured, they ordered he be transported to the command vessel and medical care as soon as possible.

"He and his men fought well in this most crucial battle of them all. "Well done Wentworth, rest now, we will take over from here," said Captain Warwick to Captain Wentworth, who then fell in and out of consciousness.

"My ship my crew, the enemy," whispered Captain Wentworth before falling unconscious again.

News of the battle won and of Captain Wentworth's deeds spread like wildfire throughout the fleet emboldened British commands to quickly clean up remaining skirmishes and take the enemy where they could. As news of the victory and of Captain Wentworth's injuries spread, many a Captain worried for his life. "Brave young captain…brilliant admiral, save HMS Valiant! Keep her afloat, tie her to my vessel…we'll bring her to port" said many a Captain.

Prince James commanded the surgeon aboard the Excalibur, with the Admiral's permission, to transfer Captain Wentworth to the command ship and attend to the young Captain Wentworth, also to see to his crew. "We pray for your young captain, admiral," said Prince James that night at Admiral Wentworth's side.

A dispatch was sent out to all fleet captains and the admiralty after many enquires:

"The seas are again quiet, England is secure, and the fleet intact and on station.

With the most crucial battle won…the young Captain Wentworth sustained serious injuries but fought on, until victory was secured, at his crew's side giving orders until relieved by three of his Majesty's ships. He has been transferred to the Command vessel for treatment. Although heavily damaged, the HMS Valiant is seaworthy and on station at this time. Her crew is being attended to by all means. Thank you for all your inquiries.

It was determined the enemy's intent here was to board and kill His Highness Prince James and our fleet Admiral and commanders, but the young Captain Wentworth, understanding the plan, instantly put himself in harm's way, intercepting the enemy vessel, placing his ship between the enemy and command vessel, fighting hand-to-hand with live cannon, shot and sword until His Majesty's ship overcame the threat and was relieved.

It is hoped the young Captain will survive his injuries, but at this time, it is still uncertain.

We have won the day and inflicted a serious blow to the enemy. We captured the fleet commander during the engagement but let it be known we are still on station, the war is on,

Admiral Wentworth, Fleet Command."

Saving the command ship with the Prince and admiral aboard was not all the effect of Captain Wentworth's deeds. His actions and those of his crew turned the tide of the battle and ended the enemy threat in that part of the seas. Captain Wentworth's bravery and valor grew among his peers. "He applied advanced tactics, displaying his mastery of them, and created new courses of action on the fly that won the battle. He showed courage beyond the call of duty. He did all this against a vastly superior enemy threat. He had won and survived through the battle maintaining command of his ship and winning the day," said Captain Warwick proudly.

The Prince, experiencing the great sacrifice made for his sake was determined to befriend Captain Wentworth, and knowing his father Admiral Wentworth well, he could see in him someone he could trust, a lifelong friend of his generation. "If he can survive his injuries, I would know him better," thought Prince James, concerned.

Many enemy ships were seized or sunk, and numerous prisoners were detained for transport to Portsmouth. The commander of the enemy fleet, having been captured, was turned over to Admiral Wentworth's custody as was customary in these cases. "He is to be treated with all the respect of a commanding officer," ordered Admiral Wentworth.

The enemy commander was brought to Admiral Wentworth, complimenting him on his command, tactics, and victory. He mentioned he would have been honoured to have served at his side if circumstances were different. His Highness Prince James, at Admiral Wentworth's side, was introduced. Prince James was impressed with the civility of the treatment of the enemy commander. The young Prince witnessed these protocols and learned the customs of treatment. "We never know when an enemy today will be an ally tomorrow," whispered Admiral Wentworth to his Prince.

The enemy commander asked, before being taken to his confinement, "Admiral Wentworth, who was the Captain who fought so valiantly to keep his ship, filled with special forces raiding teams, from the command vessel? What a struggle it was. At one point all was in the balance," said the enemy commander.

The Admiral mentioned, "It was my son's, first command, the ship HMS Valiant."

"Apt name; like father like son, I see," said the enemy commander. In respect, the enemy commander asked about the health of his son.

"Captain Wentworth is seriously injured. It is our hope he will survive and recover but as yet we are unsure," replied Admiral Wentworth.

"My hopes are with you Admiral and your son," replied the enemy commander in a sincere tone.

The commander bowed to Admiral Wentworth and Prince James as he was escorted away.

The command ship and several damaged vessels and wounded were relieved and recalled home to port after news of the victory reached the Admiralty and that all was secured on the high seas. Since the threat of battle in this part of the sea had all but been suppressed and enemy forces broken, this ended the immediate threat. Fleet forces were put on patrol status to ensure no enemy incursions went undetected and unchallenged, while most of the fleet needing time for repairs slowly withdrew from the station and made for port before taking up stations again.

"My dear Anne we, your son and I, survived the crucial battle, although I have to tell you our young Captain is gravely injured. He is aboard my ship and is being tended to by our most able fleet surgeon. Please do not come to Plymouth, since I do not know when we will reach port and the condition our son will be in at that time is not something a loving mother should bear. Although he is strong, I cannot tell you not to worry at this hour.

Please send your prayers since that is all we have to hold onto.

Will write again soon,

Your loving husband,

Frederick"

Reaching port, Frederick II was rushed to the naval hospital and given all the care possible. Admiral Wentworth was debriefed by the Admiralty on the battle and the success of the tactics employed. "All the hard work paid off Wentworth, well done," announced Admiral Extese. "Your strategies and tactics have been absorbed by all fleet commands and are being employed as of now," commented Admiral Chambers.

With the debrief over, all formality was dropped as each Admiral presented themselves and asked about the health of his young son. "This could not have been easy Wentworth, watching your son in a mortal battle before your very eyes and knowing you could do nothing to help," said one Admiral.

"I wished it would have been me and not my son," replied Admiral Wentworth. With that Admiral Wentworth begged his leave to check on his son at the naval hospital.

"Go Admiral, be with your son. All is secure here," ordered Admiral Turnbull. "We have a carriage standing by for your personal use." A young ensign in awe of the superior Admiral Wentworth then escorted him to the carriage.

Admiral Wentworth stopped by the base church to say a prayer for all those who perished. Friend and foe alike he prayed and sent a special prayer to his departed friend Admiral Croft, "past but not forgotten ole friend," thanking him for his advice and guidance these last years, knowing the day would come when it would bear fruit. He said a prayer for his son.

"Please God, have mercy on such a young and brave son," implored his father.

News of the victory broke out in the newspapers across the country as Anne read of her husband and son's exploit. "Hero!" it said. That afternoon a dispatch arrived for Anne from Frederick detailing the latest news and more importantly that he and their son were in port at Plymouth. Frederick II was in hospital as a result of sustained injuries and was not conscious as yet.

"My dear. Please do not endeavour to travel to Plymouth at this time since it is chaotic with post-battle undertakings and not a place for a lady. I am well aware, that what I ask is the hardest of requests since all a mother wants is to hold her child when they are hurt even in the smallest ways," pleaded Frederick.

"I will send dispatches of the latest news and will personally watch over our son."

Margret Anne and Fitzwilliam stayed in close contact with Kellynch Hall at this time since the Captain's fate was still not known.

A day later Frederick II awakened, though tired and drawn. To his father asleep at his bedside he whispered, "Father…father…"

"Son, I am right here. Shall I call the surgeon? Are you in pain?" asked Frederick.

"No surgeon please, just some water, perhaps some hearty soup and more rest," said Frederick II. After a gulp of water, "I hope I did not botch up the battle too badly father."

"No son, you did well, quite well indeed. We are all very proud of you," replied Frederick as he ordered hearty soup, bread, and tea be brought at once.

"I shall rest now father. I am still weary. My ship, my crew?" asked Frederick II.

"Your ship and men are in Port. Sleep now son, all is well," replied Frederick as his son's eyes closed and he drifted into a sound and restful sleep.

Frederick wrote a dispatch to Anne and the children,

"Anne, our son woke up for a few moments this morning asking for water, hearty soup, and no surgeon. This is a good sign indeed. All he could talk about were his worries of 'botching up' the battle. What courage and compassion a father feels in these moments. Knowing your son was in mortal danger and had come through it….Will write soon, Love and

Warmth to all of you,

Frederick"

The Admiralty had confidence in Wentworth's abilities but also his most special ability to elicit the loyalty and trust of fellow officers, "that is the powerful combination that wins battles," said one Admiral.

"Admiral Wentworth will be given a fortnight to take his son home and return to fleet operations at Plymouth station gentlemen," the Admiralty ordered.

"Now that an attempt to kill him has been repelled it is known he is the mastermind of this war's sea defences and must be protected. Post marine guards with his person, his son, and at his estate at Kellynch Hall immediately. A marine guard is to travel with him to and from Kellynch and Portsmouth," ordered Admiral Chambers.

His Highness the Prince relayed the story of Admiral and Captain Wentworth to his father the King and asked that Admiral Wentworth be given leave to escort his son home to Kellynch Hall when possible. The King himself asked the Admiralty for leave to allow Admiral Wentworth to escort his son home, and also to keep this request confidential. His Majesty's command was obeyed immediately.

Admiral Wentworth visited his son at the naval hospital. Still asleep, the surgeon informed the Admiral this was quite normal. "Your son has been awake and ate again early before dawn. He is young and strong, and I see every indication of recovery but this will take time. He will need much rest and recovery though and in the way of a quiet life for the foreseeable future." The Admiral still in dress uniform stayed at the hospital all night at his son's bedside.

"Kellynch will provide the quiet life. Gain your strength then we will travel there soon," thought Frederick watching his son breathe in between reading dispatches from the front, answering them, and handing them to a group of ensigns standing by, with armed marine guards, for his written replies.

Captains Benwick and Harville visited to check on the progress of their young Captain as other fleet Captains visited to pay their respects. Hospital staff concerned at the growing crowd of men flowing through the halls requested that quiet was of the utmost importance. "Stay as a group, not too large, and don't interfere with the care on the floor," barked nurses and doctors.

The admiral promised to send word to the captain's corp. on any changes. "But friends of the family may go through to his room. The admiral is there with his son," directed a nurse proud to be caring for two of His Majesty's heroes.

The next day at dawn, just then when the sun hit on the horizon, Captain Wentworth awoke, gazing at his father's tired eyes as he stirred in his chair. "Father, me and my crew did all we could. I relive the battle hoping I did not make a mistake," said Frederick II in a less frail tone.

"You and your crew fought to your namesake valiantly. Congratulations on your victory son," said the Admiral.

"They almost won. I was worried but fought on. I am famished!" said Frederick II.

"Nurse more sustenance, please," requested Frederick of the nurse.

"Would it cause a commotion if I could be made to sit up for a short while? Perhaps some pillows?" asked Frederick II of the nurse but Frederick hopped to it quickly, finding three pillows on an empty bed nearest him. A nurse propped Frederick II up carefully using the pillows and placed a tray of food on his lapboard.

"Did you know the crew on that ship was made up of a special forces raiding team of a kind more highly trained and equal to our best marines? They were specially trained for the grim task. Your crew of regular sailors fought so well that it was inspiring. I believe it was because they trusted you completely. Your tactics and firing canon on the vessel killed most of them below deck. Although still overwhelming, your crew maintained their poise," said Frederick.

"They fought brilliantly and with much courage," said Frederick II.

Frederick smiled. "Many of the Captains Corp. want to meet the 'Sea Lion' that turned the winds of war in our favour. You are up for commendations on actions in battle, and the H.M.S. Valiant is ordered to be repaired. How do you feel son?"

"A bit bruised father and very weak. And of course, I feel this hole running through the back of me to the front. With some rest and perhaps a cup of tea I will be right as rain and ready to take on the repairs to the Valiant," replied Frederick II.

"Not so fast son. You will recuperate at Kellynch Hall, and I will escort you tomorrow if you're strong enough. Your mother and sister are eager to nurse you to health. I can't tell you how relieved I am," said Frederick, before calling to the nurse.

"Yes, Admiral," replied the ward Nurse.

"Can we have a cup of tea for my son, please?" asked the Admiral.

"Of course and right away sir," replied the nurse.

Just then Benwick and Harville entered the room.

"Admiral, we thought to visit for a short time to look in on you and our young sea lion. I see there are guards posted inside and out of this hospital. Are you well sir?" asked Harville.

"Yes, these are just the normal precautions, considering our enemy wants us quite dead. Please do come in, our Captain is awake," motioned Frederick, tired himself but happy his son was awake and with all his senses.

"Captain Wentworth, how are you? You gave us a frightful scare here," said Captain Benwick, smiling but concerned as the nurse brought in a hot cup of tea with the surgeon at her side.

"Well Frederick, have this cup of tea then we will see if you can keep down some more hearty soup this time before you rest again. This will bring up your strength. Will you try?" asked the surgeon.

"Yes of course," replied Frederick to a great-sized bowl of meaty broth filled with beef chunks, potatoes, and carrots, with buttered bread placed on the tray.

"I am as grateful to be alive gentlemen. I assure you. Thank you for your assistance in the battle. It could not have been more welcome and timed," said Frederick, regaining his strength with each spoon of broth taken, as the nurse guided the next spoon into his mouth.

"Not at all Captain, if we could have been there sooner," mentioned Harville as Captain Warwick entered the room.

"What a fright! We thought our brave Captain was done. As you fought the enemy with a sword a coward presumed to run you through from behind. I am glad to see you improving, it is truly a blessing," said Captain Warwick.

"So many guards!" mentioned Captain Warwick looking at Admiral Wentworth as he entered the room.

"It seems there is a price on our heads now," replied Frederick as his son finished his tea and soup, looking much better but tiring.

"Better rest then," said Frederick II as the nurse adjusted him down.

The Admiral sent a dispatch to Anne of her son's recovery and plans for a pending arrival at Kellynch Hall.

"My darling wife, it will be tomorrow or the next day when we will leave for home. Our Captain is gaining his strength, and our travel will depend on his progress. I will stay a fortnight with you and then be posted to Plymouth for the remainder of the war."

There was a dispatch for Elizabeth from Captain Warwick. Anne explained to Margret Anne the latest news, since she enquired after reading of the battle in the paper, "How can I help Mother?" asked Margret Ann.

"Come home for a while dear," replied Anne.

Anne employed all her organising skills to the house staff in readying Frederick II's rooms, while Margret Anne set about contacting and briefing the surgeon of the pending arrival and recovery notes prepared by the navy surgeons. Margret Anne also instructed the cook on the special foods her brother would need.

Members of the admiralty and other captains visited Captain Wentworth at the hospital, wanting battle accounts and admiring him for his bravery and experience gained, "the Navy is truly a family, and now the family knows of your deeds, they will surround you while you recover son," said Admiral Wentworth to his son. A special ambulatory carriage was readied for the Wentworths as Captain Wentworth was organised for the trip home.

The next morning at Kellynch Hall all was quiet as Anne, Margret Anne and Fitzwilliam sat for breakfast together. It will have been almost two years since Kellynch Hall had seen all of them under the same roof, a bittersweet moment but also a blessed one. "To see dear Frederick and our Captain will be a happy event for me, both alive and safe," thought Anne in anticipation.

After breakfast, Margret Anne personally inspected Frederick's rooms in readiness for his arrival. She organised house staff on attendance, treatment, and food. "All is set," thought Margret Anne.

The surgeon arrived in plenty of time in the early afternoon and spoke with Anne and Margret Anne about what they knew about the latest condition of her son. Within the hour, there was a commotion just outside as a special carriage arrived with a marine guard escort taking up positions throughout the estate grounds.

A servant announced the arrival of Frederick and his son, and Anne was already out the door, closely followed by Margret Anne, Fitzwilliam, and the surgeon. Anne greeted her husband warmly then quickly turned to her son guiding the surgeons to Frederick II's room and taking charge to settle her son as he was carried closely behind. To Anne's surprise, tea hearty meaty soup, and strong bread were waiting in the room, with one servant and Nurse Rooke standing by and ready to assist in any way.

With the house in an uproar, Frederick II was readied to be removed from the stretcher and carefully placed in his bed. Anne, Margret Anne, and Fitzwilliam, a little shocked, greeted Father and Frederick II. One could see in his weakened state Frederick II needed some refreshment and then rest and quiet to recover from the trip. Briefed on the details of treatment, the local surgeon offered assistance to the navy surgeon. Nurse Rooke also offered help in any way.

Anne could see Frederick was exhausted as well, from his war work, tending his son, and the trip home. With Frederick II settled and receiving all the attention needed, she turned to Frederick.

Worried, she focused on her dear husband, determined to make the next few precious days of peace for her warrior husband. She would work to give him his breath back - that was most important - keeping family visits to a minimum and short in duration for the next fortnight.

Frederick needed much in the way of rest himself and fattening. "Come dear heart; let me take you to your bed. It is time for rest and fattening for you this fortnight. We can do all the talking and catching up tomorrow," directed Anne gently. Frederick slept soundly for the better part of two days.

On the third day, Frederick II was able to take short visits from family and sit up in bed for a few hours, as the surgeon, Nurse Rooke, and Margret Anne watched over him throughout the first few days and nights. The Naval surgeon stayed as a guest, taking his turn to monitor Frederick until he was stronger, before taking his leave to return to Portsmouth. At night Fitzwilliam would stay in the same room as his brother. Marine guards could be seen from the window below, watching for any threat, while others patrolled the grounds.

"There are signs of regaining strength and vigour," said Fitzwilliam at one breakfast with mother and father in attendance.

"He will recover but it will take time. The wounds are deep and he was close to the brink of perishing," said the surgeon, bringing home the gravity of recent events at sea.

Anne and Frederick, aware time was short, and with Frederick II settled, proceeded to spend the next couple of days together as much as possible, before he returned to the Admiralty and Plymouth to assume fleet command. Anne was relieved her Admiral would not be ship-bound and in battle directly, but at Plymouth giving orders and setting plans. "He will be as safe as one can be in war. And once our son is out of danger, I may travel to Plymouth and support my husband with short trips, perhaps," she thought.

Frederick related all that happened, that he dared not write about in dispatches that brought them to this moment. He talked of his son's bravery in battle, and the cost paid. Anne, overwhelmed with pride and grateful for her son's life, teared up and upon hearing the accounts of their brother's exploits at sea, Margret Anne and Fitzwilliam devoted themselves to Frederick's recovery.

Elizabeth, the Musgroves, and William Elliot even arrived to offer assistance and pay their respects as is only right of family and a national hero. Anne gave Elizabeth her Captain's dispatches. Later that evening Frederick talked to Elizabeth confidentially of Captain Warwick's mission and status. She did not talk about it to anyone else but was grateful to Frederick in a way that changed her tenor to him, she almost loved him like a brother in her treatment thereafter.

So quickly it was time for Frederick to return to Plymouth and take up his duties. "Son, I am off to Plymouth once more and grateful that all is well here at Kellynch. I may now focus on the war to its end. Take your time, recover, and regain your strength. Send me a note on your progress I will be interested in hearing from you, as a father more than a commander," said Frederick.

"Good luck and God's speed to you Father," replied Frederick II. On his way out to the carriage, "My dear if but I could stay. While I am here men are in harm's way and I can do something to increase their chances of coming home too. So I must leave you again," said Frederick as he hugged and kissed Anne, Margret Anne and shook hands with Fitzwilliam.

"Fitz, take care of our family," said Frederick gravely.

"I have and I shall father," said Fitzwilliam.

"There will be several marine guards stationed here while Frederick II is recovering and the war continues," said Frederick waving as the carriage bolted up the lane and out of sight of his family again.

Anne focused on her oldest son, but in the back of her mind, she wanted her husband home too. Frederick II reminded his mother how his father would save many lives because of his command abilities, "He will be home soon, have no fear of that," said Frederick II as he held his mother's hand. Anne lived for these comments more than she would tell. They gave her hope.

"I have some final work to complete at finishing school. It will take me a fortnight and no longer. I plan to leave tomorrow," said Margret Anne to her mother

"I was going to ask you if you would return to school to complete your work but was glad for any extra moments I had with you," replied Anne.

"The headmistress and teachers have specially accommodated me because of my father's and brother's status in the realm. This is a very short stay, and I will be back as soon as I can, and for good I am afraid," commented Margret Anne.

"I will be glad of it Margret Anne. I love you dearly you must know this," said Anne.

CHAPTER 8

Margret Anne

Captain Wentworth was recovering nicely at home. He received weekly dispatches on the progress of the war. It all seemed to be going well as he sent his hearty congratulations to Captain Benwick on his promotion to Admiral. "The war will end before I am well again," wrote Frederick II to his father. With that realisation Frederick II focused on his recovery.

One morning a single horseman and five marines arrived at Kellynch Hall. This was not normal so Anne thought perhaps her Admiral had sent a special dispatch. Walking to the front door Anne stepped out to His Royal Highness Prince James. Immediately curtsying, "Pray your Royal Highness, please excuse me...I did not expect...please do come in," said Anne leading the way as a servant fumbled and stumbled at the sight of their future King.

As Anne and Prince James entered the drawing room, Fitzwilliam recognised the Prince immediately and without delay stood and bowed and stepped to the side to give way to his Royal Highness.

"It is a great honour for me to be invited into this home and to meet you, Lady Anne. Please would all of you be at ease? I have a great fondness for your husband, the Admiral, and your son who saved my life at sea so recently. What more can be done to assist in his recovery pray tell me ma'am?" asked the Prince.

"All that can be done is being done sir," replied Anne nervously not used to the circumstances.

"Please do not be alarmed at my personage, it is I who am in awe of you dear lady, and your husband and son. I'm here to pay a call on your Captain Wentworth. It is a great pleasure and honour for me. Is he well enough for a visit Lady Anne?" asked the Prince.

"I believe so your Highness, I will go to him now and prepare him for your visit. If you would excuse me for a few moments," replied Anne as she left the room to prepare Frederick II.

"Is it Fitzwilliam?" asked Prince James.

"Yes it is Your Majesty," replied Fitzwilliam standing.

"Please sir, sit and be comfortable," commanded the Prince as a marine officer entered the room to hand the Prince a dispatch. Reading it the Prince found a nearby desk and pen and ink and responded sealing the note and handing it back to the marine for delivery to the palace and his father, the King.

Anne returned to escort Prince James to Frederick II. The Prince again mentioned it was an honour to visit this place of courage and loyalty to his father and the realm. "Please dear lady be at ease in my presence. Let me not make you uncomfortable in the least," said the Prince, now entering Frederick II's apartments.

"Frederick ole fellow, how are you getting along?" asked the Prince.

"I am stronger each day and hope to be out of bed and resting in the garden thereafter," responded Frederick II smiling.

"Stopped by on my way to my father for a visit and thought this not to out of the way in my journey," said the Prince.

"I am honoured for this visit sir," replied Frederick II, a little overwhelmed now.

"Be at ease, you saved my life, overcame great odds in the most crucial battle, and almost made the ultimate sacrifice on behalf of the King and country. It is I who am honoured. There are few I can trust, but I believe we will be great friends, trusted friends," said the Prince.

"Thank you for the compliment your Majesty," replied Frederick II.

"In private call me James," mentioned the Prince.

"A great honour indeed," thought Anne.

"May I come and visit you regularly as you recover?" asked the Prince.

"Yes, it would be an honour, James," replied Frederick not used to using his Majesty's first name.

"Good this is settled. The ride here is not so out of the way of my travel between town and Plymouth. Ma'am would you be so kind as to offer me a small room where I may lay my head should I stay the night during my visits?" asked Prince James of Anne.

"Of course, this can be arranged with little effort sir," replied Anne.

"I will leave you for now and see you in a few days," said James as he stood to leave.

As Anne returned with Prince James, he related, "I should like to visit regularly, however, due to threats on my life, would the family keep my presence here confidential?"

All agreed as tea was served. The Prince asked Anne if he might return to Frederick II privately."

"Of course sir," replied Anne.

For the next hour, the family waited in the drawing room downstairs while the Prince was with Frederick II. It was not until this moment that Anne and Fitzwilliam realised just how much of an impact Frederick II had on winning the battle that day and how brave he acted. "He has the heir apparent visiting him, Mother," said Fitzwilliam in a hushed tone.

"We must protect this secret so the Royal visitor may come and go as he likes. It is our duty," said mentioned Fitzwilliam.

"It was not just a battle but many lives, including His Royal Highness Prince James and Fredrick who depended on his action and that of his crew. Now, we have His Highness asking leave to visit with him, indeed this is extraordinary," related Anne.

An hour passed and Prince James entered the drawing room to take his leave of the family, thanking Anne for the lovely cup of tea and time with Frederick II. "I would like to return lady. Do I have your leave to visit?" asked Prince James.

"Of course, Your Highness. I have already arranged an apartment for your particular use should you require it," replied Anne as Prince James thanked them and left, escorted by the guard he arrived with.

Anne assembled all the servants asking them not to mention even to their families of the Prince's comings and goings. The butler was directed to instruct all the grounds folks of their discretion as well.

Margret Ann finished with the final school business and returned for good to Kellynch Hall this morning. Anne and her family greeted her as if any other day. "What is it mother?" said Margret Anne. "You are such a beauty now and very accomplished. I am so proud of you daughter," said Anne.

"Why thank you, mother," replied Margret Anne.

Margret Anne had Anne's grace and humility and her father's mental capacities and intelligence, making her formidable in every way.

"Where is my brother and hero then?" asked Margret Anne.

"On the patio this morning, enjoying the sun," replied Fitzwilliam. Margret Anne headed straight for Frederick II before anyone could alert her of his special guest.

Margret Anne burst onto the garden patio. As she approached her brother his guest asked him "Who is this person approaching?"

"My sister Miss Margret Anne, sir," responded Frederick II as Prince James discreetly waved off a marine guard about to intercept her.

"Would you introduce me only as James?" asked Prince James.

Frederick II nodded in agreeance as he sat up to greet his sister warmly.

"Sister, I would like to introduce you to James. James, this is Margret Anne," said Frederick II.

"A pleasure to meet you, sir," replied Margret Anne.

"James was an officer on the command ship during the renowned battle that led to all of this," said Frederick II.

"So James is it true this talk of hero and my brother Frederick II?" asked Margret Anne of Frederick II's guest. "Yes, very true indeed. He is the truest of heroes and defender of His Majesty, the King, and the realm," replied James sincerely.

Margret Anne asked every question needed to satisfy her lack of knowledge of the events. Every so often, James would comment as Margret assessed him, as she did with all men. She could find no fault in him though. His mind was quick and his thoughts brilliant, his speech intelligent, and his manner impeccable. "He must be a fellow Captain," she thought satisfied.

"I will see to lunch brother," said Margret Anne as she took her leave of Frederick II and his guest to organise the kitchen staff.

Anne, walking toward the drawing room to find a servant to have lunch brought out to the patio for her Captain, herself, daughter, and his guest ran into Margret Anne, having the same idea and coming unto the patio, "Mother, why do we have so many marines stationed about the house and grounds? It is quite unusual. Is our Captain in danger even at Kellynch Hall?" asked Margret Anne as they walked out together with servants carrying lunch and tea on trays behind them.

"There are always guards here, but it is true today more than normal. They are for His Royal Highness Prince James of course," replied Anne.

"What Prince?" asked Margret Anne stopping to face Mother to be sure of what she just heard as the servants carrying lunch passed them and began laying lunch at the patio table.

Looking toward Frederick II and James, she exclaimed "James! Mother why was I not told of this? I treated His Royal Highness as a commoner.

"It is true, James is His Royal Highness Prince James, the heir apparent," replied Anne discreetly and with raised eyebrows.

Margret Anne's knees weakened momentarily at the news as she tried to employ all the skills she had just learned these last years at finishing school. "I was conversing with my next sovereign and so unaware of his personage, how embarrassing," thought Margret Anne, helping to lay trays of food and tea on the table in proper order with her mother.

"Do not be concerned dear. All is easy here. I am sure he would have said who he was if he wanted a formal tone," mentioned Anne.

"I feel embarrassed," replied Margret Anne.

William Elliot walked out from the drawing room to attend lunch with Frederick and Prince James, smiling at Fitzwilliam's jokes about how the Prince dispenses with formality when he is here at Kellynch Hall, but that one should not forget their station to that of his even in these circumstances. "His Highness has extended this family a great trust, we must keep Margret Anne," said William.

Margret Anne served lunch and tea to her brother and Prince James as if nothing in her knowledge had changed about who he was, and she used all of her poise and will to remain calm, but the Prince and Frederick II noticed her change in character.

Serving lunch to all and sitting quietly Frederick, sensed Margret Anne's unease and asked, "You must know James' true identity?" as Prince James looked on.

"Yes brother," said Margret Anne.

"Do be at ease, Miss Margret Ann. I am surrounded by so many who fear, are in awe, or want to use my title to some advantage of their own. It is wonderful to be among those who respect the weight of my office yet can be open and friendly with me. It is a great gift, truly. Can we be friends then?" asked Prince James extending his hand in friendship.

"Of course Your Royal Highness," replied Margret Anne blushing as she bowed and took James' hand.

"Please call me James," commented Prince James. Margret Anne, smiling, agreed and all reverted to how it was when she first arrived, conversation was keen and lively and in a friendly air, save Margret Anne was aware now of whom she was associating with.

In the next weeks, Frederick's recovery progressed well. The regular war dispatches indicated the war was beginning to wind down. A number of Captains and members of the Admiralty visited Kellynch Hall, all too often finding marines stationed about and Captain Wentworth with His Royal Highness Prince James discussing some topic or other or about the grounds. Frederick II, on surgeon's orders, must begin to walk about in his treatment to gain strength again. "Walking is still an effort but I am showing some nimbleness and this is a triumph these days," laughed Frederick II with Nurse Rooke at one side and Prince James at the other, guiding the exercise should assistance be needed. "I still tire easily but I am determined."

The Navy visitors were very cordially welcomed, and many friendships were developed over this time.

The Admiralty related to Captain Wentworth and family that it seemed the initial battle set the tone for the whole war. The enemy sent their best and was not able to overcome regular Royal Naval forces. For the rest of the war did all they could to avoid battles where they could, while in other cases surrendering after short and quick engagements.

Captain Wentworth's actions won the crucial battle that settled a fear of engagement over the sea, saving many lives on both sides in the long run. Frederick II, not strong enough yet to travel to Portsmouth, would wait for his commendations depending upon his health improvements, as the surgeon sent regular reports on his progress to the admiralty.

Frederick II realised he had a special friendship with the future King of England and took this trust seriously. He was respectful of His Highness and kept his confidences safe and without question. Prince James knew his experiences with the Admiral and Captain Wentworth were indeed a fortunate set of events. He gained great friendships, loyalty, and trust here.

Prince James noticed Margret Anne over time thinking, "She is intelligent, beautiful, and kind, a completely unaffected girl."

Frederick II noticed his discreet glances, wondering where it would lead, but did not comment. Margret Anne found ways to be around Frederick II more often than normal when James was visiting. James asked Margret Anne not to call him His Highness or Sir but rather James, a singular distinction. Margret Anne relented and began to call him simply James in private company.

One day the Prince talked to Frederick II about his sister's character and manner. Frederick II realised the Prince would like to invite the family to a royal function as a pretense to introduce Margret Anne to the royal court and his Father, the King, and Mother, the Queen, hoping Margret Anne would make a good impression with them. "Well sir, that is a high distinction indeed. However, father is with the Admiralty in Plymouth, and it would not be proper for Anne to go unescorted in this case," replied Frederick II.

"I have asked friends in the Admiralty to grant Admiral Wentworth leave to attend my family in town for this function, which by the way, many of the members of the Admiralty will attend by order of the King," said Prince James.

"Well, then sir, it is settled, but one more hurdle, that is mother. It would be proper to speak to her of this intention. It is only honourable," suggested Frederick II.

"Yes, this is only proper. Is your strength enough to travel to town and have one evening as the Royal Family's particular guest Captain?" asked Prince James.

"I believe so Your Highness. I have been walking much these last few days, and it has done me good. I cannot dance and must sit often, but I believe this will be a pleasure to move about different surroundings, thank you for asking," responded Frederick II.

"Shall we inform Mrs. Anne of the decision?" asked Prince James.

"Yes, let's do it.

That evening Frederick II talked with Margret Anne, telling her of James' plan. "I believe him to be an honorable man and open in his intentions," said Frederick II.

"Yes, Frederick I have noticed. Perhaps this is a girl's intuition," replied Margret Anne in a superior but gentle tone.

"Is this agreeable with you sister?" asked Frederick II.

"Yes I should think so," responded Margret Anne in a more agreeable manner. Frederick thought perhaps Margret Anne had not thought out what this would lead to and the being away from Kellynch Hall, a place she so loved.

"It is not my place but to support my sister's endeavours, and I do," thought Frederick II, looking deeply into his sister's eyes.

Royal inquiries were made about the family and Margret Anne. One couldn't help but notice the investigation with questions in the village and the parish. Investigations at the admiralty of the admiral and Captain Wentworth's career, schooling, friends, and associations were also not so subtly asked about. Sir Walter's family line was not above some looking into, and even the charity work was scrutinised closely.

One bright afternoon, a carriage arrived at the main court of Kellynch Hall, and who stepped out of it but no other than Admiral Wentworth. "What a surprise dear," said Anne breathlessly, as instantly Fitzwilliam stood at his father's side.

Frederick explained he was to be home for a fortnight. With the war coming to a close it is a matter of time before he will be home for good. "My orders are to attend, with the family, a royal function in town at the royal residence," commented Frederick.

"Ah yes, it seems His Royal Highness Prince James is paying particular attention to Margret Anne," responded Anne as Fitzwilliam smiled.

"Yes, I see. I was wondering about the attention given to investigating Frederick II's naval records of late. All I was told was that it was a royal inquiry. It all makes sense now my darling. Pray, tell me of our Captain's progress and health," said Frederick.

Frederick noticing marines stationed about asked, "Is the Prince here today?

"Yes, my dear. He is with my Captain and Margret Anne on the garden patio," replied Anne.

"I have to pay my respects, my dear, would you walk with me?" asked Frederick.

"Of course, my dear," answered Anne.

"Your Royal Highness," said Frederick as he, Anne, and Fitzwilliam bowed.

"Be at ease Admiral. Would you sit with us and join our conversation?" asked Prince James.

"It would be a pleasure," replied Frederick sitting.

"Margret Anne and I shall see to lunch and tea. If you will excuse us," said Anne as the men stood for the women.

In the house, Anne asked Margret Anne, "Dear do you fully understand the nature of this invitation to the royal palace and the meeting of His Majesty the King?"

"Can anyone know the mother? I understand it but it almost seems I am just a player in this set of events," replied Margret Anne.

"Do you love him?" asked Anne discreetly.

"Yes, I do but I am torn with what this would mean to my life here and with our family. Everything will change," commented Margret Anne.

"Then you do know the gravity. Your father and I are here for you. Be damned with society's rules in this case. I only care about your happiness. If you say you will be happy then I can be satisfied," said Anne.

"That is what I am wondering as well Mother. Time will tell, it is too soon to know," replied Margret Anne as she and her mother directed the servants in organising the lunch trays and tea.

"How are you father? What news of the war?" asked Frederick II.

"Very well son. Hostilities are coming to a close and not too soon. Naval forces are already being recalled from many positions thought unthinkable only six months ago. I will be glad for a peace and the living of life again," answered Frederick.

"Gentlemen, this is not widely known in government and even in the admiralty, and I trust the both of you implicitly and Fitzwilliam as you are a Wentworth, and that namesake is greatly respected by His Majesty, I will give you a bit of news ahead of most. An informal framework for peace has been signed, and it is left to some details now on the disengagement of forces. It is expected that this time next month all operations and the separation of forces will have been completed. Both sides will have turned over all prisoners of war and a formal end to the war will have been made public some weeks after," said Prince James as they stood for the approaching women and servants returning with tea and lunch and changing the subject to that of Captain Wentworth's career.

"Admiral, shall we turn our attention to that of your son's career? Since many in the Admiralty are of the age to retire and as the war draws to an end they must be replaced with competent, experienced, and dedicated officers. Would you not stay on at the admiralty to guide Frederick as Admiral Croft in his time guided you?" commented Prince James to the astonishment of Frederick in knowing this little-known fact.

"Frederick and I have been corresponding on just such topics for some time now. We have resolved that when he is fully recovered I will have entered him for assignment to three crucial admiralty committees for planning and readiness similar to that of Admiral Croft's guidance of my career," replied Frederick.

"Excellent sir, I should like to know of one or two officers in the service of His Majesty's Navy should my assent to King come sooner rather than later. I realize this is a heady conversation but one in my position one must look to the Kingdom and its service constantly," commented Prince James to silence and respect.

The conversation moved to a lighter topic and the evening at the palace and town. "It will be a pleasure to greet all of you at my home. I look forward to this event," said James.

"It is our pleasure and honour to be asked, sir," replied Frederick.

"I see you will need time to visit with your family Admiral, and so I shall leave you to this. It has been a pleasure being so welcomed here," said James standing as all stood for him.

"Thank you for the excellent lunch. I do enjoy this time here at Kellynch. I see why you love this place so," commented Prince James to Margret Anne. "Right then, I shall expect you all at the palace this Saturday?" remarked His Highness.

"Of course, sir," replied Frederick as Prince James was escorted to his carriage. As he entered his carriage, he paused for a moment to look at Margret Anne but said nothing and the carriage sped off down the lane surrounded by marines on horseback. At that same moment, a dispatch rider arrived with a letter for Admiral Wentworth. "By Royal Invitation…." it said.

Frederick II commented on the invite telling the mother and father of the Prince's intent. "In these cases the Prince's wishes take precedence," said Frederick.

Margret Anne, still unaware perhaps emotionally of the gravity of this royal invitation was cautioned by her father, explaining where this could lead and that her wishes if not aligned with that of the Royal Family may be considered willful in these cases and could cause her reputation damaged in the general society.

"I believe James to be a very honourable man, and he would protect you in every way from any injury in society if a possible union between the two of you would not be acceptable to you," commented Frederick. "I understand father. It is quite a lot to take in, and he has made me no offer. Perhaps, I shall just enjoy the moments and assume it is the two heroes in the family the royals which to honour," smiled Margret Anne, lightening up the moment.

Margret Anne was made to realise her next actions could help or hurt this family materially. Father gave her the protocols of action when with the Royals. Margret Anne took this all in and endeavoured to act with the utmost decorum following society's expectations for a lady in these circumstances.

The family decided to plan their trip to arrive in town Friday afternoon. The travel to London was uneventful save the marines ever watchful of the safety of those in the carriage. On the day of the royal function, the Wentworths took in a sight or two while in town then returned to the let townhouse close to the royal palace. They rested and refreshed themselves in preparation for the evening. Late in the day, a royal carriage arrived, waiting upon them, to take them to the Royal residence for the evening's events.

"Dear, I suppose we are finally ready. Shall we brave this parade of events?" asked Frederick.

"Yes, we must. It is a duty," replied Anne smiling and looking radiant for her husband's sake. Anne knocked on each of her children's doors, "We are ready."

Frederick II was assisted down the stairs by two servants, so he didn't attempt the effort without help. "One day I will be fully recovered and not soon enough!" commented Frederick II in full dress uniform looking like his father's younger self.

"Brother, you are making a good recovery. Let us not push too hard so we do not re-injure ourselves," said a worried sister standing by him.

Arriving at the Royal Palace, they were escorted to the great hall into the royal court and announced to many onlookers aware of them and their deeds. "Look dear we are being looked at by many a lord and lady," said Anne discreetly smiling.

"Yes, it seems so my dear," replied Frederick.

Members of the royal family greeted those arriving, in a line, introducing themselves and making small talk until it was the Wentworth's turn, whereupon a different tack was taken, and they were treated with extra attention and greater civility. "Thank you for coming Admiral and Mrs. Wentworth, it is a pleasure having you here," said Her Royal Highness the Duchess of Cornwall and Lord Keys.

"Captain Wentworth we understand you are not fully recovered from your war wounds and at my father's request we have a special chair set aside for you so you might not over-strain yourself this evening."

"Might I escort our war hero?" asked Lord Gresham, carefully taking Frederick II's arm as servants quickly flanked him to assist the Captain's comfort, walking through a crowd that separated at her approach and bowing slightly in honour and recognition.

"Miss Wentworth it is a pleasure to finally meet you," said Princess Stephanie presenting herself and smiling to a surprised Margret Anne. "My mother, father, and brother have not yet presented themselves at court as is customary, they enter after all have arrived," said Princess Stephanie, curtsying.

"It is a pleasure to meet you, your Highness," replied Margret Anne meekly. Not used to such affairs, Anne and Margret Anne stayed together as Frederick guided the girls through this formality. He had been to many a royal affair as part of the duties and rank of service.

Princess Stephanie was adept at these events and did all she could to put Margret Anne at ease. She especially singled out Margret Anne to be her escort, at least until her brother James was presented at the court. "Princess Stephanie, I would like to present my brother Fitzwilliam," said Margret Anne, whose beauty stunned most men.

"Your Highness," said Fitzwilliam, bowing.

"I have another brother, may I present our Captain Wentworth? We know him as Frederick II. He is just there sitting as he is still recovering from war injuries," said Margret Anne walking toward Frederick II with Princess Stephanie as onlookers bowed to Her Royal Highness whose focus was Frederick II.

Upon arriving, Frederick II was slow to stand and Princess Stephanie, realising the pain he was in said before being presented by Margret Anne "Dear Captain Wentworth, please be at ease with me. Perhaps it is I who should stand in the presence of such courage and bravery and to the man who saved my brother, the future King of England, from a fate unspeakable."

"Madam, I thank you for your compliments, but I assure you I am merely a man who was very lucky on that fateful day," replied Frederick II attentively.

"May we sit with you?" asked Princess Stephanie.

"Of course, Your Highness," responded Frederick II as he stood until both ladies were seated.

"Would you do me the honour of calling me Stephanie even in this formal of settings?" asked Princess Stephanie to a surprised Frederick II and Margret Ann.

"Yes, of course, if you wish it so, Stephanie," responded Frederick II with Margret Anne at his other side.

"I wish it so sir," responded Princess Stephanie.

"Would you tell me your account of this battle that has taken on such a legend Captain Wentworth?" asked Princess Stephanie, giving him her full attention.

"You may call me Frederick II" he requested as Princess Stephanie smiled at his gesture. Margret Anne, listening had never before heard her brother talk of the events directly that caused such great injuries to himself and the attention of a grateful King. She listened deeply to his words of the events of that day. "Well, it began with intelligence warning fleet command of a build-up of enemy forces just over the horizon…" described Frederick II humbly, yet in a manner befitting a Captain in the Royal Navy.

Periodically talking through the story an admiral or captain would politely interrupt to enquire on Captain Wentworth's health and then quickly leave. "Captain if there is anything I can do to assist you, you only need to ask," they would say.

It seemed not even Margret Anne realised the breadth of love and respect Frederick II had gained in the war and the truly daring and valiant actions he took on that fateful day. With tears in her eyes, "How close we were to losing you, dear brother," said Margret Ann, wearing her tears well; only Stephanie noticed, discreetly handing her a handkerchief.

Princess Stephanie began to form an attachment to Frederick II more so than the typical men she encountered each day in her duties, and those trying to attract her attention even at the ball. She could see Frederick II was someone to take special care of. She could see into him and instinctively knew his nature.

"Pray be upstanding," was announced throughout the hall.

Princess Stephanie's father, mother, and brother arrived to open the evening's events. Princess Stephanie on one side and Margret Anne on the other side Frederick II lent an arm to help him to his feet to allow him to bow, as is customary when the Royal family entered the room.

"Frederick II will you excuse me a moment as I greet my family?" asked Princess Stephanie.

"Of course Your Highness," replied Frederick II.

"Call me Stephanie," replied Princess Stephanie with a smile as she took her leave.

"Brother, Princess Stephanie pays you a great compliment in sitting with you and asking you to call her by Christian name. Are you sure you have not met her before?" asked Margret Anne.

"No sister, I have not been formally introduced. I did see her once at Portsmouth when I was standing with a number of captains and Prince James arrived to take his station aboard the command vessel under Father's command. However, I know nothing of her directly I assure you," replied Frederick.

"I am surprised as you are sister. She can be with any man in the room but sits with me to talk over the crimes of war and battles past now," responded Frederick II.

"Brother, this is the first time I have heard you talk of this battle so widely known and described by others. I didn't realise your pure bravery and dedication and fortune in surviving such an assault. I am deeply impressed and grateful you were returned to us," said Margret Anne with tears and hugging Frederick II, not realising His Majesties and Prince James and Princess Stephanie, were approaching with Frederick, Anne, and Fitzwilliam.

"I am still your brother sister, that will never change. I am still here and in full command of all my faculties," commented Frederick II as Princess Stephanie arriving, first standing at Frederick II's side, presented Frederick II and Margret Anne for the first time to her mother and father.

"Mother, father may I present to you Captain Frederick Wentworth and Miss Margret Anne Wentworth," announced Princess Stephanie as all bowed in the presence of their King.

"Miss Margret Anne, I see you have tears in your eyes. What has distressed you so? How can I help you?" asked the King.

"Sir please forgive me. It is nothing but the caring of a sister for her brother. For the first time, this evening, I was witness to the story of my brother's exploits in battle from him personally and was overwhelmed with gratitude for what he did and that we are fortunate to have him still with us," responded Margret Anne, composing herself now and holding Frederick II's arm tightly.

"Yes, I see Miss Wentworth. We, are very fortunate indeed to have the Admiral and Captain Wentworth here," said the King sincerely.

"Frederick II, please sit as I understand your wounds are not completely healed as yet and standing is quite painful. Please be at ease here in our presence. The Queen and I would like to thank you for coming and for your dedication to the crown. It has not gone unnoticed," said the King.

Her Majesty the Queen asked, "Sir, do you have everything you need for this evening?"

"Why yes Your Majesty," replied Frederick II.

"Mother, I will sit with Frederick II this evening and assure you this is so," commented Princess Stephanie.

"Thank you, daughter, I will be relieved then that all is well here. Sir, may I have the pleasure later to visit again since at the moment there are dignitaries, diplomats, and guests to meet as you can imagine," mentioned the Queen.

"Of course your Majesty and at your leisure," replied Frederick II as many watched the honour accorded the Wentworths.

As Frederick, Anne, Margret Anne, and Fitzwilliam stood amazed at the affection shown by this highest of families to Frederick II. "Then I shall not be concerned. Frederick II, thank you for saving my son and standing in the breach changing the fortunes of the sea war," said His Majesty, showing a genuine father's love for a son.

"Margret Anne, may we have the pleasure of your company this evening?" asked Her Majesty.

"Of course," replied Margret Anne bowing then taking the side of the Queen.

Margret Anne noticed she was being shunned by many women in attendance, so much so that she felt slightly uncomfortable for the first time in her life. Her Highness, noticing this, explained discreetly the circumstances to Margret Anne of the disappointment many of these women would have over their plans to court and perhaps marry into the royal family, and they considered her to be an obstacle to their designs and a nobody at that. But you are a somebody, a very important someboby. Margret Anne realised she was not at Kellynch Hall in the countryside anymore and trembled at the thought.

"Margret Anne, tell me about yourself," asked the Queen as she performed her duties through the evening.

With the events now coming to a close, Princess Stephanie, having spent the evening with Frederick, recounted the love and respect many naval officers paid to Frederick II. His tireless response and engagement with each officer, in turn, thanking them for their compliments. "He is very well-mannered and sharp of mind. He has caught my interest this day," thought Princess Stephanie still at his side assuring he was wanting for nothing.

"Princess, many a gentleman's heart is broken that you stayed at my side this evening," said Frederick II.

"Perhaps sir, besides your brother and mine, your father and mine and the officers, there were few if any true gentlemen in attendance," replied Princess Stephanie, smiling in a now familiar way. Her meaning was well understood.

Anne and Frederick arrived to determine how to get Frederick II to the carriage and the townhome. "I will not be carried out of here since I am not invalid as yet. I have sat all evening and have enough of it," said Frederick II, standing slowly but steadily.

"Sir, would you take my arm and allow me to be your escort?" asked Princess Stephanie sincerely as Anne and Frederick looked on surprised.

"She treats him with such tenderness and only met him this evening," noted Anne.

Seeing Captain Wentworth, a number of Captains stood close by to be of help if needed. Even an Admiral feigned talking to Frederick just to be near to assist if needed. "Shall we try?" asked Frederick II, walking at some effort slowly but well enough as the group followed just behind.

Once in the carriage and carefully placed, Princess Stephanie stood waving with her brother at her side until the carriage was out of sight. "Sister, do I see an attachment forming here?" asked James.

"Perhaps, maybe; why not? He is such a man as I have ever met. He is true and steady; calm and sure; unaffected by the politics of the world., from a good family. Any girl would be attracted to this," replied Stephanie.

"Then I take it I will have to find a reason for you to arrive at Kellynch Hall soon?" asked James.

"Yes, please brother," replied Stephanie.

"Perhaps if you make particular friends with Margret Anne?" suggested James.

"That would be easy since I feel she is a dear sister already," replied Stephanie.

"Father and mother could not help but notice the broken hearts all evening and the special attention you paid the Captain. They will ask you. It is a matter of time," mentioned James smiling.

"I am not worried brother. He is very eligible if it comes to that," replied Stephanie.

Arriving at the letting house, the Wentworth family were served tea. Before retiring, they reviewed the evening, being presented at court, all was easy and respectful. The King recognised the Admiral and Captain Wentworth as heroes, while Anne and Margret Anne received the special attention of the Queen. Frederick II received the special attention of Her Royal Highness Princess Stephanie, and Margret Anne and Princess Stephanie became particular friends.

"Her Majesty chatted with me and Margret Anne about a number of common topics when suddenly she mentioned her son's interest in her and her thoughts on the matter. She also asked if Margret Anne had noticed ladies at the gathering avoiding and shunning her. Margret Anne said yes, I suppose I have inadvertently broken some rules of society. My dears she said, you are quite well connected and good enough. Your men serve the crown and are heroes deserving of much. They shun you because His Royal Highness Prince James has favoured you with a personal invitation. Do you know how they boil with jealousies that they were not so honoured?" said Anne to the family, relating her experiences.

"I could see Margret Anne realised now the gravity of the moment, with Her Majesty saying have no fear, my dear, you are under our protection as sure as your men protected James in the heat of the fiercest battle of this last year's war, "Tell me of yourselves" after a while Prince James asked Margret Ann if she might dance with him with the floor clearing and only the two out there, "he could feel my nerves rise but simply said, have no worries, I will not let you down" related Margret Anne.

"Of course, it was only right to accept the dance. I trembled inside at the sights and the general splendour of the surroundings and personages at the ball but danced well enough. James sensed this, mentioning I was the equal of all there, calming me, commented Margret Anne, smiling.

On their return to Kellynch Hall, the Royal family made it known the Wentworths were charming, and they were glad to know them. Late in the evening at the palace and just before retiring, Prince James related the events of the war to his father the King, and other close relatives in the room. His sister Stephanie added her opinion of the Captain. Surprised at the valor and bravery described, the royal party retired with a favourable impression of the Admiral and Captain Wentworth and the sacrifices made on behalf of the Crown.

CHAPTER 9

Knighthood

After a few days, Prince James asked the King if he would consider knighting both Admiral and Captain Wentworth for their actions in the war. "Father, they in their way secured victory at sea, risking life for His Highness and the excellence of service to the Crown. James related particular events leading up to war with the designing of superior tactics and strategies by Admiral Wentworth, of the briefing of captains and the Admiralty before the breakout of hostilities at Kellynch Hall, at his own expense and of that day and events of the sea battle where Captain Wentworth turned the battle and was credited for demoralising the enemy, impacting the rest of the war saving life and ship. His description was as if it was just yesterday.

"I shall consider upon your request son," said His Majesty as he ordered a report detailing the full account to be drawn up on the request for knighthood of Admiral and Captain Wentworth, drafting a note to the prime minister to look into the matter on his behalf.

Several weeks later the Admiralty presented the King with the Admiral and Captain Wentworth's records accounting for all their deeds, answering questions of service and special commendations made. "It is agreed that the recommendation for knighthood proceed," said the King.

All of the preparations were to be made to notify the Wentworths of the coming honour to be bestowed. Prince James asked his father to give him leave to break with protocol and allow him the honour of delivering the King's dispatch personally. The King, having lived longer than his son, took note of the special relationship his son had with this family particularly Margret Anne and Captain Wentworth, and consented to the request.

The King commanded Prince James as his envoy to announce the Royal decree of knighthood to be bestowed on the Admiral and Captain Wentworth. The ceremony would take place in a month. Additionally, the King asked his Scotland Yard to scrutinise the Wentworth family once again. He knew little of this distinguished family and could see he would want to know more about them, especially considering his son's attentions to a certain daughter and perhaps even his daughter with a certain Captain.

A morning like any other since Anne and Frederick took possession of Kellynch Hall, this one was serene and relaxed. The air was thick with mist, but it would be a sunny day. The patch of land Kellynch was situated upon was beautiful in Anne's estimation with just the right amount of tree and brush, bird and deer and fox accented with the loud cries of peacock in the wood.

Anne, paying special attention and enjoying every moment of her family and life at Kellynch Hall, noticed the early arrival of Prince James' carriage. She quickly received him, expecting he would want to visit with Frederick II, but he requested the privilege of seeing the whole family in the drawing room. Anne complied by asking the servants to find and instruct family members to gather in the drawing room at Prince James' request. This would usually be an unusual request but when Prince James made a request one was only to follow the royal command.

In quick fashion the admiral and captain - walking much better now - entered, Margret Anne came from the garden; and shortly after Elizabeth with her Captain Warwick entered the room, with Fitzwilliam trailing behind.

His Highness began with, "Good morning to you all. I have in my hand a communication from my father His Majesty the King. It says, 'By Royal Decree on this day of Dec 1821, it has been determined that the Admiral and Captain Wentworth are to be knighted, at my pleasure and one month from today I will receive you both and your guests at the Royal Place where I will perform this ancient and solemn ceremony. The King'."

The Prince looked up to a room completely silent and surprised. Frederick absorbing the moment responded initially with a bow, and a thank you to His Highness. Captain Wentworth bowed as well and said, "We graciously accept this great honour, Your Royal Highness."

"Then all is settled, we shall expect you at the palace in one month and according to the details outlined in this invitation," said Prince James, handing the invitation to Admiral Wentworth and a second copy to Captain Wentworth.

"And so you shall," said Anne holding Frederick's hand ever so tightly now. "My two best men being honoured," thought Anne.

The Prince begged his leave as he had a number of engagements for the crown these next few days, but wished to personally present his compliments to the Wentworth family. Margret Anne walked with Prince James to the awaiting carriage.

Returning to the drawing room, Margret Anne overheard her mother say, "The invitation-only gives us one month to prepare for this rare and great honour. Attendance at the palace for this solemn event requires all the pomp and circumstance of society. We must plan this immediately."

"There is the letting of a residence in town to be settled, travel, and proper dresses for the women, dress uniforms for the admiral and captain, a gift for the King and Queen to be sent ahead of time as is customary, family and guests to be invited, and notice of the ceremony to be made public," said Anne.

"And there are the papers to report on the honours," said Margret Anne.

"We have much to do," said Anne

"Where do we start mother?" responded Margret Anne as they engaged in planning and lists.

Anne, excited for the news of her husband, and son congratulated them both with hugs and kisses as they were surrounded by family. The family was notified of the coming honour and were excited as well, putting all the attention upon Frederick and his son. A dispatch from the Admiralty arrived expressing their congratulations over the wonderful news.

"Mother, we must invite the Benwicks and Harvilles, as well as members of the Admiralty, since they are known to the King as is right for their station and duties to the crown," said Margret Anne.

"We should invite the Dowager Viscountess Dalrymple, even if her health won't allow, and the Honourable Miss Carteret and Cousin William," said Fitswilliam.

"Of course, as well as Mrs. Croft, the Musgroves, and other family members. We will get this invitee list right and review it to be sure we have not slighted any in the invitation," said Anne to Margret Anne.

The servants were made aware of the events to come. "First, is to organise a dinner with family and close friends that are to be invited to the Honours. During this evening Anne and Frederick would relate the day's events, particulars, and expectations of the occasion and the society they would be in. This dinner must go well," said Anne to the housekeeper.

Anne and Margret Anne would go to town to settle on a house to let, and dress for the after-ball in honour of husband and son. "Anne, may I accompany you and Margret Anne to town to shop for a gown and help with the arrangements?" asked Elizabeth.

"Yes, please be welcome. Thank you for asking," said Margret Anne. Mary arrived and was also invited on the shopping trip. All was settled as Henrietta and Louise made their way into the plan and were also invited.

The admiral and captain took their leave to travel to Plymouth for a short celebration staged by the admiralty. Captains throughout the realm arrived in Plymouth to pay honour and respect to the Wentworths. This was the first time Captain Wentworth had been outside of Kellynch Hall healthy and to the admiralty at Plymouth since arriving there with grave injuries sustained in the battle. There was the question of commendations to be presented and congratulations to be made still not paid.

Admiral Benwick and Captain Harville greeted the Admiral and Captain Wentworth as they arrived at Admiralty Hall. Soon they were overrun with Captains they knew, and some never met, but those hearing of the Wentworth's extraordinary exploits and wanting to meet them personally and present their compliments. All were greeted in turn as congratulations were passed frequently. Both Admiral and Captain Wentworth were steady and patient with each officer returning the compliment and thanking them.

"Son, this was the perfect opportunity to gain friends and acquaintances with the officers. How is your strength holding up?" asked father.

"I am a little tired but no pain," replied Frederick II.

"Let us rest now and refresh ourselves while we can," directed Frederick.

"Ah, it is time to board the carriage son. Are you ready?" asked Father in full dress uniform.

"Yes father," replied Frederick II. They left for the ball.

The evening's events were packed with speeches of honour upheld, courage and valor sustained, and remembrance of those lost. Many Captains, now friends, talked of Admiral Wentworth's dedication to the navy leading to unique strategies and tactics that saved many lives and won the seas. They talked of Captain

Wentworth having the same bloodlines as his illustrious father, courage, honour upheld and valor unequaled. They also spoke of Captain Wentworth's tendency to strategy and tactics like his father, of saving His Royal Highness Prince James and his father the Admiral, as well as the command ship resulting in winning the first major battle decisively that day over superior forces by all estimations and to great personal peril. The Admiral and Captain Wentworth made their acceptance speeches short after a long evening of speeches, all were grateful for the consideration given adding to their respect for the pair.

The Admiral and Captain Wentworth met many fellow Captains, friends, and admirers this evening. They didn't realise their exploits were now required reading at the academy, which was mentioned more than once. Underclassmen attending were in awe of the admiral and captain. Each meeting was made personal as the Wentworths took the time with each group returning the honour.

Frederick mentioned he opened the doors for his son's entry into a number of committees within the Admiralty just as Admiral Croft had done for him.

"I will be ready when you are father," responded Frederick II.

"You have paid the price, son. You have proven yourself. This is the next step in your career," said Frederick proudly.

"Now that you are back to health, and the country is at peace this is the best time to build one's connections and plan for the inevitable coming of the next conflict. Like the Admiral, you will gain trust and reputation as a master tactician and strategist. You are ready," said Frederick.

"I would be honoured to take your advice father," said Frederick II.

With the evening, a complete success in all respects and all the proper civilities observed, the Wentworths took their leave of Plymouth and returned to Kellynch Hall to find all the women were off to town to settle on their long lists of tasks. Fitzwilliam was in town to greet the ladies, guide them, and lend his protection.

"It will be two days before their return to Kellynch Hall," said Frederick II.

"The next day or two will give us some much-needed rest before, in another week, we are all off to town and the honours at the Royal Palace," commented Frederick.

The local papers published the events at Plymouth and the coming knighthood and paying of honour to the Wentworth family, explaining the events leading up to this honour, as well as the long-standing charitable work done in the parish by Anne and Margret Anne, on behalf of the family.

The King received the report detailing the Wentworth family history. He read of Sir William and his link to the nobility of the royal family, of services to the nation, and charitable works by the women. He was most interested in the special attention his son had paid to Captain Wentworth and the particular attention James had paid to Margret Anne Wentworth; her finishing school, charitable works, and connections. "She is an unaffected girl of a family in good standing," whispered the King.

The King saw nothing of concern and related to the Queen "I would be glad to know of this family my dear. Have you read of Lady Anne's charity work throughout the parish they reside these last years?"

The Queen read, "It is very impressive, with schools, surgeries, food, clothing, apprenticeships, organisation, and chairmanship of the charity committee. I will be happy to know her better. Our brief visit to the ball gave me a very positive impression of Lady Anne. She is bright, capable, and able in personality and character I can see," said Her Majesty.

Captain Warwick arrived at Kellynch Hall that evening and would stay the next day, awaiting Elizabeth's return from town with the women.

"Many a young captain endeavored to meet you Frederick II. Did you know this in Plymouth last?" asked Captain Warwick.

"Why should they aspire for so little my friend?" responded Frederick II smiling, his face buried in the papers.

"Your actions in the crucial battle cannot be taught surely. It even impressed the most experienced of sailors and captains. The next generation of navy officers will measure themselves by you and see they will act at least in this way at the appointed hour, that they will have the courage and strength to face the fires. We never know for sure until that time, whether we have what it takes," mentioned Captain Warwick.

"Has your father talked of getting back to work at the Admiralty with important committee work that will shape the next generation of navy?" enquired Captain Warwick as Frederick II looked on.

"Yes, I am engaged now in the committee and am grateful for this guidance. Are you offering to lend your experience as well sir?" asked Frederick II of Captain Warwick.

"I will assist you and the Admiral in any way. All you need do is ask," replied Captain Warwick.

"Thank you sir for your generosity, I value your opinions and advice, and I ask," said Frederick II.

Anne and the women arrived from town with everything settled and with much conversation over tea and biscuits. "Frederick, we rented a house for the fortnight. It is near the palace, with rooms big enough to entertain and in a respectable area of town," said Anne.

"I trust we have enough room for family members. We will need larger drawing rooms as we will be obligated to entertain at least twice while there," explained Frederick hinting this is certainly the domain of a woman. "Send me to war and I am much more comfortable," he added.

"Here here," Frederick II chimed in, in agreement with a smiling group of women ready to help their men in the endeavor.

"The Viscountess has apartments in town; she and the Honourable Miss Carteret are settled in this respect. They will be invited to one of our functions, which would be in addition to the knighthood ceremony and the after-ball at the Palace you know. We still have much to organise," said Elizabeth with Margret Anne, and Mary nodding in agreement.

"Several dispatches have arrived from town," said Frederick.

"Oh?" commented Anne.

"They are invitations to a number of gatherings where our presence is requested from a number of illustrious personages," explained Frederick, handing the invitations to Anne.

Margret Anne, looking over Mother's shoulders, volunteered to send out responses in the morning. Anne grateful for the help commented, "We will have to schedule our occasions around the invitations and get these details settled."

During supper that evening Anne and Frederick agreed to spend the next day together just the two of them. "It has been so busy these last weeks it is time to catch up and just be a couple," said Anne to Frederick.

Later in the evening Anne and Margret Anne finished the final arrangements for travel to town, the invitation lists, occasion dates and the sending out of invitations and acceptances, as well as servants were to go on ahead to town to ensure the house was ready to receive the family.

"I am glad all this organising is done and lists are written. Now we can enjoy ourselves the remainder of the time," said Anne happily.

Looking at Frederick, both women mentioned how much more a woman has to do these days to keep the house running smoothly, to Frederick's confirmation.

The next day, Anne and Frederick organised themselves, determined to spend the day together. "For the first time in a while all the children are at home and will supper together this evening, a rare treat," said Anne as she and her Admiral walked the country lanes around Kellynch talking and catching up on all manner of topics. They lunched in the local village and shopped, not buying anything, just being together. The locals, sensing this was a precious time, gave way to their honoured neighbours, not interrupting them in the least.

"Mother, father we haven't seen either of you all day today!" exclaimed Margret Anne entering the drawing room to tea just arriving for Anne and Frederick.

"We spent the day together," responded Anne.

"What did you do then?" asked Margret Anne.

"We had breakfast in our rooms this morning, took a walk to the village and back, had lunch, shopped and bought nothing, visited Mary and Charles where we found Louisa and Henrietta, and now it is tea time and supper with all of you for the evening," commented Anne.

"You were quite busy then," replied Margret Anne.

"We wanted to catch up and be a couple again," mentioned Anne to an understanding Margret Anne, lifting a cup of tea to her lips.

At supper, the Wentworths caught up on each other's news. Anne, pensive, looked over at her husband.

"Why the tears my dear?" asked Frederick, handing her a handkerchief.

"How time marches on, the children have grown, and soon it will be you and I again," replied Anne.

Frederick, ever the optimist stated, "We have a lot of life ahead of us my dear, and the prospect of you and I is not so bad really, is it?"

The next day was spent working through the final arrangements for the trip to town. Anne asked Mrs. Croft if the arrangements were complete. "Yes, all is in readiness, Anne. Thank you for taking me to town with you and the family. It has been long since I have had the opportunity to visit with old friends in the navy," commented Mrs. Croft.

"Not at all dear lady, you are family and are always welcome," replied Anne.

"Thank you dear Anne for your kindness to me, especially since my Admiral's passing," mentioned Mrs. Croft.

"Not at all, truly," Anne responded.

Anne crossed a short lane on the grounds of the estate to the small cottage where Harriet and old Nurse Rooke resided. Anne and Harriet had been close friends since school but more since Anne employed Harriet and Nurse Rooke to help Lady Russell and her in raising the children. Harriet, used to society until her husband passed away, was able to live life quite successfully through the Wentworth's kindness and was grateful to Anne and Frederick. They lived on a beautiful estate and had the use of a cottage all these years while earning a modest income through the family. "What more could one want?" thought Harriet.

Anne arrived at the cottage knocking at the door, to Harriet answering. "Hello Mrs. Anne welcome, please come in, a cup of tea?" asked Harriet. "Yes please that sounds lovely" responded Anne.

"How are you these days Harriet? We must catch up dear friend. I have been quite busy, as you know," mentioned Anne.

"I am very well, thank you for asking. As you know, I have been taking care of Nurse Rooke these past few months as her health is deteriorating. The old age, you know. However, she is comfortable and that is all any of us can ask. She is resting at the moment," said Harriet.

"Hmmm lovely cup of tea, thank you, Harriet. I will not stay long as I am determined to spend as much time with Frederick and the children as I can. We have so few moments lately and the next few days will be quite busy," said Anne.

"Congratulations on the knighthood honour, how very exciting and truly deserved. I could not have imagined such a grand future for you Anne. You must be so proud of your men folk," expressed Harriet.

"I am very proud of them and grateful they are home and safe," replied Anne, sipping tea.

"I brought the list of items for the management of the hall while we are away. The servants and the groundsman have been informed that they will answer to you during this time we are away. Each of them has their instructions as to what I would like them to do and to come to you with any decision. They are very competent and I don't expect much for you to do in this respect but here are their lists just in case. I asked the housekeeper and head groundsman to visit you to talk over their lists and report any problems during the week.

"About the Charity ball, as you know this year it will be quite impossible to attend the yearly event in the village, as we will be playing to His Majesty in town. This is a disappointment since we work so hard, and it is the time to say thank you to all those who give of themselves in this effort throughout the parish. Will you represent the family and give all our thanks?" asked Anne.

"Yes, of course, it is my pleasure" replied Harriet gulping.

"I have sent notes to all those to be thanked so really it will be a formality but also important. Words of thanks mean a lot to those who sacrifice so much. It gives them breath to employ themselves another year in this way. We all want to be needed," added Anne.

"I would be an honoured to represent the Wentworths, thank you for asking Anne," said Harriet.

"You're most welcome Harriet, thank you," responded Anne.

"Here are the ball details. I have sent word to Mrs. Thrussell of the village organising committee of your standing in our stead. She will visit you in the next day or so to complete final arrangements for the gathering," explained Anne. "Well, Harriet it's time to go. We will have tea when I return. Thank you for giving me leave to visit with you and taking on these engagements," expressed Anne.

"Go safe Anne. All will go well here have no worries. I look forward to your return and telling of all the stories of your trip to town and the palace," replied Harriet smiling at the cottage door.

Back at Kellynch Hall, "Frederick, I have completed my last task for the day. Shall we walk to the village together then? We have so much to talk about," said Anne.

"That would be wonderful," responded Frederick.

Meanwhile, Margret Anne, Frederick II, and Fitzwilliam got wind of the adventure as they entered the library and asked to accompany Anne and Frederick.

Along the walk and down the lane many an acquaintance and stranger expressed their congratulations over the events to come in town at the palace. "We have come so far Frederick," said Anne

"What do you mean my dear?" responded Frederick.

"I remember a time when I went unnoticed to the village, recognised only as the mistress of Kellynch, and now people step aside for my sake, chat with us over stories of how the Wentworths might have helped their families and of course the knighthood to come, and the granting us great privilege. We have come a long way since those days of quiet and not being noticed," said Anne.

"This is true dear but through no fault of our own. We have done the best we could in life and tried to be an example to all and be compassionate in our actions. We have positively affected folks around us, and I am glad for it," replied Frederick, walking at Anne's side.

"We have worked hard and risked much to be of service and we have been very fortunate indeed to have our family restored," replied Anne as she watched the children just ahead laughing and talking.

"See," said Frederick pointing to the children.

"Yes, I do. It has been a long time since they have just been together like this; all of us as a family. I fear it may never happen again. All this business with Margret Anne and Prince James" commented Anne.

"Don't be concerned dear. He is a good and honourable man with the best of connections. However, it is true; her life will change profoundly forever if she accepts him."

"She will have great responsibilities and little time for us. My little girl," said Anne with a quiet sadness in her tone.

"Yes dear, it is difficult when children grow up and go off into the world. We prepared them as much as we can and hope they never leave us, but there it is the road leads from our hearts into the unknown," replied Frederick.

In the village, the family decided to take tea at the local Inn. Entering, a hush came over the room, as they were led to the best of tables. Some folks came up to thank them for their charity works and congratulate the family on their fortunes of late.

"Bless you surely Lady Anne," said one patron on the way out.

"Congratulations gentlemen," said a Subaltern. But mostly, the family was granted quiet and made the most of it, telling each other of the latest news.

"Anne I am so proud of you and the charity work you and Margret Anne undertook. It is such a surprise to see so many folks in the parish humbled to be near you. While my son and I were at the wars you did your part on the home front, and I am glad of it. I could not have imagined such an impact surely. Fitzwilliam you used your skills to enable such effort and contribute in that way. This is so good of you. In the next days, in town, Frederick II and I will be knighted and I for one am proud to share this with each of you. A toast!" said Frederick lifting his teacup.

"Here here," said Frederick II, along with his brother, sister, and mother.

Mrs. Thrussell, taking tea and seeing Anne just across the room took the liberty to walk over and congratulate Anne and the family, as well as to finalise a detail or two for the charity ball. Anne mentioned her dear friend Harriet Smith would step in for the Wentworths and that she would await her visit to make final arrangements. Mrs. Thrussell thanked Anne, "God's speed and safe return from town. Have no worries about the charity ball. It will go well."

After tea, the Wentworths set off to stroll along the lane toward Kellynch Hall. "The weather is too very fine today, neither too hot nor too cold a breeze," said Margret Anne."

"How the village has changed since our growing up," said Frederick II.

"All these conveniences and modern inventions, what say you father?" mentioned Fitzwilliam.

"It is true, life is moving along like the currents of the sea ever flowing. Let us pledge to hold on to each other no matter how life changes around us. Always and forever bound, we must have each other," expressed Frederick as Anne held tightly to her Admiral's arm at his sentiment.

They all agreed, more with their eyes and standing together than with the word, wishing the moment would last, but in sight was Kellynch Hall now and soon tomorrow's adventure into town would begin and in the wider world for a fortnight.

Anne invited Mrs. Croft and Harriet to dine with the family this evening before they traveled to London. Speaking to the servants, Anne wanted a particularly special supper tonight. She likened this to a special occasion. All was readied in quick order and to her wishes.

Anne secretly purchased a present for Frederick. It would be something special, something linking the both of them and only sentimental to them as a couple.

Anne did not notice Margret Anne, who loved books, reading in a windowsill just beyond the corner of her sight. Finally, Margret Anne asked to a startled Anne "What you are about their mum?"

"Oh! Margret Anne, I did not notice you there. I am wrapping a present for your father."

"May I see mother?" asked Margret Anne.

"Of course," said Anne.

Reading the note Margret Anne commented "so lovingly framed, so tenderly cared for, so specially arranged. Mother, this is the note Father wrote to you of his proposal. You told me about when I was a little girl. And all these years you have kept this so well. What are these smudges?" asked Margret Anne looking at her mother intensely now.

Anne explained, for the first time, her history with Frederick and the eight years lost to the persuasions of her society of the day. "These smudges are records of my tears of joy as I read this note," explained Anne.

Margret Anne, so touched by the description of the loving memory had full tears in her eyes and asked no more but simply helped her mother wrap the precious framed note.

The connection between mothers and daughters can at times never be explained perhaps just recognised. This moment would be perfectly understood and never to be forgotten. "Father will love this mum. Thank you for sharing this tender task with me. I better understand both of you and the trials you faced. I know of the love that connects you. I have lived it. It created me and my brothers and I honour it."

"I will give this to your father tonight at supper," said Anne.

An hour before supper, an unexpected visitor arrived at the door. Prince James entered through the portal. He was escorted to the drawing room by one of the servants and announced nervously before the family, "Sir, please excuse us as we were not expecting you this evening but were making preparations for the trip to town tomorrow," said Frederick.

"Have no concerns, Admiral. I wanted to personally escort the family to town tomorrow. I rushed here with no plan or notice for proper arrangements as is customary to be sure, and I apologise for it. Would you offer an acquaintance lodging and supper this evening?" asked Prince James.

"Of course Your Royal Highness you are most welcome here," replied Anne.

Margret Anne, at Anne's hinting, rushed off with a servant to prepare rooms for Prince James.

"I will personally inspect them upon completion," said Anne to Margret Anne's nod.

Frederick II welcomed the Prince as Anne offered him tea.

Prince James related the excitement felt by all in the Palace to honour the Wentworths. It had been long since the crown had honoured true heroes. He also mentioned how much he had learned from both the admiral and captain on his visits to Kellynch Hall and at the admiralty.

"Perhaps he also wanted to be near Margret Anne, as his glances would move to the women folk chatting and doing needlework in the background, but quite attentive to the conversations of the men," thought Frederick II.

He could tell, as the twin and brother, Margret Anne sat up just a bit taller and moved with just that bit more grace. He wondered where this would lead; hoping whatever the circumstance it would secure the happiness of a beloved sister.

With the announcement of supper served, the family and guests entered the dining room to sit at the table. Prince James did not take a customary seat at the head of the table as reflecting his station but sat across from Margret Anne, hoping no one would comment or notice. No one commented but everyone noticed, passing the knowledge from one glance to the next in a respectful way.

Margret Anne, never one to be intimidated, touched Frederick's hand as he squeezed hers with confidence and power for support. She felt at ease again.

Conversation was amiable with much said of the day and of the coming days. At the end of the meal and before it was right to leave for the drawing room, Margret Anne watched Mother pull out her precious gift, so lovingly cared for over the years and made in like manner. Anne stood as all listened quietly to get all the attention asking all the men present to be seated. "Dear

Frederick, my love, it seems just yesterday we started our lives together. We married; you took me on a voyage to Spain and Italy a little and meek village girl who barely visited town let alone another country and all the business sea voyages. The experience changed me. Upon our return, we began life at Kellynch Hall, a surprise wedding present, suddenly three wonderful children were born, a war, and tomorrow we set off to town where you and my Captain are to be honoured by the King himself. Today, we have the honour of the company of His Royal Highness Prince James and our dear and close friends Mrs. Croft and Mrs. Smith.

"I wanted to tell you in some feeble way perhaps a woman's way, my way, how grateful I am for you still dear husband, my dearest friend in the whole world. I love you more for coming home to me and bringing my Captain home safely, restoring this family whole again," announced Anne with tears in her eyes now.

Margret Anne, being a woman and a daughter to her mother, had the same tears of love and respect for her father, and stood with her mother. Anne handed a wrapped gift to her Admiral and kissed him on the cheek. Frederick surprised, looked over the package then began to open it ever so carefully so as not to rip the paper and being respectful of Anne's effort.

Prince James, not used to such openness of form looked at each member of the family engaged in the moment. His eyes, falling on Margret Anne, discreetly offered her his handkerchief to dry her tears as she took her seat focused on her father now. He, the Prince, was deeply moved by the true emotions, the obvious connections of this family to each other and honoured them in his heart of hearts for showing him that love expressed is not a weakness but a strength indeed.

The package unwrapped, Frederick knew immediately what he was reading as he relived in the blink of an eye the moments of uncertainty, his happiness in the balance, standing on the streets of Bath outside Camden Place waiting to find Anne, her running to his side and the loving answer to his proposal those many years ago now seemed like yesterday. "It seemed like yesterday, only a moment ago," thought Frederick.

Looking up and into Anne's eyes, as if everything in the room faded away and he and Anne were the only two, he could see in his mind's eye both just there again on the street at Camden Place so young and full of hope.

Looking at Anne earnestly she said, "My dear, I am in receipt of your proposal and I accept as I did those many years ago and still today."

The Prince stood up, at that, and proposed a toast to the Admiral and Lady Wentworth. "Sir I often wondered at the root of courage and valor. It seems I know now. Love is the root. Love that special strength so fine as to be invisible yet so strong as to be unbreakable; a toast, to the Wentworth's."

In the drawing-room, Margret Anne, Prince James, and Frederick II played a game of cards while they talked about the affairs of the day.

"The Prince obviously has an interest in Margret Anne and is taking all the proper steps expected of any gentleman in wanting to court a woman of family and connections," said Mrs. Croft to Harriet.

"Yes, it seems so. I hope our Margret Anne is up to the weight of the offer to come," said Harriet.

"She certainly is strong enough as we have seen in her growing," commented Mrs. Croft.

Entering the room through the gardens Frederick, with Anne on his arm said "There are marine guards posted in the gardens, we bumped into a couple on our short stroll about."

"Please forgive this dear lady, Admiral," said Prince James. "It seems this is a requirement of the office these days. There are those who would harm the future King it seems. I promise they will be as unobtrusive as can be while I am here."

"Not to worry your Highness it was meant in jest. We are honoured by your visits and that of the marine guard," replied Frederick.

The next morning after a light breakfast all the carriages were readied, while Prince James, Frederick II, and Fitzwilliam readied their horses since they rode into town in this way.

"Frederick II, although you are in full health if the riding is too much, and you need to rest, please stop and tie the horses lead to one of the carriages and sit with us in comfort awhile," mentioned Anne, fussing over her son.

Soon the party was on their way with marines leading and in tow.

Mrs. Thrussell, who would meet with Mrs. Smith, said to her husband "The Wentworths travel to town today for a fortnight, attending assemblies, balls, and plays with the King bestowing a great knighthood. I do wish them well and God's speed, they are truly deserving of such singling out."

"Is that not Prince James, Fitzwilliam, and the marine guards with the Wentworths, come quickly, see? Just there through the hedge, they are passing in the lane. See the marines escorting the carriages," commented Mrs. Thrussell.

"Yes dear, right you are," said Mr. Thrussell, in awe of the company being kept at Kellynch Hall these days.

Mrs. Thrussell, calm again, focused on her task to visit and complete arrangements with Mrs. Smith for the charity ball in the village.

Upon arriving in town the Prince escorted the Wentworths to their let house and then begged his leave to pay respects to his father the King and oversee the ceremony, as well as ensure the after-ball arrangements were complete.

"Are you free to dine with me and my parents tomorrow night?" asked Prince James.

"Of course Your Highness," said Frederick.

"Right then, this is settled," responded the Prince.

James took his leave and set off for the palace with his guards.

The first evening the door was so busy with dispatches, and congratulations arriving that the doorman made it a point to place a chair the outside where he could sit in comfort in anticipation of receipt of the many dispatches, reducing the commotion these events inevitably excited to an otherwise quiet neighbourhood and house.

Every so often, the doorman would come in and place numerous letters in the proper tray just outside the drawing room where one of the Wentworths would pick them up and take them into the drawing room for opening and reading.

The next morning when the Wentworths awoke to all the hustle and bustle of a big city, and all before breakfast, Anne said to Frederick "How I love the countryside, so quiet in the morning."

"Yes, truly. This town is for the young folk leaving the rest of us to the country and the calm quietness surely," responded Frederick.

At breakfast, Margret Anne commented, "Do people not sleep in town? There is so much movement; all this coming and going can't be good for the health!"

With the invitation to dine at the palace this evening it would be fine to spend the day quiet and indoors, but with that said a knock announcing the arrival of Admiral James Benwick and Captain Charles Harville. There were smiles and congratulations. Just behind them in the street, a carriage was stopped to let out Elizabeth and Captain Warwick, who would be staying at the house.

Anne invited both Charles and James in to sit with Frederick entertaining them. While servants organised bags and rooms for the Warwick, Anne escorted Elizabeth and Captain Warwick into the drawing room. Benwick spoke of his true intention this morning. He invited the Admiral and Captain Wentworth to lunch with naval officers today at the customs house, and they represented the official invitation. Arrangements to have a carriage fetch both were settled and would arrive in a couple of hours.

"Dress uniforms gentlemen, we will return at eleven this morning with your conveyance," commented James as he and Charles prepared to leave.

"Good morning to you gentlemen," said James Benwick.

"Good morning to you sir," replied Frederick.

A Royal dispatch arrived at that moment, freezing Benwick and Harville in place. It was no ordinary communication but a dispatch from the palace. The royal courier was announced and escorted into the drawing room where Frederick accepted it and read the note. "This is a royal invitation asking the family to dine with the King and Queen this evening, at the Palace," read Frederick.

A response was sent back with the courier saying, "accepted with pleasure."

"More happens here in one morning than in a week at Kellynch Hall!" commented Anne.

"This fortnight should be quite active and exciting to be sure my dear, although I will long for the peace and quiet of my Kellynch Hall," said Frederick to the agreement of all there.

"Cannot the women come to the eleven a.m. gathering at the customs house?" asked Anne as Margret Anne listened intently.

Benwick responded "I don't think it will break any protocols to observe in the gallery, but there is one portion of tradition that belongs to naval officers only and is not a public ceremony. These private ceremonies are performed twice, at the beginning and the last fifteen minutes or so, at the end one is invited to enter and view the final proceedings. It would be an honour to escort you both and guide you through the luncheon." commented Benwick.

The women intrigued and with nothing better to do, agreed. "It would be a pleasure, Thank you" responded Anne.

"Then it is settled," replied Benwick.

At the appointed time that morning, a carriage arrived at the residence ready to take the family to the naval luncheon. During the carriage ride, Admiral Benwick talked through the proceedings with Anne and Margret Anne. "This should not be a trail of endurance and mindless rituals," said Benwick.

"Can no one tell me why a wife and daughter should not see her husband and son be so honoured?" commented Anne.

"Quite right my dear, I am glad for your attendance. These will be the last days of the Navy for me. My time had come and now is almost gone," replied Frederick as Frederick II stared out the carriage window, miles away.

"I have much to be grateful for," thought Frederick II.

Arriving at the customs house, they disembarked from the carriage. Admiral and Captain Wentworth left Anne and Margret Anne in the capable hands of Benwick as they entered. The ceremony started with closed doors as Benwick described the proceedings to Anne and Margret Anne just outside the chamber doors. In what seemed a few moments Admiral Wentworth came through the door to invite his wife and daughter to enter into the luncheon, thanking Benwick as they all entered the hall together.

In this esteemed place, one could feel the history of the Royal Navy exudes from every board in the hall. One generation to the next carrying the torch of courage and valor to the next. England is a seafaring nation. The empire lives on the seas. Seated now, there were many toasts and short speeches made until everyone present had their turn at the accolade. Lunch was not so much grand as to express recognition of the honour and credit the Wentworths had brought to the navy in this generation.

On their way home, the conversation was of reconnecting with old friends not seen since the conflict, "How fortunate and grateful that most came home safe and victorious," commented Frederick.

"By the grace of God," responded Frederick II as Anne nodded in recognition.

The subject turned to the hustle and bustle of town life and how grateful they were to live the quiet country life.

"We must attend church before the knighthood ceremony, my Admiral," commented Anne.

"Of course my dear, where do you suggest?" replied Frederick.

"Perhaps St. Paul's? Do we know the Arch Bishop?" mentioned Margret Anne.

"I found a small church, All Saints Church, just several blocks from our let house where I confirmed details with the vicar. He seemed pleasant and willing. I thought this would be less intrusive and more personal," said Anne.

"Then All Saints Church it is," replied Margret Anne.

The evening came quickly as seemed to be the way in town.

The family prepared for supper and an evening at the palace. Margret Anne sat with her mother, who described what she would see and do in this particular society. All was ready as the royal carriage, conveying the Wentworths, arrived at the palace gates.

Prince James greeted the Wentworths. "Thank you for accepting our invitation to dine with us this evening. All was very cordial as the Prince escorted the party to one of the many drawing rooms in the private part of the palace. "This is a drawing room for the particular use of the family," explained Prince James as servants adeptly provided refreshments to the guests.

"The furnishings came as a gift from…" stopped Prince James as he was interrupted by father and mother entering the room. All stood and bowed and curtsied as is proper and customary in the presence of their Monarch. After all the civilities, Her Majesty talked with Anne and Margret Anne, while His Majesty gathered around the men in the room. The men talked of war and the business of the empire, while the women talked of children, society, charity, the weather, and the condition of the roads.

Sooner than expected, notice of supper being served ended their time in the drawing room as the party was led to the connecting dining room through now-opened giant mirrored doors and a seat at the table.

Prince James made it a point to sit across from Margret Anne. With great poise and ease Margret Anne sustained polite conversation with James and at times was queried by the Queen on a subject or two. Princess Stephanie, apologising for being late and knowing of Captain Wentworth, made it a point to continue her most amiable conversations with him as now he was fully recovered and showed her respect, but never the false compliments she endured at open court with many a man.

The evening went very well and His Majesty very astute in matters of society aptly entered into good relations with the Wentworths.

Back in the drawing room the Queen and Princess Stephanie made it a point to know Lady Anne and Margret Anne very well indeed through conversing in the easiest and most relaxed manner, yet maintaining all the necessary form expected of their respective stations. With the supper evening soon coming to a close and the hour late, Prince James proposed a toast to the Wentworth expressing the recognition and gratitude of the crown for the valor and courage displayed on behalf of His Majesty, the King, and the Empire.

A carriage came to convey the Wentworths to their let house for the evening where for the first time one could see the town at night through candlelights in windows, and street lanterns lit and a slower pace. "I believe this to be a very amiable evening and the royal family to be very cordial indeed," mentioned Frederick.

"This is true. The Queen, at least in my case, made a great effort to know of me and my interests throughout the evening. Did not Princess Stephanie pay you great attention Frederick II?" asked Anne.

"Yes, mother I have to agree. She is quite a woman, very intelligent, witty, and yet very kind in her nature. She pays me great attention," replied Frederick.

Back at their let residence, the Wentworths talked of their experiences at the palace. Elizabeth and Mary who waited in the drawing room during their absence listened intently to all the going's on. "Had you been there tonight you would have enjoyed the moment," said Anne.

"I look forward to a visit at court for the knighthood ceremony and ball next evening," remarked Mary.

Elizabeth asked Margret Anne for all the details of Prince James at the dinner and conversations, drinking in all the descriptions and the telling. "It must have been wonderful. I look forward to tomorrow," exclaimed Elizabeth.

Retiring for the evening, the night flew by and the dawn turned to early morning very quickly. Anne lay awake thinking of all the tasks to be done this morning to ensure they were ready to travel to the palace on time. Frederick, not one to sleep long hours said, "Good morning dear."

"Good morning my Captain," replied Anne.

"It has been long since you have called me by that name. What is this?" asked Frederick.

"I also whisper this name to you. It is etched into my heart my dearest Captain. I just avoid confusion by calling you Admiral, a much-earned rank mind you, I am quite proud to be sure," replied Anne rolling to Frederick's arms.

"We have much to do this morning with the ceremony. How do you feel about it all," asked Anne. "I have learned to let society heap their awards and accolades. It eases the conscience of a society that asked so much as a result of the politics of the day. Let us just enjoy the moment, so we can be off to Kellynch and our lives again. I have missed you these last years and want to know my dear heart again," said Frederick as he lay with his love in the quiet morning hour.

This day would entail knighthood, tea with the Royals, and then a return to the Palace for a celebration ball this evening as a special guest of His Majesty. The family breakfasted discussing the day's events as a dispatch arrived for Margret Anne. A royal courier stood to raise eyebrows from across the table so early this morning.

The dispatch was from Prince James inviting Margret Anne to a royal function this morning, before her father and brothers ceremony. She would be the particular guest of Her Majesty the

Queen. As is customary, Margret Anne agreed and with pleasure. A carriage would pick her up in one hour. Miss Wentworth would then join the family later for the knighthood ceremony at the Royal Palace.

"Mother, I must prepare. I have very little time," said Margret Anne.

"I will help you, Margret Anne," replied Anne, leaving breakfast with her daughter to waiting servants.

Frederick commented "My dear Margret Anne. This is a great distinction indeed. You do realise the Prince is singling you out and presenting you to the royal court and the royal family?"

"Yes, Father I do. This is not a common invitation. If you will excuse me, I must prepare. I have less than an hour before the carriage arrives," replied Margret Anne taking her leave and walking with Anne, who would assist Margret Anne with her preparations, with Elizabeth and Mary in tow to help as well.

After an hour and moments before, the royal carriage arrived and Margret Anne made her appearance to her father and that quickly was whisked off to the palace for a morning of official royal functions. "Obviously the royal family is assessing her as a possible daughter-in-law dear," said Anne.

"Are we sure this is what Margret Anne wants?" commented Frederick.

"Perhaps in a day or so we should talk about this, the three of us," said Anne.

"Yes indeed, it is best to go into this knowing what to expect rather than not knowing. It leads to unhappiness if one is not aware and prepared for the sacrifices," commented Frederick.

"If she is determined, we shall support her of course," said Anne.

"Yes, of course," replied Frederick.

Several hours later, the Wentworths departed to the palace for the knighthood ceremony. Along the way, they were uncommonly quiet. Prince James greeted the Wentworths at the palace just as he did a couple of days earlier, except this time Margret Anne was at his side. Anne, acutely aware of the scene, felt a ping of pain at her dear Margret Anne married and living in town away from her and Kellynch Hall. She snapped out of it with the exiting of the carriage and a quick escort to the throne rooms and the imminent preparations of the knighthood ceremony. A palace member advised them as to protocol and ceremony.

Admiral and Captain Wentworth were separately escorted to the staging area and organisers explained in detail the formalities.

With some pomp and circumstance, the room filled with dignitaries from around the realm. Members of the Admiralty entered and finally the Admiral and Captain Wentworth walked in from the left side of the room, to approach the throne standing to the right.

With trumpets blaring and to perfect timing of doors opening, dressed in royal robes, His Majesties and Prince James entered the room to 'God save the King". Having dinner with the Royals only a night earlier and treated with such relaxed grace it made one lose their breath at the sight of His Majesties in the full glory of the empire on display.

The ceremony was a blur. The sight of the sword touching the Admiral's shoulder and then Captain Wentworth's was the moment of note. Just that quickly each was now distinguished as Sir Frederick and Sir Frederick II. With the exit of His Majesties, they received many congratulations from the guests and the meeting of many illustrious personages of the realm. Benwick and Harville stood at Anne and Margret Anne's side just close enough to be of assistance and far enough not to intrude. Anne, aware was grateful for the support. Both Frederick and her Captain were engaged with well-wishers of the moment as was only right, greeting each person and graciously accepting their congratulations.

A royal servant announced the time for the Wentworths to visit with His Majesties. This time it was different. The first visit was so much at ease. The Knighthood ceremony, being an official function, required the power and majesty of the empire to be on display. In a small room Frederick, Anne, Frederick II, and Margret Anne entered, waiting on a servant to direct them to the royal family. Instead of a servant, Princess Stephanie herself entered the room and after all the proper greetings acceptable under the circumstances, she guided the family to her father and mother while walking with Frederick II, it did not go unnoticed.

The royal family congratulated the two newest knights of the realm and expressed their sincere gratitude for all that was done to earn this distinction. Princess Stephanie stayed by Frederick II's side throughout, talking and making light of this and that. Frederick was aware she was paying special attention and did nothing to discourage it.

Soon after the meeting lunch was served. Only a particular guest and the Wentworths were invited. Here all was relaxed and the ease of conversation returned like an old friend. His Majesties made it a point not to intimidate honoured subjects of the realm, especially since they were not regulars to the court of Saint James.

Lunch flew by and they were about to leave when Her Majesty asked Sir Frederick and the Lady Anne if they would spare their daughter for a fortnight further. Margret Anne would be a particular guest of Her Majesty, assisting her with royal obligations, staying at the palace and under the protection of the crown. "Of course Your Majesty it would be a great honour for Margret Anne I am sure," said Sir Frederick.

"Well then it is settled, if your daughter would only accept?" asked Her Majesty.

"Of course, I accept with pleasure," replied Margret Anne meekly.

Margret Anne walked with her family to the carriages as arrangements were made for her clothing and personal effects to be brought to the palace. Just in entering the carriage, Anne looked at Margret Anne with just that look that only a mother and daughter share, becoming suddenly tearful. "I shall write mother and in a fortnight be home at Kellynch Hall. It will all go by quickly."

"But not quickly enough," thought Anne.

The carriages left the palace. Margret Anne, taking Prince James' arm walked to her royal residence for the next fortnight.

James noticed Margret Anne's uncommon quiet and her emotions so close to the surface he made it a point to be especially gentle with her, walking slowly and talking softly to her, "Have no worries dear I will personally escort you to Kellynch Hall in a fortnight. Mother has a number of functions you would attend with her, and some may even be fun. She is always about helping the people in some form or other. This will be a great opportunity to know of the Queen and our lives here," smiled James calming Margret Anne.

Sir Frederick, Anne, and Sir Frederick II returned to the palace for the celebration ball that evening, with the Warwick and Fitzwilliam in tow. They were announced at the door with all eyes upon them.

The general splendour of the ballroom was breathtaking. Such a large ballroom, with so many well-wishers, music, dancing, food, and great conversation.

"But where is Margret Anne?" asked Anne.

"Perhaps she will enter with the royal family," remarked Sir Frederick.

The next moment, mirrored doors opened and His Majesties entered the room. Anne and Frederick, to their astonishment, all noticed Margret Anne at Prince James' side.

Margret Anne was wearing a gown so opulent it could not have been purchased by the Wentworths. Could the Queen have given her a gift? A necklace and earrings glistening in the candlelight, she looked magnificent. Every male eye in the room focused on Margret Anne. Single women present with plans to press themselves upon the Prince now knew this would be a futile attempt since Margret Anne was formidable indeed.

As the evening progressed, Margret Anne made her way to her family, greeting them warmly. Anne and Margret Anne sat in a quiet corner and talked as mother and daughter, as the men greeted guests and all who wanted to meet the Wentworths.

"Are you well daughter?" asked Anne.

"Yes, mother but missing you and father very much even though it has only been a few hours," replied Margret Anne.

"As we miss you," replied Anne. "It is only a fortnight, and you will be busy with crown business as the particular guest of the Queen."

"I am grateful for the honour but will be glad to be back at Kellynch Hall," said Margret Anne thinking that she was not yet ready to give up her country life, her country home, and her wonderful family.

Princess Stephanie, in a not-so-subtle, but still dignified manner, made it a point to pay particular attention to Sir Frederick II, leaving many a man standing and without her company, since she was engaged with Captain Frederick II and now knight of the realm.

A few days later and back at Kellynch Hall, Sir Frederick talked of obligations to be discharged due in part to his new title and rank. "All these new titles, whatever will we do?" asked Anne.

"How I miss my sister," mentioned Sir Frederick II.

"Ah, there is a letter from the Palace," commented Fitzwilliam, walking into the drawing room. "It is addressed to you mother."

Anne flew to the letter while Frederick had tea brought in and remained silent, knowing Anne would be engrossed. "It is from Margret Anne, she is well enough and is off to a ceremony in the morning hours with Her Majesty in the north of town and preparing for an evening gathering with visitors to the palace," said Anne.

"She is missing Kellynch and the family. That is to be expected really under the circumstances," said Anne, looking for assurance.

Frederick squeezed Anne's hand tightly, in silence, wondering where the time had gone from a dear child to an adult woman.

"She will be home in a few days dear and I will be glad of it," commented Frederick.

"It would not be soon enough since one day soon we will lose her forever. Our time will be precious now indeed," replied Anne, gazing at the fire.

"We will not lose her dear. We will gain a son-in-law," smiled Frederick.

Depending on which Wentworth, your perception of these days went by fast or slow. But alas Margret Anne was to return today and all anticipated her return to Kellynch to be an occasion. Early afternoon a carriage escorted by a marine guard arrived at the front door where His Highness followed by Margret Anne stepped out of the carriage. With them was Princess Stephanie as a particular guest of Margret Anne. Anne saw more here. Her Captain spent much time dancing with Princess Stephanie at the ball a fortnight ago. "It seems we have a growing attachment?" said Anne to Frederick waiting to greet their guests.

"It seems so my dear," replied Frederick smiling.

After tea Prince James took his leave of the Wentworths and was escorted to his carriage by the family but mostly by Margret Anne when he took his leave of her. "I suppose all we wait for my dear is the announcement of engagement," Anne commented discreetly to her Admiral holding his arm tightly.

The family found Frederick II occupied with interest in Princess Stephanie as they returned to the drawing room. As is only right, Princess Stephanie engaged Margret Anne, eventually taking a turn about the house and the grounds learning its secrets and history. "I have heard so much of this Kellynch Hall. By all accounts, it is as described. This is such a peaceful place I would never leave it," said Princess Stephanie.

"Indeed it is a haven, and I have missed it," replied Margret Anne, walking along with Princess Stephanie.

In the drawing room, Frederick and his son were talking about the navy and the latest news of the committees and the admiralty.

A knock at the door interrupted their discussion with Anne, Margret Anne, and Princess Stephanie entering the room. Both men stood and bowed in greeting to the women.

"Sir Frederick you and Sir Frederick II have spent so much time this day in the study. May I entreat you both to sit with us over lunch and perhaps a country walk afterward where you may offer your protection?" asked Princess Stephanie smiling.

"It seems our ladies have come to rescue us. Shall we not take up their cause?" asked Sir Frederick.

"Of course, we should take up this cause and with pleasure," responded Frederick II as they all walked to the dining room for lunch and then a country walk.

Frederick and Anne talked over their daughter and son's interests of the heart, wondering where it would all lead, "Dear; Frederick II is doing well with his assignments with naval planning committees in the Admiralty at Plymouth. I will guide him as much as he will let me before I retire from service. In a day or so Admiral Benwick will arrive for the crucial meeting and appointments," said Frederick.

"He is so much like you. Tall and straight, his character and his exploits in the navy," commented Anne.

"Yes, I can see this clearly," replied Frederick.

"I will be glad to see our friend Benwick," said Anne

"Margret Anne is so much like you Anne in character but very confident and accomplished in so many ways," said Frederick.

"She has your tallness, intelligence, and social skills," remarked Anne.

"Have we not done very well with these children dear?" asked Frederick.

"Yes, we have been very fortunate Frederick," replied Anne.

"And of course there is Fitzwilliam. He is so much the businessman. Did you know he has almost doubled our estate through very clever investments? I have notes from a number of prominent persons and neighbours, some of whom I have never in my life met, asking to visit with him at Kellynch Hall, and all to ask estate advice. Of course, what he did with the finances of the charity made it possible to serve so many more in the parish. He is brilliant, to be sure, in his own way," commented Frederick.

"Each has their own individual character and excellence, and yet they stand with each other and are connected. I have no worries when the day is upon them that we are gone. They will have each other," said Anne.

"Let us have no more talk of being gone one day my dear. Today is upon us and we are here and well and I for one am glad of it!" replied Frederick.

As lunch came to a close, Anne suggested, "Shall we take a tour of the countryside then? The weather is glorious with sun and warm and light?"

"Yes, let's do a walk," replied Princess Stephanie.

Frederick noticed that this freedom was intoxicating to Princess Stephanie. She would normally be locked away in the palace with many functions and obligations, but here she could be free and easy." Frederick could relate to this attraction, when he is with the admiralty his obligations are many leaving little time for himself.

Along the lane, Frederick II lent his arm to Princess Stephanie as Margret Anne walked on her other side. Anne and Frederick walked up ahead and at a slow pace. Marine guards followed and led at some distance as to render service if needed but not so close as to intrude on the privacy of the moment. "I have only been here a short time, but I love this place Kellynch. I find I will be able to sleep and wake to such, quiet and calm. It is as if I can breathe," mused Princess Stephanie, taking a deep breath of country air.

"Well, then my dear friend you must visit as often as you please. You are very welcome here," replied Margret Anne.

"Yes, very welcome," said Frederick II tenderly.

"Where is this local village you talk of?" asked Princess Stephanie.

"See, just there between the trees; see, the cottage roofs." pointed Frederick II.

"When next we walk perhaps we can walk there," said Margret Anne.

"It would cause a stir in the village at the sight of you," stated Frederick II.

"Shall we, for today, point ourselves up this lane and back in the direction of Kellynch Hall then?" pointed Frederick to the group.

Anne and Frederick's eyes fell upon Margret Anne as she walked into the drawing room. "Margret, may we speak with you?" asked Anne.

"Of course mother, father what is it?" replied Margret Anne.

"This business with the Prince, is it serious?" asked Anne in all earnestness.

"It seems so mother," replied Margret Anne.

"Is this what you want child?" asked Frederick earnestly.

"I believe so father. I understand the great responsibilities and pressures as much as someone my age can perceive. Mostly, the greatest hardship will be being away from all of you and Kellynch Hall, that will be the difficult part," said Margret Anne taking a deep breath.

"Is there an understanding as yet?" asked Anne.

"Yes, but not in a public way but all seems a matter of time, the royal protocols are many, leaving a lot of navigation" responded Margret Anne.

The conversation was interrupted by Anne's tears as Margret Anne consoled her. "I will miss you, daughter. It was only yesterday I held you, and now you are about to enter the wider world. We are very proud of you," said Anne.

"Mother, father if this does come to the expected end I promise to visit often and invite you to town regularly as you are able. I will never live in such a way that you are left behind. I promise this. You will not lose me. I need the both of you. Rather you will gain a son and one day grandchildren," replied Margret Anne.

Princess Stephanie and Frederick II walked into the drawing room from the garden startled at the scene of tears. "Mother, what is it? How can I help you? What can I do?" asked Frederick II at once a powerful commander showing the love of a son for his mother.

"My dear these tears are of your growing up and how proud father and I are of you both. I fear there is nothing to be done with the growing up and as for being proud of you that is as it is too, and we are glad for it," explained Anne.

"Then at least let us all sit with you and endeavour to support you," replied Frederick II.

Fitzwilliam arrived describing his exploits in town and the successful conclusion to a number of transactions.

Princess Stephanie was in wonder at such a family. "They serve the crown so well and yet are so unaffected. They love openly, living in a quiet country rooted in the heart of this England, they are England in many ways," thought Princess Stephanie wishing the weight, and the burden of responsibility could be lighter for her parents, that they might have time for moments like this and for living but this is not to be for the empires monarchs.

At supper, Anne mentioned that tomorrow would bring some charity work and a tea to be held at Kellynch with guests to come. "Margret Anne would you assist me?" asked Anne.

"Of course mother," replied Margret Anne. Princess Stephanie, intrigued looked at Margret Anne in that way as to ask a question but without saying a word.

"Princess Stephanie would you like to be the honourary chair of our county charity committee?" asked Margret Anne.

Anne, surprised looked up.

"I would love to assist in any way if this would be acceptable to your mother?" responded Princess Stephanie enthusiastically.

"I have heard only good things about this charity work you have undertaken for these many years. My mother has taken a keen interest in your organisation, programs, and the handling of volunteers and those that are being served."

The rest of the supper all engaged in lively and amiable conversation about everything and nothing. Toasts were made and the evening flew by.

The morning hours of the next day were spent in preparation for the charity committee's arrival. "Today's goals are to settle on the year's activities to be undertaken," said Anne to Princess Stephanie.

Anne and Margret Anne, having done this for some years now, saw this day as a routine event. But Princess Stephanie was all alight with fervor and energy, as this was new to her. "What would you have of me Lady Anne, for the committee meeting?" asked Princess Stephanie.

Anne and Margret Anne sat with Princess Stephanie to detail all the planning activities and decisions to be made during the session. Princess Stephanie offered some new ideas that would be proposed and took note of ideas that were working. "My mother is chair of the charities committee for the empire and should know in more detail of your work. What you are doing here would be well received Lady Anne," commented Princess Stephanie.

"You asked what you may do, by being the honourary chairperson to the charity this will highlight support in a grand way," said Anne.

"Yes, it would be an honour. There are of course protocols that have to be followed to make this official, but I see no impediments. Thank you again for allowing me to lend a hand," replied Princess Stephanie.

"We must be sensitive to Princess Stephanie and her position in society and as a member of the royal family. Members of the charity committee may be overwhelmed with your person. So let us be gentle with these folk, some of whom will recognise Your Royal Highness. Others may not recognise you and are not high in society. Also, let us protect our Princess," said Anne to Margret Anne.

"I shall walk in first and begin an informal conversation," said Anne excusing herself.

As the final charity committee member arrived it was time to call the meeting to order. After some informal chit-chat, Princess Stephanie, not known by most, walked in with Margret Anne and remained in the background while working with Margret Anne on the final details for chairing the meeting.

Anne led the group into the study since they would not be disturbed there and Frederick would not mind. "Shall we bring this meeting of the charity committee to order ladies? We'll start with a prayer, God save the King, and then committee business," commented Anne. "I would like to nominate a honourary chairperson for our charity. May I introduce, our nominee, to you Her Royal Highness Princess Stephanie." There was a hush as all took a moment to take in the information and the gravity of the personage in their presence. Princess Stephanie took up the main chair at the head of the table, smiling, as the group bowed and curtsied.

"Please ladies, be at ease," encouraged Princess Stephanie.

"Do I have a second nomination?" asked Anne as Margret Anne quickly raised her hand with all others there following her lead. "Shall we put this to a vote then ladies? All in favour?" asked Anne.

It was unanimous the charity committee had its first honourary chairperson. "On to the next order of business… said Anne.

Nothing seemed to express the awe of the Princess's presence and the weight she brought to the meeting. When she realised her presence was overwhelming these kind and gentle folk, she spoke, in the gentlest of words "Please ladies it is an honour for me to assist you in any way that I can. I hear of your charity work and haven't until now had the opportunity to recognise the good works. Through my most fortunate connections with the

Wentworth, we can know of each other and me of you and the work you do. Thank you for having me. Be at ease."

With that, the members were all able to relax a little, which set the tone for the rest of the meeting. Motions were discussed, votes were taken, and issues were resolved. The conversation flowed easily. Suggestions and concerns were all taken up and addressed. The meeting flew by much more quickly than expected.

Anne and Margret Anne were unexpectedly surprised by Princess Stephanie's manner and caring nature toward all the women there. "She was so gracious to each member, spending time to talk with each, representing the power and majesty of the crown as well as its compassion for its subjects. She was interested and focused on concerns making suggestions and offering options. This is truly an extraordinary person," mentioned Margret Anne to her mother.

They thought they knew her well enough these last days but to their surprise, she had shown a great depth of caring and poise for the common person of which they were unaware. Margret Anne took special note of her gentle and kind ways while maintaining the status of Her Royal Highness Princess, a fine balance to be sure.

At one point Fitzwilliam was invited to enter the room and present a financial report and proposal. "With your permission Madam Chairman, ladies?" asked Fitzwilliam to a startled Princess Stephanie. "Please sir, proceed," replied Princess Stephanie.

"Ladies thank you for having me and congratulations to all of you for all the good you do. As some of you know, my role is to endeavour to raise funds for the charity. I connect funds and your charity work to the advantage of all. So I would like to present to your committee on behalf of the Wentworth Fund the sum of £3,000 for use as needed this year. We have an additional £50 donated by various families in the neighbourhood for this purpose as well. It is my hope that you will be able to assist those in the county in a way that makes a difference. Remember to consider each penny and how it may make a lasting difference. As well, you are not bound to spend all of it," announced Fitzwilliam to cheers and gasps at what could be done with such a sum. "Thank you, ladies," replied Fitzwilliam as he stood to take his leave.

Having settled all the business of the committee this day, the members complimented and thanked Anne and Margret Anne, and curtsied to Princess Stephanie for hosting them.

The committee presented a surprised Anne with special recognition of her work and sponsorship over the years. They provided a second award to Margret Anne, reading a true account of the results of the work of the charity committee. It was a touching moment as the women sat together sipping the last of the tea and finishing their sandwiches as all chatted about various folk they were able to lend assistance.

"It was voted that perhaps this year you would come to your charity ball in the village?" asked Mrs. Thrussell of Anne.

"This is my hope ladies. Perhaps we may invite Princess Stephanie?" replied Anne.

"I didn't realise the depth of experience you have in this area and the sure results you gain in helping to raise the human condition. I am truly honoured to know you," mentioned Princess Stephanie to Anne and Margret Anne.

"Thank you for your compliments" returned Anne and Margret Anne alike.

"If you are interested you may remain honourary chair of our committee. It would mean you attend meetings twice a year only. One meeting is light and just before the annual ball here at Kellynch. All the members would be happy for your participation. Would you think about it? Mind you, it is a country ball and not so sophisticated as that of a ball at the palace," remarked Anne.

"I do not need to think about it, I would be honoured. There are formalities of course since the crown does not lend its name readily, but I see no impediments," replied Princess Stephanie.

All the committee members and guests would be sure to have stories for family and friends these next days of the goings-on at the big house up the lane. As the final members bid their leave, Princess Stephanie asked Anne and Margret Anne how they came to start this charity work. Anne began with her stories of the great Lady Russell and her coming to the realisation of how little it took to help someone and quite by accident found joy in this. They became determined to organise assistance for the less fortunate in the village, asking Fitzwilliam for his financial genius to guide this aspect. At first, we started in the village, and then they expanded to the county, to finally grow to as it is today with sponsoring schools, apprenticeships, healthcare, housing, and more. "We are more a hand up not so much a handout," commented Anne.

"Many want to help but just need encouragement and organization. We provide the means," remarked Margret Anne.

"I see, absolutely brilliant work," replied Princess Stephanie.

"Margret Anne has been involved ever since she was able. Starting at about seven years old, doing at first the simplest of tasks in visiting the poor and later running sub-committee meetings focused on children's matters and women's health. Harriet, who helps with the charity, is acquainted with society but having fallen because of the loss of her husband, lives on the estate. "She is a dear school friend who has helped raise the children. Lady Russell and I were very much known in these parts for charity work. It has been a while since I recollected this, it seems like yesterday but there is quite a history now. It has been a blessing to help where one can," said Anne with a smile.

"A helping hand is a blessing," commented Princess Stephanie.

The men arrived to escort the women to the dining room. "Supper is served and each of you has worked so hard today on behalf of others can we now serve you the rest of the evening," said Frederick.

"That is kind of you Sir Frederick," replied Princess Stephanie with a smile.

This next day brought the arrival of Admiral Benwick and a discussion that would be important to Captain Wentworth in securing the second half of his naval career.

Still morning and with breakfast complete, Princess Stephanie took a short morning walk with Frederick II. Of course, her marine guards were also in attendance. It became their time and anyone in their right senses could see they were forming an attachment, with the benefit of both being refreshed and more amiable afterwards.

While Frederick II and Stephanie were out on their usual morning walk, Admiral Benwick had arrived.

"This is very good that Captain Wentworth is on a walk with his guest. It gives me a chance to catch up with my dear friends. How are you both?" asked Admiral Benwick.

"Very well thank you, James," responded Anne as she served tea.

"And you my friend?" asked Frederick.

"Very well, although the years are finally catching up, and I will not be too late behind you in my retirement ole friend," replied Benwick.

They talked about the days in town and those leading up to now. "It is commonly thought that your daughter will make the most fortunate match with Prince James," commented Admiral Benwick.

"Yes, it seems so, but there is no formal understanding or announcement as yet sir," replied Frederick.

"And I will miss her so," responded Anne.

"As you know, Captain Harville will be promoted to Admiral next month. A dispatch is to reach him today with the news. What happy news it will be. I wish I could see his face," said Admiral Benwick.

"I have sent my congratulations and of course will attend the promotion ceremony," commented Frederick.

Just then Captain Wentworth and Princess Stephanie walked into the room to the startled look on Admiral Benwick's face.

Anne and Frederick neglected to inform him that their guest was the Her Royal Highness Princess Stephanie.

"Your Royal Highness, please excuse me. It seems my dear hosts did not inform me of their guest" said Admiral Benwick with a shy smile jokingly. As he stood to bow, tea spilled down his coat due to his hurried actions.

"Admiral Benwick, please be at ease here. It is my pleasure, truly. May I have the pleasure of refilling your cup of tea?" asked Princess Stephanie.

"Yes, of course, Your Highness."

After a short round of conversation, Princess Stephanie took her leave of the party. Knowing the men must complete their business by suppertime, Anne decided to invite Admiral Benwick to dine with them this evening, as is her right.

Admirals Wentworth and Benwick engaged Captain Wentworth in a discussion that led to a number of agreements to participate in and lead at least three Admiralty committees.

"Captain Wentworth, considering your actions in the war, honoured by His Majesty and connection to Admiral Wentworth, you are very well respected throughout the navy. It was thought that your involvement in these key committees to be the next step in your already impressive career and would demonstrate great leadership and commitment to the Navy. I realise this may result in you having to leave other committees but that cannot be helped. Your father and I would be happy to guide your steps if you let us. The work done is considered first-rate and will not be wasted in the least," said Benwick.

"Thank you, sir, I am sensible of your proposal and welcome your advice and guidance along the way. Let this be settled then," replied Frederick II.

Both Admirals pledged to guide him as long as they were able. "It is in peacetime that preparations for war are made. When war is upon us, it is too late for the planning, it is the time to act," related Admiral Wentworth.

"True," added Admiral Benwick.

"It is my honour to follow in your footsteps. I am at full strength now as you can see and am playing my part willingly," replied Captain Wentworth.

"Good man!" reported Admiral Benwick.

"Let us then talk of your attachment here, " said Benwick, no longer acting in the official capacity of the Admiralty.

"Be open, we are all friends here," added James.

"Well, she is very impressive, well-mannered, intelligent, and beautiful. Not to mention well connected," said Frederick II.

"To be sure sir!" replied James.

"And there is love in this case?" asked Benwick.

"Yes, I believe so gentlemen," commented Frederick II.

A knock at the door and the ladies entered to announce supper and welcome James again to stay and dine with the family and guests. "How can I refuse to be in the company of such accomplished ladies!" remarked Benwick in his fun way of expressing such compliments as to be acceptable to the ladies in a harmless way.

Over the next few days, Princess Stephanie, having completed her fortnight stay at Kellynch Hall, returned to town and the palace. "Goodbye for now. I will write to you of my exploits in town," said Princess Stephanie.

"I look forward to your notes. I will find an excuse to visit the town in the next few weeks?" replied Frederick II, kissing Stephanie's hand and helping her into the carriage.

"I will write to your sister asking her to invite me again very soon," said Stephanie discreetly.

CHAPTER 10

Fitzwilliam

A month gone by…

"The Royal family is said to be visiting a cousin whose estate is just ten miles from Kellynch Hall. They are expected to stay a fortnight," said Frederick.

"How do you know this dear?" asked Anne.

"There is a notation in the weekly Admiralty letters. It said marines have been dispatched to the Claxton estate for a fortnight. There is only ever one reason for those orders," commented Frederick.

"Since they are in the neighbourhood expect an invitation any day now dear," exclaimed Frederick.

"Do the other children know of this?" commented Anne.

"No, not yet, let's wait until an invitation arrives before we tell them," said Frederick.

Later that day a royal courier arrived with an invitation to spend the day with the Royals at the Claxton Hall in two days. As expected, Margret Anne and Frederick II were excited upon hearing the news, but Anne worried about the ten-mile ride to Claxton and back.

"My dear, the roads are quite good between here and the Claxton Hall. This ride should be nothing, especially during these summer evenings. The weather has also been quite calm of late so this should be nothing on that account. I remember you crossing the wide sea to Spain and Italy without worry in that case. This should be nothing to that," commented Frederick.

"Well, you will be at my side, and that is what matters," replied Anne.

"Now, that's the spirit my Anne!" commented Frederick.

"Benwick will lunch with us today. We have to settle on final matters where Frederick II is concerned. We have refined our plans for his engagement with the Admiralty. Benwick and I will give him a good start and then retire from the service. It is a business for the young, and we are past our prime I'm afraid," said Frederick.

"Good morning mother, and father," said Fitzwilliam upon entering the dining room in search of breakfast.

"Good Morning Fitzwilliam," responded Anne.

"Father, remember the £10,000 you were so kind as to lend me for a business venture?" asked Fitzwilliam.

"Yes son, I do," responded Frederick.

"I would like to return it with interest. I have turned that ten thousand into one hundred thousand on your behalf," commented Fitzwilliam.

"Son, I am not so business-minded, as you know. It is the lot of the females in this society. Notwithstanding this fact would you explain this good fortune in lay terms?" asked Anne.

"Why of course Mother, before I asked Father for the funds I looked over a number of investment schemes that showed interesting returns. They were short-term in nature and of manageable risk. The investments turned out as expected and these were the returns allowing me to pay back the original loan with interest and leaving me seed money for my next investment opportunities," explained Fitzwilliam.

"Son, with all the work you have done with our family finances why not keep the investment in a safe bank account in reserve," commented Frederick.

"Are you sure father?" queried Fitzwilliam.

"Of course I am. We are in no danger of financial ruin thanks to you. Anne and I have all we want and live in moderation and economy," said Frederick.

"As you wish Father, but these funds are at the disposal of the family," replied Fitzwilliam.

"Son, I have been hearing quite a bit about your exploits in the business world. Many a gentleman in society is paying close attention to you in the matters of business and finance. Once thought to be a trade but no longer since it is a necessity," commented Frederick.

"Yes, true father, I get dispatches every day asking me to look over one investment or other on behalf of some lord or prominent person. It is becoming distracting since it takes time out from my efforts to increase our wealth and security in that way. However, on the other hand, it is always good to have connections of these types in society. Doors are opened where they were closed.

"Father, I have been tracking an investment opportunity that I believe will bring substantial returns, with little risk, and within a timeframe of eight months. I have a bit more work in research to do as yet. If this turns out to be real, shall I invest some of the money I am holding in reserve for you? Do I have your permission?" asked Fitzwilliam.

"You have a great talent in the way of a business son, and I honour your judgment. If you think this investment will return you have my permission to proceed. Son, what are these investments, specifically?" asked Frederick.

"Well father, as you know, the navy will be commissioning the building of almost an entirely new fleet of war vessels. Indications are, the news tells me, that inquiries have begun with a number of shipbuilders. Since this group is a limited number, and they will need cash to begin the efforts, I expect significant returns for the initial investors. It is safe because it will be backed by the government, leaving only work to be done on the style and honour of the management of the companies," explained Fitzwilliam.

"Yes, I see. You are correct. It was supposed to be a secret, but it is true, inquiries are being made at this time. It is not so visible an opportunity until you explain it, then it makes perfect sense and is obvious. You do have a way of seeing these things ahead of most. You will be very successful Fitzwilliam," commented Frederick.

"I invest in businesses that need capital to grow to the next step. It is safe since the business is the collateral, I can measure the need and understand the management team. At this, I can make a decision based on market and demand and risk to me, quite simple and complicated all at once really.

"The growth of the business community increases opportunities for people to work and raise the standards of living. Not everyone is born into wealth and privilege so many must work to live. My investments return to the investor, support the growth of the business, and secure a standard of living in the empire," commented Fitzwilliam.

"Remarkable," commented Frederick.

"It makes me proud to know Mother and I have part of your life," said Frederick.

"Yes father, you and mother are a very great influence in my life, and I am grateful to the both of you, and of course Margret Anne and Frederick II," replied Fitzwilliam.

Changing the subject, "What of this business with the royals? It seems they will have my brother and sister," commented Fitzwilliam.

Just then Margret Anne and Frederick II strolled into the dining room; "Who will take your brother and sister?" asked Frederick II.

"I can't help but notice Prince James' and Princess Stephanie's interest in the both of you. If this interest takes its course, I see changes for the Wentworths," commented Fitzwilliam.

"Brother, I see things differently. You will gain a brother and perhaps a sister if things run their course. Yes, that would mean some changes, but we are bound, the three of us," replied Frederick II as Anne and Frederick listened intently but did not interfere.

"Fitzwilliam, we will never be so far apart as to ever be strangers," added Margret Anne.

"I do hope so, life would indeed be a lonely place for me without the both of you," commented Fitzwilliam.

Admiral Benwick arrived at Kellynch Hall and would be staying for dinner. First, he and Frederick would conclude their naval business with Frederick II. Louisa came along to visit unexpectedly and was very much welcomed. She spent time with Anne catching up on all the goings-on in the Benwick household and at Uppercross.

Margret Anne, a great friend of Louisa, listened to the conversation intently, commenting only sparingly so as not to interrupt the flow of news yet displaying her interest in events. Fitzwilliam had a number of dispatches to attend to. He spent most of the morning writing business correspondence at the desk in the drawing room.

Louisa turned to Fitzwilliam to comment, "Fitzwilliam. I hear from the men folk how able you are in business investments and was wondering if you would advise us on matters in this way?" asked Louisa.

"What are the concerns that bring up this question dear cousin?" responded Fitzwilliam.

"I am one for economy and moderation, as you know. However, the expense of keeping a house, servants, a ball once or twice a year, trips to Bath, and children can be quite a drain. With Admiral Benwick's pending retirement, we have a lot to consider," commented Louisa.

"Yes, I see. I would have to talk to James as well, but, yes of course, I would be happy to look at your circumstance and advise you as I see it and suggest the best course," replied Fitzwilliam.

"James and I discussed this but were not sure if you had time to speak with us and advise us on these matters. I am very glad and grateful for your consent," commented Louisa.

"You're welcome, I will always have time for the Benwicks. I will speak with your Admiral later this evening if you would like. I can gather some facts and perhaps I may review your current finances. I can devise a plan that would present growth with little risk to your fortune," said Fitzwilliam.

"Thank you Fitzwilliam, you are very kind. We are not destitute mind you, but we should know our limits and course to take. Your reputation for good business is quite renowned. The advantage is you're in the family. Thank you," expressed Louisa sincerely.

"Not at all cousin, if I can help, I will," responded Fitzwilliam returning to his dispatches.

All the while both Anne and Margret Anne carefully watched the proceedings. Anne was just gaining an understanding of Fitzwilliam's skill and reputation in the business world. She could now see Fitzwilliam separated and individual in his own right to that of his older twins. Margret Anne was so proud of Fitzwilliam. Even though his manner and dress were to that of Sir Walter, he had a genuine kindness and generosity that were endearing.

"My brother is growing up," she commented to Anne and Louisa.

"Indeed," responded Anne.

Fitzwilliam focused on his correspondence, not missing the comment altogether.

"Yes, indeed," commented Louisa.

Frederick, James, and Frederick II came strolling into the room sooner than expected but that was just perception. Time had flown by so quickly the afternoon had passed. Tea was served and soon all were for supper. James thanked Fitzwilliam for his offer to look at the family's finances, and advice as to course and investment. They scheduled a date certain to chat about the matter.

"It seems we are finding out more about our son's prowess in business matters of late," commented Frederick.

James mentioned he was off to visit the Lions tomorrow at the invitation of His Majesty. "And so are we. Shall we travel together?" asked Anne to Louisa.

"That would be lovely. What do you think James?" asked Louisa. "Fine idea dear" replied James.

"Then this is settled," commented Frederick.

The evening ended with all in high spirits.

The next morning, the dawn was upon them all before they knew it. "Frederick, are you awake?"

"Yes dear, what it is?" responded Frederick.

"Fitzwilliam is so changed in my eyes these last days," said Anne

"Yes, also in mine. I thought he lived a quiet life but his business prowess is catching a lot of attention. I have neglected to mention to you the dispatches I have received from many a personage of late thanking me for Fitzwilliam's time and advice in matters of finance. He is becoming renowned for this expertise. I did mention to Fritz my admiration of his skill in this area," commented Frederick

"Each of our children has their way and is excellent at some endeavour. What more can one ask for?" asked Anne as Frederick lay quiet.

"Soon they will be living their own lives. I hope they will not forget us. How we will miss them," said Anne.

"Dear, they are as much a part of us. We are them and they… are us. The children will always need us and each other. Let us not have any more of this, let us be grateful, enjoy each day together, and enjoy each other. We have known since the beginning children are on loan. Tomorrow will come and we will face its pain and pleasures," added Frederick.

Everyone was in high spirits at an early breakfast that morning.

"It is a privilege to receive an invitation from the Royal family, especially when they are on holiday," said Anne.

"This is a rare and special invitation indeed," returned Margret Anne.

"In the morning hours the men will go shooting with the King and Prince," said Frederick II.

"It is my understanding, that the women will take tea and a tour of the Hall, learning of its historic secrets," commented Anne.

"It will be best to leave shortly after breakfast so as not to be late. We wait on the royals by all means," commented Anne.

"You see the Benwicks have arrived," commented Frederick.

The rest of breakfast was a blur with everyone in a world of conversations of the day's events in anticipation. The Wentworth carriage arrived at the front, and all was readied for their departure. Along the way, Anne, Margret Anne, and Louisa chatted about the Prince and his intentions of late.

"He pays you special attention," commented Louisa.

"Yes, he pays me special attention," commented Margret Anne.

"The Prince will have to declare himself soon as is only right," commented Anne.

"Do you expect otherwise Margret Anne?" asked Louisa

"No, but these circumstances are quite unusual considering this is the royal family. All is done carefully and at a pace that is all their own, requiring patience," responded Margret Anne.

Frederick, James, Frederick II, and Fitzwilliam, riding in the second carriage, conversed about what interests men.

"Now that we have set the war to right let us move on to the state of government and attend some changes there," said Frederick II.

"I think the empire would do well to slow its growth of conquests and solidify the empire," commented James.

"Consolidation is always a good strategy. It lends itself to the fixing of all manner of social ills. What say you Fitzwilliam?" asked Frederick.

"Well gentlemen, it is true, consolidation is good in this way of the fixing of social ills and trade between the partners, but there is a balance that can be struck between the growth of the empire and the attending to the needs of the societies therein, whereas England should consider all our options and select the best of paths for supporting the Empire and her people," said Fitzwilliam as everyone listened to his breathtaking perspective.

"So, you say there are more options to investigate on the subject of growth and maintenance of our empire?" asked James.

"Yes sir, but this development of options will require some broadmindedness in the gathering of truthful and trusted information where decisions may be made using common sense and care. Many times the doing of what is right is not always easy on the popularity," replied Fitzwilliam.

This morning was heavy with mist and fog moving in. One could only see a few yards in front of the carriages so extra lamps were lit so those on or near the road could take notice of the caravan of two carriages and horses. Traveling was likened to that of traveling through a cloud. It created a muffled quiet, bringing one a sense of serenity.

As the carriage whisked along the Kings Highway one could see the faint hint of rooftops and church steeples in the small villages, and farmhouses along the way. After an extended period of countryside and road a great house there. Visions of Camelot came to mind at the approach to the Claxton Hall estate. Just there on the hill half above the mist, one could see the ancient turrets of a time-long paste and the Royal standard flying proudly in the upper breezes announcing the royal presence.

Quietly slowing almost with reverence the horses pulled the carriage along the lane toward the main house. They could now see marines and palace guards in the woods along the way and at the front door watching their approach. Arriving at the entrance to Claxton Hall, servants waited outside in preparation to assist the guest. When the carriages stopped the servants jumped into action by opening carriage doors and greeting the group with much ceremony and care.

"Miss Margret Anne, Sir Frederick, Mrs. Anne, Sir Frederick II, Admiral Benwick, Mrs. Louisa, and Mr. Fitzwilliam, His Majesties are waiting on you in the drawing room, having just now finished breakfast. I would be honoured to escort you. This way please," pointed Prince James in a relaxed tone.

Marine guards at the entrance snapped to attention as required in the presence of His Royal Highness and the company's rank demanded. Anne, surprised was reminded of the high rank her husband and son held in His Majesty's Service. Louisa was relieved to have the addition of the Wentworths in greeting the Royals since she was not used to such company.

Louisa was quite grown up now but still had that child-like excitement for those special occasions. She was always close to Anne and shared that connection with Margret Anne. As a result, Louise walked closely with Anne and Margret Anne.

"Quite a charming day with all this mist about, it reminds me of being at sea," said James to Frederick and Frederick II.

"Hunting should be very interesting. All of us navy can find our prey while the others will not be able to see a thing through the pea soup. Let us be resolved to be safe and aware of those carrying shot and not knowing how to act in this condition," responded Frederick.

"Well the company of his Majesties, who are able in these conditions, but let us be mindful as well of those that are not so able in these conditions. Pray let us not keep them waiting much longer," declared James smiling, as a servant led the way.

Claxton Hall was one of the old estates. The old estates were built to defend against long sieges and had battlements as a matter of course in the architectural design and positioning along critical passes. Inside were unusual artifacts dating back to the time of Uther, the Pendragon, and even before the Roman occupation. Tapestries hung from the walls depicting historical events mostly forgotten by most. Suits of armour lined some halls, and spears and swords of a bygone era were displayed. In a corridor or two, against intricately carved wood, paneled archways with painted images of history one-noticed carvings depicting the beginnings of England faintly visible in the soft candlelight. One could not help but see the priceless value of this place, a museum in many ways.

"The women would have much to talk about with their exploration and touring of the estate house. Like a history book, they will turn each leaf discovering perhaps forgotten moments that made the difference on the path to empire and the current day," said Anne to Margret Anne.

"Truly Mother," acknowledged Margret Anne.

Even with the burden of history, the home seemed light and full of life. "Some old estates are so dead and gloomy," remarked Louisa

"But this home seems so full of light, richly adorned but not heavy in atmosphere," commented Margret Anne.

"It is a precious jewel in the pages of England, and it will be wonderful to discover some of its secrets this day," commented Anne

Prince James, Sir Frederick, and Admiral Benwick leading the women, came to a stop as the escorting servant paused to knock. Receiving a signal, they announced each visitor before entry to the occupants therein, "Sir Frederick and Mrs. Wentworth..., Sir Frederick II, the Honourable Miss Wentworth...The Admiral and Mrs. Benwick, the Honourable Mr. Fitzwilliam Wentworth."

"Please be welcome here," announced the King, as the Queen moved to greet the women and take them to her corner of the room for tea, refreshments, and conversation. His Majesty greeted the men, offering refreshments and introducing guests who were staying at the Hall and had arrived previously.

All was relaxed, as the crown was in the cupboard, and the Royals were on holiday. The only reminder of the royal power was when a courier escorted by royal marines arrived in the room to present the King with seemingly important dispatches of Empire business. The King, whose demeanour changed in a flash to that of the Monarch of the Realms where he quickly wrote several notes in response to urgent dispatches, sealed them with wax and impressions of his ring then placed his correspondence into a royal crested pouch and quietly instructed the courier with delivery instructions.

As soon as the courier left the room, the King's demeanour changed to that of smiles and relaxation again. "Gentlemen, even in the relaxation I must often deal with the business of the Empire, be at ease," commented the King.

"Not at all father, we are at your pleasure here," replied Prince James smiling in support.

Conversation was amiable as the royal family, very experienced in these arts comfortably guided the gathering. "Sir Frederick I see your son is taking up the responsibilities at the Admiralty. I hear good things of him, of his dedication and application of his skill to the crown," said the King.

"Admiral Benwick and I are guiding him while we can, your Majesty," responded Sir Frederick with Benwick at his side in agreement.

"Sir Frederick, I see my daughter Stephanie has paid special attention to your son. I give my leave for them to court with your approval of course. Even now they talk privately of who knows what young people have to say," remarked the King as Sir Frederick nodded in recognition but without saying a word.

Prince James and Margret Anne were in animated conversation in a quiet corner of the room, visible to all yet private in overhearing. They hadn't seen each other in a few weeks and were obviously catching up on all topics not mentioned in the many letters they wrote to each other.

Her Majesty's group, which included Anne, Louisa, and others talked of touring the house, discovering its secrets, and learning some of the old history of England's beginnings. "This should be a profitable day for the mind ladies. This hall is one of several quiet and protected places used to store much of our realm's history," said Her Majesty.

"I have never known of this estate or its treasures before this..." commented Anne.

"This would be true. The estate is closely protected because of its place in the history of this island. One day it will be open to the public, in a way as to preserve its value and charm and also its treasure of records of past deeds and artifacts. For now, though it is under the direct protection of the crown. In our tour, you will see why," responded the Queen.

Lady Hamish approached the group, begging Her Majesty's leave as she curtsied, which was granted, "I would like to introduce to you Lady Hamish. She will be our guide, giving us many of the points of interest and legend of this ancient estate and what it contains."

"It would be my honour to guide you today," said Lady Hamish as all made room and welcomed her.

One could hear the dogs and horses assembled at the side of the house in preparation for the hunt. The men gave their leave, so they could change cloth to that of hunting attire. In a matter of half an hour, the entire party of men was outside selecting horses and shooting for the hunt. Quickly, they were off and into the thick mist, not to be seen for the next few hours.

"Finally, quiet! Shall we have our guided tour ladies?" announced the Queen.

"Yes please," replied Louisa forgetting, her place to smiles at Her Majesty and the ladies present.

"This way ladies," guided Lady Hamish, arriving at what seemed an older part of the house to begin the tour. "Around 1010, to the best of our knowledge, this part of the house was the only standing structure, notice the stonework so unique for its day...," described Lady Hamish as the tour sped along in between pauses and descriptions of paintings, artifacts, and carvings, leaving enough time for the group to satisfy all their questions.

The men, at the hunt, galloped overhill and through wood but to no avail. The fog was thicker now than early morning. The challenge soon came in finding one's way and staying with the group. At one point the guide led the party to the outskirts of the local village. He loses his way but quickly regains his bearings. Sir Frederick, Admiral Benwick, and Frederick II, used to these conditions at sea, discreetly instructed the guide as to direction and time. It didn't go unnoticed by His Majesty's, both grateful for the assistance rendered.

The guide mentioned a wood, if it were clear could be seen to the southeast of the house at about two miles where game was plenty but in the thick mist making it impossible to see and get his bearings. Only after asking, Sir Frederick and Admiral Benwick took up the challenge to assist the poor guide in a way they could salvage the hunt by the lending their skill well-honed in the service of His Majesty. Both men agreed and announced to the party they would "guide the guide" using superior naval skill and an accurate compass, in the fog, gained through years of experience.

After a good laugh, the party lightened up and made their way to the woods for a truly interesting hunt. It was also agreed that no one was to shoot unless all were accounted for and out of the way so as not to have any accidents that day. Fitzwilliam remained close to his brother. Being inexperienced in this endeavour, and with the fog, making him more unsure, "Have no worries, brother you are with me," said Frederick II in the calmest of voices. He kept his gun unloaded so as not to cause an accident but vowed to learn to become an expert shooter one day soon and try this sport again in better conditions.

The women made good progress through areas of the house, gaining a great appreciation as to why the crown granted its protection of this estate.

"This estate is such a treasure, Your Majesty," remarked Anne.

"This day call me Mary dear Anne," replied the Queen.

"Yes your Majesty," replied Anne smiling.

"It is not so much the value in gold and silver as it is the value in history and remembering," commented Anne.

"Yes, Anne and there are several of these estates quietly protected and kept quite out of the way and those that would take and spoil these priceless places," remarked Mary.

It was lunch and the women were escorted to the dining room for tea and a meal. Each talked in turn about the surprises they encountered on the tour thus far. The group of women enjoyed lunch with easy conversation and a secret longing to get back to their investigation of English history. As lunch concluded Lady Hamish announced a continuation of the tour of the house after all the women were refreshed and ready.

The men, reaching the wood in good time and with a grateful guide, proceeded to use the dogs to flush out their prey. Of course all refrained from shooting, allowing His Majesty to bag a number of birds for supper that evening.

Frederick found the opportunity to bag a bird but Frederick II made what seemed a lucky shot and bagged two birds with one shot, becoming the talk of the hunt.

"Frederick II, now tell us again, was it a lucky shot or were you intending to bag both birds with one shot?" asked his friend Prince James.

"I can see I shouldn't say and leave it at that," replied Frederick II.

They were all smiles on the way back to Claxton Hall with supper in hand and honour upheld. The mist was as thick as ever and Sir Frederick, Admiral Benwick, and Sir Frederick II, to the guide's delight, pointed the party safely back to the Hall and led the way.

Entering the hall as conquering heroes, the women were nowhere to be found. His Majesty commented, "Where are our woman folk?"

A servant responded to the King's inquiry, "On the tour of the house your Majesty,"

"Her Majesty and guests, I believe, are at the south corner of the premises," said another servant.

"Well, then gentlemen let us be at ease here until their return. Shall we have refreshments?" remarked Prince James as servants gathered all the birds in preparation for the evening's supper.

The women returned with Lady Hamish leading the way after about an hour. The men standing bowed, as is customary, at their entry, save the King, who received all the courtesies due his office but paid careful attention to his Mary.

"Gentlemen, will you not relate your adventures to your ladies?" asked the Queen.

"Of course my dear, we were lost in the fog and ended up on the outskirts of the local village.

Sir Frederick, Admiral Benwick, and Sir Frederick II pitied the poor guide, using superior naval skill in the pea soup fog, and guided us to the wood where we bagged enough birds for the evening's supper. Sir Frederick II made a singular shot bagging two birds but won't tell if it was luck or skill! We decided it was skill and left it at that. With honour upheld we left it at that and returned to the hall," related the King.

"Will not the woman relate their day's adventures on the house tour?" asked Prince James.

The women recounted their adventures through the house, the history discovered, and the many interesting artifacts they came upon. One recollection talked of Avalon and the lady of the lake.

"Dear there are some artifacts of the time and place I would like to show you before we are gone from this place and back in town," mentioned Her Majesty to her husband.

"Hmmm…, this is a very interesting topic for me, as you know, I have a passion for the Empire's history," remarked the King.

Tea was served as the party broke into groups and talked about the many moments of the day. Prince James and Margret

Anne, Princess Stephanie, and Sir Frederick II coupled while Anne, Lady Hamish, and the Queen talked of their children, the war, and much of her charity work. Her Majesty, focusing on the charity works and guiding the conversation, finally asked Anne if she would be interested in an honourary position with the Royal Charity Trust, chaired by Her Majesty herself. Anne was surprised, and accepted the offer.

"We meet four times a year at the palace to discuss issues, decide on sponsorships for the year, and set agendas for discussion with members of Parliament," said Her Majesty.

His Majesty, sitting with Sir Frederick and Admiral Benwick, asked about Fitzwilliam. "It is my understanding your son is a very skilled businessman in finance?" queried the King.

"It seems so Your Majesty," replied Sir Frederick.

"You sound surprised," commented the King.

"Anne and I can see ourselves in the twins but Fitzwilliam blazes his trails with a bit of us in him, his grandfather Sir Walter in manners and a great skill for business that we cannot quite account for," said Frederick.

"I believe Anne has it right. Sir Frederick, I wanted to gain your opinion on my considering Fitzwilliam for a post in the government, focusing on growing our commerce and business base throughout the empire. Many of the Lords and Ladies have commented over a period of time about his singular ability to see an opportunity where most see nothing or have seen no hope of recovery. He could help so many people on behalf of the Crown. What do you think sir?" asked the King of Frederick.

"I think he would accept, let us ask him. Shall I motion for him sir?" asked Sir Frederick.

"Yes, no time like the present," replied His Majesty.

Frederick motioned to Fitzwilliam to approach and sit with them. Arriving, he performed the courtesies required of any in the presence of his King.

"Please sit Fitzwilliam and be at ease here," commented the King. "Fitzwilliam, I have come to understand much about your talents with finance and business. Many a Lord and Lady have commented on your excellent abilities in this area. However, more your generous spirit and helpfulness," said His Majesty.

"Thank you sir for the compliment. What is this all about?" asked Fitzwilliam.

"I wanted to offer you an opportunity to serve the people, the Empire, and your King. After speaking with your father about this first, the Empire requires that her people have opportunities to make a living and raise a family to a standard that reflects the decency the Crown expects. To accomplish this, we realise we must stabilise and grow our commerce base. The economy is a complex and heady topic. You seem to grasp this discipline more than most. I have secured the most proven business leaders and politicians in the land. It is a very small group to be sure. You are the last, but not least, of those I wish to secure for this work. The goal would be to raise the standard of living, education, and opportunities for our citizens not only here in Britain but around the Empire through smart and common-sense economic planning. This special group would propose not only programs but also a means to self-sustaining living through ventures of sensible financial planning and approaches. That is where you come in Fitzwilliam, your instincts are first-rate in this area. Would you accept this offer and join this team?" asked the King.

There was silence for a moment as all could see Fitzwilliam deep in thought, considering his options. Snapping out of it he looked up, smiled, and accepted the opportunity.

"Good man!" said Prince James with a smile and a great nod from His Majesty.

The royal family withdrew to get ready for supper, as all the guests were provided rooms to refresh themselves before the evening dining. As each group was ready they went to the drawing rooms to meet with others attending the supper party.

Sir Frederick and Anne walked into the drawing rooms. Prince James approached them for a private word. They entered a side room to the drawing rooms and sat by a fire.

"How may I help you Prince James?" asked Frederick as Anne looked on.

"Sir, I have this night proposed to your daughter, and she has accepted me. I would like to ask for your blessings and permission to make the announcement tonight," said Prince James.

"Are you certain about my daughter sir?" asked Sir Frederick.

"Yes sir, very sure indeed, I will honour and keep her always," remarked Prince James.

"Do your parents know? And are they accepting of this offer of marriage?" asked Anne.

"Yes, Lady Anne, they know and give their approval with all their hearts," replied Prince James.

"Then sir you have our blessings and congratulations. If I could make one request, would you and our daughter not be strangers to Kellynch Hall? Anne and I have found it hard with the children growing and moving away. At our stage of life, what is there to live for but our children," said Frederick.

"Of course sir, Margret Anne has expressed the same sentiments. And I love the place of Kellynch Hall and its quiet. It shall be so as much as we are able," commented the Prince as they walked out of the side room together.

Anne and Frederick found Margret Anne and sat with her. "I take it, you know of the offer made to me?" asked Margret Anne.

"Yes," replied Frederick holding Anne's hand. "I have given our consent and also asked that you not be such a stranger to us once you are married. It was agreed."

"Are you sure Margret Anne, your life will change completely?" queried Anne.

"I am sure," replied Margret Anne.

Anne looked at her daughter with such eyes that only a mother may bestow on a daughter "What is it mother?" asked Margret Anne.

"I remember the moment of your birth, holding you for the first time…and now you are a young lady engaged to the Heir to the throne of England. I could not have imagined such a life for you. But here we are, you are about to embark on one of life's greatest journeys through the most precious of promises that can be made. I wish you happy dear child," exclaimed Anne.

"It would be a good idea to tell Fitzwilliam and Frederick II," remarked Frederick calling each to their side.

"You may give Margret Anne your congratulations," commented Anne to her boys.

"Margret Anne, do you have some news?" asked Frederick II.

"Yes, I was made an offer this day by Prince James and have accepted him. Father and mother have given their consent, and His and Her Majesty have given their blessing," said Margret Anne to a deep hug from Frederick II and Fitzwilliam both at her side now.

After Frederick and Fitzwilliam gave their heartfelt congratulations and wishes for every happiness, they walked together to the dining room, wondering what else the evening would make of this moment. Other guests and the royals were just present so no time was lost to getting to the meal.

Supper began as expected in society of this type. All was punctual and formed in the serving and eating. During the dinner with all at ease, the King stood to propose a toast. "I would like to propose a toast to a young couple who have only just announced their engagement. To the honourable Miss Margret Anne Wentworth and our son Prince James."

Everyone lifted their glasses to the couple, wishing them all happy. The guests knew this was a special moment because no one outside this room knew of these latest of events. Furthermore, they were the first to be introduced to the future Queen of England.

"The announcement will be posted at the palace gates in the morning," said the King.

Supper had ended and the Wentworths and the Berwick's bid their goodbyes for now. Louisa and James left first in their carriage, then the Wentworths to theirs. Halfway home they were wondering if this day was a dream or real. Anne and Margret Anne talked of all to be done and noticed a marine guard on horseback at the side of the carriage.

The fog had lifted and the sky was clear this evening. Anne and Frederick held hands like newlyweds do. Anne related the offer Her Majesty made to join the charity committee and Fitzwilliam related the King's offer to attend his economic committee.

"Looks like we will be bound to the royal family," commented Anne.

"We have always been bound to King and country my dear," replied Frederick as they arrived at Kellynch Hall.

There were marine guards at the gates of Kellynch Hall with a small group of men standing at the side. It was too dark to tell who the group of men were. As the carriage came to a stop two marine guards were standing at the front door and another two patrolling the grounds as if this was a normal routine.

The marines, noticing Admiral and Captain Wentworth, snapped to attention and saluted him. "Who is in command here?" asked Admiral Wentworth.

"I am in charge Sir," replied a marine guard stepping forward.

"What is all this?" asked Admiral Wentworth. "His Majesty announced the engagement of His Royal Highness Prince James to the Honourable Miss Margret Anne Wentworth. She is now under the protection of the crown sir," replied the Guard.

"I see, Carry on then," commanded Admiral Wentworth.

"And that group of men at the gates?" asked Captain Wentworth.

"They are from the London Times and other papers sir," explained the guard.

We shall have the house servant attend to your needs for food, drink, and shelter," commented Admiral Wentworth.

"Thank you, sir," replied the guard.

"We will have to get used to this dear. It comes with the role," commented Frederick to Margret Anne, and Anne.

"With great privilege comes greater responsibility," said Anne.

"Let us have a cup of tea before bed. These times of a quiet Kellynch are coming to an end," remarked Fitzwilliam.

The next day the Wentworths decided to spend the day together after Anne and Margret Anne's charity committee meeting scheduled for the morning hours.

"Let us all meet in the drawing room at 1:00 pm and take a walk up the lane together, come back for afternoon tea, and dine at home tonight to the quiet," announced Frederick at breakfast.

Anne and Margret Anne met with Harriet, who was organising the charity meeting. Harriet, Anne, and Margret Anne went through the agenda of topics to be discussed and decisions to be made. They remembered the days when this effort was a small affair and a walk to the village, and a meeting over a cup of tea would do the trick. Today, this effort requires management and insight into needs so that funds and resources are best used to the benefit of those in need.

"And soon, I will no longer be able to participate in this endeavor," thought Margret Anne with melancholy.

"Harriet, the Queen has asked me to join her charity committee. They meet four times a year to consider the needs of the whole of the Empire," commented Anne.

"Mother! You mentioned this on the carriage ride home, only now do I realise the honour here. Congratulations!" replied Margret Anne.

"This is a very great honour, Anne, congratulations!" remarked Harriet.

"My goal is not to be a bull in a china shop, but I will bring a little of our knack for getting real results with limited resources to the table. I will not give up our charity work here. This offer is just additional," said Anne.

With all ready, the first charity committee guests arrived at Kellynch Hall for the morning's meetings.

"The charity meetings went well, and all were satisfied that the business needing to be addressed was addressed," said Margret Anne as the meeting was concluded with all the resolutions being modified that were needed and passed so the work may continue.

"Finally, we are all here. Are we ready for our family walk?" exclaimed Frederick

"Shall we go dear?" replied Anne.

"Yes, dear we are ready," replied Frederick.

The day started with rain but by afternoon the sun was out and all looked to be a pleasant day. As they walked along, Fitzwilliam commented on the marine guards in front and behind by some yards.

"Not interfering but able to lend assistance should it be needed. See sister what you have done!" commented Frederick II.

They all laughed at the turn of events, so unexpected.

"I could not have imagined this when we were but young children playing in the neighbourhood. We are at the stage where we will find our own way in the world but let us not be strangers in the rush into life make time where the family may reassemble a few times a year, so we may remember our beginnings and celebrate the love we have for each other. What say you all?" asked Anne.

All agreed and promised to reconnect at Kellynch Hall a few times a year as Anne held tightly to Frederick.

The evening's dining was as old times. The humour and goodwill were back in force as if the realisation of the coming changes would not present challenges to this close unit.

"A toast, to the Wentworths, let us never forget our beginnings and the love we have for each other, and for coming together as often as we can here in this place," proposed Frederick II. They all sipped from their wine glasses with this fervent hope.

There was a knock at the door and within a few moments, a servant announced the Musgroves, Mary and Charles, James and Louisa Benwick, and Henrietta and Charles Hayter. At almost the same moment the guests were standing in the dining room.

James remarked "Ah Frederick, Anne, we were in the neighbourhood and chanced to visit with you and family since we are family. I do hope this is not inconvenient for you?"

"No, not at all, you are always welcome here. Please do come in and make yourselves comfortable! Will you all supper with us?" asked Frederick.

"We are half-starved and since I have been ill the surgeon said the only cure for me is to eat regularly, I am quite ill you know," said Mary as servants rushed to place table settings, and the kitchen scurried to provide additional food for the newly arrived guests.

Anne organised the housekeeper and kitchen staff to ensure all would be acceptable, and they could provide a meal in quick order. Returning, "Tea will be brought out and meats and bread and all good things in just a moment."

"Please sit," announced Frederick as he called for more food and drink.

The conversation was amiable as everyone assumed their roles and enjoyed each other's company. Mary was on about her recent illnesses; Louisa and Benwick on eyeing a new property upon James' retirement. There were questions about the marine guards now stationed on the estate and Margret Anne's wedding plans to Prince James, himself being speculated but not officially announced through the palace as yet.

There was even time to discuss Anne's appointment to the Queen's charity committee and Fitzwilliam's appointment to the King's Royal Commerce Committee. The Musgroves were sufficiently impressed although Anne and Fitzwilliam never sought approvals.

"It seems I will be the one left home after I retire! I shall have to take up the gardening I suppose," exclaimed Frederick to rousing laughter.

The evening concluded with the lateness of the hour and the guests boarding carriages back to Uppercross and other neighbourhood estates.

"Good evening and thank you for the visit," said Anne.

The next day, a royal dispatch arrived from the palace summoning Margret Anne for wedding planning. The courier, Prince James, would escort Margret Anne to town and the palace.

"It was a good excuse to abandon state business, however, brief, and visit Margret Anne and this wonderful place of Kellynch Hall. It seems to have the power to help me catch my breath, and so I am glad for the short time I can spend here," remarked the Prince to Sir Frederick.

"Mother, I will have to go to town for a week. I will be staying at the palace working on the state wedding," commented Margret Anne as Frederick and Prince James entered the room. "There is much to do," added Margret Anne excitedly.

"Mrs. Anne, I have a personal note from my mother to you," said the Prince James handing Margret Anne the sealed note.

"Fitzwilliam I have a note for you from the Lord Chamberlin on behalf of my father."

As Anne read the short note, "It looks like I will be going to town with Margret Anne to attend my first charity committee meeting at the palace this coming week," exclaimed Anne.

"And I shall accompany the woman, father," responded Fitzwilliam to Frederick, as I will be introduced to the Lord Chamberlin on behalf of the King.

"Prince, you have taken both my women!" said Frederick with a smile

"Sir they will be under the protection of the crown, and I will personally escort them back to Kellynch safely at weeks' end, upon my word sir," replied James.

"Fitzwilliam may have to spend a fortnight at his duties for the crown though," replied Prince James.

"This will not be a problem, Prince James. I will be honoured," commented Fitzwilliam.

"When shall we leave for town James?" asked Margret Anne, the only one to call him by his Christian name.

"Tomorrow morning I am afraid," replied Prince James.

"Then sir if you will excuse, mother and I have much to do if we expect to also dine with you this evening," commented Margret Anne as she and Anne gave their leave.

The supper was very enjoyable. The royals certainly knew how to socialise and make all feel at ease. A note was sent earlier in the evening to the Musgroves, Mary and Charles as well as the Admiral and Mrs. Benwick and the Hayters since they were in the neighbourhood. It seemed only proper to extend an invitation to dine with Prince James and the Wentworths.

The next morning all was in readiness for the departure of Anne, Margret Anne, and Fitzwilliam to town.

"The navy men will be left to their own devices," said Anne to Margret Anne.

"Yes, I see mother. Upon our return, we expect Kellynch Hall to be as intact as it is now and for each of you to still have all ten fingers and toes. So mind you well father, brother, and take good care," exclaimed Margret Anne with a sly smile.

"Like mother like daughter, " exclaimed Anne smiling, but she never liked leaving Frederick's side.

Traveling to the royal palace was easier now. This was a trip on familiar and well-constructed roads. In addition, the security of being under the protection of a marine guard and having their assistance on hand if needed couldn't but help one's courage with the travel thought Margret Anne. Anne though, of a different notion, was always agreeable to staying on at Kellynch Hall with her husband and family, charity work, and the infrequent trip to the local village colouring the scope of her daily life.

"I can bear this travel to town four times a year as long as I can see some good in the charity work. Let us be patient…" thought Anne.

Fitzwilliam worked on business matters the length of the trip, only looking up to comment occasionally. Margret Anne and Anne chatted back and forth about the week's adventures to come. The carriage finally slowed as it arrived at the palace gates.

CHAPTER 11

Royal Events

As expected, the Wentworths were greeted and quickly conveyed to their guest apartments in the palace where they refreshed themselves after the long trip. There was a knock at the door and a servant announced the entry of Lady Elton. With all the courtesies performed, tea was brought in as Lady Elton talked of her mission.

Addressing Margret Anne, "I am here to help with planning the wedding. As you can imagine this will take a staff of people, and they have begun the work. There are the royal protocols, deciding on your Royal title. I believe it will be Her Royal Highness the Princess Margret, then the church to be selected. You have a choice of St Paul's or Westminster Abbey, even Windsor Castle is a possibility but not likely in this case. There is the invitee list of dignitaries, family, lords, and ladies, and the people who want to see their new Princess and Queen someday through events leading up to the wedding. There are do's and don'ts, practicing at the different venues, troops of all the services to line the streets along the way, decisions on food and drink, fireworks in the evening, the ball, and still more.

"The good news is we have experience in what works and have done much already. We will take care of many of the trivial decisions, planning, and execution. The bad news is you will have to turn over your schedule to us, so we may fit you into the many meetings and decisions to come.

"You must know what to do and when, royal protocol is very important you know. The people depend on it. You have dresses to select for the wedding ceremony, the ball, and the honeymoon. There is a choice of tiaras, introductions and the meeting of people, the buying of gifts and much more. You will have help all along the way.

"Behind the walls of the Palace, we must fulfill your wishes for the special day. The rest is for show. It is expected by the British subject," exclaimed Lady Elton regally.

Before Margret Anne could respond, "This week I prepared a schedule of events for you. There is the church to decide on, an inspection of ball plans, food and drink menus, a carriage to take you to the churches, the setting of a date for the selection of gowns, a wedding dress to choice, honeymoon clothing, rings, presentations, and speeches," explained Lady Elton.

"I have clothes" commented Margret Anne.

"No, no that won't do. You will be a member of the royal family, a future Queen, and you must be able to meet with the highest officials in the land and for that fact the world, as well as the lowest personages. Every detail leading up to the day of the wedding to your return from honeymoon will be planned for you. A personal secretary will be assigned to you. The press will be positioned for you and Prince James. The Empire will want to know how the lucky couple is doing throughout," explained Lady Elton.

"I have a number of tutors who will increase your knowledge of English history, faith, politics, current affairs, Royal protocol, and more dear. For the next several months you will be quite busy. I have apartments for you, and family members set aside at Kensington Palace. Royal protocol dictates that you may not stay at the palace where the Prince resides as this will be looked upon badly.

"I have also set aside offices for a staff of three people who will be at your disposal. You will have a secretary to schedule your days in coordination with that of His and Her Majesty, and your soon-to-be husband Prince James. You don't shop; others do that for you and present you with acceptable choices here in the palace. There are transportation and security details to be organised.

"We have more but I can see you are overwhelmed. Have no fear, Margret Anne, I will guide you every step of the way and am at Her Majesty's pleasure to assure you this. I have a list of tasks, events, and meetings for the week. Each day is laid out with descriptions, locations, and precise times. I will leave these with you. We will start tomorrow at precisely 9 am. I will see you then, good day to you ma'am, good day Mrs. Wentworth."

Fitzwilliam was preparing for the evening when he received an invitation to dine with the King. This would be informal, but of course, nothing was informal with the King at the palace. The servant bringing the invitation would wait on him since he would not know where to go and the palace being with so many rooms. "I will return to escort you sir at precisely 7 pm," said the servant.

Fitzwilliam was led through a gallery of halls, up several staircases, and through a portal into a set of rooms that were obviously the private quarter of His and Her Majesty. They were opulent beyond description, with gold and all manner of precious objects from every corner of the empire preserved as if newly laid. Fitzwilliam, used to wealth in some manner, was overwhelmed and startled at the sheer grandeur of the royal palace and the display of the power of the Empire.

The servant paused for a moment, then knocked softly at the door and awaited leave to enter. "You may enter said a commanding voice." The King.

The servant turned to Fitzwilliam and mentioned that he would be waiting for him at the end of the evening to escort him back to his guest apartments. Entering the room, the servant introduced Fitzwilliam, "Your Majesty, Mr. Prime Minister, Ministers I would like to present to you the Honourable Mr. Fitzwilliam Wentworth, son of Sir Frederick Wentworth of Kellynch Hall." Fitzwilliam was warmly greeted as the door closed softly.

"I hope you are hungry Fitz," said the King.

"Quite famished as a matter of fact your Majesty," replied Fitzwilliam.

Fitzwilliam was amazed at the rank of those in the room and did all he could to make this seem a normal occurrence in his everyday living. They were the highest in the land, and they wanted to know of him and were seeking his counsel and advice, thought Fitzwilliam. He also knew they were assessing him. "Can he be trusted? Does he have Sir Frederick and Sir Frederick II's loyalty and dedication to serving the crown?" Fitzwilliam surmised.

As the evening progressed Fitzwilliam commented, advised, and counseled where expected. The guests present assessed him. They as brilliant and refreshing as he, found he could be trusted and with a family as the Wentworths he would be respected by the House of Lords and members of Parliament, as well as leaders around the commonwealth. "He is quite brilliant," thought the Prime Minister.

The King was in good spirits as he could see the ministers were of his opinion. "Fitz, a great responsibility of the King is to rule his people, by looking after their welfare in many areas. My people have need of better business opportunities throughout the empire but lacked the skill to get to the challenges, as well as the opportunities with ready plans that give my governors the information to make good decisions that encourage economic growth. You see conditions and develop strategies well before any. That lead time is just what we need.

"I believe the Crown can use your talents, if you are willing, to help your King and his governing Ministers to assist the people in this way. Will you help me?" asked the King as the ministers in attendance stopped, for the moment, to review Fitzwilliam's response.

"I am at your service your Majesty, of course. How might I help the Crown?" replied Fitzwilliam respectfully.

The King looked at the Minister of the Exchequer, who related several stories of those lords and ladies whose financial stability was very much in doubt with no one holding out much hope for their retrenchment plans. "Then you Fitzwilliam changed their situation with amazingly carefully thought out strategies for recovery. You in some cases revitalised businesses that were being mismanaged and in other cases reinvested assets in less risky investments where none were known. You have a bit of your father in you. Where others are blind you can see. You take action where some fear, and assess in a most sensible way through the investigation of options to best suit the circumstance," related the minister.

"You see Fitz. The people are suffering needlessly. We can make this right. If only we had the correct opinion. More than not, we don't know the critical questions and the available options of good choices to study a topic and that is where you come in. The clarity you bring to the group will lead to decisions that would grow commerce, increase work, stabilise pay, enhance treatment, and more. This is a very exciting moment in the history of the empire.

"Expanding conditions would enable the addition of schools, health, and care for our people throughout the Empire. The commonwealth would thrive and be an example. This is what is wanted and needed," explained the Minister of the Exchequer.

Fitzwilliam sat there dazed but taking it all in, looking up, he responded "Where do I start sir?"

"Good man Fitz, I knew we could count on you. My wife the Queen said I am a good judge of character and in this case, she is correct," remarked His Majesty to confirmation by the minister's present.

With dinner over, the evening ended with a very amiable conversation. "Tomorrow we will start Fitzwilliam. We will expect you at our offices at Parliament for lunch and then a number of meetings in the afternoon," Commented the prime minister.

"Yes, of course, Minister."

"Fitz I have apartments set aside at Kensington palace, at the pleasure of the King, while in town on the Crown's business, this is at your disposal," remarked one of the Lords present.

Taking his leave to retire for the evening the servant awaited Fitzwilliam to escort him back to his guest apartment.

At 8 am precisely, the next morning, a knock at the door, and servants brought in a lovely breakfast of tea, scones, kippers, creams, and jams. "Will sir be having breakfast with you Ma'am?" asked the Servant.

Anne looked a bit confused. "Fitzwilliam, is his meaning mother," commented Margret Anne.

"Oh, yes of course. Yes, he will have breakfast with us this morning," replied Anne.

"The bone china cups are extraordinary mother, see the designs," pointed Margret Anne.

Shortly after breakfast was served Fitzwilliam entered the room to breakfast. "Good morning Mother, good morning Margret Ann," exclaimed Fitzwilliam.

"Good morning dear," replied Anne

"Good morning Fitz, you were out late last night. When I went to say good night you were not yet back in your apartments. Where were you?" asked Margret Anne.

"I was with the King, the Prime Minister, several of the cabinet ministers, and a lord or two. We talked about my role in helping to plan and put into action business works that will increase commerce, and investment and create new business throughout the Empire," replied Frederick.

"That is extraordinary, truly. You certainly have the ability to help in this case son," commented Anne.

"Thank you mother for your confidence in me," replied Fitzwilliam.

"Margret Anne what are you and Mother to do today?" asked Fitzwilliam.

"I have a wedding dress, church, tiara, and tutors today brother," replied Margret Anne.

"I am off to Parliament to lunch with the Prime Minister and several ministers," explained Fitzwilliam as a servant announced her ladyship, the Lady Elton presented herself.

At Kellynch Hall, Frederick and Frederick II made preparations for a trip to Plymouth where Frederick II began his work at the Admiralty. "Father, we are ready to leave. I shall await you in the carriage.

On their way, Frederick said "Son, you will be watched closely now, more closely than before. The Admiralty will assess your abilities in the areas of strategy, tactics development, dedication to the service, and ability to elicit the confidence of your fellow Captains."

"Yes, I see," commented Frederick II

"You made a splash when last you captained a ship. You changed the course of a battle and saved His Highness and your father. These are things of legend, many will be in awe of you while others will be jealous and find any reason to knock you down. Be gracious to all and work for the success of others, friend and foe. That will be the saving grace. In time many will rally to your side, and you will have built a loyal following," explained Frederick as Frederick II listened intently.

"Father, I have not been idle these weeks past but worked on the next generation of strategy and tactics that build on your strong foundations. I am ready to show these plans to you and James while we are in Plymouth," commented Frederick II.

"Your work did not go unnoticed son. I was hoping you would show the initiative that it takes to be a leader. This is something that one is born to and cannot be taught. Many in the Admiralty are hoping for your success. The next generation of officers will see things differently, and adjustments now will be a key to the Navy's success in the next conflict. One must someday hand off the torch to those to come in turn and my hope is you will be one of the trusted. Benwick and I believe you have all the makings and will hand off our whole experience and advice to you," said Frederick.

"Thank you, Father. I will pay great attention and respect to you and Admiral Benwick," responded Frederick II.

"I have reports Prince James is in Plymouth for a couple of days on Crown business. He has taken his sister Princess Stephanie with him. How are you and the Princess?" asked Frederick.

"Well father, if the King and you are agreeable I should like to propose to my Princess. She is hinting that she expects a question soon. I have delayed so as not to overshadow Margret Anne's day. I will miss her sorely as she takes up greater responsibilities," replied Frederick II.

"Have no worry, son, I believe she will make time for the family. Margret is realising now the great weight of her new role and will balance that role with that of her family and former life. We will all benefit much from our connections to the Royal family and that of the Empire," related Frederick.

Arriving at the Admiralty in the later afternoon, Admiral and Captain Wentworth signed into quarters where an invite to that evening's dining and audience with His Royal Highness Prince James and Princess Stephanie was waiting on them.

"So, it looks like you will be seeing your Princess this evening after all," commented Frederick.

"Yes, it seems so father," smiled Frederick II.

"Benwick ole fellow!" exclaimed Frederick.

"Sir Frederick, Captain Wentworth!" retorted Admiral Benwick.

"Why so formal among friends Benwick?" asked Frederick.

"Well, we are at the Admiralty after all," responded Benwick with a smile.

"Are you ready to take this navy into the future young Captain?" asked Admiral Benwick.

"Yes sir, and with your and father's guidance it will be successfully done. I have already drawn up preliminary strategies and tactics I believe to build on Father's methods but now take advantage of the advances in naval vessel designs and firepower," commented Captain Wentworth.

"Great start, your father and I look forward to your presentation and commenting on these designs. We start tomorrow," exclaimed Benwick.

"I look to your advice and counsel Admiral," said Captain Wentworth.

"For tonight let us dine together as friends catching up," exclaimed Admiral Benwick.

"That would be very acceptable, but we have here in our hands an invitation to dine tonight with His Highness Prince James and Princess Stephanie," commented Sir Frederick.

"Well then, we shall all go together then, since I have an invitation myself to this evening's event!" replied Benwick.

At the Palace, Lady Elton had what she considered a successful day with Margret Anne. They accomplished all the tasks on the list for that day. Lady Elton began to understand Prince James' attraction to Margret Anne and was gaining the opinion of Margret Anne to be a very sweet-tempered, considerate, intelligent, amiable, and capable young lady, a credit to her family and herself.

"Margret Anne," called Lady Elton.

"Yes, Lady Elton,"

"Can I have a word with you before I leave you free for the evening?" asked Lady Elton as Anne was just entering the room.

"Oh I did not mean to intrude," exclaimed Anne.

"Don't be at all concerned mother, you never intrude," commented Margret Anne.

"You are perfectly welcome Mrs. Anne. I was about to offer Margret Anne advice and counsel on palace personages."

"Oh, I am just learning of these affairs myself and could use any advice. May I listen Lady Elton?" asked Anne.

"Of course," responded Lady Elton.

"Margret Anne with great privilege comes great responsibilities and even greater jealousies from those around you. You will quickly learn there will be those you can trust and others who just want your privileges but not the responsibilities that go with the role. They are hangers-on. These people are at court because of titles one is born to and as such society dictates that titles be respected. To this end, all due is paid but no more than that. They are left out of the most inner and trusted circles. They do very little to help the crown whose purpose is the welfare of the Empire and her people. As you have probably noticed today your role is one of giving," explained Lady Elton.

"Yes I see," replied Margret Anne.

Continuing, Lady Elton mentioned, "Tomorrow we will be in the company of some of the greatest personages in the Empire, perhaps, not so much in the title as in the deeds done. These are the very trusted lords and ladies who work for the raising of the Crown and the Empire. They are no saint by any means mind you but when it comes to King and Empire their priorities are straight.

"The day after tomorrow we will be in mixed company where some of the hangers-on will be present and the tenor of conversations and decisions will be quite different. Take note and be aware. You will see that type of friendliness that invites you in and for no good. Be conscious of those who want your friendship only to stab you later in the dark of the night. Trust but verify with this sort. I will identify them for you and advise you if you wish?" offered Lady Elton.

"Yes, of course and thank you for your consideration dear Lady Elton," responded Margret Anne.

"Thank you, Lady Elton," commented Anne.

"I fear you have met with these sorts Lady Anne?" inquired Lady Elton.

"Yes, I have this day. Her Majesty guided me through these waters well," replied Anne.

"Her Majesty is the best to pick out the character of a person very quickly. She can see far sooner than most. She will be a great mentor. I am also assigned to the Royal Charities Trust Committee but am relieved of these duties while I assist Margret Anne with the wedding at Her Majesty's pleasure," said Lady Elton.

"As I become acquainted with Margret Anne, I see this will be a pleasure for me as well. She is a well-bred young lady of standing and family connections," said Lady Elton discreetly.

"Thank you for your compliments Lady Elton," commented Anne.

"Not at all dear, I am glad of it. Now if you will excuse me," said Lady Elton as Anne and Margret Anne stood to bow.

Fitzwilliam's day was exceedingly successful from a number of points, and he wanted to relate his experiences to his mother, "Hello mother, Margret Anne, how was your day?" asked Fitzwilliam.

"Very good dear," responded Anne.

"How about your outing at Parliament?" asked Margret Anne.

"Very Good, don't you think it rather strange we are staying at the royal palace while in town?" asked Fitzwilliam

"This takes some getting used to, but we are on the Crown's business and it is only right and proper to accept an invitation from His Majesty," replied Anne.

"Don't forget we dine with His Majesty's this evening," commented Margret Anne.

"I met with the Prime Minister and the Minister of the Exchequer. I was given the opportunity to join a small team that would advise the Crown and the highest government official on where and how to apply resources to encourage commerce and industry throughout the Empire. I was given a staff of four and will be paid, quite a handsome sum by some standards and commit to a two-year appointment," related Fitzwilliam.

Anne and Margret Anne were excited for Fitzwilliam.

"Is this not the opportunity you have waited for? The opportunity to help those less fortunate in a way that gives them the opportunity to work for their own and their family's success?" asked Anne

"It seems so. I will certainly commit myself to this endeavour," said Fitzwilliam.

"I wonder how father and Frederick are doing?" asked Margret Anne.

"They should have arrived at Plymouth if all is according to plan," commented Anne.

"Have you been visited by Princess Stephanie?" Anne asked Margret Anne.

"Why no mother, she did leave me a note to say she will be back from Plymouth before the end of the week where she attends with her brother on crown business," commented Margret Anne.

"Perhaps my Captain will see his Princess while at the Admiralty?" related Anne.

"I would expect so mother. Why doesn't he propose already?" said Margret Anne.

"It could be that he does not want to overshadow your wedding," replied Anne.

"Well mother, I am sure James - would not take any offense but wish Frederick and Princess Stephanie all the happiness, truly. Although I would expect some protocols in this case, I would not presume to deny the happiness of a beloved brother and sister. Is this then what Frederick is thinking?" asked Margret Anne of Anne.

"Yes, I believe so," replied Anne.

"I will write Frederick II directly and send him our wishes for happiness and tell him my thoughts on the matter Mother. Why should he not be happy but for me and James in the way," commented Margret Anne concerned.

"I see you are determined. Send my love dear," said Anne as the servant entered and announced himself there to escort the Wentworths to dine with His Majesty.

The Admiral and Captain Wentworth arrived at Admiralty Hall to dine and spend the evening with His Highness Prince James and Her Royal Highness Princess Stephanie. As they were announced, many naval friends rushed in that way so as not to seem improper but with all speed to greet old friends. Frederick II spotted Princess Stephanie, whose eyes had caressed him well before he found her position in the room. As he greeted old friends and made new ones, he worked his way to her side after a time, and all were satisfied with the greeting.

Captain Wentworth excused himself from conversations after a short while, not too soon as to be considered rude or inconsiderate but not so long as to hurt Princess Stephanie's feelings. As he turned to Princess Stephanie, he could see a number of men working hard to capture her attention, which was ignored politely.

"Princess Stephanie, how are you this evening?" asked Frederick, bowing and kissing her hand.

"I am well Sir Frederick II. Come sit with me; tell me all the news of late. I have missed you," commented Princess Stephanie, leading the way to a quiet and comfortable corner.

The rest of the evening was a blur as Frederick and Princess Stephanie talked of all they did while they were apart, of all the activities so common but always amazing to each other's ears to hear and minds to imagine when love is the close companion. Every so often, a captain or admiral paid their compliments to Her Highness the Princess as well as greeted their own Sir Frederick II.

"And of Mrs. Anne and Margret Anne, how are they? Well, I hope?" asked Princess Stephanie.

"They are at the palace. Margret Anne is busy with wedding details and her mother with the Queen's charity and Trust committee work. Moreover, there is Fitzwilliam about the King's Royal Commerce Committee work," commented Frederick II.

Both smiled at the turn of events. "It seems dear Frederick II the Crown is in need of the Wentworths in many areas. What say you?" exclaimed Princess Stephanie.

"Yes my Princess this seems so," replied Frederick II.

"Frederick II, I would like to invite you to the palace in a fortnight to visit with me and my family. Will you be free to join me?" asked Princess Stephanie.

"Yes, of course, dear," replied Frederick II.

This was the first time Frederick II lovingly called her dear, and Princess Stephanie noticed.

"I shall send a formal invitation to Kellynch Hall," commented Princess Stephanie with a smile and a glint in her eye.

"Shall we tell your father of our wishes?" asked Frederick II.

"Yes, it is time," replied Princess Stephanie.

At the evening close, Frederick II and Princess Stephanie set time to dine the next evening at the royal residence in Plymouth. All the guests, although not ignored nor treated in anything resembling an improper manner, could see the special relationship between Sir Frederick II and Princess Stephanie. Frederick II tall and handsome, almost fully recovered now, and Princess Stephanie fair-skinned, with bright green eyes and soft auburn hair caressing her face, was a beauty to be sure. Each seemed so well suited to each other in style and temperament.

"So ole chap, when can we expect the next royal wedding?" commented many an Admiral and friend discreetly throughout the evening.

Frederick just smiled and nodded in recognition and politely refrained from an answer, changing the subject to that of navy affairs and the latest politics.

Lady Anne was to work with the charity committee that day and prepared, at first being briefed on issues facing the people in the empire and then asked for her opinion on priorities, her idea for relief programs, and then helping in the planning efforts for relief efforts this year. Members were genuinely interested in her successes and lessons learned with her work at the county level. Even the Queen took note of what worked well and where the challenges were.

"People want to live a good and productive life, given the opportunity. I found when helping to ask if help was wanted and a hand up not so much a hand out. Sometimes, even where there is a need, help is not yet wanted. So we keep in mind to help where wanted to give those in need the freedom to accept the assistance and to be careful to provide the right assistance," advised Lady Anne.

"Well, said Lady Anne," replied the Queen. "We have upon too many occasions been unwelcomed with ready help leaving us wondering what could have gone wrong. A handout, as it were, I have often wondered why," commented the Queen.

"It is true that a charity should be keenly aware of children and mothers. They are so vulnerable and often need and want help. Our society does not afford a woman the means to sustain herself without a man and should an accident or death befall a family they may be left with nothing but the poor house or begging as their option. This group is very appreciative when help is provided. In the end, women given a hand up will raise well-mannered and strong men for our women in later generations, as well as polite, unaffected girls," commented Anne.

Lady Elton, listening intently gained respect for Anne. "I now know where Margret Anne gets her sensibilities," thought Lady Elton.

"For what reason did you start the charity work in your county Anne? You certainly had no cause to be of service to the people. With a large income, an impressive estate, and a wonderful husband and hero to the Empire, you could have easily retreated into your own world, like most today. However, something made you aware of needs you could fill. What was it Dear Anne?" asked Lady Elton to the attention of all assembled there.

Anne, surprised with the directness of the question thought a minute. This was a crucial moment as the group of women stopped to listen intently as tea was served, "Thank you for your compliment, Lady Elton. I assure you I am no saint. However, some years ago when my mother passed away, I was befriended by my mother's dear friend and neighbour the Lady Russell. Some of you may remember her. She has since passed away. In her day, she took me on, for my mother's sake, and guided my life through all the ups and downs to be expected of any young lady of the times.

"At first she had opinions about my husband Frederick, which were not my own, since I loved him dearly from the start. But, Frederick at the time was without fortune, family, or connections. He was a young naval officer going off to war and this circumstance made his marriage proposal quite out of the question. Eight years later Frederick returned to my life through the circumstances of his sister Mrs. Croft letting our home at Kellynch Hall. By now Frederick - Captain Wentworth - was quite wealthy and much admired in the way of the navy. After a time and some trials, Frederick again asked me to marry. The match was eligible and after some convincing with family, we married and moved back to my beloved Kellynch Hall.

"During this time Lady Russell's opinion of Frederick had changed. She realised Frederick was a man of honour and he loved me truly. This wasn't just a marriage of convenience. Frederick also treated Lady Russell with great respect and honour for my sake. This won her over.

"Like her daughter, the Lady Russell talked of all matters important and not so important, as women often do. One day on a walk to the village we noticed the hopelessness of some of its residents and decided then and there to assist. At first a box of food stuffs here, and clothes there, then we asked a number of acquaintances in the village if they would help us to understand the need better.

"What was shocking was the realisation that it took very little to help someone. The effort developed into organising volunteers and expanding the reach of assistance. Our surgeon offered free a surgery once a month. Extra food was donated, used clothes in very good condition, and sometimes work and apprenticeships were made available to the unemployed through charity. The goal is to assist where wanted, help folks to help themselves, and ask those helped to help the charity in return. Quite a cycle when you see it in action the first time.

"Most of the volunteers have wanted to be of service to their community but needed someone of rank to recognize them and organise the work to be done. Once a year we hold a ball at Kellynch Hall for the volunteers. It is a way to say thank you. We recap the year of good work and successes and recognize special folks. Other meetings take place at a regular time once a month. Since a very modest beginning, the charity has expanded to a countywide effort affecting the entire shire. It has been a blessing.

"The Lady Russell passed away when the effort was small, it was then I realised the full nature of her compassion and determined that I would organise monthly meetings for those directly helping the needy and quarterly meetings for gentle folk supplying funds and other resources at Kellynch Hall. It was in these discussions, that we learned to focus efforts and understand trends in the local communities. Sometimes we worked with local counsels to ensure success.

"I organised what I called area organisers with a reach beyond the local village. Area organisers would own an area of the shire. This might mean several villages and groups of volunteers. I thought this level of organiser would be good for meetings and sharing what was working as well as what challenges we faced in helping. Our patrons were mostly gentlefolk. They don't mind donating resources as long as one can prove the benefit and give them recognition. Our annual ball is where we recognise all hear stories of success and see some of the results of the effort. This seems to renew the group to pledge another year of effort.

"I found a number of truths, they are these; given the opportunity most Christian people will be of service as long as they know their efforts, work, or resources will go to good use and make a difference. Sometimes it takes reminding of our fortune and of those less fortunate. It really takes so little to help. In helping, we get back so much in the filling of our hearts. One day we see the results of just giving a hand and its surprising results. When giving, ask if assistance is wanted, and finally, when assisting do so with great care and dignity to those receiving.

"On a final note…on my wedding day, at the local parish and completely to my surprise, the county came out and lined the lane throwing flowers, cheering good wishes to me and Frederick with such happiness and best intentions. It brought tears to my eyes. I had no idea of the love and respect people had for me. It was in the work that I revealed I did not realise I had a hand in changing so many lives and giving so much in a way of hope.

"Later I asked a few folks why they would have come out just for my marriage. A young lady said to me 'Ma'am, we lost our father to an accident at work. My mother had nothing but three children and was about to be thrown out of our dingy one-room home when your charity workers found out about us and the circumstances and helped us in so many ways that it can't be described". She detailed her life now as the village teacher and charity volunteer. What could I do but feel humbled by her recounting," said Anne.

With that, Anne looked down at the work before her and the light in the room seemed somehow brighter full of possibility.

In the preceding moment and for a few moments after, the room was completely silent as each member of the committee digested what they had just heard. Even the hangers-on, just there for image's sake, realised the great trust and responsibility of the Queen's committee. The hope and faith of people yet unknown was placed in them and the good they could do could be immense indeed.

"It doesn't take a lot," thought Anne.

Several of the members walked over to Anne and nominated her to organise the drawing up of plans for this year's trust activities, with many enthusiastic members raising their hands in agreement and wanting to help. Anne, surprised at the events unfolding, found many a Lady asking to assist her in any way, and at any time, she was only to ask and every door would be opened to her. Many a husband was a Lord or member of parliament and had an influence that could be used if needed. The group of women, for the first time, bonded and Anne was the catalyst to notice the Queen.

"Anne, we must do something about your title. You see we, here are all titled. Your husband and son are knights in the realm, and I believe Lady Anne of...... would be much more becoming and fit for someone of your level in society, being the daughter of a baronet, as well as your deeds prove this," explained Her Majesty.

All the women present agreed and called for Anne to be titled.

"I shall go to my dear husband and ask him that this be done with all speed," commented the Queen.

"Thank you, truly," said Anne.

Her Majesty, usually in the forefront now in the background, was in awe of Anne. With a smile looking at Anne as they made eye contact communicated in a single glance her purpose had been fulfilled. The Queen needed someone to bring the diverse group of women together in a common cause to bond them and help them to believe they could make a difference.

Anne was the catalyst the Queen needed to bring out the volunteer spirit, and this was now unfolding before her very eyes. "Thank you, Anne," said the Queen discreetly.

"Let us keep the work simple; focusing on basic goals and we will be successful in helping people. We can work to build charity organisations throughout the empire in a number of ways. Let me explain. Local groups would manage on the scene and knowing the circumstances would be able to decide the best need for and application of resources and the course of the actions to be taken.

"Each group is assigned a leader who reports on the use of resources, describes needs, and answers to the committee member assigned that territory. The committee member with limits may decide on the granting of aid requests. For territory-wide programs, these decisions would be made with this committee for the granting of aid and support to the territory. The committee would also intervene where needed and provide special help. Food, health, shelter, education, job training, and apprenticeships are all areas that can be improved. Upon their improvement life is better for all.

"There are many that want to help but have no means to do so. We can give them the organisation, the direction, and the means to help. With a good start, we can build upon these successes and make the needed changes that make our efforts more effective in all the areas where we find the reason to do so. Remember ladies this is a vast empire, and we cannot solve all the problems, so let us start small and gain the confidence of local folks through small consistent successes at first and then build upon this success little by little to larger programs as we gain confidence in ourselves and those observing our efforts," said Anne.

It was so simple but it took someone like Anne, with all her experiences, to say these words. The charity members were enthralled and ready to begin organising. Anne started with coordinating the committee with the agreement on the Trust's goals, creating territories and assigning members to them, and discussing common territory goals, starting with the protection of children, women, men, families, education of children, and training for men as a good first step.

Each area was explored and made understandable through simple goals and priorities.

"Now ladies, let us devise programs for each of our goals. We can do this by applying Trust plans to each while each area may in turn have an area-specific program unique to that concern and where common we can leverage plans from other areas. We may begin to then draw up plans for coordinating volunteer organisations that are on the ground and support a means to help while this committee then focuses on the review of requests from the area who represent the teams that meet with committee members who run these areas. Does this make sense ladies?" asked Anne.

"Yes, it does, please continue," replied the Queen.

"In the next days, we could set a small group here to the task of coming up with a fair criterion for the granting of the means to help. We will follow up with all those where help was given in search of results that can be used to guide present and future assistance. This is so we can determine if the resources did what was intended and to our charity's goals.

"Lady Elton, would you volunteer to manage responsibilities for England as a trust territory? Lady Hamish, would you take on Ireland as the assignment? Lady Cort, are you not of Scottish bloodlines? Would you take on Scotland? Volunteers for Canada, and the East Indies? Any for the West Indies" asked Anne of the group.

And this went on until all the territories were assigned. In one day more was decided and with such enthusiasm than since the founding of the Trust.

"Ladies, we have made such progress," announced the Queen "Let us break for today, take lunch together, and consider what we have done. Tomorrow we will meet again. Anne what should be the agenda for tomorrow?" asked Her Majesty, smiling with triumph.

"Learning about each territory and their needs. We can talk about organising local charity organisations for each region that are represented at the territory level with group leaders who answer to the assigned committee member and volunteers under the group leaders at the lower levels in the villages and towns. We should agree on guidelines for how groups communicate at the territory level and how the territory communicates to the Royal Trust, as well as criteria for the granting of aid at this level to distribute and list initial programs to sponsor. A date to get started and finally, agree on a reporting method to capture results so we may be sure aid is making a difference," outlined Anne.

"Remember the local organisation provides a place for the volunteers to serve but the Royal Trust, once the organisational charters are drawn up, will provide the means to help. Next is to draw up a plan for discovering what needs exist and what ways will best serve the people on behalf of the crown. We have to be very careful to assure visible success, especially at first, so those looking from the outside with a skeptic's eye may gain confidence and respect for this organisation, even becoming a supporter" commented Anne.

"Thank you, Anne, you have certainly made a very positive impact on this committee," exclaimed the Queen.

"We are adjourned ladies. Let us lunch then," announced Lady Elton.

The Queen, at Anne's side, pushed away invitations to dine for Anne, stating that she had Anne's time all week with wedding and charity work. Undaunted, many a member mentioned dates later in the year. Each member wanted to befriend Anne and to show they valued her with a growing friendship and respect. The Hangers now having a change of heart about Anne wanted to know Anne as well.

At supper, the Queen mentioned Anne's triumph at the committee meeting that day. His Majesty commented "Well done Anne. I have had high hopes for the Trust to help the lowliest people in the kingdom. You are just what we needed. Thank you for your graciousness in serving, and your efforts in these matters. I and my wife Thank you on behalf of a grateful kingdom.

"I received a request to provide you with a title, not that you need a title, dear lady. I have thought upon this matter carefully and have just this evening signed a decree to title you. And with your leave, from this time onward you will be known as the Lady Anne Wentworth Duchess of Glastonbury," announced the King.

"I am humbled and grateful for the opportunity to serve the crown and the honour Your Majesty's have bestowed upon me this day. Thank you," replied Anne.

"Not at all Lady Anne, this is much deserved and long overdue," replied the King

The next days were much like the days before for Margret Anne. She worked on the many details of a royal wedding assuring all the decisions; choices and the entirety of questions were answered to everyone's satisfaction. She realised this life would have its privileges, but it would be a life of service as well and would take some getting used to.

Lady Elton, having gained great respect for Lady Anne and Margret Anne, opened up to them more than before, telling them of the inner workings of the palace, the royal family, and the government. These insights helped Anne and Margret Anne to better chart their course through palace politics and interactions with the royals.

One afternoon, the Queen came to the guest apartments quite by surprise and unannounced. Her Majesty wanted to thank Lady Anne personally for her involvement in the Trust committee. Members had sent notes to Her Majesty mentioning how Lady Anne had revived the member base and infused the team with energy for the work ahead.

"Your organisational skills, experience, and grace give members leave to input and be involved. I have even received notes from those who want to be members and help in some way. Thank you,

Anne, truly. This will be a banner year and get this trust off the ground, and you are a major reason," commented Her Majesty.

"All we need now is to put plans in action and see some success, then the energy will be self-sustaining," commented Anne.

"Mother, you didn't tell me of your committee's success and new title. May I become a member of Your Majesty? I have assisted mother since I can remember with county charity committee work," added Margret Anne.

"Yes, of course. I was hoping you would volunteer. For the moment though you have the wedding, and this will take up all your time," replied the Queen.

A servant entered the room and motioned with a note for Her Majesty. "I must leave you both for now. Good day," exclaimed the Queen, leaving the guest apartment.

In the morning hour, Admirals Benwick and Wentworth accompanied Captain Wentworth to his meetings with the Admiralty. As a formality he was granted leave to involve himself in the work he requested and was assigned to the committees he requested leave to join. Captain Wentworth met with each member of the committee to introduce himself formally as required by naval custom and settled details for beginning regular work in each area. As expected he would commit to one week a month at Plymouth to work on behalf of the Admiralty.

"Admiral Wentworth I was quite impressed with your son today. I got a hint of his draft plans for new strategies and tactics. They are very impressive. His ability to be at ease while listening closely to instruction when given will take him far indeed gentlemen," commented Rear Admiral Chelsea.

"I second that!" Captains Wilson and Montgomery exclaimed with Admiral Benwick listening.

In the evening Captain Wentworth, Prince James, and Princess Stephanie dined together. This was no normal supper though. "Brother, I have accepted Captain Wentworth's offer of marriage. What say you?" announced Princess Stephanie with a probing look.

"Congratulations to you both. This calls for a toast! To my dear sister and brother! This is not really a surprise. One could see the love you have for each other. I wish both of you happy. That fateful day you saved my life on the high seas I knew we would be bound, my friend. I am pleased that in this life you have found happiness with my sister. God bless you both," responded Prince James, extending his hand in friendship. "Sister you could not have chosen a worthier man in my eyes."

"Thank you, sir," commented Captain Wentworth.

"Do father and mother know the news?" asked James.

"No, I will tell them in a few days' time when Frederick is to dine at the Palace at my special invitation," replied Princess Stephanie.

"Then sister I will change my plans, so I am there to support the both of you. Though, I expect a happy response," said James.

"Word is Lady Anne and Margret Anne are making quite a positive splash at the palace. Mother is very excited for Lady Anne and her work with the Trust committee, and Lady Elton has advised me I have chosen very well with Margret Anne, and you know how picky she is in all affairs great and small," mentioned James.

"Excuse me, sir, you mean Anne Wentworth, my mother?" asked Frederick II.

"Ah, you don't know. Father bestowed your mother with the title 'the Lady Anne Wentworth, Duchess of Glastonbury', and just a few nights ago," explained Prince James.

Frederick II was both speechless and proud.

"Well then my dear Lady Anne it is!" exclaimed Princess Stephanie with a smile and the raising of glasses to it.

"In a communication with the prime minister, Fitzwilliam seems to have acquitted himself with distinction for his acumen with respect to business and commerce. So you see all should go well," said Prince James.

"Brother I want to keep this news within the family until after your wedding. I and Frederick II have decided not to take the light from you and Margret Anne," requested Princess Stephanie.

"Well then, let it be so," replied Prince James.

The evening went along famously and with easy conversation. "Shall I see you tomorrow my Princess?" asked Frederick II.

"I am off to town early tomorrow my Captain. I have completed crown business and must-see my dear friends, your sister and mother. I will tell them in confidence of our plans," commented Princess Stephanie.

"I will miss you then," replied Frederick II.

"You have Admiralty business to attend to, and I will see you for the announcement of our happy news to the family in a fortnight. In the meantime, I shall write to you of my boring exploits and silly things," exclaimed Princess Stephanie as Frederick II kissed her hand and cheek at departing.

"Congratulations Frederick II, I am so happy to hear this news. Does mother know of it?" asked Sir Frederick.

"No, not as yet; Princess Stephanie will be off to town tomorrow morning and will visit with mother and sister to announce the happy news," commented Frederick II.

"They will take this well. Your sister's friend is to marry a beloved brother. Happy news indeed sir, happy news indeed," said Sir Frederick.

"We are to keep this in the family so as not to overshadow Margret Anne's wedding plans. In a fortnight, I am summoned to dine at the palace where it will be announced to the family formally," said Frederick II.

"Then it shall be so," replied Frederick.

Fitzwilliam in London "Let us consider the long-term solution to financial stability gentlemen. It is not in the immediate fix that one derives the full benefits. They tend to be short-lived, leaving the same problems one set out to resolve. In the resolution of a problem for the long-term benefits we can derive long-term benefit with a strong and self-sustaining foundation."

"It only makes sense. Now that we can see the facts and options, resolution can be quickly decided and made painless. Without your brilliant insight, we would have still been in a stalemate Fitzwilliam. Thank you for accepting this post," said the prime minister with the Minister of the Exchequer looking on approvingly. Other cabinet members smiled in agreement with the King's choice.

Princess Stephanie arrived at the Palace late that night. Tomorrow was Friday and she could spend some of the day with Margret Anne and Lady Anne.

"Welcome home Your Royal Highness," said the doorman.

"Please would you have my bags sent to my apartments? Are mother and father up?" asked Princess Stephanie.

"No ma'am, they are off to sleep gone an hour Your Royal Highness," answered a servant.

"Thank you all, good night," commented Princess Stephanie as she made her way to her apartments.

The next morning came all too quickly but Princess Stephanie was determined to breakfast with her mother and father. "Good morning mother, and father," exclaimed Princess Stephanie walking in to breakfast.

"Good morning dear," replied Mother in a surprised tone.

"You're not surprised I am here?" asked Princess Stephanie.

"Nothing happens much in the palace without our knowing of it dear. We are very pleased you are here," said Father.

"How was your trip from Plymouth?" asked Mother.

"Uneventful, all went to plan," replied Stephanie.

"Mother, Father I have an announcement I would like to make, first to you. Captain Wentworth has proposed to me, and I have accepted him."

"It's about time dear. I have been waiting for what seemed forever," replied the Queen.

"Congratulations my dear, Sir Frederick II is a worthy man," exclaimed the King.

"That is a coincidence. It is essentially what James said," commented Stephanie.

"I have asked Frederick to dine with all of us in a fortnight Father. He will ask for your blessings and a formal announcement. We would like to keep this news between both families until after James' wedding. Would that be considerate?" asked Stephanie.

"Yes dear, that is very considerate indeed," responded the Queen.

"I will try to catch Lady Anne and Margret Anne this morning before they finish breakfast," commented Stephanie.

"You had better leave now then dear, both have been quite busy on the crown's business."

"Yes mother, father, bye," said Stephanie.

"They grow up ever so quickly. I hope for her happiness," said the queen.

"Frederick II is quite the man. His exploits in the war, our son's opinion of him, and our friendship with this family have been a blessing. Stephanie should be truly happy I expect," said the King.

"Dear Lady Anne and my friend Margret Anne, good morning to you both. I hope I do not intrude on your breakfast?" asked Princess Stephanie.

"No, not at all! When did you arrive?" asked Margret Anne.

"Last night, late," replied Princess Stephanie.

Fitzwilliam walked in, not expecting Princess Stephanie at the table. Awkwardly, he bowed and performed all the courtesies required.

"Please Fitzwilliam sit, have breakfast, and be full at ease here," commented Princess Stephanie.

"Lady Anne, Margret Anne, Fitzwilliam I have an announcement to be kept within both families," exclaimed Princess Stephanie.

"What is it?" replied Margret Anne.

"Frederick has proposed to me, and I have accepted him," said Princess Stephanie confidentially.

"Many congratulations dear Princess Stephanie," responded Lady Anne, all smiles.

"I wish you and Frederick all the happiness one can have sister," exclaimed Margret Anne.

"I wish you happy Princess," said Fitzwilliam raising a cup of tea.

"We don't want to overshadow your wedding dear Margret Anne. So this is to be kept between the families for now. In a fortnight, we will have Frederick to dine with us here at the palace and formally announce our plans to Mother and Father, although I asked them to keep this in confidence this morning, and they agreed and are very happy for us. I shall leave you now and find you later in the day before you leave for Kellynch Hall. Until later then," said Princess Stephanie.

"Good day Princess Stephanie," said Lady Anne as Margret Anne and Fitzwilliam stood and bowed at her leaving.

Her Majesty was on the schedule today and Margret Anne was excited to visit with her. Since first they met formally the Queen had been very gracious and open with Margret Anne, giving her advice and guiding her along the way. Today's tasks would include a review of the wedding plans with her Ladyship, Lady Anne and Lady Elton, lunch together, and a selection of jewelry from the Royal Vaults, as well as a discussion on the royal title after marriage.

Lady Elton arrived on time to take Margret Anne on her first appointment with the dressmakers and tailors to finalize measurements for her dress.

"Margret Anne, we will go to Westminster Abbey for practice ceremony and title investiture protocols, then lunch with the Queen where we will review wedding plans, the final selection of jewelry, and the royal title. Then you will be free to take tea with Her Royal Highness the Princess Stephanie."

"Thank you Lady Elton for your kind assistance; right then, shall we get started?" replied Margret Anne eagerly.

The morning flew by without any delay of note, and it was time to visit with Her Majesty the Queen.

"This way to the Queen's private apartments," motioned Lady Elton.

They went up a staircase, surrounded by opulence that now seemed quite normal and unspectacular but impeccable none-the-less. Entering an outer room to the private apartments, this part of the palace seemed warmer somehow, very personal and inviting, hinting at the secret lives of the King and Queen being all but quite normal.

Her Majesty walked in with her private secretary, notepad in hand, greeting Lady Elton and Margret Anne warmly. "Please do come in," invited the Queen as she escorted her party into the inner rooms of the private apartments.

Very discreetly Lady Elton mentioned to Margret Anne this was only the second time she had ever been invited into the private apartment of the Majesty's. "This is quite a privilege indeed Margret Anne," said Lady Elton.

"Ah, we are here. Please sit. As you can see, we are all at ease here in one place," commented the Queen. A servant approached Her Majesty and handed her a menu for lunch for her approval.

"With that settled let us review the wedding plans, shall we?" asked Her Majesty, giving her full attention to the matter.

Lady Elton handed the Queen the wedding plan details, and they reviewed all points. As they completed the review Her Majesty approved of all the details. "Are there any special details you would like added to the ceremony that would be tradition for your family Margret Anne?" asked the Queen earnestly and to Lady Elton's surprise.

Startled, Margret Anne replied, "Yes, when mother and father married the ceremony was at Kellynch parish church. I have often dreamed of my wedding day including two hymns that were played on their day."

"Lady Elton, would you make arrangements for these hymns in the ceremony," commanded the Queen. "Is there anything else Margret Anne?"

"Nothing I can think of at the moment Your Majesty," replied Margret Anne.

"Please let me know if there is any other accommodation, and we will do our best to make it so," smiled the Queen.

"I would like to give my opinion on a matter your Majesty," stated Lady Elton.

"Please do," replied the Queen.

"For so young a person I find Margret Anne to be very patient, kind, and generous in all her dealings," said Lady Elton.

"These comments seem consistent with my reports of her character. Since I didn't want Margret Anne overstrained as she is not used to court, I have been keeping an eye that she is not overwhelmed. Thank you Margret Anne for making these activities at least bearable to all who just wanted to please you and the crown. You have gained many loyal subjects already," said the Queen.

Margret Anne blushed at the compliment.

"Would you walk with me?" asked the Queen as they made their way to the next room. The room was laid out with tables along the length. Upon the tables were silk cloth nests within which were differing arrangements of jewels laid out. It was time to select the jewels for the wedding. As each was viewed the Queen talked of the history of a particular setting. All the jewelry was exquisite, making it difficult to pick. Each had its merit.

Margret Anne commented "Any will do, what is the difference. They are all exquisite truly."

"In that case, my favourite are these, since this is what I wore to my wedding, it seemed to have brought me very good luck," exclaimed the Queen.

Margret Anne looked at the choice and knew that was what she wanted too. This arrangement was beyond words.

"This will do just fine Your Majesty," said Margret Anne.

"Good, then this is settled," said Lady Elton.

With jewellery matters settled it was time for lunch, where conversation and talk of the week's adventures were reviewed in detail. Margret talked of her tutors, Lady Elton's help, and the happy news of her brother and Princess Stephanie's confidential news. The Queen asked Lady Elton to keep this news confidential as no one but her outside the families knew of the engagement.

"I have considered your title after marriage. It will be Her Royal Highness the Princess Margret officially. I received advice from our historians to ensure all was in order. What do you say Margret Anne?" asked the Queen.

"What is one to say Your Majesty save yes," replied Margret Anne with a smile.

It was soon time to go. "Until next time dear," commented the Queen.

"Tonight we are off to Kellynch Hall. Thank you for having us as your guest," replied Margret Anne.

"Not at all dear," replied the Queen as her secretary led her away.

With an hour in total to sit with their mother, Margret Anne was suddenly aware of all the time she had been from one appointment to the next during the week.

"It has been so busy. It is bliss just to sit in peace with your mother," commented Margret Anne.

Princess Stephanie entered the apartments. "I hope you don't mind I took the liberty to order tea and sandwiches for us."

"Not at all, thank you," replied Lady Anne.

"Now, tell me all of your dealings and adventures this week long," said Princess Stephanie.

"Only if you promise to tell me of this business of your proposal," replied Margret Anne.

Soon two hours had passed, and it was time for Lady Anne and Margret Anne to leave for home.

"Good evening then, have a safe trip. I will be seeing the both of you soon," said Princess Stephanie.

"Thank you very much for your hospitality. Send our regards to His and Her Majesty for their graciousness and hospitality," commented Lady Anne.

"Oh! Lady Anne, congratulations on the investiture of your title. It is quite an honour, although I believe you have always been a Lady all your life. I shall convey your regards and bye for now," replied Princess Stephanie leaving the apartment.

The carriage ride flew by with an easy conversation between Anne and Margret Anne. Arriving at Kellynch Hall in the late afternoon, Anne realised they had arrived before Frederick and son. Fitzwilliam would stay in town tonight and return tomorrow afternoon.

"Shall we have supper started for our men?" asked Margret Anne.

"Yes, dear that would be lovely," responded Anne, thinking how much Margret Anne had grown, and just so suddenly.

Sir Frederick and Sir Frederick II arrived at Kellynch later in the early evening and just before suppertime. Anne and Margret Anne greeted them at the entrance.

"My dear husband, how I have missed you," exclaimed Anne in a deep hug.

"As I dear Lady Anne!" replied Frederick.

"Where is my Captain?" asked Anne

"Here mother," responded Frederick II with hugs and kisses for Mother and Margret Anne.

"I see you are to be married," commented Margret Anne.

"And mother is Lady Anne Wentworth, Duchess of Glastonbury! Congratulations Mother," exclaimed Frederick II.

"We have just enough time for tea before we go in for supper."

"Ah, perfect dear," replied Frederick.

"I second that," commented Frederick II.

"Now tell me all about this engagement," said Anne as everyone listened intently to the events leading to the asking and the acceptance of Princess Stephanie.

"Would you grace us with the story of this new title dear?" asked Frederick.

At supper, Margret Anne and Anne related their experiences at the palace during the week. "It seems you have both been very successful," commented Frederick asking Anne "What did you like about Her Majesty's Trust Committee?"

"Well, you know I have a passion for helping people, and I believe that given a chance people want to live a happy and productive life. The scope of work that I do here is at the county level and very valuable work that I will continue to support. The work of the Royal Trust spans the scope of the empire. We discussed children, education, women's matters, food, clothing, and organising areas of responsibility and coordination with local charity representatives where they exist. Where they don't exist we will work on a plan to create these entities. It is challenging work to be sure but the good we can do is beyond the imagination," sighed Anne.

"Mother," commented Margret Anne. "Over tea with Her Highness, she mentioned how very pleased she was to have invited you into the Trust committee. She said you changed the character from one of overwhelmed females to one of hopefulness and action. She was humbled at your ability to transform capable women who were once frozen into inaction at the immensity of issues that of capable women taking on each challenge, putting a plan down, and moving to solve it. The committee began to believe they would make a difference in the lives of the people. I was humbled at the description and that this was my mother," said Margret Anne with all looking on with pride.

"I only talked about what we do here in the county dear. I suppose we have learned a lot in these last years that can be applied more broadly and to the benefit of the Empire," added Anne.

"And you Frederick and my Captain! Tell us of your successes at the Admiralty," said Anne.

"I have much to be thankful for Mother. With the guidance of father and Admiral Benwick, every door was opened for me. I presented the preliminary draft for naval strategies and tactics improvements that build on my father's work, and they were well received indeed. Many of the officers there were in awe of my exploits in the last engagement, making working with them a challenge. I had to stop and tell them I was but a man. I commanded great respect, for which I was grateful. I also received the special attention of His Majesty Prince James, and yes of course Princess Stephanie, that kept me in awe in the eyes of many at the assemblies," related Frederick II.

"Dear sister, I have missed you these days away. I hoped for your successes and prayed for you," commented Frederick II.

"I too brother, I suppose it is true twins are more connected to each other than the normal sibling," replied Margret Anne.

"I believe I will miss you very much when you are off on your new life," admitted Frederick II.

"I am fighting all the tears of pain that I should ever leave Kellynch, often asking myself what was I thinking to have set into motion these events," said Margret Anne with a tear in her eyes. "I never wanted to leave this place of such happiness and peace for me."

"You're overly tired dear. Let me take you to bed. All will not seem so hopeless in the morning," said Anne as the men watched, wanting to help but staying out of the way of the women.

The next day, the family rallied around Margret Anne, supporting her in ways that words could not proclaim but clearly stating she was gaining a husband not losing her family! Frederick II, closest to Margret Anne, spent the day at her side, and sometimes just there in sight. Mother and father planned family events for the next couple of days to lighten the atmosphere. They would dine with the Musgroves, invite a number of friends, and picnic on the estate, while Anne would do things that were common to the women folk, even though there was a constant presence of marines now.

Fitzwilliam arrived early afternoon from his exploits in town in a very cheery mode. "Welcome home son," exclaimed Anne.

"Frederick, Princess Stephanie bid me to deliver her love and this note to you!" as Fitzwilliam handed Frederick II the precious papers.

Frederick II noted Princess Stephanie's tales of her last day's activities and how she missed him. "If only a certain someone would invite her to the estate as a guest," wrote Princess Stephanie. With the hint taken Frederick II asked mother and sister if they would invite Princess Stephanie to Kellynch Hall. They agreed. Prince James, on the other hand, is in the neighbourhood on crown business and would stop by on any pretense of visiting Margret Anne.

"Margret Anne, I know of your concern of leaving your beloved Kellynch and family. Have no fear, between responsibilities we will spend as much time here as allowable. I love Kellynch and your family too. There is a great peace here and that is something not so readily found," said Prince James to Margret Anne.

This seemed to lighten Margret Anne's mode quite a bit. "Thank you, James," she said many a time.

When Princess Stephanie arrived at Kellynch Hall, Frederick II and Margret Anne were like children again. They would chat for hours, walk the country lanes, smile, and laugh. Princess Stephanie was obviously in love with Frederick II but had a dear friendship with Margret Anne as well, soon to be a sister.

It was time for Frederick II to spend the day in town and dine with the royal family. Princess Stephanie especially made this date for the marriage announcement, and for it to remain within the family until after Margret Anne and Prince James' wedding. "I like the sound of it, I am engaged to Sir Frederick II," said Princess Stephanie.

Princess Stephanie planned events so she would ride back to town with Frederick. Of course, he was quite pleased with her plans. Margret Anne was invited on two accounts, to not provide a reason for improper behaviour, and her brother sent her a confidential note asking her to please bring Margret Anne. The three talked all the way to town of everything and nothing.

That evening's dining was a wonderful experience. Sir Frederick II was congratulated and invited into the family. Prince James related his respect and friendship with Sir Frederick II and His and Her Majesty talked of how the Wentworths have revived the royal family with all their little ways of being. All too soon the evening was done, and Frederick and Margret would stay the night and in the morning be on their way back to Kellynch. "Please invite me back soon," commented Princess Stephanie.

"Let us settle this now and place it on your schedule," said Margret Anne.

A month later brought the events Margret Anne has set into motion more than a year ago; the marriage of His Highness Princess James to Miss Margret Anne Wentworth of Kellynch Hall. All the arrangements completed, the Wentworths arrived at Kensington Palace with many bouquets of flowers and notes from well-wishers from all over the world. The next days went by in a blur and just that suddenly Margret Anne was Her Royal Highness Princess Margret and married to Prince James.

"Mother we will leave for our honeymoon tomorrow morning. How I will miss you and father, all of you," said Margret Anne.

"We will think of you both each day and send our love and prayers for your happiness," replied Anne.

"Good luck, God bless dears," as the families sent off the newlyweds this morning, with many hundreds of thousands of subjects sending their good wishes.

Two weeks later the Palace announced the happy news of the engagement of Sir Frederick II to Princess Stephanie, the wedding to take place this summer month of June 25th.

CHAPTER 12

The Autum Years

"Frederick, it is almost three years since Princess Stephanie and our Captain married, and now with Stephanie just pregnant, it is only good tidings. I wonder if it is to be a boy or girl," commented Anne.

"Whatever the child we shall love it just the same dear," replied Frederick.

"Of course we will. Margret Ann arrives tomorrow for a much-needed rest and is to stay with us for the week. She is bringing our grandson, Prince William," answered Anne.

"I noticed the marine guard taking up positions around the estate this morning. With such a twenty-four hour signal Margret Anne need not send a dispatch to us of her pending arrival," commented Frederick with a broad smile.

"And it's almost two and one-half years since you retired from the royal navy my dear," mentioned Anne.

"It almost seems like a different lifetime when I think of it," commented Frederick.

Life at Kellynch Hall had become Sir Frederick's world with visits from old naval friends and colleagues who themselves had retired or were about to retire, as well as visits from family and friends making life varied at least.

"It was announced Captain Wentworth would be promoted to Admiral. Like his father, his involvement in Admiralty affairs and the positive effect of his efforts made the promotion possible. Sir Frederick II, I would like to propose a toast. I wish you all the success in your naval career. You have certainly made good in your turn thus far," toasted Frederick.

Sir Frederick II and Princess Stephanie took on Claxton Hall just ten miles on a good road, practically in the neighbourhood, and were frequent and very welcomed visitors to Kellynch. Anne had become as close to Stephanie as any mother. It was one of the charms of Anne that she could befriend someone quickly gain their confidence, and be a positive in their lives.

On one visit Stephanie sat with Anne talking about when the child will be born, "Is it not strange Stephanie that we plan so hard for our children's success only to find they will walk their own path one day," commented Anne.

"I suppose, but we are bound to it anyway," replied Stephanie.

"Sir Frederick naps a bit more these days, does he not madam?" asked Stephanie, changing the subject.

"Yes, I worry for him. The surgeon said this is what comes with older age. I would lose my heart if I were to lose him from my side too soon. I remember his proposal and the happy days following like it was yesterday. In those days Frederick could stay up for two or three days and not at all show signs of tiredness. You know that navy training requires a lot of our men. However, now we are both at the twilight of our lives and so quickly to even comprehend.

"Dear Stephanie, enjoy every moment. Fight hard not to end your days so readily. Hold your Admiral close because these are your days, your days of pure joy, of pure happiness. Soon enough you will look back to these moments and wonder where they have gone," said Anne with her eyes wet with tears as if her heart were breaking just then.

"Ah, my love," said Frederick to Anne strolling into the room. Princess Stephanie, how are you and our grandbaby?" asked Sir Frederick.

"Very well sir," replied Princess Stephanie.

"I was wondering is your husband about?" asked Frederick.

"Yes, in the study I believe. He didn't want to interrupt your nap," replied Stephanie.

"Damn naps; they are a necessity in this time of life but such a waste of time. My love, shall we all take lunch together today?" asked Frederick of Anne.

"Of course dear," replied Anne.

"If you will excuse me, ladies," begged Frederick as he bowed and walked away in the direction of the study.

"He looks well and seems to have all his faculties," said Princess Stephanie to Anne.

"That is all we can ask for," commented Anne.

"Frederick II, I have been looking for you. I wanted to comment on your last note. You asked for my advice on your latest battle tactics and details. I think they are brilliant. I could never have dreamed of such ways or means in my day, and you know how hard I worked and tried to stay ahead of the times," explained Frederick.

"Thank you, father. I feel confident now to present these plans to the Admiralty. Father, you are much talked about and admired at the Admiralty still today," commented Frederick II.

"Thank you, son, give my respects to all. Your sister will arrive tomorrow. Did you notice the marine detachment and the taking up of positions? I believe she will bring little Prince William. You and Stephanie are very welcome to visit anytime or stay if you wish" said Sir Frederick.

"I noticed the guard but didn't know she would be bringing William. Of course, we would be happy to stay, if it is not inconvenient. Is it not almost lunch? Let us settle the affair then with the women," commented Frederick II.

"Father, on a more serious note Mother is concerned for your health these days. You are well, are you not? It is as if she can see the pending time when you will not be with us," said Frederick II sincerely.

"Yes, I can see. It is true I am reaching the end of my days. We all are, but today I am here and I would suggest we enjoy the moments we have! Who knows Mother may leave me first!" commented Sir Frederick with a smile.

"Then father, we live in the moment, because that is what we have," exclaimed Frederick II.

"To lunch then with our women?" asked Sir Frederick as they both walked to the drawing room and the women.

At lunch Frederick broke with convention and sat next to Anne, holding her hand where it was convenient, as if to tell her he would always be at her side. Stephanie and Frederick II were moved by this but tried to act as if it were nothing.

The next day, as expected, Her Royal Highness the Princess Margret and Prince William arrived. "Welcome daughter, how do you do young Prince," said Frederick, shaking hands with his young grandson.

The women surrounded Margret Anne and William, leaving Sir Frederick and Frederick II standing in the wings. "Let the women have their private confidences, Father. We can visit with them later. Are you up for a walk this morning?" asked Frederick II.

"Yes, I am," responded Sir Frederick.

"Sister," said Margret Anne to Stephanie. "Father and mother send their love and a note."

"Prince William is growing so very quickly," exclaimed Anne.

"Are you raising him more in the style of the Wentworths or has palace protocol taken him from you with a governess and such?" asked Stephanie.

"I am with him as much as I can be, in between official duties. I believe he is getting the best one can give with a working mother and father," replied Margret Anne.

Just then Sir Frederick and Frederick II walked past the open door on their way for walking. Prince William bolted for the door to be with the men. "Father would you like to take William on your walk?" asked Margret Anne as tea was brought in for the women.

This would be a serious female discussion and no interference would be best.

"Yes we would be happy to take William with us," replied Frederick II. At that two marine guards attached themselves to the men for the whole of their walk.

The women settled down to tea and conversation. They talked of palace happenings, marriage, politics, child-rearing, and of course their men.

"Sir Frederick is doing well for his age," said Stephanie.

"He has slowed quite a bit these last months, resting more than ever. I worry for him," commented Anne with saddened eyes. "We enjoy each day and I am grateful for all the moments more than ever. I don't know what I would be without him. He saved my life," exclaimed Anne.

"We will rally around you dear mother when that fateful day comes. Nothing can replace Father, he would be dearly missed, but we need you too," responded Margret Anne.

"Then let us resolve to live only in the moment," commented Anne.

It was time for lunch and the women fussed over details since this would be the first time in a while the whole family would be together. Fitzwilliam arrived and would stay for a week visiting with all. Frederick, Frederick II, and Prince William came into the house full of mud and hedge remnants. "You three look so wild from your walk. If we didn't love you so, we would send you to the servant's entrance for bathing and changing," commented Anne with a smile on her face as the men stood with mused faces.

Margret Anne and Stephanie, looking at the sheepish trio of men, confirmed Anne's comment with their appraising looks upon such a scene while offering just a touch of compassion upon the men.

"What an example to give to William. You have undone many months of palace training in manners and courtesies," exclaimed Stephanie as she winked at Margret Anne for concurrence.

"Well then ladies are we not fortunate to be so loved by our women? Let us wash our hands and faces for lunch," exclaimed Sir Frederick.

"Father, did you walk through the hedges row or crawl?" asked Margret Anne with her brilliant smile.

"We did try to walk, truly" responded Frederick II.

At lunch, Frederick sat at Anne's side and somehow, although engaged in the general conversation that comes about in any family meal, he and Anne were in a separate world, a world that only they knew, that only a lover and his love may know. It is that touch of a hand, a glance of the eye, a soft whisper that signals a connection. Still, everyone noticed how young they became in each other's presence.

Princess Margret suggested that all be determined to spend more time at Kellynch Hall together and not waste their life on pursuits that bring no true value. "Is it not family and connections that make us breathe?" asked Margret Anne at the lunch party.

"Yes, it is family. We have all the material things, and we give back to our Empire, why not spend the best of our time with each other?" commented Margret Anne.

"Yes, let us be determined," replied Stephanie, now so much a part of the family, a truer sister and daughter there could not be.

In the next year, the family found every excuse to come to Kellynch and spend time with mother and father, gathering all those many moments that are stored in the memory for a lifetime.

Prince William grew to a young gentleman, speaking already with great forethought and loving his grandfather dearly, spending many a day in the garden on some adventure or other, both full of hedge row at their return to the scorn of their loving women folk as they smiled at each other's reactions.

Frederick II and Fitzwilliam found excuses to ask father for advice, giving them leave to be at Kellynch and of course bring the women, as it would be improper not to do so for Anne's sake. The family spent many a meal talking of times past, the day's affairs and just enjoying each other's company.

"Frederick II it looks like action?" queried Sir Frederick.

"Our hope is diplomacy will rally a solution Father," replied Frederick.

Stephanie leaned over to Anne with a tear in her eye, "I now know what you suffered when your Captain was off to war. The sleepless nights just looking at your husband hoping that memory would not fade if the worst would befall your beloved," commented Stephanie.

Anne squeezed Stephanie's hands "Let us pray for our diplomat's success then," replied Anne.

"What are you women whispering about?" asked Frederick II

"Nothing dear husbands. Can we not worry for our men in peace?" responded Stephanie

"Father and I are off to Bath for a fortnight," commented Anne.

"When are you off?" asked Frederick II.

"Next week," responded Frederick.

"I can accompany you as far as Bath, and then I am off to Plymouth for Admiralty business and may, in fact, be able to meet you in Bath for a day and your return journey. Shall we settle on this plan?" asked Frederick II.

"It would be wonderful to travel with you Frederick II," said Anne.

Bath became like days of old for Anne and Frederick, with evening assemblies and visits to the pump rooms where they met with long-forgotten acquaintances. They visited all the sentimental places and noticed the growth of Bath since the last they visited some years ago. One evening Anne and Frederick dined with the Honourable Lady Carteret, now aged and a widower. They talked of days past and the ceremony that had gone since.

Frederick II arrived a day early and spent the day with their mother and father. "Son it has been such a long while since I have seen you in uniform. I am startled at your form. Just like your father when he would wear his clothing in that manner and in his day," said Anne.

"Thank you for the compliment, Mother. I am bound to wear it since so many navy reside here in Bath. One must keep up the navy while away from her ships and ports."

"I remember those days," commented Frederick with a grin.

The trip back to Kellynch was filled with lively conversation and all the changes to the countryside, the size of the villages, the condition of the roads, and the weather. Arriving at Kellynch Hall all was as it was left. "Sweetheart, I will spend the coming week in town at the palace on Trust committee business. Will you be ok without me for a week?" queried Anne.

"Yes my dear, it will be a quiet week I fear, but I shall occupy myself with reading, walks, and letters to my dear children."

At breakfast the following week, "I am off to town this morning dear and will be returning Friday. I will travel with Margret Anne, Prince James, and Fitzwilliam," commented Anne.

"You will be missed dear. Will you send me a dispatch of your safe arrival?" asked Frederick.

"Yes, I shall," answered Anne.

"Please rest and protect yourself from the drafts," said Anne.

"Of course," responded Frederick.

Later that week Frederick felt overly tired and went off to bed early. The next morning came quickly but Frederick didn't have the strength to leave his bed. Since no one was home but the servants it wasn't until late morning the next day before it was noticed by the staff that Sir Frederick had not yet risen. They called in the surgeon who came as quickly as possible.

"Sir Frederick, Sir Frederick speak to me. How are you? Are you in pain?" asked the surgeon.

"No pain, just very tired. I could sleep the day away," replied Frederick.

After some examination, the surgeon instructed, "Here, drink this Sir Frederick."

Turning to the servants, the surgeon ordered new linens for the bed, and a general tidy-up of the room. "Where is Lady Anne?" asked the surgeon to the servants.

"She is in town at the palace sir," answered one of the servants.

"I must send word to her quickly."

Just then a carriage carrying Princess Stephanie stopped at the entrance.

The surgeon greeted Princess Stephanie, apprising her of the situation with Sir Frederick. Stephanie ran to Frederick's side. He was awake and sitting up as she entered the room. "Princess please excuse me for not performing the natural courtesies when a gentleman greets a lady," said Sir Frederick.

With tears in her eyes, "Sir Frederick, will you not stay longer with us? We are not ready to let you go so soon. You have been like a father to me since I first came to this beloved place. I am now bound to you in heart sir," Princess Stephanie tearfully.

"I am trying dear child. Whatever will face us, let us have courage together," replied Frederick.

"What can I do to help you?" asked Princess Stephanie.

"Would you call for Anne? She is in town, at the palace."

"At once sir, I will order one of my guards to fetch the Lady Anne immediately, and in the meantime, I shall attend you day and night," exclaimed Princess Stephanie.

"Guard! Come here please, I send you on an urgent commission to fetch the Lady Anne and Her Royal Highness the Princess Margret from town. They are at the palace with my mother and father the King. You are to give them each these dispatches, and take charge of their arrangements, and assure a safe and swift return to Kellynch Hall. Take these notes to them at all possible speed," commanded Princess Stephanie.

"Immediately ma'am," responded the guard, running for his horse.

"Servant come to me," commanded Princess Stephanie. "I would have these dispatches sent immediately and at all possible speed to Fitzwilliam, Elizabeth, Mary, and Prince James begging their return to Kellynch Hall. See to this now, and thank you."

"Yes ma'am," replied the servant.

"Carriage man, quickly go to fetch Sir Frederick II, hand him this dispatch, and bring him to Kellynch Hall."

The carriage man boarded the carriage when just at the moment Frederick II on horseback was entering the grounds. Princess Stephanie ran to him before he could approach and Frederick, alarmed, quickly dismounted his horse. "My dear, what is it? Are you well?" asked Frederick.

"Your father Frederick, is bedridden. I sent one of my guards to town to fetch Lady Anne and our sister Margret, as well as dispatches for the return of Fitzwilliam, Elizabeth, and Mary," replied Stephanie.

The surgeon was waiting in the entry hall of the home when Frederick II entered with Princess Stephanie. "What is the condition of my father sir?" asked Frederick II.

"Well, I believe Sir Frederick suffered a stroke, thus his weakness, but he seems to have come through it. My fear is he is now on the decline and loved ones should stay close to home. It will not be long now I fear," advised the surgeon.

"How long do you estimate Sir?" asked Frederick.

"In my experience, it could be anywhere from a week to a month. One never knows in these affairs sir," responded the surgeon.

Frederick II and Stephanie entered Sir Frederick's room. He was sitting up in bed reading quietly, "Ah son, I am glad you are here, thank you for coming. My dear daughter Stephanie has taken very good care of me," said Sir Frederick.

"How are you father? I can fight battles with nerves of steel, but I fear it will break my heart if you leave us too soon," commented Frederick II.

"Son, I will never leave you. I am in your heart and mind forever and always, know this truth," said Sir Frederick looking in his son's eyes deeply. "Daughter do you have time to send word to my Anne?" asked Sir Frederick of Princess Stephanie.

"Yes sir, I sent my personal guard. I also sent word to Margret Anne and Fitzwilliam, Elizabeth, and Mary," replied Princess Stephanie knowing the stroke can affect memory.

"Thank you child for your kind attention to me, would you have tea brought in? I fear I haven't the strength to dress and walk to the drawing room," commented Sir Frederick.

"Of course father, at once," said Princess Stephanie asking a servant to bring tea.

After tea, Frederick was clearly tired and needed rest so Frederick II and Stephanie removed themselves to the drawing room, checking on him often. "I knew these days would come but still there is no preparation. I will miss him so, he has been a good father and mentor to me," commented Frederick II to Stephanie.

"He is not gone from us yet and your strength will be in much demand these next days and weeks. Sir Frederick is correct in saying that he is in you. You and he are so alike in manner and temper. He will never leave you," said Stephanie.

Very late that night, Anne and Margret arrived. Stephanie had the servants ready with tea and food. Frederick and Stephanie met Anne and Margret at the door. "He has not gone from us yet has he?" with tears asked Anne. She looked so small and frail herself at that moment.

"No Mother, he is resting, and we took tea with him this evening in your rooms. We have been checking on him regularly. I will take you up to him," said Frederick II.

"Thank you Stephanie for all you have done," said Margret, squeezing Stephanie's hand.

"Sir Frederick is sleeping well Lady Anne, Princess Margret. I feel confident he will have a better day tomorrow," commented the surgeon, bowing.

"I will sit with him tonight," commented Anne.

"Mother, perhaps if I take turns with you. I would worry if you were up all night. The strain, you need to rest too. See I am young and can stay up for days. Let me stand watch. I will have tea and food brought up to you," implored Frederick.

"We can all take turns since we will all shatter if we just sit in wait," commented Margret.

"Perhaps if we bring Mother a bed into the room," suggested Stephanie.

"I will sleep in my husband's bed like I have these more than thirty years," responded Anne.

"Will you not take some refreshment first Mother?" asked Frederick II.

"No, I am not hungry dear. Perhaps some tea can be brought up," responded Anne as they all walked to the dining room where a late supper was prepared and waiting.

It was early morning when Frederick, looking at Anne through the early light of dawn, said "My dear I thought I had died and gone to heaven. You are all I ever wanted in my life, and you have been everything to me since. I am sorry for this worry upon you.

"I was very careful not to over-exert. I just felt tired more than normal. The next morning I was not able to find the strength to get out of bed you see."

"I was worried that you might have left me without saying goodbye. I worried I left you at the wrong time my dear," said Anne.

Margret Anne was listening in the corner of the room, keeping watch over Father this hour, touched by their words and not trying to intrude. "I will not leave you so soon if I can help it dear, and if I am to leave first then one day I will stand at that heavenly doorway waiting for you, I promise," said Frederick as they cried in each other's arms.

Margret, with tears in her eyes as father reached out his hand to her, "My two most special girls in the world. Thank you for having me in your life. I love you both so very much."

In the full sun, Frederick sat up in bed, and met with Stephanie, thanking her for fetching the family. Frederick's sons were there with all their attention to father and mother. Sir Frederick had time to speak with Frederick II, "Son. You will be head of this family soon. Everyone will depend on you, and this will present even more challenges for you with naval commitments but have courage. Today I am feeling better, I wonder if I can retreat to the chair there."

I wonder what the surgeon will say to that," commented Frederick with a broad smile.

Dispatches were coming from everywhere and everyone as word came out that Sir Frederick was gravely ill. Anne brought some to Frederick; these are special dispatches from His and Her Majesty, the prime minister, lords and ladies, and just enough of them not to be tiresome.

Family members came and went throughout the day. Mostly, everyone wanted to be together, while also giving Anne and Frederick the privacy they needed, that lover's need. The day went by so very fast, and in the blink of an eye, everyone was ready to retire for the evening. Frederick had a good day. The family had a good day together, saying things normally left unsaid.

Anne lay with Frederick listening for every breath, noticing every movement. Sometimes, although asleep, Anne could hear Frederick softly call her name in the dearest of tones. "How I wish I could turn back time my dearest love, my life. How I will miss you all the days of my life," said Anne softly in tears, thinking to herself, "Be brave, be brave."

Morning came so quickly, "I love you, my dear," would be her first words to him.

This day was different than the other. One could almost see Frederick was between the worlds now, trying hard not to leave and being pulled by a force stronger than time to go. He was in and out of consciousness. Anne was at his side praying, holding his hand, loving, and hoping somehow she could bear this moment and the rest of her life without him.

Then Frederick opened his eyes, completely clear-minded. He looked at his Anne and the children, "I love you all, thank you so very much for being in my life, for the privileges." Then looking at Anne through tears, "I will wait for you, my love. I will never leave you. I promise. I love you now and forever and ever. Live for me, celebrate life for me, and love for me. I will know and I will bless those moments and wait for the day you return to my arms, truly."

With that, his eyes closed and in a most peaceful way, Frederick was gone from this world.

CHAPTER 13

Honors For Anne

Anne wrote in her diary, "It will be a year since my Captain's passing. How lonely I have felt without him by my side. It's the little things I want to tell him. How William has grown. The roses are wonderful this spring; Stephanie has given birth to a beautiful son, and she named him Harry Frederick, he looks like you already in his young life, and I miss talking to you about what only a husband and wife can share.

This last year has flown by really. I lived but a half-life. The kids have been wonderful to include me in their lives, but I cried this entire year, an observer not really a participator. I keep remembering your last words to me 'live for me, celebrate life for me, and love for me". I am trying my love. I will try harder and with all my heart."

This morning it was raining, like many a typical English spring day. Anne rose from her bed, prepared herself for the day, and made her way to breakfast of tea and toast. "Stephanie will be visiting with Harry. I will find the strength to be bright and cheerful. I will just be light, love, and hope today. I will live in the moment and enjoy each of them as best I can. I will just give into life and trust, what will be," she thought in a determined way with just a bit more of a healing in her heart.

"Good morning Mother," said Stephanie as she entered the room with Harry.

"Granny, Granny!" said Harry at once on her lap.

"Good morning Stephanie. Thank you for coming today despite the rain. Cup of tea?" asked Anne.

"Yes please and how are you today? You seem brighter. Your face has a light I haven't seen in it since your Frederick's passing?" said Stephanie inquiring earnestly.

"I woke up this morning thinking of Frederick's last words to me. He said, 'Live for me, celebrate life for me and love for me". I haven't had the strength this last year to answer his call until now. I awoke with these words on my lips. For the first time, I feel strong enough to take perhaps weak steps at first toward these goals. I am determined. I will enjoy each moment and be grateful for all of you and life," said Anne.

"I am a glad mother. We have all worried about you, missing you so very much, and praying for you. We need you, all of you in our lives. We can never replace Frederick but we all need you more since his passing. You give us the strength to live our lives in an ever-changing world. We are grateful to have you," said Stephanie.

"I am sorry I have been…away really this last year. I lost the rock in my life. Frederick meant so much to me, and suddenly he was gone. All that I lived for was for him. I was glad for every moment, and then I had to live for myself. I cried every day this last year, but now I am determined to honour my husband with a life that celebrates him, us," explained Anne.

"How can we help you? We all need you and depend on you, your advice, and just your presence in our lives," said Stephanie.

"Well dear, I was going to write a note to your mother asking if I may resume my efforts with her charity trust as a start. What do you think? Is it too soon?" asked Anne.

"No, not at all, Mother has quietly asked about you often as well as many of the ladies of the committee. They are praying for you. She would be so very happy to hear from you. You have such a positive way with people. It is a wonderful idea. I will help you in any way," commented Stephanie, smiling with hope and squeezing Anne's hand. "I shall write a letter later today then, without delay."

"Right then, how is your Admiral these days? When will I see my son?" asked Anne.

"Frederick II is well. He has been spending more time at the Admiralty. It looks like a conflict is on the horizon. I am so worried about him. War means many of our men are in harm's way and many will not come home from it. He will be landbound. It is our hope the diplomats will be able to find some way to avoid this path. Father is working with the prime minister and members of the parliament to find better ways than war in this case," explained Stephanie.

"Your father is very formidable dear, and if there is a will there will be a way. I am sure of it," replied Anne.

"Frederick II, I and the child will visit with you this weekend. Will that be inconvenient for you?" asked Stephanie.

"Of course not, it is never inconvenient child! You are always dearly welcomed here!" responded Anne with a rare smile these days.

"I will be so happy to tell Frederick II of your light and your smile returning. He will be very happy at the thought of you returning to us. We have missed you so," said Stephanie.

"Thank you dear for your love, your patience, I love you too," answered Anne.

The next day Anne received a dispatch from Her Majesty the Queen in response to her note sent just yesterday. It said "My dear Lady Anne; I was so happy to receive your note this day I was determined to reply this minute. You are very welcome to return to the charity trust! Our next meeting is May seventeenth, and I invite you as my particular guest to stay at the palace. Beyond the charity, I have to say I have missed your friendship and am glad you are back with us. So many of our members have missed you and ask for you often. I will leave it a surprise of your return to us all. I am sending a palace carriage and marine guard to convey you safely." Your dear friend, The Queen."

"Mother! Where are you?" cried Fitzwilliam.

"Here dear, I was not expecting you until the weekend," answered Anne, receiving kisses on the cheek. "I have called for tea in the drawing room, come walk with me."

"I heard of this transformation in your mother and wanted to see it for myself. It is true; you have come alive to us again. And we are glad of it. This last year has been hard on the whole family with father's passing, but we also felt we lost you too and that was an unexpected blow to all of us. We love you, need you, and want you in our lives as long as we can have you, mother," explained Fitzwilliam looking deeply into her eyes.

"I am truly grieved my dear for neglecting my children this last year. The loss of Frederick was so hard on me, that I couldn't find my way out. I grieved the whole of this last year, but now I am determined to honour his memory with his last words to me. He said to celebrate him by living and loving life, and I intend to do just that. Just this day I received a note from Her Majesty granting me leave to return to the charity trust and to be her particular guest at the palace," commented Anne.

"That is a wonderful mother! I am so glad for you. When is your next meeting? May I escort you to town? How can I help you?" asked Fitzwilliam.

Overwhelmed with emotion, Anne answered, "Her Majesty is sending a palace carriage with a marine guard to convey me, but you may accompany me to town."

Stephanie and Frederick II also arrived unexpectedly in the late afternoon. "Mother, what is this transformation I am hearing about?" asked Frederick II as Harry ran into Anne's arms.

"Well, dear I am determined to get back into life by honouring Frederick's memory and his last words to me to celebrate him - love and live life," commented Anne.

"I can see the difference in your mother. Your light is back. Your face is full of smiles and I am glad of it, truly," commented Frederick II. "We miss Father but we thought we lost you too," added Frederick II.

Marine guards began to take up positions around the hall grounds. "I believe sister must be coming sometime today. I did send her a note of your renaissance yesterday," mentioned Stephanie.

"I am always glad of all your visits to Kellynch Hall. The more the merrier," mentioned Anne.

Conversations over cups of tea were easy as the children caught up on all the affairs in their lives and only paused when it was clear a royal carriage was arriving. Anne and the children walked to the entrance to find Margret Anne drawing up, and she had brought young Prince William with her.

"Hello mother, Stephanie, Frederick II, Fitzwilliam," cried Margret Anne as all the formalities were observed, with the bowing of the men and courtesy of the woman.

"How did you know to come dear?" asked Anne.

"Well, the Queen who rarely comes to my apartments visited me over her excitement of your return to the Charity Trust. She talked of how she missed your friendship and how the group of women asked after you. Then I received a note from my dear sister Stephanie where she explained the most amazing transformation in you of late, and well I had to come and see it for myself. I have missed you so Mother. It has been hard with father passing, I thought you were lost to us as well," explained Margret Anne.

Back in the drawing room over tea, Anne commented "I apologise to all of you for my manner this last year. I missed Frederick so very much. All I could do was cry every day. Although I still miss him, I feel I have the strength to honour his last words to me. Thank you all for supporting me even without the hope

I would come out of my grief and tears. I will live. I will love… all of you and I will be in life, to honour Frederick. Be assured of this," said Anne.

"I for one am glad of it Mother," said Frederick II.

With the two boys, William and Harry, playing together the adults caught up on all the news of late and each other's affairs. "How long will you stay dear Margret Anne?" asked Anne.

"For the week if you will have me Mother?" answered Margret Anne.

"Of course I will have you dear and as long as you like," commented Anne.

"Then let us make this a family reunion of brothers and sisters too!" exclaimed Fitzwilliam.

The next days brought much in the way of fulfillment. With the sun shining, the family walked the nearby country lanes together, and had suppers and lunches. They caught up on all their doings. One day it was so warm and inviting that they walked to the nearby village to many a resident's surprise. While there, many passersby sent their love and respect to Anne and the rest of the family.

"The marine guards did have to earn their income on these days of adventure," said Princess Stephanie. And of course, the party didn't linger too long for fear of disrupting the commerce of the village for too long a period of time.

It was good for Anne to have this time in public. It gave her confidence again and with the family at her side cheering her on, she could not fail to regain her poise. Once on the way back, they all stopped at the village churchyard to visit Sir Frederick's resting place. Anne battled with the Admiralty for the right to bury her Admiral in the family plot rather than to lay him to rest at sea which is customary for admirals. Anne could not stand the thought of Frederick's remains so far away from her, so she made it a point to have him placed in the family section of the churchyard.

This was only the first time she had visited him since the funeral. It was only now she had the strength.

Having picked wild flowers from the hedge along the way she, Margret Anne, and Stephanie placed their bright bunches of flowers on the grave. The family all held hands and prayed for a moment as some villagers paused to view the touching site and hoped Anne and this beloved family would return to public affairs once again.

"Bless you, bless you," could be heard as the party walked back in the direction of Kellynch Hall.

"Today was a good day. The best day since Frederick's passing" wrote Ann in her diary.

With lots of friends hearing of Anne's rise in spirits, there came many a note and surprise visitors every few days now. "Thank you Harriet for helping Stephanie hold up the county charity works while I was not able to help. I see you have been assisting my daughter. I have always appreciated your friendship and loyalty to me," commented Anne over tea with Harriet.

"Thank you dear Anne but I cannot take all the credit. Princess Stephanie stepped right into your role and organised, encouraged, and participated in all the ways you would have. She is quite a lady and has been very gracious to me at every turn. We missed you, Anne. I am glad for the rise in your spirits," said Harriet.

"I am glad for it too Harriet," commented Anne.

The Admiralty sent a dispatch to Anne via Admiral Wentworth II. In it, it said "It is at His Majesty's pleasure that we announce the christening of H.M.S. Wentworth on the twenty third of August in the year of our lord 1827. You are invited as His Majesty's and the Admiralty's particular guest for the ceremony in honour of the Admiral Sir Frederick Wentworth."

In an open portion in His Majesty's own handwriting it read "Dear Lady Anne, please know of my glad step in knowing of your rise in spirits. Do come to this ceremony as the Queen and I have missed your company dearly. I will send my personal carriage to convey you and your family to Plymouth," warmest regards, His Majesty, the King.

"Of course you must go, mother. I will come arriving the night before in His Majesty's box. The whole family is invited. Father and you served this Empire well and many want to say thank you," commented Frederick II.

"I feel strong enough to go, son, will you be my escort?"

"Of course Mother it could go no other way. I will personally make all the arrangements for you and the family. Be assured," responded Frederick II, so grown up and competent now.

"Just like his father," thought Anne.

"Next week I am off to London on Her Majesty's charity trust business for a few days. Fitzwilliam will escort me there and back," said Anne.

"I am glad for it mother. You do so much good there. You are not only helping the people the charity is meant for, but you help the charity volunteers in so many ways. I would think everyone will be glad of your return," related Frederick.

A few days later it was time to travel to town, "Mother, the palace carriage is out front and ready to convey us to town. It is time we left. Do you have everything you will need?" asked Fitzwilliam.

"Yes dear, I am sorry for my delay. This is the first time I am leaving Kellynch Hall since your father's passing. I am a little apprehensive as you can imagine," said Anne as she entered the carriage.

"Mother I have, at the request of Frederick II, looked at the family's personal finances and find we have increased our wealth significantly through a number of sound investments father and I engaged in some years ago. So the family is doing well in that respect, and with your high spirits, we are very well off indeed. Thank you for coming back to us mother, we dearly missed your enthusiasm for life. The reason I mention this is you were keen on the setting up of schools and trade training for the young people in the county and wondered about the family funding such an endeavour. Well, we can now afford the funds. All it will take is the organising of the endeavor. I volunteer to look into the financing of it, and Princess Stephanie and Frederick II will draw up the plans," said Fitzwilliam.

"Thank you Fitzwilliam. We can look to this endeavour upon our return in the next few days then. I love you all very much," said Anne as the carriage slowed in arriving at the palace gates.

"I shall return to the palace this Wednesday evening to escort you back to Kellynch Hall," commented Fitzwilliam.

"Yes right then, I shall be waiting dear," replied Anne.

The palace servants, ever so efficient, conveyed Anne to guest apartments where to her surprise Her Majesty the Queen and Princess Margret were assuring Anne's every convenience. "Your Majesty's," said Anne in a courtesy.

"Dear Anne, I am so glad to see you again. I and your daughter are so excited you are here. We wanted to personally ensure everything was ready in the apartments. We hope we do not intrude?" said the Queen.

"Your Majesty I am overwhelmed with your kindness and am very grateful for your attention, truly. There is no intrusion surely," replied Anne.

"I will leave you with our daughter for now Lady Anne, but tomorrow you are mine the whole of the day," commented the Queen.

"Yes, of course, Your Majesty," replied Anne as the Queen left the apartments.

"Mother, I am so glad to see you out and about again. I cleared my schedule of duties, so I can be at your disposal throughout your stay. Tell me, mother, how are you?" asked Margret Anne sincerely.

"Thank you, dear. I was a little worried leaving Kellynch Hall for the first time since my Captain's passing but the trip to town was very pleasant and Fitzwilliam is so humorous these days. Have you noticed?" said Anne.

"Yes, Fitzwilliam has a keen sense of the human condition and the gift of talking about serious problems in a way that puts all his listeners at ease. He has been a great asset to His Majesty," replied Margret Anne.

"Mother would you like to dine with Her Majesty and I this evening, quite informal mind you, just three friends catching up on all the news and happenings in each other's lives. We will leave all the royal titles in our rooms for the evening. What do you say to that?" asked Margret Anne.

"I accept with pleasure, being alone is still a bother for me with Frederick no here," answered Anne.

"Dear Anne, thank you for accepting supper with me and your daughter this evening. I have missed you and not just because of your extraordinary work at the charity but as a result of a deep and abiding friendship," said the Queen.

"Thank you your Majesty for this great privilege, surely," replied Anne.

Supper went famously as if no time had passed. The ladies caught up on all the latest news and happening. These types of conversations had a way of binding friendships and renewing spirits. "Anne, about tomorrow's charity work, I will dispense of the scheduled items. Our group of women will want to welcome you back. So many have missed you and worried you were lost to us, so rather than act like everything is normal many have asked me if we could just celebrate our friendships and your return to this meeting as a reminder that we are all bound in some way and care for each other, and I agreed," relayed the Queen.

"It really is overwhelming all the sentiment your Majesty. I didn't realise the effect I had on so many," replied Anne.

"You have a great influence mother, and we are glad of it. Only today did many find you had arrived at the palace and sent a note to ask if you would be strong enough to attend the charity tomorrow and can they help in any small way. You have many friends here," commented Margret Anne, with the Queen agreeing in gesture.

"Thank you, thank you all so much," said Anne.

The next morning went well, starting with Margret Anne having breakfast with Anne. Later that morning Anne was scheduled to meet with the Queen, then the Charity Trust committee members for tea. Of course, the Queen mentioned she would dispense of the formal work and have a more informal get-together since everyone missed Anne.

"Your Majesty," said Anne.

"Anne, good to see you; how was your evening?" asked the Queen.

"Very good your Majesty, I spent time with our daughter and had time to catch up on everything and nothing," commented Anne.

"Anne, on a more serious note, the events of the last year has brought to light something important that is a responsibility of the Monarch but fell, by the wayside. For years many members have given time and resources in the effort to build up the Charity Trust, however with no recognition, no honour for the extraordinary efforts put forth. It is my duty to say thank you, from a grateful Monarch and grateful Empire. Before we visit with the committee for the afternoon His Majesty and I would like to honour you with a distinction for exceptional service to King and Country," explained the Queen.

"Your Majesty I am quite honoured but there is no need truly," responded Anne.

"Lady Anne that is why it must be so, and by royal command," replied the Queen.

"Then, it must be so your Majesty, and I will accept gratefully," replied Anne.

A servant entered the room; he motioned to her Majesty at the readiness of her next appointment. "Anne would you walk with me please," asked the Queen as Anne complied. They walked through a number of corridors and down a number of grand staircases to a mirrored set of doors stretching from ceiling to floor. This area of the palace was not unknown to Anne, since she had been here once before many years earlier. "Do you remember this area of the palace Anne?" asked the Queen.

"Yes, many years ago. This is where Frederick and Frederick II were knighted by His Majesty just on the other side of these doors. I sat just there so proud of my men," said Anne.

"Yes, quite true," commented the Queen.

At each side of the door were palace guards dressed in opulent costumes, sword and breast shields polished to perfection. They had paused when suddenly as if on cue trumpets blared and the doors began to open slowly. "Anne have you ever been to the throne room?" asked the Queen. "No your Majesty," responded Anne meekly.

Once in a while the full power and glory of the Empire was on display and today was one of those days.

"Anne I will walk at your side and guide you through this ceremony," related the Queen.

"Your Majesty, what ceremony pray?" asked Anne.

"Why your honour dear friend," replied the Queen. "Right then, let us walk in slowly and pause to the right," commanded her Majesty.

Anne realised the Trust committee, naval representatives, Order of the Garter, and various Lords and Ladies were in attendance. "For me your Majesty?" asked Anne meekly.

"Yes, for you Lady Anne," replied the Queen.

The King stood up from his throne where he stepped forward and addressed the assembly. "Lords, ladies, and knights, today it gives me the greatest pleasure to honour a British subject whose work on behalf of her King and Queen and the Empire has earned her great distinction. Her efforts have benefited the Empire and enhanced the lives of countless subjects. She is quiet and modest but her impact is profound. Walk forward with me Lady Anne," commanded Her Majesty.

Her Royal Highness the Princess Margret, dressed in the full regalia of her rank, with Princess Stephanie at her side, arrived to stand with Anne so that the Queen was to the right and they to the left and back of Anne. "Lady Anne, enjoying the general splendor of this place?" asked Princess Stephanie in her regalia, smiling slyly.

"I know of the pomp and circumstance but this is so magnificent, truly," commented Anne discreetly.

"Enjoy this Mother, you deserve it," replied Princess Stephanie.

Anne could see in the audience, Fitzwilliam, Sir Frederick II, Elizabeth, and Mary. "You kept this secret well daughters," said Anne just loud enough to be heard and appreciated.

"Let us approach the throne," commanded the Queen as the King held the sword of England in his right hand. With all very quiet now and not a sound to be heard, "Lady Anne Wentworth approach your King," commanded his Majesty.

"Don't forget to kneel there Lady Anne," mentioned the Queen. Anne approached and kneeled just there as marine guards quickly came to Lady Anne's side to assist her in this way, gently holding her arms for support.

"At the pleasure of your King it is with great honour I bestow upon you honourary membership into the Order of the Garter. This distinction for your lifetime of charity works on behalf of the Crown and the Empire," said the King tapping her shoulders twice with his sword. "Please stand with marine guards assisting, I would like to present Lady Anne Wentworth as a member of the Order of the Garter," said the King to much applause.

Anne was quickly surrounded by servants who carefully put over garments of the order on her person as a rite of passage. "You look well, Lady Anne. I am glad to see it!" commented the King.

"Thank you, your Majesty, Thank you," replied Anne.

As the King, Queen, and Princesses withdrew, attendees surrounded Anne asking about her health and how radiant she looked, of their concern for her, and congratulations for the honours just given. The Admiralty representatives reminded Anne of the planned celebrations at Plymouth in August. "God willing I will be there," said Anne. The charity committee members then escorted Anne.

And so the gathering moved to a nearby ballroom where tea and sandwiches were laid out for all to enjoy. Conversations flowed from one to the other as the evening quickly approached. "Anne we missed you so, and are so glad of your return," commented Lady Elton.

"Thank you Lady Elton for your kindness," replied Anne.

Princess Margret, watching her mother, assured her she did not overstrain herself with all the well-wishers. So many wanted a word with Lady Anne, and Margret would bring tea and food to Anne.

Soon it was time to say goodbye to the gathering. Anne was clearly tired and needed time to retire before dining this evening. "Welcome back to the Trust committee, tomorrow we will resume normal business, thank you all for coming and welcoming Anne back," exclaimed the Queen. With that Princess Margret and Princess Stephanie escorted Anne to her guest apartments.

"Mother how are you?" asked Margret.

"A bit tired but good in spirit. At any age, that ceremony would have been taxing," replied Anne.

"Yes, of course, mother, that it would," commented Margret Anne as they walked into the guest apartments. "Here rest now for a while. I will be back later this evening to sit with you for supper with His Majesties. In the meantime, Princess Stephanie will stay with you."

Supper went very well with much in the way of amiable conversation and the catching up of ole friends.

So quickly the next days flew by and Fitzwilliam would be here in less than an hour for the escort back to Anne's beloved Kellynch Hall.

Princess Margret and Princess Stephanie stopped by for tea and a final goodbye for now, joined by Fitzwilliam. They all fell into a familiar chat.

Without noticing, His Majesty and Her Majesty were standing at the threshold of the apartment when suddenly Anne stood up "Your Majesty's, please be welcomed," said Anne as they all performed the proper courtesies.

"We stopped by to say safe trip, Lady Anne," said the Queen. "Husband, do we have time to take tea with Anne before she leaves for Kellynch Hall?"

"I am King. I suppose I can command this to be so if Anne would have us?" asked the King.

"Of course," said Anne.

After easy and lively conversation, one with less small talk and more of true friendship, Anne was on her way to Kellynch Hall with Fitzwilliam. With her head on his broad shoulders sound asleep, "You seem so frail and small these days Mother," thought Fitzwilliam.

The next month and a half were idyllic. Summer at Kellynch brought out its best in colourful plants, bushes, and wildlife. Anne loved the outdoors and could be found in the gardens when the weather permitted. "Mother," cried Stephanie. "Harry wants to find you."

"I am here Stephanie by the lavender clumps. Harry, Harry," called Anne, as Harry slipped to her side easily.

"What are we doing granny?" asked Harry.

"Let us discover lavender plants," replied Anne.

"What colour are they granny?" asked Harry.

"Purple," commented Anne.

"Granny, the plants before you are purple," commented Harry.

"Yes dear, these are lavender plants. Notice the smell, and the colour and rub them in your hands."

As tea was brought to the porch, Anne and Stephanie talked over the coming weeks of events at Plymouth.

"You look wonderful and healthy mother. The garden suits you well," exclaimed Stephanie.

"It is true we have had a glorious summer this year, and I revel in it. Have you also noticed the many butterflies?" asked Anne as they watched Harry in the lavender hedge.

The following week would be busy with preparations for leaving for Plymouth. All the children stopped by save for Frederick II who is in Plymouth. "Frederick II will accompany the royal carriage arriving tomorrow afternoon. He will be your escort to Plymouth and throughout the week's events. Mother, we will be leaving for Plymouth tomorrow morning. "Frederick II will then leave for Kellynch II to come fetch you. By then I and Harry will be settled and ready for your arrival tomorrow evening," said Stephanie.

"Thank you dear, I will be quite calm at the knowledge that you are there and ready to receive me. At my age, as you can imagine, it is not so easy to travel about the country as when one is young," replied Anne.

"Fitzwilliam will be arriving this morning to stay with you so you are not alone this evening and assist you in any way. I believe he may be accompanying you and Frederick II to Plymouth tomorrow," commented Stephanie.

"I will be glad for that. To have my two men at my side will be a great comfort indeed," explained Anne.

The next morning went as expected as the servants prepared all the bags for travel while Anne and Fitzwilliam breakfasted on the porch to a lovely August sun and warm temperatures. "We have had an exceptional summer Mother," exclaimed Fitzwilliam.

"I have loved every minute of my time in the gardens. Stephanie has been so kind to visit, frequently bringing Harry. We have had many adventures in the wilds of the nearby wood. Sometimes young Prince William would attend our conquests. Truly so much fun, it seems it is the simple things that matter now," replied Anne.

"This business of Plymouth brings up many memories of your father," said Anne looking as if into another world. "How I miss him so. I talk to him every day, as if he were at my side, and write to him as if he has gone away to Plymouth. Yes, Fitzwilliam your mother is a bit out of the mind," commented Anne.

"No Mother, you are the sanest person I know. You and Father have a rare love, a true love. I ask him for advice all the time. I assure you we all miss him too. However, we are glad you are with us. We need you too," said Fitzwilliam as a servant came in announcing Admiral Wentworth's arrival.

"Son!" exclaimed Anne.

"Mother" cried Frederick II with a kiss on the cheek, then turning to Fitzwilliam, "Brother! Mother, how are you today?" asked Frederick II.

"Quite well thank you."

Brother, will you be joining us on our journey to Plymouth?" asked Frederick II of Fitzwilliam.

"I believe so if you will have me brother?" queried Fitzwilliam.

"Of course!" responded Frederick II.

"Tea and food first, then we journey. I asked the servants to load all the bags," commented Frederick II in the meantime.

On the way to Plymouth Frederick explained the agenda of events and what to expect. "Son, the last time I was in Plymouth, I was with your father. It will be strange without him, but it is a comfort to be with my two boys," explained Anne.

"Thank you mother it is an honour to be your escort," exclaimed Frederick II. His Majesty is looking forward to seeing you, and both send their warmest regards for your safe conveyance."

"All of you have taken time to visit with me many times these several months, Thank you. I have had a wonderful summer. Tell my daughter how much her frequent visits with Harry have meant to me," commented Anne.

"Yes, Mother I will. It is always a pleasure to be with you," responded Frederick II with a concurrence from Fitzwilliam.

Arriving just outside of Plymouth the carriage was surrounded by naval cadets on horseback. They were fully uniformed. "Here man, what is this?" asked Admiral Wentworth as a young cadet approached saluting.

"At ease cadet, what is this about?" commanded Admiral Wentworth.

"Sir, it would be with the greatest honour and respect to accord Admiral Wentworth's widow an honourary escort. May we escort the Lady Anne Wentworth, Duchess of Glastonbury to your apartments at Plymouth sir?" asked the cadet.

"You have our leave, let us proceed then," commanded Admiral Wentworth to shouts of commands.

As the carriage approached Plymouth it did not go unnoticed as it worked its way slowly through the streets. Wherever there were officers they would stop and salute. Many servicemen and the general populace began tailing the carriage along the route to Admiralty quarters until the crowd was quite large. "Father had many friends," said Anne.

"So does the Lady Anne, whose charity work helps sailors and their families throughout the empire," said Frederick II.

As the carriage approached Admiral Wentworth's apartment, Princess Margret and Stephanie and young Prince William and little Harry came out to greet them. The house was surrounded by officers and cadets who wanted to form a guard that then lined both sides to the front door in honour of Lady Anne, making a clear lane to the front door and the Princesses and Young Prince waiting.

"Son, did you know of this? It was unnecessary," commented Anne.

"This is a surprise to me, mother. It seems you and Father made quite a splash those many years together. I am glad for it. Father and you did so much in the day. You deserve it," replied Frederick II.

"Quite overwhelming," commented Fitzwilliam.

Upon exiting the carriage, Margret Anne and Stephanie surrounded Anne. "Mother, how are you? How was your trip?" asked Margret Anne and Stephanie.

"Very good, the weather was fine and the roads smooth the whole way through and the boys kept me laughing throughout," responded Anne, turning to wave at the crowd in thanks for their kind and surprising reception.

Once inside the house, tea was served and the women talked of all the notes and dispatches that had been arriving all day from every corner of the Empire. "You are quite a famous mother in your own right," commented Margret Anne.

"Your father was the hero. He saved my life and brought all this upon the family. Even in his passing his light shines on us all," replied Anne.

"Frederick II, what will be the events for tomorrow?" asked Anne.

"At midday, we are to go to the yards to rehearse the christening ceremony. I will be your escort, then it is lunch with the royals, and the evening will be a presentation and ball at Admiralty Hall," commented Frederick.

"The next day starts with the christening of H.M.S Wentworth, then a tour of the ship, the meeting of dignitaries, and finally a quiet night with your children. Then the next day we travel back to Kellynch Hall," said Frederick II.

"Dear, would it be so much out of the way to spend a day in Bath with you all on the way back? This will be my last opportunity to visit this beloved place. I would like to take you all on a tour of places your father and I knew so well in our day. Camden Place where he proposed, the café where we spent the day planning our future, and the house, we announced our engagement. There is so little time to tell you, to explain your beginnings," asked Anne.

"Of course mother! It would be an honour to escort you," replied Frederick II as each, in turn, agreed to clear their schedule. It did not go unnoticed that Anne talked in terms of time being short for her as everyone bravely acted as if they had not understood, but in the quiet of each of their hearts, tears fell.

These days brought much in the way of accolades and awards given in honour of her dear Captain Many came to her and talked of their dealings with them and the honour of knowing him and now her. His Majesties honoured Anne with dining and a toast in praise of her late husband, as well as honourary admittance into the Order of the Garter. The young cadets opened doors and lined entries wherever they visited, in the hopes of acquitting themselves with honour.

At the sending off of H.M.S. Wentworth Anne presented a surprise gift to its Captain in the form of Frederick's personal dress sword. The Captain was clearly taken with the gesture, thanking Anne personally. "He called this his war sword and never took it out of his sleeve save in the heat of battle; and now Captain I pass it to you and this magnificent vessel," said Anne.

The Captain was seen carrying the heirloom with reverence and respect to his quarters, promising to pass this honour on to the next captain in turn.

All was as it should have been, Sir Frederick II appointed himself with the utmost dedication to his King, his country, and his family. The events of these days went flawlessly to schedule and with naval precision, but also displayed a gentleness when hardened naval officers softened at Anne's presence and the giving way of their spirit to an English lady in their presence.

"So we are off to Bath Mother?" asked Margret Anne.

"Yes, and I am so very glad of you, Stephanie, and the boys coming with us. How did you get away from royal duties daughter?" asked Anne.

"Well Mother, I can do this with the escort of marine guards and little fanfare, so we may travel quietly without drawing crowds," replied Margret Anne.

"You must have guards in place at Bath already?" commented Frederick II.

"Yes, they arrived last night and have taken up a post in all the areas we know we will visit. They are dressed in plain clothes so as not to attract too much attention. Quite an affair this royal rank," exclaimed Stephanie as Margret Anne smiled in agreement.

"Shall we ladies?" exclaimed Fitzwilliam, escorting the party.

At Bath, the group stopped in for tea at Camden Place. "Thank you Elizabeth for your invitation," said Anne.

Afterward, they began their tour of Baths. "This is the corner where I accepted Frederick. I received a note here at Queen's Square in which Frederick announced his true feelings to me and I ran through the streets to find him. I was quite out of breath but had just enough to tell him of my acceptance. This is the café we spent the day. We talked of our past, the time lost, our future, and the surprise it would be to the family of my engagement. We were so very happy in those days. It could not be otherwise," said Anne.

"Mother, is it true Lady Russell was not keen on Frederick at first?" asked Margret Anne.

"Yes, quite so, it was war you know when Frederick asked me to marry him, and I loved him so but he had no family, no connections, no fortune and was about to set to sea and I the daughter of a baronet. We lost eight years. During that time Frederick worked his way up the ranks of the navy and amassed a fortune in Spanish gold. I kept track of him during this time through the papers, but we never wrote letters and I had little hope of knowing him again.

"When the family retrenched in Bath, Frederick's sister, a dear soul she was, let Kellynch Hall, and Frederick became known to me again. He was angry with me at first and ignored me. Later he said I almost broke his heart being persuaded to change my mind about the engagement but despite it all he had always been constant," explained Anne.

"Did you know Frederick never told me of his dealings with Sir Walter in the purchase of Kellynch Hall? It was a wedding gift to me from him? It was such a surprise. That was a happy day indeed. After the month-long honeymoon he surprised me and that night we had our first supper with the family present. During the dining, I promptly fell ill a surgeon had to be called, and it was announced I was quite pregnant."

"Did you know it was going to be the twin's mother?" asked Margret.

"No, not until later in the pregnancy did the surgeon hear two heartbeats. What a surprise and how terrifying all at the same time. Frederick would not leave my side," explained Anne.

"Here is where I bought my wedding dress, and that is the shop where I first met Frederick in Bath. William Elliot was escorting me home and was paying special attention to me at the time. How much this vexed Frederick. He was beside himself with fear of losing me, but he did not worry, I loved him just as much and wanted him to ask for my hand," said Anne.

"In those days the pump rooms were an important assembly place for those with status. During the day, many would meet and in the evening the setting was staged for plays and concerts. Today it is more in disrepair. Times have changed surely," explained Anne.

"Mother shall we take tea at Camden Place, refresh ourselves, and then take our carriage ride to Kellynch Hall?" asked Frederick II.

"Yes of course dear," replied Anne.

"Dear Harriet and Nurse Rooke informed me of William Elliot's misdeeds in his plan to assure my father's title and the setting up of his mistress Mrs. Clay in town," said Anne.

"Did he not propose to you Lady Anne?" asked Stephanie.

"Why yes he did. I would not answer in the hopes of Frederick's proposal. Almost immediately I received his letter of offer and that changed my life," related Anne.

Conversation flowed at tea and much of the family history before the children was related to some of it for the first time.

"Shall we be off to Kellynch Hall then? We will arrive late in the evening," said Frederick II.

The street in front of Camden Place elicited a moderate crowd of onlookers. With opulent royal carriage and marine guard, what would one expect as Lady Anne, Princess Margret Anne and Stephanie, Admiral Wentworth and the Honourable Fitzwilliam boarded? Waving, the carriage was off with its detachment of guards.

A week later, at Kellynch, the conversation turned away from the wonderful happenings of Plymouth and Bath. Both were a success and the family needed this time to remember its roots. They were never closer than now. Frederick II quietly reminded all of Anne's sudden tone of implying how little time is left to her in this life and that they should all stay close to home, visiting frequently in case time is short. Everyone agreed.

Fall can be a wonderful time in the English countryside and this year like the summer it was glorious with little rain and warm weather for many days. Anne had the opportunity to spend time with the grandchildren in the gardens and have tea and dine with her children. One could see that Anne's chapter was drawing to a close.

"Life will be so lonely without you dear mother," thought Frederick II, with Stephanie and Harry at his side, each missing her already.

CHAPTER 14

Anne Is Gone from Us

The winter months were long in length and short in daylight and too cold for civilised activity in the out of doors. Just when Kellynch Hall's residents were about to lose their minds spring had come with a vengeance. Every plant seemed to break out in colour as green painted the background, spring bulbs bloomed and flowers shot up from the ground. The gardens were magnificent.

Anne couldn't wait to sit in the outside. She so loved the gardens. Since traveling about at her age was simply not practical, the garden was her haven. A bit of sunshine, a comfortable chair, and a spot of tea would make her happy indeed these days, with the occasional visitor.

"She sleeps quite a bit more these days. Always a signal of the coming time," related Frederick II to Stephanie.

"And how I will miss her. Thank God I have you and Harry. My heart is breaking," said Stephanie tearfully.

"It would indeed be a lonely life otherwise," said Frederick.

"She has become a mother to me. She is the sweetest of person. Your family is blessed in that way. It all came from this little Anne," commented Stephanie.

"Well, she is here today so let us enjoy her light and radiance every moment we can, and make it count," said Frederick as they entered the garden porch.

"Hi dears, thank you for visiting. How are you both?" asked Anne.

"Very well dear lady and you?" asked Stephanie caringly.

"Very well dears, I am up and in the sun enjoying the day. Shall I call for tea?" asked Anne.

"I have done so mother," said Frederick II.

"Mother we planned to stay at Kellynch Hall for the next few days. I am not so busy and Stephanie and Harry are free as well. We want to be with you."

"That is darling of you sweetheart. I am happiest with my children about me, please stay as long as you want," replied Anne as tea was set at the table.

Stephanie poured and chatted with Anne as Frederick II looked far away.

Frederick II could hear Anne tell Stephanie a story of a dream she had last night, "I was young again. You know that age when all is so very new and life is such an adventure. When sleep is short and every moment, every sound is new to the ear. I got out of bed on what seemed like a warm sunny day deep in summer. Suddenly, Frederick's voice sounded 'Anne, are you up. Breakfast is ready, come down dear. Let us spend the day together". I rushed down as if wings on my feet, how I missed his voice. And there he was so young and strong. You didn't know him in those days of power and the glory of love, the navy, and for me and in that order. I stood frozen as if all my breath had left me relearning each curve of the hair and shoulders, his stance, and the eyes that reached into my very soul to caress my being. We talked of so many things, of so many things. How I have missed him, so I cannot say."

Frederick and Stephanie, with tears in their eyes, looked at Anne, "Frederick II. What is it dear? Are you alright?" asked Anne with Stephanie, taking Frederick's hand.

"It seems your time is coming mother with dreams of father at your side. How I will miss you dearly all the days of my life," Frederick said quietly, holding Anne's hand.

A few moments of stillness left only the sounds of the garden and of birds, and Harry playing alongside.

"Dears have no fear of life's nature. You will never lose me. I will love you forever and ever. My love and Frederick's are with you, all of you all the days you breathe. And one day I believe we will meet again, all of us.

"Look, see their Stephanie and Harry, they live on your love and protection. There is Fitzwilliam and our lovely Margret Anne and young William too, looking to you as head of the family. I am also here with you today. Let us not grieve for tomorrows that are not yet here. I know you love me. Son, you are so like your father. Did you know how proud of you he was, just to know at his passing you would protect me that gave him the strength to let go of this life. Let us talk of life, not my passing before it even comes," said Anne.

"True mother, let us celebrate life and enjoy the moments we have," replied Frederick II.

"Mother, there is a chill in the air, shall we retreat to the fire-warmed drawing room?" asked Stephanie.

"Yes dear, I feel cold suddenly. Frederick would you lend me your arm to the drawing room?" asked Anne.

Frederick quickly moved to her side in assistance. They withdrew to the drawing room and a warm fire. "Ladies if you will excuse me a few moments I will see to supper with the kitchen staff," commented Frederick II setting Anne by the warm fire in a comfortable chair.

When Frederick II was out of the room, "Daughter, my time is short. I know this. I have written letters for each of you. They are on my personal desk in the study. Keep this confidential until my passing. It seems I see my Captain more than I say. I fear soon I will not be able to resist this wondrous place in the countryside where he resides and I will go to him forever. How much I long for this now. Please don't think me selfish, for wanting my love, my life with me again," said Anne.

With misty eyes "Not at all Mother. How we will miss you so," replied Stephanie.

"I believe perhaps this is just a stopping place for us all. Perhaps our true home is this place I see every night now. Whose beauty is beyond all description. I also believe we will all meet again on a summer's day in this place and laugh over cups of tea telling of our many adventures. Living and loving again each other.

"It is at least my hope and prayer. I will tell Frederick of you and Harry and of James and Margret Anne, of Frederick and Fitzwilliam, of your mother and father, even of the HMS Wentworth, all love and light," said Anne.

"Mother it's a wonderful dream. I hope it is true, how I wish to see us all together again someday on that sunny day, I pray this too for you," replied Stephanie as Harry stopped playing and approached to hold his mother's hand in that most quiet moment, somehow sensing the preciousness of the time.

Frederick heard the conversation standing outside the arch to the drawing room, not seen or noticed, composing himself with all his strength, his heart breaking. Gathering himself, he walked into the drawing-room, "Ladies, supper is secured." I have a few more tasks and shall only be a moment longer, pray then I shall escort you to supper."

Frederick quickly headed to the study to write Margret and Fitzwilliam individually. "Perhaps it is convenient for you to come to Kellynch now, your loving brother Frederick," he wrote.

Calling a servant he handed him the dispatches. "Have these sent to Fitzwilliam and Margret Anne at all possible speed."

Frederick II returned, "Ah shall we dine then?" asked Frederick as he entered the drawing room holding back emotions better left unsaid for now. At supper, they talked of the many points in life that teach us better ways. They talked of the surprises of James and Margret Anne, and Frederick and Stephanie, the charity Trust, and how blessed it was. "It saved me from thinking of the loss of Frederick," commented Anne.

The last trip to Bath and Plymouth was such a highlight. "The whole family together and so amiable the mood, we just enjoyed each other, and I had the opportunity to share with you the early days of your father and me. I was glad to visit these places one last time. Precious memories," said Anne.

The next day brought some confusion as Fitzwilliam and Margret Anne arrived at Kellynch Hall. Frederick was sure to meet them first while Stephanie kept company with Anne on the garden porch. "I think Mother is coming close to that time and didn't want to wait until the last minute. I wanted you both to enjoy every minute we have with her," said Frederick II, relating the last couple of days and Anne's dreams.

"Thank you, brother, this is the right thing, and I am glad for it. Let us enjoy mother together while we have her," said Margret Anne.

"Agreed," said Fitzwilliam.

"Mother, look who arrived this morning and will be spending time here with us," announced Frederick

"I am so glad to see you both. Margret Anne, where is William?" asked Anne.

"He will be coming along tomorrow with his father. Is it inconvenient that we stay at Kellynch?" asked Margret Anne.

"No, of course not dear, God knows all the rooms we have," commented Anne.

"How have you been mother?" asked Margret Anne as Frederick and Fitzwilliam set for tea and then played with little

Harry in a nearby hedge of lavender just in sight but out of earshot of the women's conversation.

"Mother, are you to leave us soon?" asked Margret Anne gently.

"I fear my time is short and have completed all the preparation one can, so the burden will not be placed on any of you at that appointed time. I mentioned to Stephanie, that I wrote letters to all of you individually. The letters are on my personal desk in the study."

"Have you seen a surgeon's mother? Perhaps I should call the royal surgeon?" implored Margret Anne.

"My dear, no one knows the moment is near and no surgeon can say. Let us be together for however long we can be. Let us just be together while we can," said Anne as tears streamed down Margret Anne's face now. "Have courage dear, I will always love you, always, and forever I promise. It is my pray we will meet again," said Anne handing Margret Anne a handkerchief.

"I wish I could walk around the garden one last time. This has been my haven for so long a time. This is Frederick and my special place. We lived and loved here best of all," said Anne…..

Anne passed away quietly a few nights hence, her family at her side. The last words from her were "My Captain, where have you been. I have missed you so…I have so much to tell you…" said the Lady Anne Elliot Wentworth, Duchess of Glastonbury."

END